SHE WAS BEAUTIFUL. HEADSTRONG. AND DESPERATE ENOUGH TO ASK A MAN LIKE HIM FOR HELP. . . .

"What'd you do, Duchess?" he joked. "Kill somebody?"

Her gaze was challenging. "Yes. I think I did."

Cain dropped his glass in surprise. It crashed to the table and bounced off. Bourbon splashed over the surface and onto her dress.

She didn't move, and her eyes never left his. "So you see, Mr. D'Alessandro, why I need your help. And your answer."

Christ, what he wouldn't give right now for a clear head. Cain knew he was on the verge of saying yes, of giving up everything to follow this woman. It was ridiculous—she was a murderess and a whore, and there was something about her cool manners that disturbed him. He didn't want the trouble she brought, didn't want to have anything to do with her at all.

She was still staring at him. . . . Hell, if he left now, if he walked out of the tavern and never came back, he knew he would remember this woman for the rest of his life. Would always regret that he didn't go.

MEGAN CHANCE

A DELL BOOK

Published by
Dell Publishing
a division of
Bantam Doubleday Dell Publishing Group, Inc.
1540 Broadway
New York, New York 10036

ISBN: 0-440-21487-4

Printed in the United States of America

Published simultaneously in Canada

September 1993

10 9 8 7 6 5 4 3 2 1

OPM

For my father, Bill,
and for Kany,
who were always there for me—
even when they didn't think they were.

Special thanks to Kristin Hannah, for giving me back my spirit when I had lost it, and to Linda, Elizabeth, Jena, Melinda, Liz, and Sharon, for making sure it stayed there.

Light breaks where no sun shines;
Where no sea runs, the waters of the heart
Push in their tides.

—DYLAN THOMAS

Chapter 1

ORK CITY
CH 1849

om the open door cut through the
ss of Cavey Davey's tavern, rousing
half sleep. He lifted his head, blinking
until his vision cleared, and found himself staring at the
woman who had just come in the door.

The sight of her almost sobered him.

She was in some kind of trouble. He wasn't sure how
he knew it, but he did. Maybe it was the way she held
herself, or the subtle panic that touched her features in
spite of her calm demeanor. She believed she was hiding
it well, he thought, but Cain had seen that kind of panic
before. Too often.

Even so, he was fascinated by the way she moved. He
watched her through a haze, watched the regal way she
held that slender, delicate body, the way her bearing
belied the blatant sexuality of the green satin dress she
wore. She was a whore, he realized, but if she'd been in
any other clothes he would never have known it.

It was her grace that caught his attention. That, and
her hair. She had more hair than he'd ever seen on a

woman. It was the color of mahogany, heavy and thick, piled on her head in a kind of loose chignon that looked ready to fall at any moment. He found himself placing a silent bet as to whether it would fall and when, and smiled at the thought.

For the first time in what seemed like forever, Cain felt a surge of desire. It was weak, drowned by bourbon, but it was unmistakable. He toyed with the idea of going up to her, asking her price, but he abandoned the notion quickly. His last coins were gone, the bourbon he'd bought with them already coursing through his vei with the numbing mercy of a benediction. Hell, didn't even have enough to buy another bottle— less a woman he probably wouldn't even be abl form for.

He closed his eyes, forgetting the woman sleep or, better yet, a free drink. He'd be this smoky, dreary place, but he liked Ca liked never knowing whether it wou not, and he wasn't sure which was better: the an of a crowd, or the irreverent talk he shared with Cavey Davey when there was no one around. There were too few places like this. Too few places where a man could get drunk enough to forget.

The problem was, he never forgot. These last two weeks, he'd tried everything to escape the latest incident, but he couldn't drink enough to dull the vision of that poor girl twisting with pain beneath his unsteady hands.

She would have died anyway. The thought winged through his mind like an elusive breeze. *Even if you had taken the leg. No one could have lived through the infection already racing through her body.* No one. That's what he told himself, anyway, though it was probably a lie, and he knew it. The truth was, he should never have said he'd help, not once he realized he would have to amputate—and he'd known that practically from the moment her father told him the problem. But he'd been drunk when the man found him, and he'd momentarily thought he was Jesus Christ or something. Besides, he needed the money.

So he'd gone to that broken-down shanty despite his better judgment, had smelled the scent of death in the air, had tasted it. He heard her weak, pitiful cries—cries that wrenched his soul, cries that begged for salvation. His demons had stared at him from that poor girl's eyes. Questioning him. Tormenting him.

And he had turned around and walked away.

Cain's fingers trembled as he relived the scene again in his mind. Leaving that room was possibly the only heroic thing he'd ever done in his life, he reassured himself. She would have died under his hand if he'd tried the operation, just as . . .

Cain squeezed his eyes shut. *Forget it. Just forget it.*

Why the hell had he even tried? Why did he ever?

God, he needed another drink. Another drink would help. It always helped. He picked up the empty bottle, tilting his head to look at it through alcohol-bleary eyes. Nothing, not even a drop. He meant to throw it down, but before he could, it slipped from his nerveless fingers and rolled across the tabletop. He dropped his head onto his arm, watching the bottle roll back and forth, barely moving . . .

"I need a man." Ana took a deep breath and plunked the small bag of gold on the rickety table. "Any man."

Cavey Davey frowned, rubbing his grizzled chin with a scarred hand, his eyes locked on the bulging leather sack. He said nothing, letting the silence grow in the tiny back room.

Ana clenched her jaw and waited, willing herself to ignore the increasing tension. This was Davey's usual game, she knew from experience. The heavy consideration, the thick silence—all calculated to drive up the price. She had no fear that he would deny her request. At Cavey Davey's, anything could be bought.

It was why she'd come.

She looked away, studying the rows of bottles sparkling in the dim lamplight, listening to the muffled sounds of the crowd outside the room. Finally her patience snapped. "Well?"

Davey smiled at her uncharacteristic discomposure. "You'd best lay low for a while, Duchess. Do somethin' 'bout that cut on your cheek." His gaze touched her face, lowered to her hand. "An' wash your 'ands too. Blood makes a man nervous."

Ana swallowed. The smell of spilled rotgut seemed overwhelming suddenly. "I don't need advice, I need you to find someone to protect me."

"I see." He studied her thoughtfully. "Then you better tell me wot kinda trouble you got."

Ana shook back her tumbling hair and lifted her chin. "I think I killed Benjamin Whitehall."

Davey turned pale. "Wot?"

"The bastard whipped me," she said coldly. Her eyes narrowed. "I hope he enjoyed it—it's the last blow he'll ever strike."

Davey looked startled, Ana noted with a twinge of satisfaction. He watched her warily, as if her violence toward Whitehall would somehow transfer itself to him. She smiled wryly at the thought.

"I don't know, Duchess." Davey shook his head. "Whitehall's an important bloke—almost as important as the bloody mayor."

"I'm not sure I killed him." She adapted quickly to his uncertainty. If she had to lie to get Davey's help, so be it.

And it was a lie. She was almost certain Whitehall was dead. The thought brought no remorse. Unconsciously Ana touched her cheek, wincing. Too well she remembered the sadistic delight he'd taken in slashing his whip across her face. It had excited him, and he'd been rough with her—so rough she still felt the scratches on her thighs and breasts, still tasted the sharp saltiness of blood on the inside of her lip.

She'd known it was coming. Whitehall had been after her like a dog in heat for months. Until tonight, she'd managed to be busy every time he asked for her. She'd heard the screams and cries from the other girls when he was with them, but Madam Rosalie wasn't in the habit of turning away such important customers—or their gold.

Ana clenched her hands, again feeling the gummy blood on her fingers. She would never forget the smug smile on the bastard's face as he fastened his trousers and announced that she hadn't satisfied him. He had no intention of paying for his abuse. Rage blazed through her at the memory, and she quashed it ruthlessly. She'd paid him back in spades. Whitehall had wanted her; well, he'd had her. If he was still alive, she doubted he'd ever forget the encounter.

Davey took a deep breath and looked at the bag of gold. "Been savin' it long? For a rainy day, maybe? Or did you steal it from 'im?"

Ana looked at him coldly. "It's money, Davey. I didn't know you were in the habit of questioning your customers."

"Just want to know wot a man's up against, Duchess."

"I need to leave the city," she said evenly. "Rosalie will be looking for me. Whitehall was the brothel's richest client." An ironic smile touched her lips. "It isn't good for her reputation to have such a prominent citizen murdered in her house."

"No, I can see that."

"She'll be looking for a single woman, not a couple. I need someone to pose as my husband."

"Well—" Davey rubbed his chin thoughtfully. "I got a friend in Buffalo, you can go up there for a while—"

Ana's throat tightened. "Buffalo's too close."

"Wot?"

"I'm not going to Buffalo."

"But—"

"I'm going to California."

It was the second time she'd startled him. It had to be a new record. Davey glowered at her, but Ana continued. "Rosalie won't follow me there."

"Jesus." Davey let out a long, low whistle. "That gold country ain't civilized, gel."

Ana smiled. "Then it's perfect. I'm one of Rosalie's highest-paid girls. What do you suppose a lonely miner would pay for a woman like me?"

His eyes lit with admiration. " 'Ow're you gettin' there?"

"I've got enough money for a steamer ticket to Panama. They're leaving every day now. The papers say it's the quickest way."

"I 'eard the same." Davey crossed his arms. "Okay, Duchess. You got a deal. I can find someone for you. Just give me a couple o' days."

A couple of days? Ana licked her lips. God, a couple of days was much too long. Rosalie was ruthless. There was no telling what the woman would do, and Ana was too young to spend the rest of her life penned up in jail like a common criminal.

Even though that's what you are.

No. She was no common criminal, only a woman doing the best she could to survive. Hadn't she always done that?

Just as she'd do whatever she had to now. Ana smiled coldly. With careful calculation, she curled her fingers around the bag of gold—one of the three she'd stolen from Whitehall. Davey's hiss of protest sent a surge of satisfaction racing through her.

"It'll take time to find someone willin' to go so far," he argued.

"I can't wait," she said steadily, not releasing her hold on the money. "Either you help me, or I find someone else. But I have to go tomorrow."

His gaze slipped to her bloody fingers. "Yeah," he said slowly. "I guess you do."

She looked up at him. "Then you'll find someone?"

"There's one man," he said, his eyes never leaving the gold clenched in her hand. "I wouldn't 'ave picked 'im before, but seein' as you're desperate . . ." He shrugged. " 'E's used to travelin', an' 'e's strong enough, an' 'e knows 'ow to keep alive."

A brief warning fled through her mind, chased by a growing eagerness. "What else?"

Davey smiled. " 'E speaks Spanish—you'll need that where you're goin'."

"He speaks Spanish," she repeated. It was too good to be true—this unknown man was a godsend. "Take me to him."

Davey motioned to a small peephole in the door. "Maybe you better look at 'im first."

Obediently she bent and squinted. The bar had grown more crowded in the last few minutes. There were people everywhere, more men than she could count. Ana sighed impatiently. "Which one, Davey?"

"See the table in the corner?"

Ana looked. The corner table held one occupant. He was passed out, his dark head rolling on an outstretched arm. An empty bottle sat beside him. "The one with the drunkard?"

"That's the one."

"I see it."

"That's 'im."

Ana snapped up. "Don't joke with me, Davey. Which one is he really?"

"That *is* 'im." Davey frowned.

Her heart dropped, hope fled. "You'd send me to California with a drunkard?" she asked tensely. "Do all your customers get such special treatment—or am I just lucky?"

"I trust 'im."

"That's hardly a recommendation," she said sharply.

Davey shrugged. "You're the one in a 'urry, Duchess. Besides, 'e's got one thing goin' for 'im that no one else 'ere does: 'E'll go."

She looked at him suspiciously. "He'll go, you say. Why?"

Davey grinned. "Because, gel, 'e needs the cash."

"What for?"

" 'Is next bottle, o' course."

His next bottle. Ana's lips thinned. Any hope she'd had that this man's drunkenness was a one-time thing disappeared with Davey's words. God, this entire evening had been a nightmare.

A drunk. Despair went through her at the thought. What was she supposed to do now? She couldn't very well journey all the way to California lugging a man too drunk to take care of himself. Could she?

She glanced at Davey. His arms were crossed over his chest, he was watching her confidently. Her choices were growing fewer as the moments passed, her chances of capture greater. She had no other choice.

Or, truthfully, there was one other choice. She could stay in the city, hiding and waiting until Rosalie found her and either had her killed or brought her to trial. She had no doubt how that would end—with her neck in a hangman's noose.

She had other plans for her future. She'd spent her life fighting, trying to survive, had done what she had to in a world limited by poverty and her mother's fatal illness. Damned if she would let some rich, sadistic bastard finish her before she'd even begun to live.

She had tarried too long. It was time to be gone, and

Davey had given her no other out. She needed a man—*any* man—and this drunkard of Davey's was the only one available.

A grim smile touched her lips. It wasn't as if she couldn't handle a drunk. She'd been handling them since the day she crossed the threshold of Rosalie's brothel five years ago. He would be easy enough to deal with.

Besides, she reasoned, if he got to be too much trouble, she could always give him his blessed bottle.

Right over his head.

"D'Alessandro, 'ere's someone you should meet."

Cain opened his eyes, struggling to remember where he was. He tried to focus on the people standing before him. They wavered and twisted until he could concentrate. Ah yes, he was at Cavey Davey's, and that was Davey and—and the woman he'd been watching earlier.

He tried to sit up, rolling his head off his arm, backing away from the table to waver unsteadily in his chair. The world spun for a moment and then cleared.

"Davey?" His voice was hoarse and croaking. Was it even his? Cain closed his eyes, struggling for control. When he opened them again, he caught her staring at him. Measuring him. The sight of her cool calculation pierced the cloud of drink.

"Cain D'Alessandro, this is the Duchess. I mean—eh—" Davey looked distinctly uncomfortable.

The woman called the Duchess didn't. She smiled—a charming smile that didn't quite reach her eyes, but charming enough to make him wonder if he'd imagined the calculation of before. She extended her hand as if she were some sort of princess. "Ana," she said in a clear, musical voice.

Cain stared at her hand, suddenly remembering the trouble he'd sensed when she entered the tavern. No wonder he'd seen it. Her fingers were covered with blood.

His gaze moved up her arm, rested on her skirt. It too was covered with blood. And there was a cut on her face. She was hurt, she needed his help. The familiar fear raced through him, but the drink blurred it, brought with it a strange sense of inevitability, even a dismal, desperate hope. Maybe this time he would fail so badly it would give him the courage to finally end it all.

Even as he recoiled from it, the thought brought exquisite relief. Without hesitation, Cain reached for the small wood and leather case he carried with him. His fingers brushed over the brass tacks that formed his initials.

"Tell m'where the pain is," he said, setting it on the table.

"Huh?" Davey grunted.

Cain glanced up. The woman—Duchess, Ana, whatever her name was—stared at his bag, then at him, with a mixture of confusion and revulsion.

"You're a doctor."

Cain frowned at the accusation in her voice. "Yes."

"He's a doctor." She turned to Davey, who looked suddenly nervous. "You didn't tell me."

"I didn't know!"

"No." She wiped her bloody hands on her skirt as if they had suddenly touched something vile. "No doctors—"

"Duchess, there ain't much time."

"Excuse me?" Cain looked from one to the other. Was he missing something here? He motioned to the bench next to him. "You're covered with blood. Sit down."

She jerked away, even though he hadn't touched her. "I'm fine," she said. "There's nothing wrong."

"You got no choice," Davey said, his expression intent. Then, when the woman paid no attention: "I can't get no one else on such short notice, gel. It's either 'im or Buffalo."

Him or Buffalo? Cain blinked, suppressing a sudden urge to laugh. Christ, he knew he was drunk, but surely even he looked better than Buffalo. What the hell were they talking about? The world was taking on sharp edges again, and he felt the familiar gnawing in his gut that told him he either needed another drink or a few hours in bed.

He glanced longingly at the bar, and then sighed. Bed was the better choice, he knew. He looked at the woman and Davey arguing back and forth in low voices. Well, as long as she wasn't hurt, he could go to bed with a clear conscience. Or as clear a one as he ever had. They could argue without him. He couldn't even remember why Davey had brought her over.

Cain rose unsteadily, planting his hand on the table to brace himself. He reached behind him for the crumpled frock coat he'd abandoned earlier.

"It's been pleasant," he tried to say, though it came out sounding a bit slurred now that he'd abandoned the effort to appear coherent. "But I'm afraid—"

They stopped arguing and turned to stare at him.

"What are you doing?" The Duchess's tone was suddenly harsh. Her eyes bored into him.

"Leaving."

"But—"

"No!"

She and Davey spoke at the same time. Cain narrowed his eyes, trying to focus. He tucked his medical bag under his arm.

"Thanks for the invitation," he said. "But no thanks."

"But . . ." Davey scrambled for words. "But Duchess 'ere, she thought you might like to 'ave another drink."

Cain stopped.

"Yes, of course." She moved quickly, spreading her shimmering skirts and seating herself on the bench. "Another drink. Please bring a bottle, won't you, Davey?"

Cain stared at her, at the way she dismissed Davey as if she were royalty, at the poised and elegant way she seated herself, and he knew in that moment that she was even more trouble than he'd first thought. He wanted to say no to the drink, he really did, but suddenly his mouth was watering and his gut was churning, and there was nothing on earth he wanted more than that bourbon.

She watched him avidly, leaning forward just enough to create cleavage between her small breasts. The black lace trimming her bodice dipped and swelled.

Cain swallowed. "Whiskey," he choked.

She flashed a smile. "Whiskey, Davey."

Cain felt for the bench and sat, shoving his coat and bag aside. She was staring at him, and he suddenly felt as if she was seeing every imperfection: his olive skin and his too-long hair, and the way he wore only crumpled and stained shirtsleeves while his frock coat lay abandoned beside him. He suddenly had an overwhelming urge to shrug into it again, and anger washed over him at the thought.

"Duchess," he said slowly, fighting to keep his thoughts and his words clear. "What d'you want with me?"

Something flickered through her eyes, but it was too dark to see them clearly, and he was too drunk to care.

"Davey said he could trust you."

"Why?"

"Is he wrong?" A tight smile played at her lips. "You feel you're not trustworthy?"

"What's it to you whether I am or not?"

"I have a proposition for you."

A barmaid thumped a bottle on the table and retreated. Cain reached for it and sloshed a good portion into his glass, downing it quickly. Its warmth spread through his stomach, into his blood. He poured another glass. "What proposition?"

"I need a partner."

Cain gulped his drink. "Didn't look to me like you cared for doctors."

"I don't need a doctor," she said quickly. "I need a partner."

"No, thank you."

She didn't take her eyes from his face. "Davey said you were used to traveling."

Cain straightened. Traveling? What the hell did that have to do with anything? This entire conversation was strange. He thought for a minute that the drink was making him hallucinate, but she was too real to be an illusion.

"He said you never stayed in one place long." She said quickly, as if afraid he would interrupt her. "I need someone to travel with me. I'll pay you well. Very well." She took a deep breath, as if the next words were a necessary evil. "How long has it been since you had a woman?"

He nearly choked on the bourbon.

Her voice dropped to a practiced purr. "What about me? Do you want me?"

Cain leaned forward. "Listen, Duchess, Ana, or whoever you are, I'm not interested, but since it looks like that won't shut you up, why don't you just come out and tell me what you want?"

She stiffened. "I need someone to pose as my husband to California. I need to leave soon—tomorrow if possible—on the next steamer to Panama, but I can't go alone. Even you must be able to see that I'll need someone to protect me on the trip."

"You don't look like you need help."

"But I do." Her voice was low and intense. "There

are—people—looking for me. They'll be looking for a lone woman, not a couple."

"Why me?"

"Davey said he trusted you. He said you could survive. And that you spoke Spanish."

"Ah." He laughed shortly. *"Chapurro."*

"What did you say?"

He shrugged. "That I get by, that's all. It's been a long time since I had to speak it."

She nodded. "Will you do it? Will you come with me?"

"It depends on what I get in return."

She shifted her body subtly, and he saw the cleavage again. Suddenly the aristocrat was gone, in her place a whore. He wasn't sure how she'd done it, but she'd replaced cold distance with seduction.

"In return for pretending to be my husband, I'll give you husbandly rights," she said, her voice low and throaty. "All yours. No one else, until we get to California."

"I wouldn't offer free medicine to a well man," he said. "What else do you have?"

She looked confused for only a moment. "I'll pay for everything. Your tickets, your food."

"I expect that. What else?"

"Your booze," she said angrily. "Cash. Enough for your next bottle, and the one after that, and the one after that."

He saw her look away, as if ashamed by her outburst. The motion told him that, drunk as he was, he hadn't misread her earlier. She was desperate. Desperate enough to ask a man like him for help.

"What'd you do, Duchess?" he joked. "Kill somebody?"

Her gaze was challenging. "Yes. I think I did."

Cain dropped his glass in surprise. It crashed to the

table and bounced off. Bourbon splashed over the surface and onto her dress.

She didn't move, and her eyes never left his. "So you see, Mr. D'Alessandro, why I need your help. And your answer."

Christ, what he wouldn't give right now for a clear head. Cain knew he was on the verge of saying yes, of leaving everything familiar to follow this woman. It was ridiculous—she was a murderess and a whore, and there was something about her cool manners that disturbed him.

He didn't want the trouble she brought, didn't want to have anything to do with her at all.

She was still staring at him, and her gaze sent an insidious, coiling heat into the pit of his stomach. There was something in her expressionless face, something that burrowed inside of him with a tenacity he knew he'd never be able to shake. Hell, if he left now, if he walked out of the tavern and never came back, he knew he would remember this woman for the rest of his life. Would always regret that he didn't go.

After all, he had nothing to lose, did he? There was nothing for him in New York. And she promised plenty of whiskey, enough to keep him comfortably numb for the next few months if he needed it, enough to keep his memories comfortably at bay.

Still . . .

"I'll go," he said roughly.

Chapter 2

Ana gritted her teeth as he tripped once again, throwing the whole of his weight onto her shoulder. She struggled to hold him before he braced his hand on the wall of the stairway and regained his balance.

"Sorry," he muttered. "M' room's not far."

She said nothing. It was late, and she was tired. The events of the day settled in her stomach like a lead weight. She glanced at the man beside her. He was very, very drunk, and a man used to being that way, it seemed. Her heart sank. What had she done? Why had she listened to Davey when he told her Cain D'Alessandro was trustworthy?

He was a drunkard, and a doctor to boot. A *doctor*. The word filled her with revulsion. Thank God he had turned down her offer of sex. She wasn't sure she could have let him touch her.

Normally she would have found a man like Cain D'Alessandro attractive enough. He was tall and broad shouldered, though he was strangely lean, his clothes too loose. His dark, thick hair fell to his shoulders. Much too long, she thought. Unkempt.

But the most compelling thing about him was his eyes. They seemed too large in the gauntness of his face, accentuating the hollowness of his cheeks, the high, broad cheekbones that suggested Spanish ancestry. But mostly, the dark brown depths of his eyes seemed to hide secrets. Haunting, painful secrets . . .

"Up here." D'Alessandro rounded the top of the stairs. His fingers were white where they grasped the corner. He stumbled at the top step and slumped against the wall. "Thisss room."

Haunting and painful indeed. Ana brushed by him, twisting the lever on the flimsy door and pushing it open.

It was a cheap boardinghouse room, like hundreds she'd seen before, with one dim lamp. She lit it quickly, glancing over her shoulder at D'Alessandro, who still leaned against the wall outside. She shouldn't have ordered that last bottle, she thought grimly. At least he'd been coherent before.

She stood in the doorway and crossed her arms over her chest. "Are you coming in?"

He blinked, pulling himself upright. He wavered there for a moment. "Of course," he said carefully, the slurring barely under control. "It's my room, isn't it?"

"I assume so."

" 'I 'ssume so,' " he mimicked. "Duchess's a good name for you. Better'n Ana."

She watched him impassively, not moving. It was the only way to deal with a drunkard, she knew from experience. Don't goad them, let them talk and fall until they pass out. Oh yes, she knew plenty about drunkards.

He walked toward her unsteadily. "You're pretty, y'know? Don't know how I'll keep m' hands off you."

A flutter of apprehension shivered through her. Ana

ignored it. It was the drink talking; only a few hours earlier, he'd told her himself that sex didn't interest him.

"Go to bed," she said evenly.

"T' bed." He smiled. "Be happy to."

He stopped even with her, a mere few inches away, and Ana found herself staring at his chest, at the crumpled vest that hung open to reveal a stained shirt. His thin silk tie was undone, hanging limp and loose from around his neck, and his collar was unfastened so she could see the tanned skin of his throat, the start of the dark curls on his chest. Ana swallowed. She raised her eyes, trying to ignore the unsettling feeling pitching through her stomach, and backed up so he had room to get by.

But he didn't move. He stood there, staring at her, until Ana looked away.

"What are you waiting for?" Her tone was brusque, more than she wanted it to be.

His voice was a whisper, his mouth curved in a sensuous grin. "I'm afraid of the dark, *querida*. Will you stay? Chase away the demons for me?"

Before she could answer, he stepped away from her and into the dimly lit room.

Ana was cold suddenly. For the first time since they'd entered the building, she felt the drafts of icy air breezing through the cracks in the walls. It was because she was standing in the unprotected hallway, she told herself. It had nothing to do with the strange feeling that had gone through her at his words. What had he said? That he wanted her to chase the demons away? It was absurd, ridiculous. The words of a man so drunk he was undoubtedly hallucinating.

But it was disturbing nonetheless. What *had* she gotten herself into? Ana stared at him, unable to tear her gaze away as he dropped his coat over a chair and sagged onto the straw mattress, flinging his arm up over his face

to shade the light. He had forgot
knew. Almost immediately she hear

Ana took a deep breath. Slowly s
behind her, latching it carefully so he
the noise. The moment it clicked behi
began to shake.

She closed her eyes and swallowed, m[illegible] silently to the other side of the bed. Rigidly, struggling for control, she balanced carefully on the edge of the mattress, listening to the music and laughter echoing from the streets, the soft nickering of a horse. The hallway creaked with the footsteps of someone stumbling to bed, a key scraped in a lock.

The day was over, or nearly so, and the images she hadn't allowed herself to think about flashed through her mind in nauseating circles—Whitehall's face contorted with malicious pleasure, the sickening crack of the vase on his head, the sticky warmth of blood on her skin, and the terrible, terrible fear. And then, finally, she saw again Davey's face as he looked at the gold.

She squeezed her eyes more tightly shut. Measuring and uncaring. The face of an accomplice but not a friend.

That memory was worse than all the others. As it had so many times before, the dark loneliness grew inside her, filling her until she was trembling so badly she clutched her arms to still it. It was all right, she told herself. It was all right. She didn't need anyone else. Loneliness was a small price to pay for invulnerability, and she didn't regret anything. She'd done what she had to do, she was who she had to be. It was time to put it all behind her and go on. Fate had given her the key to her escape, and she would make the most of it, just as she always had.

Ana clenched her teeth, staring stonily ahead into the darkness, listening to the soft snores of the man beside her as she forced herself to imagine leaving on the

, moving on. He *was* a godsend, and because of New York would soon only be a painful memory—a memory her California riches would make easy to forget. She would be in control of her life, dependent on no one. Everything would be fine.

Yes, it was all over now.

But still she shook long into the night.

He had to be dead.

Cain cracked open his eyes, then squeezed them tightly shut against the sunlight slanting through the window. He was dead, and he was in hell. Nothing else explained the pain that shrieked through his skull, or the scorching heat against his left side.

He knew he should expect to be hung over, but he always forgot to. It used to be—not so long ago, it seemed—that he felt fine after a night of drinking, that these blinding headaches were the exception. Not anymore. He knew that if he moved, even a little, the nausea would rise to his throat, the world would spin crazily. God, he hated this.

Now there was nothing to do but lie there and wonder how long it would be until he gained strength enough to reach his flask.

Cain took a deep breath, throwing his arm over his eyes to block the light piercing his eyelids. His elbow brushed something heavy, a body. He froze. There was someone in bed beside him. Christ, what had happened last night?

There was only a cold blank where memory should be, as well as a familiar panic. Fear raced through him, nervous sweat bathed his skin. Not again. Please God, not again. But his desperate effort to remember brought only the dim recollection of stumbling into Cavey Davey's last night. What happened after that?

Carefully Cain turned his head and opened his eyes. Dizziness assailed him, but he forced himself to focus on the woman at his side. Her face was turned away, so all he saw was hair. Lots of hair. Heavy dark brown strands dancing with red highlights in the morning sun. It covered her shoulders, spidered over the coverlet.

Cain closed his eyes again. Who the hell was she? Nothing about her brought back any memories. Normally he avoided women and the problems they brought. He was usually too drunk to even feel desire. But perhaps there had been something compelling about this one. Perhaps he propositioned her. In that case, he hoped he'd been sober enough to perform. If he had been—he smiled briefly—it was doubly a pity that he couldn't remember.

There was no other explanation for her presence, was there?

He groaned, trying to keep the fear at bay. He'd been having blackouts for the last year or so, on and off, but they had grown more frequent lately. Now, when he picked up a bottle, he was never sure what might happen, and that thought was alternately frightening and soothing. He hated the memory losses, but more, he hated the recrimination of morning, hated wondering if he'd done something he couldn't forgive himself for.

Had he done that last night?

Steeling himself, Cain glanced again at the woman beside him. He wished to hell he could see her face. Maybe then he'd have some memory, some clue. Even as half of him wanted to wake her just to find the answers, the other half dreaded it. He wasn't sure he wanted to know what happened last night, and he was damn sure he didn't want to know how she ended up in his bed. Should he be boasting or apologizing?

It didn't matter, he realized. Sooner or later he'd find out, and it was better sooner than later. Taking a deep breath, Cain rose to one elbow.

The world spun. He stared at the wall until it stopped dancing, then, pinning on as gentle and caring a face as he could master after such a night, he leaned over and touched her shoulder.

Her hair was soft and silky beneath his fingers, her skin warm. He moved closer until his mouth hovered just above her ear, and caught her scent—sweat and stale smoke, with an underlying perfume that had once been fresh and citrusy. He swallowed, curling his fingers around her shoulder.

"Querida," he whispered. His voice came out hoarse and choking, and he cleared his throat softly. *"Querida,* wake up. Wake up."

She moaned a little and tried to shrug his hand from her shoulder.

Cain let his finger fall to brush her collarbone. "Ah, *mi amor,* would you sleep the day away?"

She jerked awake so violently her elbow speared his gut. Cain fell back, helpless beneath the onslaught of dizziness and pain as she tossed aside the blankets and scrambled to her feet. The bed rocked.

"What in the hell do you think you're doing?"

Cain tried to open his eyes, but nausea clawed at him, and he knew that if he did, he'd disgrace himself even more than he had obviously already done. He struggled for breath. "W-waking you up."

"What's wrong with a simple 'good morning'?"

Christ, she was a strange one. He tried to open one eye. "I—I thought you might prefer a more—romantic—"

"I don't."

"I'll remember that."

"Please do."

He opened his eyes and his stomach clenched. She stood beside the bed, both hands on her hips, the long, tangled mass of her hair falling to her waist. She was wearing a crumpled green satin gown, with a bodice that needed badly to be adjusted. Her small breasts were ready to pop out of it.

The thought nearly brought a smile to his lips, until he saw the blood staining her skirt. Ah Christ, what had he gotten into? This woman looked like a whore and spoke like a lady, and she was either badly hurt or had hurt someone else. Fear bubbled inside him, a need to know that was more intense than his desire to save her feelings. She would figure out soon enough that he didn't remember her.

Dread crept into his voice. "Who are you? What are you doing here?"

"You're having second thoughts, then?" The mild annoyance he'd heard in her tone turned to irritation.

"Second thoughts?" Cain winced at the loudness of his own voice. His stomach lurched, the pounding in his temples grew more furious. He closed his eyes again. "Second thoughts about what?"

"About our deal, Mr. D'Alessandro."

A deal. Hell, what kind of deal? Had he killed someone or watched her do it? What happened last night? What had he bargained for? Her body?

He took a deep breath, trying to banish the panic to some far part of his brain, fighting queasiness as he pushed off the blankets to get out of bed.

He stopped short at the sight of the whiskey-stained buff trousers still covering his legs. "I'm still dressed." He was so startled he spoke the words aloud. Thankfully, he saw no blood on his own clothes. His relief disappeared in a wave of confusion. "What the hell happened last night?"

"My God, you really don't remember, do you?" she asked, surprised. Then, when he shook his head: "You were very drunk."

"Now that's easy to believe." Cain rested his head in his hands. "Just tell me—that blood on your dress—"

"Has nothing to do with you."

"You're sure?"

"Yes." Her voice was very cool, very calm. He looked

up to see her studying him carefully. "Are you often . . . that drunk?"

Cain shrugged. "When I can afford it."

"And when you can't?"

"Lady," he said, rising from the bed and making his way to the frock coat on the chair, "I always try to afford it." He fumbled in the pockets, pushing aside bits of bloody cord and his folded scalpel until he remembered he'd left the flask in his valise last night. He went to the bag and pulled it open, lifted out a small, willow-covered flask and uncorked it. There was maybe one swallow left, and he thought about saving it, but then the smell of bourbon wafted up to him, sweet and soothing. The ache in his head seemed to ease just at the scent. He closed his eyes and gulped it, sighing as deliverance sped through him.

He turned to look at her. "I'm sorry, *querida,* but you have me at a disadvantage. You seem to know who I am, but I don't remember you."

Funny, he had the strangest feeling he'd seen the look in her eyes before. Her measuring, cold gaze was calculating, almost too reasoned. It contrasted strangely with the way she looked, with the soft brown hair, the pretty face marred only by a single, shallow cut, and her slender, delicate body. And more than that, her eyes were the wrong color for such a cold stare. They were tawny, a golden-brown color that reminded him of pralines and sherry and gypsies . . .

"Ana," she said. "My name is Ana."

It was the way she said it that made him remember. She'd said it exactly that way the night before, with that same look in her eyes.

The evening came back to him in bits and pieces that began to make sense. Relief—so strong he was sure she felt it—overwhelmed him, banishing his fear. He remembered her now. Yes, he remembered her, and remembered that she had asked him to go somewhere with her. Somewhere—

"California," he said suddenly.

Her eyes widened. "You remember."

"A little."

"Do you remember what we talked about?"

Clasping the flask, Cain walked to the bed and sank down onto it. The straw in the mattress rustled and shifted, the bed ropes creaked. He leaned his head back on the wall, staring at the ceiling. "You wanted me to go to California with you," he said after a moment. "I agreed—for what reason, I can't imagine."

She straightened. "I offered you cash. Enough to keep you drunk all the way there, if you want."

Of course. It explained, all too well, why he had agreed. Cain looked at the empty flask in his hand. He could get by without it today, but sooner or later, the dreams would come . . . Hell, he would agree again. Her offer was the answer to a prayer. "What else did I agree to?"

"That's all," she said. "You agreed to pose as my husband until we reach California. Once we're there, I don't care what you do or where you go."

"As long as I'm away from you, right?"

"I only need a partner for a short time," she informed him. "I can take care of myself after that. You would just get in the way."

He smiled wryly. "Probably I'll get in the way long before then."

"Probably," she agreed.

"Then why me?"

She turned away in exasperation. "I explained it all to you last night."

"I don't remember. Explain it again."

Her face hardened. "I told you. I killed a man." She clenched her skirt as if the words pained her, but Cain saw no such emotion in her eyes. They were muddy and cold as an ice floe on the Mississippi.

"You killed—"

"They'll be looking for me now," she went on as if he'd said nothing. "But they won't be looking for a couple, and it's safer if I have a 'husband' during the trip." She sighed impatiently. "Anything else? You said you'd go with me, you consented to the price. Are you coming or not?"

He leaned his head back. Hell, he wished he could remember more. Something told him he should be careful, should ask more questions, like who she killed and who would be looking for her. But the pounding in his head drowned out everything else. He should care about this, and he knew that if he felt better he would care. But it was all he could do to keep from throwing up, and all he wanted was enough whiskey to dull the pain.

One thing did seem important, however. He motioned to the bed. "Last night, did we . . . ?"

She didn't pretend to misunderstand. "I offered my body last night. You turned it down."

He'd been that intelligent, at least. Strangely, as much as he agonized over it earlier, the information didn't make him feel better now. Cain slammed the cork into the flask, suddenly wishing he'd left it buried in the bottom of his valise. "Really?" he said. "Do I get a bonus for that sacrifice?"

"You get two hundred dollars," she answered. "And all your expenses. That seems more than adequate to me."

"Of course it would." Cain smiled thinly. He had no problem with her conditions. It would be ludicrously easy to do as she demanded. And truthfully, it had been so long since anyone needed him, he felt oddly willing to do whatever she asked.

But he knew himself well enough to know that it wouldn't really be that easy. He wasn't well—or in control. As much as he hated it, he knew he needed to be protected. The morning was too clear in his mind; the rough panic and fear of his blackouts still gripped him.

He would never survive the trip to California, not without her help. It was difficult to admit, even more difficult to ask. He knew already that she cared about no one but herself, that putting himself in her hands meant a degree of trust she probably didn't deserve.

Cain took a deep breath. "I need something else from you."

She looked at him as if he were a bug she wanted to squash. "We have a deal. Or are your promises so easily broken?"

"I'll do what you want," he said. "I'll be your husband until we reach California and then I'll leave. But I want your promise that you'll stay with me until then. No matter what happens."

She regarded him coldly. "No matter what happens? What does that mean?"

Cain's jaw tightened. "Sometimes I drink too much."

"Really," she said dryly.

"And I forget . . . things." The admission was hard to make, and when the words were out, he closed his eyes in relief, waiting for her response. She said nothing. The silence in the room grew until he could hear the sounds of morning in the streets—the dull smacking of horses' hooves, the squeak of wagon wheels, and the harsh shrieking of women screaming at husbands still drunk from the night before.

He opened his eyes. She wasn't looking at him anymore. Instead, she stared at the window, at the broad stripes of sunlight glaring through a thin, tattered curtain that shivered in the draft. She looked thoughtful, her fingers rubbed the cut on her cheek. For a minute he stared at it, at the angry, swelling red edges, and he thought, *It was a whip that made that wound.* His fingers itched, and he glanced at the medical bag lying abandoned near his frock coat on the floor. But something kept him from grabbing it and ministering to her. Something he couldn't really remember—

She turned from the window, dropping her hand from her face and crossing her arms over her chest. "Very well. I promise I'll stay—"

A knock on the door interrupted her. She spun toward the sound and motioned impatiently to Cain. "Answer the door."

Christ, the woman was ordering him around already. "Get it yourself."

"I can't."

Cain looked lazily at the door. "Who is it?"

"It's Davey. For Christ's sake! Let me in."

She was at the door, turning the latch in a second. Davey barreled in, his breath short, his gray-black hair tousled. "Morning, Duchess," he breathed.

The Duchess stepped forward. "Did you get the tickets?"

"You're leavin' this afternoon," he said. "Managed to grab 'em from some bloke who changed 'is mind. Will you be ready?"

She laughed shortly. "I'm ready now."

"I'll be bringin' by a few more clothes in a bit."

"More clothes?"

"When I do a job, I do it right," Davey said. "An' one look at those fancy skirts an' the whole ship'll know exactly wot you are."

"He's right, you know," Cain said. They both turned to stare at him, and he got the uncomfortable feeling that he was too unimportant to consider. "You don't look much like a wife."

She turned back to Davey. "Very well, then, where will you get them?"

"I got some stowed away."

The Duchess's voice lowered with warning. "Don't tell anyone about this, Davey."

"You paid me well enough not to." The bartender spoke in hushed tones. "Now listen. You're goin' to 'ave to be careful. Rose's lackeys are already out, lookin' for you. 'Eard the rumors this mornin'."

He didn't want to know, Cain thought. No, he really, really didn't want to know what they were talking about. Before he could say anything to contradict that thought, Davey had turned to him. The question in the man's face made Cain nervous. Damn, he wished he could think straight. This was all too confusing, and his head was throbbing.

"You've got to get 'er to the docks by noon—without them seein'. Can you do it?"

Cain tried to concentrate. He looked at the Duchess, at the hair that cascaded over her shoulders, the cut on her face, the green satin stained with blood. She looked like a whore who had just committed murder, about as far from respectability as she could get.

He got unsteadily to his feet, bracing his hand on the wall and making his way to the door. "If you put up your hair and change your clothes, maybe."

Her lips tightened, but she said nothing.

Davey reached into his pocket. " 'Ere are the tickets, then."

Ana reached out to grab them, but Cain stepped in front of her, clumsily grabbing them from Davey's hand.

"Wait a minute!" she protested.

Cain stuffed them into the inside pocket of his vest, swaying a little at the sudden movement. "Remember your promise," he said softly. "This is just a guarantee."

"Promise?" Davey seemed confused.

"You don't trust me?" She looked offended.

"Do you trust me?" When she didn't answer, Cain smiled. "I'll hold the tickets."

"Wot's goin' on 'ere?" Davey asked.

"It's nothing, Davey," Ana assured him. "Just get

him a few bottles before we leave. Enough to get him to the next port."

The contempt in her voice sank into him, much as Cain wanted to ignore it, and he found himself wishing it wasn't there. The thought angered him. Why was it that it mattered to him what this slender, cold whore thought?

It didn't, he told himself. It didn't at all. And damn, did he want a bottle of bourbon so he could prove it.

Chapter 3

Ana stared at the chaotic dock, somewhat reassured by the people thronging the wharf, all talking, laughing, screaming or trying to get through to the steamer *Delilah*. There were so many that she was just another nameless face in the crowd. But she didn't let herself relax. Ana knew—too well—the skill and determination of Rose's lackeys. The madam paid them well for that talent, and they would be watching for a disguise. Ana took a deep, calming breath. There were only a few steps between her and the ship. Only a few steps to freedom.

Those few steps were taking an eternity.

She glanced at her partner, who wavered as he shifted the valise Davey had procured for her to his other shoulder and readjusted his own. As slowly as he moved, freedom might as well be a hundred miles away.

"Hurry," she said as softly as she could over the roar of steam and the rumble of handtrucks moving over the planks.

He looked down at her, his long hair falling into his face. "Whatever you say."

She lifted her skirts and straightened her shoulders, moving into step beside him, forcing herself to walk at an even pace past the rag-covered women hawking cigars and candied almonds and the gangs of newspaper boys calling out their headlines. Her gaze darted, her fingers clenched on the rough wool of her skirt. If D'Alessandro was moving even a fraction faster than he had before, it was impossible to tell. He lumbered along, looking strained, as if merely walking—slowly—was the extent of his strength.

It just might be, she thought irritably. God knew he looked like hell, though he wasn't shaking as badly as he had that morning. Her lips compressed into a tight line.

"Could you please—"

"I am hurrying," he said implacably. His face looked ashen, his eyes dark and unreadable. "Unless you want to be the one carrying these bags, be quiet."

"Mr. D'Alessandro," she said in a low voice, "do I have to remind you there are people—"

"Looking for you. Yes, I know." He opened his mouth to say something else, then stumbled as a would-be miner crashed into him.

"Sorry," the man said quickly, flying off.

D'Alessandro gritted his teeth, pulling back the valise that had begun to slip on his shoulder. Sweat broke out on his brow in spite of the chilly weather.

Ana bit back a sigh of frustration. Gathering her thin wool cloak around her, she glanced again through the crowd. She saw no one she knew, which was surprising in itself, since most of Rose's younger girls came to the docks on steamer days, waiting to catch the eye of a would-be millionaire. But then again, they hung on the fringes of the crowd, and Ana was in the middle of it, and well disguised, thanks to Davey. Her money had been well spent. She darted a glance at D'Alessandro. Mostly, anyway.

The wind coming off the bay was chilly, the morning

sunlight had long ago been replaced by low, gray clouds. Cold cut through Ana's cloak, the wind nearly lifted the fussy black silk bonnet from her hair. The large satin bows tied beneath her chin blew into her mouth, the dyed ostrich feather smacked into her eyes.

"Damn hat," she muttered.

"But, Duchess, you look so—respectable—in it." D'Alessandro's deep baritone was touched with amusement.

Ana didn't bother to look at him. He was right, she did look respectable, as she hadn't for the last five years. She'd nearly forgotten what it felt like to wear a bodice buttoned to the throat, much less a corset. Luckily, whoever had owned this before was a bigger woman than Ana, especially in the bust, so at least she could breathe. Running a finger inside the collar of the fitted rose wool, she eased it from her throat. The fabric was uncomfortable and scratchy. She was used to the soft smoothness of satins and taffetas. No wonder respectable women were so irritable.

But she said nothing. She hated the idea that D'Alessandro shared her secret, that he mentioned it at all. She cleared her throat, glancing furtively around. "Please, don't call me that here."

"Call you what?"

"Duchess," she whispered.

"No?" He shrugged. "Well, I suppose I could call you my *esclava del amor*, but it seems a little long, don't you think?"

"That's fine until we're out of the harbor," she said. "What does it mean?"

He grinned. "I called you my love slave."

Even hung over, he had an exasperating sense of humor. It was time to nip that intimacy in the bud. "How charming." Her smile was brittle as she looked at him over her shoulder. "You look terrible. Your head must be pounding."

He paled at the words. "Thanks for reminding me."

Before she could say anything more, the men in front of her stopped dead, as if someone were asking questions. Ana turned her head so the wind blew the ribbons of the hat into her face again, hiding it from any curious onlookers.

"When we get to the gangplank," she instructed D'Alessandro quietly, "I'll put my hand on your arm."

He winced and shifted his weight, looking ill. "That'll be a neat trick, seeing as I'm carrying both our bags. I don't *have* a free arm."

"Mr. D'Alessandro—"

"Cain."

"You are not—"

"Or darling, if you prefer."

"—cooperating." Ana sighed. "I hired you for a reason," she said. "It is very important that you act like a loving husband now. They'll be watching."

"They?" A bell rang, and he winced as if the sound battered him. "Who are *they,* Duchess? Who's looking for you? You never said."

She winced. "Rosalie's men. Maybe the police."

"Oh. Who's Rosalie?"

She turned the iciest gaze she could muster on him. "The madam of the house where I worked." His sober curiosity disturbed her. She was willing to tell him what she had to so he understood her urgency. But that was all. Luckily, the crowd moved before D'Alessandro could ask another question, and Ana moved ahead gratefully, feeling a swift surge of relief as she stepped foot on deck. She grasped the handrail and turned to look at her partner.

D'Alessandro was breathing heavily, as if the walk up the gangplank had exhausted him. He was still feeling the effects of liquor, she thought, watching the way he squinted to focus and the gray pallor of his skin. Now that they were on the ship, her disguise would be easily penetrable if they weren't careful. He could be a terrible liability—right now he looked too sick to even pretend.

Ana glanced at her valise. The three bottles of bourbon settled at the bottom of it might prove to be her most valuable assets on this part of the journey. She remembered last night, when he'd so readily agreed to her proposal. She was beginning to think she liked him better drunk. At least then he didn't ask so many questions.

He stumbled ahead of her, and Ana moved back a few paces, letting him lead the way across the deck, remembering that as a dutiful, respectable wife, she should allow him to look like the one in control.

She followed him past the door that led belowdecks and down the narrow stairs, into the darkness of the ship. Ana caught her breath at the strong stench of sweat and smoke, the hot, stifling air that made it hard to breathe. Her forehead was suddenly damp with perspiration beneath the band of her hat.

"Wait here while I check our tickets." D'Alessandro moved to the side, and she saw that the corridor had widened slightly, and a crowd of men stood waiting. D'Alessandro shrugged the two bags from his shoulders and wiped the perspiration from his brow. Ana thought she saw his hands shake slightly, and she frowned.

But at least he was trying to look competent now. She hung back, waiting while he made his way through the crowd to the steward, watching the men who hovered around her.

For the first time, Ana noticed that there were *only* men. Men outfitted in every imaginable way: topcoats, pea jackets, mining outfits, Mexican sombreros . . . All taut with anticipation, all carrying heavy trunks and valises.

She tried to remember if she'd seen another woman board. She hadn't, she was sure of it. Ana stiffened, searching the crowd again. No women. This was a man's journey; she knew from the papers that most of them thought of it as a temporary absence, a way to bring back riches to support their families for years. Of course no women were on this ship. No respectable women, anyway.

Thank God she'd thought to hire a husband. At last, the dream she'd hoped for every second of the last five years—and before that, even—was coming true. She wanted to run her own house. A place where she could work for a few short months—long enough to make enough money to get out of whoring and live her life her way. In California, there were no memories, no Rosalies, nothing but a past she could invent for herself—and a future heavy with the bright lure of gold dust. This time, no man would stop her.

Especially a man like Cain D'Alessandro.

She glanced up, finding him easily in the crowd. He had made his way to the front and was already handing over their tickets. When the steward smiled at her, she nodded back what she hoped was an appropriately demure acknowledgment, then stiffened at the slight frown that crossed his face. He spoke a few low, hurried words to D'Alessandro, and her partner looked over his shoulder at her quickly, shrugging his answer.

She forced herself to remain smiling. There was no way to tell what they were saying; she could only hope D'Alessandro could handle the steward's questions. Apparently he had, because D'Alessandro turned, shoving the tickets back into his pocket, looking as if he hadn't a care in the world. But when he reached her, she noticed that his pallor had increased, and his hands were trembling slightly.

"What was wrong?" she asked.

"He was a bit concerned about our accommodations."

Ana frowned. "Our accommodations? Why?"

He looked down at her and smiled weakly. "He's

afraid the trip might be too rough for a woman as delicate as my lady wife."

"Too rough?" Ana snorted. "I've faced far rougher than this."

Her raised one dark brow. "I told him I thought you could handle it easily."

His words made her hesitate for only a second. Regardless of what he thought, there was nothing worse than the tiny room she'd had at Rosalie's, nothing rougher than the shanty where she and her mother had lived. She followed Cain down the narrow, dimly lit companionways, trying to ignore the men hurrying by them, talking and laughing. The hum of the engines increased, the floors vibrated.

She struggled to keep her footing, running her hand along the warm, smooth walls for balance as they went deeper into the bowels of the ship. She pulled at the heavy collar at her throat. It was hotter down here. Hot enough so that the rose wool dress itched uncomfortably. The smell of oil and damp wood made her slightly ill.

D'Alessandro stopped at the end of the hallway. Ana nearly bumped into him in the dimness. He stepped down. His foot slipped, he fell clumsily against the wall. "Be careful," he said hoarsely. "It's a bit trickier now."

Ana glanced beyond him, to the narrow flight of steps that descended at a steep angle, disappearing into a dim gloominess.

"This way." He stood back, motioning for her to go in front of him, and Ana stepped forward unsteadily. In the dim light it was hard to see the slats before her.

"Ummph!" Her foot slipped from the deck toward the narrow stairwell. She flailed for balance, the doctor's kit flew through the air, and Ana fell backward, with nothing but darkness below her.

Cain dropped the bags and grabbed for her. Before he

could brace himself, she crashed into him. The force of her weight slammed him backward down the stairs.

His shoulder cracked against the stairwell, and he grunted in pain. But it was nothing compared to the pain he felt when they thudded to a stop at the bottom of the stairs, and Ana's full weight landed on him, knocking his breath away.

From some part of his mind, he heard the steady tap of footsteps on the stairs and the gasps of concern. But he lay there, unable to move, the press of Ana's body making it hard to breathe. Pain ricocheted through his shoulder, joining the headache he'd been nursing all day.

Cain opened his eyes in time to see Ana lift her head. He wanted to laugh at the way her hat had twisted around so the ostrich feather drooped on her shoulder, but his ribs hurt too badly. He groaned as she shifted her weight and pulled away.

"Señorita!"

The footsteps grew more rapid, Cain turned to see a blur of motion as a young, thin man dressed in a flashy bottle-green frock coat hurried forward. Cain found himself staring at a pair of shiny black boots.

"Ah, *señorita,* are you hurt?" The Panamanian knelt, offering Ana his hand.

She took it with a dignity that belied her unsteady rise. She shoved at the hat, the feather limped to the other side of her head.

"No," she breathed. "I'm fine, thank you."

"Pardon my saying so, but you do not look fine." The Panamanian looked her over, his eyes dark with concern. "That fall, it was terrible. Terrible!"

"No, really, I'm—"

"Who was it who did this to you? Him?"

Cain found himself staring at an accusing finger. He cleared his throat and rose to one elbow. "Now, wait just a—"

"Shall I hurt him for you, *mi amiga hermosa?*"

Ana's laugh was strangled. She threw Cain a glance. "You're very kind. But he—"

"I will even kill him, if you wish it."

Christ, Cain thought, the man hadn't let either of them complete a sentence. He rose a little farther. His head ached in protest, and he put a finger to his temple to ease it. "She's with me."

"No!" The Panamanian's tone was incredulous, his dark mustache twitched as he stared at Cain. "You cannot be serious. It is a lie."

Irritation stabbed into his headache. Cain did his best to stare coldly at the man. "I am—"

"I assure you, it's no lie, sir," Ana said quickly.

Cain felt even more irritation at the slight smile on her lips. It was obvious she found the whole thing amusing.

"Perhaps it is time to find a new protector, then, *cariña.*" The man bent low over Ana's hand. "Allow me to take over."

Ana went rigid, the amusement in her face died. "I don't think you understand—"

Cain heard the ice in her tone. This was trouble, and he was damned if he wanted trouble—especially when it was undoubtedly going to fall to him to fix it. Groaning, he sat up, swiveled around until he faced the man glaring at Ana.

"Wait a minute," Cain said, trying unsuccessfully to ignore the pain of his shoulder and the throbbing of his head as he climbed to his feet.

The Panamanian ignored him. "How much does he pay you? Whatever it is, I offer more."

Any hope Cain had of ending this peacefully died. There was no way he could let the insult lie, much as he wanted to. If he ignored it, every man on the ship would then know how to treat her, and she had hired him to prevent that very thing. He swallowed and stepped in front of her protectively. A shaft of pain went through him at the movement.

"You have just insulted my wife, *señor,*" he said quietly. "Apologize now, or I will have to force you to do so." Christ, his head was pounding. *Don't let there be a fight,* he prayed silently. *Let the hothead apologize and beg for mercy.* He was in no shape for it. The rough jouncing he'd taken on the stairs had only increased the effects of his hangover.

But then he saw the Panamanian's mouth lift in a sneer. "I see no ring, *señor.* You are a liar."

Cain froze. "You will wish you had apologized when I am finished with you."

"*¡Cochon!*" The Panamanian lunged forward, his fist connecting evenly with Cain's jaw. Pain exploded through his head. He reeled back, slamming into Ana and crashing back with her against the wall.

"My God." She gasped into his ear. "Watch—"

"*Bastardo,*" the man hissed, charging again. "This time you will be sorry, *hijo de la puta!*"

Cain shoved Ana to the side, twisting so the Panamanian's fist collided with the wall. His scream of rage echoed through the passageway as he lunged again. Cain doubled over, losing his balance before his opponent could strike, falling to the ground.

The man smiled and drew back his hand. He leaned forward, his face only a few feet from Cain's. "Are you scared, *señor*? *¿Tomes las de Villadiego?*"

Cain launched forward, grasping the Panamanian by the throat and throwing him back until he thudded against the stairs.

Gripping his side, battling nausea, Cain bent over him the man and smiled grimly. His jaw ached with the effort. "*Vas su a huir?*"

The Panamanian groaned, rubbing his neck. "*Sí. Sí.* You have it."

"To the lady."

The man turned his head slowly. He smiled, charmingly, sheepishly, as if embarrassed by the last few moments and hoping they were forgotten. "I most humbly apologize, *señorita*—"

"*Señora*," Cain corrected.

"*Señora*. I am a fool. It is obvious you are a lady."

Ana smiled thinly. "There was no harm done."

The ship's gong sounded, and the Panamanian rose, wincing at the sound. "For my sake, *señora*, I hope I do not see you again this voyage. Your beauty is too much a temptation." He smiled again. With a small bow of farewell, he left them, still rubbing his neck.

Ana brushed off her skirt, reaching for the abandoned doctor's kit as if the last minutes had been nothing more than a mild diversion. "What was it he said to you?"

Cain rubbed his knuckles. He had the uncomfortable feeling that what had just happened was going to be happening a lot more often. "Something no lady should hear."

"I am no lady," she reminded him.

"For this trip, *querida*, you are," he said gently, holding out his hand to help her to her feet. "He needed a damn good lesson in manners, that's all. I was happy to give it to him."

"I hope you don't feel the need to do so often," she said. "Now, where's our room?"

She stared at him expectantly, and Cain swallowed his response. There was no gratitude in her voice or her bearing, no relief, no "thank you." In fact, he got the odd impression that his effort was not only unappreciated, but unwelcome. He smiled wryly. "I imagine you're used to being fought over."

Her tawny eyes darkened, he saw the flash of something that looked like sadness—or regret—cross her face. But it was gone quickly, and she gave him a tight smile. "Of course," she said coldly. "Where's our room?"

So much for being a hero. Here he was, with bruised ribs and a head that felt as if a sledgehammer were bouncing off his skull, and all she could say was "Where's our room?"

He glanced at her again, at her stiff body and emotionless face. Could it be she honestly didn't know? A trickle of mean-spirited amusement made him smile. He picked up the valise and started around the corner, slowing until she was beside him.

The moment the room opened before them, she froze. Cain stopped, steeling himself for her anger, but when she was silent, he turned to see why. Her lips were compressed in a tight line as she surveyed the long, wide hold before them.

Cain tried to see it the way she would. It was dimly lit, even though metal ship's lanterns hung gimbeled every few feet. There were no windows, and the press of smoke and sweat was already almost nauseating. But he'd been in such places before; his money situation had rarely been good enough for him to buy more than steerage.

But she was a woman. He glanced over at her, watching her gaze travel the room, taking in the berths that stretched three tiers high and three wide, with two feet between. Actually, to call them berths was a compliment. They were nothing but rough canvas hammocks slung on undressed lumber.

The makeshift beds stretched on either side. Down the narrow center corridor ran a long plank table covered with oilcloth. Already men were crowding the room, hunting for their assigned berths—sitting, lying, and spitting on the table that was supposedly going to hold their food.

She shook her head briefly. "I didn't expect this," she said.

Her voice was even, unemotional, but Cain felt a rise of compassion all the same. He should have warned her.

He felt a momentary regret that he hadn't and then brushed away the feeling. He had the feeling that any sympathy—like his heroism—would be disdained.

"Look at it this way." He leaned close, injecting a teasing tone into his voice. "Now you won't have to share a bed with me."

Her eyes were overbright. "That was my first thought," she snapped. She motioned to the bunks. "Well? Which ones are ours?"

Cain smiled, feeling a strange relief at the rapidness of her recovery. He pulled the tickets from his pocket and glanced at them before making his way down the narrow aisle between the table and the bunks. Behind him, her boots rapped sharply on the deck and Cain slowed when he realized that they were drawing the interested stares of the other men.

His stomach clenched, sudden tension made his shoulders tight. Not for the first time, he wished he had his hands on one of the bottles in her valise. She attracted attention like honey attracted bees—it was going to take a hell of a lot of concentration to keep incidents like the one he'd just dispelled from happening again. And damn, it was concentration he didn't want to maintain. It took every ounce he had just to keep himself alive.

But it was what he'd agreed to, and he wasn't the kind of man who backed out on a deal—especially when there was a bottle of bourbon on the other end of it.

He stopped, and when she was even with him, he twined her arm through his, smiling at the cynical lift of her brows.

Glancing ahead, he looked for the numbers on the berths, watching for theirs. It was the bottom tier, on the end, ten rows back. He counted silently, trying to ignore the pounding of his head and jaw, trying to concentrate despite the sickness clamoring in his belly and the growing need for drink. Eight, nine, te—

He stopped so suddenly, she stumbled.

"What is it?" she asked. "What?" She gasped in surprise.

Their berth partner stood there, staring at them in shocked dismay.

It was the Panamanian.

Chapter 4

"—He is like a dog with two masters." Jiméne Castañeras laughed, slurping a spoonful of thin mush and swallowing the lukewarm cereal rapidly. "One screams for water while the other wants tea, and he must answer them both."

Ana smiled, tearing off a hunk of the hard, gritty bread they'd been given for breakfast. Jiméne was working hard, trying to amuse her while the stormy gray skies and tossing seas kept them belowdecks, presumably trying to make up for his earlier bad behavior. It was unnecessary; she didn't have the heart to condemn him for seeing through her disguise, and in spite of D'Alessandro's obvious distaste for their berth partner, Ana found she liked the quicksilver Panamanian. He was like so many of the men she'd known—anxious to please, entertaining.

"Damn Mormons," Jeb Wilson said from his seat beside her. He spat on the floor and hunkered down further into his coffee. "Can't see why they need to have more 'an one wife, anyway."

Jiméne's dark eyes sparkled, he pulled a handkerchief from his coat pocket and wiped delicately at his mustache. "A man can grow tired of only one, *amigo.*"

Before anyone could answer, the ship pitched. Men grabbed their bowls, and Ana braced her elbows on the table, trying to keep herself from sliding off the bench as the sidewheel tossed and thrashed, trying to gain purchase.

Nausea rose in her throat. She closed her eyes and fought it back with sheer force of will, ignoring the stumbling of men to their bunks, the white-faced vomiting of others who had already lost control.

Jeb Wilson steadied his cup of coffee, watching the activity around him impassively. "Feels like a big sea's on."

"There is no worse time than winter for sea travel," Jiméne offered, leaning close to his bowl and shoveling the last few spoonfuls of mush into his mouth. "It is an unfortunate time to go looking for gold."

Ana frowned. "That's not what the papers say. I heard it's a paradise in California—nothing like New York in the winter."

"That is true enough." Jiméne nodded. "But to get there is not so easy. You are a delicate flower, *cariña*. Do not tell me you would come this far if not for *su esposo*'s wish for riches."

" 'Su esposo'?"

Jiméne waved impatiently. "Your husband, *amiga*. That . . . That—" He paused, as if searching for a word horrible enough to describe D'Alessandro. "He is a selfish man, forcing you to come with him."

"It's not—" The ship plunged, Ana's stomach lurched, and she inhaled deeply, waiting for it to steady.

"Where is D'Alessandro?" Jeb asked curiously. "Ain't seen him about for a while."

Ana pursed her lips, looking away so neither of her breakfast companions saw her disapproval. She knew exactly where her partner was. On the other side of steerage, buried in cards and spending her money, just as he'd been since their second day out.

She thought back to the first day, when he'd spent every moment hovering about her, growling at anyone who came close. For an hour or so, she'd appreciated it. It was true that discovering their tickets were for steerage had surprised her—more than surprised her. But her worries about spending eight days as the only woman in a group of men were quickly allayed. Her deception worked. After their initial shock, most of the men treated her with the respect due a married woman. She grudgingly admitted D'Alessandro had done his best to initiate that respect.

That alone was worth the price of his ticket, she reasoned, though once it became clear she could handle things on her own, D'Alessandro's protection was annoying. She had no intention of spending eight days cooped up with only a dissolute doctor for company, and when Jiméne had tried to start a tentative friendship, she had welcomed it.

Once Jiméne began to talk, D'Alessandro had retreated.

She glanced toward her partner. One or two of his group had been lost to the ravages of seasickness, but D'Alessandro wasn't among them. He was probably used to the sight of the world spinning before his eyes, she thought wryly, noticing the glass in his hand. He probably hadn't even noticed the pitching of the ship.

Though he didn't seem drunk now—and hadn't seemed that way since they'd boarded the ship, in spite of the fact that he drank as much as the others. The thought made her frown. For a moment, she wished she hadn't brought him along. She'd had a bad feeling about him from the beginning. There was something in his eyes, something that made her vaguely uneasy. She liked it better when he was across the room, too far away for her to see his measuring gaze—the gaze that made her wonder what he was seeing when he looked at her.

Probably nothing, she told herself. Probably it was just her imagination. But then she remembered how he had looked standing on the steps leading to his hotel room. She'd had the same feeling then, as if there were secrets behind his eyes.

Ana tore her gaze away, staring at the gray bread in her hands.

It was too bad she hadn't met someone like Jiméne first. He would have made a good partner. He was honorable, dependable. Ana turned her gaze to the wiry Panamanian. "You don't seek gold, then, Jiméne?"

Jiméne took a huge sip of coffee and swallowed, shaking his head. She thought she saw a flash of sadness in his eyes. "I am no miner," he said. "I am only anxious to see *mi familia* again. I have no interest in California."

"Why not?" Jeb asked. "You're single. Seems to me a young man with no ties could make a fortune there."

"Perhaps." Jiméne shrugged. "I will leave the gambling to you and the others, Wilson. It is no place for me." He glanced at Ana. "It is no place for a woman of your beauty, either, *cariña*. You belong in Panama, in the moonlight."

Ana ignored his ready, familiar compliments. "Do you think it's true, what they say, Mr. Wilson? That California will soon be full of millionaires?"

Jeb stroked his gray-bearded chin. "I'm betting on it, Mrs. D'Alessandro. Isn't that why you're going? Or does your husband have other ideas?"

"Ideas about what, Wilson?" It was D'Alessandro's voice behind her. Ana didn't bother to turn around.

"We're just talking about California, D'Alessandro," Jeb said easily. "About getting rich."

"Ah yes," D'Alessandro said. "Getting rich. I'd forgotten."

"Forgotten?" Jiméne twisted around, his eyes full of

challenge. "It is not even that important to you, yet you would force your beautiful wife to go?"

Ana tensed. "Jiméne—"

"I'm not forcing her to do anything," D'Alessandro said. "She wants to go. Just ask her."

"She would only defend you. It is not—"

"Jiméne." Ana glared at him. "Please." She turned to look over her shoulder, but D'Alessandro wasn't looking at her. His gaze was pinned on Jiméne, his mouth tight.

"What's the problem, Castañeras?" he asked slowly, his fingers clenching the cigar he held.

"I do not like her alone," Jiméne said stiffly. *"Someone* should care for her."

"That's why I'm here."

"But you are not always here, *señor."* Jiméne's voice held more than a trace of scorn.

"Excuse me, please." Jeb got to his feet, pushing past D'Alessandro. "I think I see a friend of mine."

Both Jiméne and D'Alessandro ignored him. In fact, if anything, Jeb's absence seemed to give Jiméne strength.

"If I were her 'husband,'" he pressed on, "I would—"

"Unfortunately for her, you're not," D'Alessandro said shortly. "Do me a favor, *amigo,* and go away."

"I will not."

This had gone far enough. Ana touched Jiméne's arm gently, ignoring her partner. "This is ridiculous, Jiméne. Please, just do as he says. It's better that way."

"Don't want to see my violent temper." D'Alessandro smiled.

Ana threw him as cold a glance as she could gather. "Really, Jiméne. I need to talk to him."

She saw his hesitation, and then Jiméne nodded slowly and got to his feet. He glared at D'Alessandro one last time before he moved off, his bootheels clacking sharply on the floor.

Before she could move or say anything, D'Alessandro

sat beside her on the bench. She caught a whiff of bourbon as he leaned close, but he didn't seem drunk. She wondered how he did it. How did a man drink so much without even looking the least inebriated?

She backed away. "You should be nicer to Jiméne."

"He should be nicer to me." He glanced at the bourbon Jeb had left behind on the table, and then looked away. "You seem to be holding your own with all of them."

"I'm used to men like them," she said shortly.

"I see."

There was something in his voice, something vaguely disturbing, and Ana turned her head to look at him. He sat very close to her, so close she could see the dark hair on his chest where his shirt was unbuttoned. He had long since abandoned his cravat and frock coat, and his blue brocade vest hung open. Thick dark hair spilled onto his shoulders and into his face. Seemingly oblivious to her scrutiny, he put the cigar to his lips and drew heavily.

The sight and smell of the smoke made her queasier than any ship's motion had. Ana suddenly couldn't bear his presence for another second.

"Why are you here?" she demanded.

He looked surprised. "Thought I'd come over and make sure they weren't bothering you. Isn't that what you wanted?"

"I don't need your help," she said sourly. "Just go away and leave me alone."

"But—"

Ana clenched her fists. "Go back to your card games, Mr. D'Alessan—"

"Cain."

"Cain," she said through gritted teeth. She lowered her voice to a dull whisper. "It's only pretend, you kno—"

The floor pitched so violently Ana was thrown sideways, into D'Alessandro's chest. Her chin cracked sharply on his sternum, she heard his grunt of surprise, and then his arms were around her shoulders, holding her steady in a world that was suddenly tossing and turning wildly. The wheel churned, iron and wood shuddered.

The steamer rocked again. The floor shifted, the bowls on the table went sliding, and D'Alessandro fell back, letting go of her, grappling for balance. Ana landed on her side, hard, her head banging against Jeb's bottle of bourbon—now spilling into a pool on the floor. The scent of rotgut filled her nostrils.

Along with another smell. Bilge water. The sickening, overpowering odor of sewage crept through steerage like a fog.

It was the last straw. Ana tore away from D'Alessandro's arms, sliding back through the bourbon, gagging on the smell filling the confined space. Her stomach lurched, she felt suddenly, horribly ill.

D'Alessandro struggled up to his elbows. "Christ," he muttered, reaching out for her. "Duchess, are you all right?"

"Get away from me," she whispered, scrambling out of his reach. God, she was going to throw up. She was going to lose control, and she couldn't stand the thought that he would see it. Suddenly she wanted nothing more than to get away from him. Far away. She didn't want him even touching her. She couldn't stand to see that mocking, knowing look in his eyes, the spiteful joy in her discomfort. He would no doubt love to see her so sick, love to see her helpless. They all did. Everyone did. *Watch the Duchess lose control.*

Well, she wouldn't do it, not for him, not for anyone. Ana staggered to her feet, grasping on to the table for balance.

"Duchess," he sat up, grabbing the half-empty bottle. "Ana, wait. Drink this, it'll help."

Ana's stomach turned over. She gasped. "I'm fine," she mumbled, her imperious tone lost in the misery of trying to keep the nausea down. "I'm all right."

"Are you?"

She couldn't answer him. Ana stumbled away, pushing past the other groaning men to the comforting, mildewed canvas of her bunk.

It wasn't until she got there that she realized she hadn't seen the mocking taunt in his eyes.

It was the fifth day on the *Delilah,* and yesterday the steamer finally escaped the cold, tossing northern waters and slid down the coast of Florida. Now they were inside the Gulf, close to the edges of the coral banks bordering the lower states. The sky was azure, the water nearly so, and the breeze was soft and warm and smelled of spice.

Passengers clustered on deck, sitting with feet hanging over the guardrail. Now that they'd hit the warmer climes, the excitement was palpable. Gold was all anyone talked about, debates held over the best ways to find it by men who had never even seen a mountain stream, much less panned one.

Cain leaned over the guardrail, wishing a bottle of whiskey were hanging loosely from between his fingers, and stared at the flat shores of New Orleans. The forest and swamp fringing the rest of the Gulf had receded, giving way to fields of sugarcane and maize that came down to a narrow levee. The stench of rotting vegetation and stagnant water mingled with the sweet scent of the blooming orange trees. It was a scent he was all too familiar with. A scent that pulled at his heart until he wanted to bury himself in a pool of bourbon.

It was *home.*

His eyes narrowed, squinting at the low, balconied planter's houses buried among the oranges, acacias, and crape myrtle, shaded and cool while the adjoining slave huts ran in unshaded, parallel rows. It was all so familiar.

He remembered playing at La Belle Hermitage when he was young, racing through the fields with Benjamin Horne. What had ever happened to Ben? What had happened to all of those boys Cain used to play and wench and drink with?

Undoubtedly, they were all wealthy landowners now. After all, they were the sons of plantation owners. Ben Horne was probably sitting on the balcony of La Belle Hermitage right now, watching the breezes turn the leaves of the acacias, sipping a fine French brandy as far removed from the rotgut Cain could afford as the sun was from the moon.

He lifted his eyes, trying to see farther, into town, where Canal Street ran muddy and barely navigable and the one-storied houses with jalousies and tiled roofs crowded the roads below. If he tried, really tried, he could probably see his father's house and the big, ugly warehouses of the sugar refinery surrounding it.

He didn't want to try. Cain closed his eyes. He should go below and grab the bottle he'd started that morning. He could imagine it—the way it ran through his veins, heated his blood. One sip and he would no longer feel the pain, no longer wonder where his father was buried or whether his aunts thought about him at all. Another sip and maybe he could actually forget New Orleans.

Or maybe he would never forget. That was what frightened him most of all, the idea that he would never live a day without the shadow of his childhood hanging over him, that he would never cease to hear his father's voice ringing through the dark emptiness of the house, demanding: *"Rafael! Rafael, come to me this instant!"*

For a while, you did forget, a voice reminded him. Yes, once—once he had forgotten the nightmare of his youth. Once the memories had disappeared in the challenge of medicine and the belief that he could do some good in the world, in the unconditional love of a man who was more a father to him than his own.

But that's all gone now. You killed it. You killed it.

Cain spun from the rail, searching the crowd gathered on deck for something distracting, something to make him forget they were anchored off the coast of the city of his childhood, waiting for passengers to be rowed out.

What he saw certainly distracted him, as it had distracted him every hour of the last five days. The Duchess —Ana, he corrected himself—was in the middle of a group of men, laughing and tossing her head as if she were the queen of some gay party. She wore the old rose wool as if it were silk, and her hair was adorned with that expensive gold comb that reminded him of a crown.

Jiméne, Jeb Wilson, Robert Jameson . . . The list went on and on. Since they'd stepped foot on board, she'd been the belle of the ball. He told himself it was because she was the only woman aboard besides the Mormon's pious, untouchable wives. But it was more than that, and he knew it. She drew men. Almost despite herself, it seemed, because she never lost her shield of ice.

Especially with him. He remembered the way she'd looked at him after they'd fallen to the floor two days ago—as if he were just slightly more than a tedious irritation. For a moment he'd been unable to believe she could be that cold.

He smiled bitterly. Not anymore. He wasn't sure why he even persisted in clinging to the illusion that he was protecting her. She could take care of herself—in fact, she *had.* Not only had she cut him dead that day, she'd ignored him every day since. More than ignored him. She had done her best to make him feel about two feet tall. Not that it was a hard thing to do, but his dear, sweet "wife" had done it better, and with fewer words, than anyone he'd ever known. Cain glanced back at the shoreline. Well, almost anyone.

Ana laughed. Cain turned his attention back to her

rapt court, noticing sourly that her smile seemed genuine.

"Jiméne, are you sure you want to bury yourself in Panama? You should come with us." Jeb stroked the stem of his pipe thoughtfully. "I could use another partner, and it looks like Robert isn't going to be much competition for gold."

Jiméne laughed, shaking his dark head. "No, no. I will leave the *oro del diablo* to you—with my blessing."

"Then you, perhaps, Mrs. D'Alessandro," Jeb urged. "Or does your husband have other plans?"

"I'm sure he does." She smiled enigmatically.

Cain was startled when she looked above the crowd and caught his gaze. He realized that she had known where he was every second. Damn, probably knew he was watching her too.

"Where is D'Alessandro?" Jiméne asked, half angrily. "He should be here, at your—"

"There he is," she said, gracefully extracting herself. "Please excuse me for a moment, gentlemen."

Cain stiffened, feeling his expression settle into a tight, defensive mask. He wanted to turn and walk away, ignore her as she had ignored him and embarrass her in the bargain, but his feet were anchored to the deck, and his hand tightened on the rail. For a brief, uncontrollable second, he felt light-headed and nauseated, and he prayed that he could hold his ground in whatever battle she wanted to fight.

She approached slowly, gracefully, as if her mere presence should be an honor. The thought sent anger spiraling through him, anger that only increased when her gaze raked him and he felt instantly ashamed, knowing that once again, she compared him to Jiméne, and that the comparison was undoubtedly unfavorable. Cain was painfully aware of his stained and crumpled vest, his limp frock coat. Damn her, anyway.

"Hello, Duchess," he said caustically. "Sorry I can't

curtsey for you, but I figure those three have done it enough for everyone."

Something flickered in her eyes. Hurt maybe. Cain almost laughed at the illusion. Christ, there was no pain in her gaze. She was indomitable, as unfeeling as stone.

And her next words only proved it. "I need to inform you of our plans," she said matter-of-factly, staring out at the horizon while her fingers moved back and forth over the highly polished wood of the guardrail.

"Our plans?"

"Yes. We're two days from Chagres. I thought you should know I've decided to ask Jiméne if he will be our partner going downriver. From what Jeb Wilson tells me, we'll need to be in groups."

He stared at her. The ice in her tone, coupled with the emotional turmoil of the last few hours, made him feel unsteady. He thought again of the bottle downstairs, and licked his lips. "Groups? Three is a group?"

"Three to four is best, he says. I'd ask Jeb as well, but he's already partnered with that fool Robert. I'd rather be alone with you than fight his advances all the way to Panama City."

"How flattering." Cain tried to ignore the insult in her words. "And I suppose Castañeras has promised to keep his hands to himself?"

She spoke carefully, as if trying to appease him. "You should learn to get along with him. He'll be with us for most of the journey."

"Fondling you?"

"You are disgusting."

"I'm not the one hanging all over every man on the ship." Despite himself, Cain reached out, running his finger down the rapidly healing cut on her cheek. "Just a warning, Duchess. Unless you want another attack like the one that caused this, I suggest you lose your harem."

She jerked away, and he let his hand fall to his side. "I've no idea what you're talking about."

"I think you do." Cain said, working to keep his voice steady. "The others're talking. About you and Castañeras."

Her spine went rigid. "What do you mean?"

"They wonder why you spend so much time with him."

"What do you tell them?"

He shrugged and stared at the horizon. "That we had a fight. That you don't like the gambling."

She swallowed quickly, stepping back, and he saw he'd shaken her composure. Probably she hadn't expected him to come to her defense, and truthfully, he wasn't sure why he had. He told himself it was because she'd hired him to do a job, but that wasn't strictly true. He remembered the sneering words he'd heard, their suggestive innuendos. Christ, even a whore didn't deserve that. Even the Duchess.

Beside him, she took a deep, shaking breath. "Thank you—for the lie."

Her admission—and the sincerity behind it—surprised him. Cain smiled thinly. "It must've hurt to say that."

She only looked at her hands, twisted together on the rail, and the submissive pose struck a chord in him.

"They don't believe you're my wife." He went on recklessly. "Let's leave Castañeras behind."

She shook her head. "I can't do that."

"Why?"

"I like him." Ana looked at him pointedly. "And I trust him to get us to Gorgona safely."

Cain froze. Her unspoken implication floated between them. "Which means you don't trust me." He clenched his hands on the rail.

"I didn't ask you to be my guide," she said in a sharp voice. "I only asked you to pose as my husband. Jiméne was born in this country. He knows what to do."

"What about me?"

"What about you?"

He turned slowly, catching her gaze, seeing something in her eyes—guilt maybe, or uncertainty. But before he could speak, she looked away.

"All you need to do is keep pretending," she continued slowly. "As long as Jiméne's with us, you only have to worry about your next bottle."

"Oh?" He felt suddenly cold, and the familiar pain settled in his stomach, cramping his gut, hurting so much he couldn't stop the words. "Ah, Duchess, what kind of a man do you think I am?"

"I didn't mean to insult you." She paused, then added as an afterthought, "You are far too drunk."

Cain shook his head. "Not too drunk, *querida*. Not yet." *Too drunk*. Ah God, he wished. He wanted to be drunk right now, anything to forget her condemning eyes and frigid words. He staggered away from the rail, away from her, hurrying to get to steerage to paw through her valise until he found a bottle—and knowing it wouldn't help, that nothing as easy as a drink could make him forget the truth he saw in her face—or the balmy, memory-tainted breezes of New Orleans.

Chapter 5

She had never seen anything like the beauty of the tropics. Every night Ana went to bed thinking the water couldn't possibly get any bluer, and each morning she was surprised when it was. The brutal beauty of the Cuban coast and the massive creamy walls of the fortress of Morro were sights she would never forget. The flying fish that followed the steamer were like something out of a fairy tale, and the soft singing of the men on the balmy, tropical nights almost made her believe in love. Almost.

Smiling wryly, Ana leaned over the guardrail. Now the coast of South America loomed beside them, the high hills covered with vegetation to the water's edge, the Darien range of the Andes towering behind the coast with their summits in the clouds. The rocky promotory of Porto Bello grew closer, and she searched the hilly shoreline for the hidden entrance to Chagres, where they would leave the steamer for the overland journey to Panama City.

"*Cariña,* there you are!"

Ana's heart sank. Much as she genuinely liked Jiméne, it had felt good to be alone for once, to not have to watch her every step or pretend laughter and interest. Sometimes the ship reminded her of the brothel, with all the men hovering—constantly hovering. She turned, pulling away from the rail.

Jiméne smiled, brushing imaginary lint from his new mustard-yellow coat as he moved into place beside her. "I have been searching for you."

She smiled tightly. "Have you? Why?"

"You wound me, *cariña.*" Jiméne melodramatically put a hand to his heart. "How can you ask such a question when you know just the thought of your smile brings me joy?"

Ana turned to look back at the horizon, too bored to even reply. She had heard it all before, a hundred times. It was a pity; when Jiméne wasn't bemoaning her lack of interest, he could be quite entertaining. "How long until we reach the shore?"

"Not long." Jiméne leaned against the rail and sighed. "Have you never been to Panama?"

"No."

"It is a lovely place," he said enthusiastically. "The jungle is beautiful—and deadly." He smiled. "It reminds me of you, a little."

"Me?" Ana looked at him quizzically. "Why is that?"

"Beautiful. Deadly."

"Ah." None of the lines were even original. How often had she heard those same things? At Rosalie's, she'd been compared to a tiger from darkest India, a black widow spider—even a jeweled stiletto. It never changed. But at least she knew how to deal with these words. At least she knew what they really meant.

That was why she felt comfortable with Jiméne. He was like all those men she'd known in New York. Easy to handle and familiar. Safe. Predictable. So unlike D'Alessandro.

The thought of her partner sent a fresh stab of confusion through her. Unwillingly, her mind went back to the incident outside New Orleans. Seeing him like that, in so much pain, had bothered her. He'd seemed vulnerable and alone, and in spite of herself, a part of her had been drawn to it, understood it.

But his bitter anger had made her angry too. She closed her eyes a moment, remembering his flat voice that hid far more emotion than she wanted to hear, the feeling she had that her words had taken something from him.

He was the strangest man she'd ever met. What had he expected from her? The reality was that he was doing exactly what she paid him to do—he was around just enough to discourage the others. She had never expected more from him. So why did she feel as if she'd somehow disappointed him?

"It must've hurt to say that." His words circled back to her. He was right, it had hurt to thank him for defending her, but what bothered her more was that he saw it. So she'd insulted him in return. Because it was safer, because his perception frightened her.

". . . miss it," Jiméne finished.

Ana pushed the image of her partner away, refusing to allow it to disturb her. She forced interest into her voice and looked at Jiméne. "I'm sorry, you were saying?"

Jiméne stroked his thick mustache. "Once again, you wound me. I was saying, *cariña,* how much I miss this place." He glanced to the green hills. "I thought I would not, but I have. I am looking forward to seeing my home again, and my family. *Mi madre,* she is getting older. And I fear she has not been well."

She heard the longing in his voice, and she knew he was waiting for her to ask the questions. Ana said nothing. Questions only led to questions, and she didn't want to see the hurt on his face when she refused to answer his.

He sighed, then went on as if she had asked. "Though I do not miss Chagres. It is a place to be missed, a—how do you say?—a pig hole?"

"Sty," Ana corrected, smiling a little. "A pigsty."

"A pigsty, then," he said. "But my house—*mi madre*'s house—is far away from there, in a small *valle* near Panama City."

She nodded, not taking her eyes from the shore, wishing Jiméne would simply shut up and enjoy the view.

He shook his head sorrowfully. "You do not care, do you, *mi amiga hermosa*? Ah, how heartless you are." He took a deep breath. "Nothing I say impresses you, Ana. Tell me how much harder I should try."

Ana didn't answer.

He bent closer, touching her arm. "Why are you with D'Alessandro, *cariña*? Leave him. Come with me."

"No, Jiméne." She withdrew her arm gently, suddenly feeling sorry for him. He *was* gallant and impulsive. It wasn't his fault he'd become enamoured of a whore.

Besides, it was true that, every day, she came a little closer to accepting his offer and leaving with him. It would be easy, so easy. D'Alessandro confused her and made her uncomfortable—good enough reasons in themselves to leave. But even more than that, D'Alessandro had become a liability. She was afraid he was going to gamble all her hard-won money away—if he didn't squander it on drink—before they even reached Panama City.

Yes, Jiméne's offer was certainly tempting. If it wasn't for the promise she'd made . . . A self-deprecating smile touched Ana's lips. A stupid promise, but a promise nonetheless. Besides, it would be too much trouble to get rid of D'Alessandro now. No, she'd wait and hope he wouldn't slow her down once they were on the trail.

But if he did . . . Ana frowned slightly. If he did, she would have to take matters into her own hands. She couldn't abide the thought that he might delay her trip. San Francisco beckoned, her new life waited . . .

"Please, *cariña?*"

She looked up at Jiméne and shook her head. "I can't leave him."

"But why? What is it he holds over you?" His hand tightened on her arm, he leaned closer until she could read the pleading in his brown eyes. "I can offer you so much more . . ."

Ana looked past him, barely hearing his words as she saw D'Alessandro stagger onto the deck. He barely spared her a glance, but she knew by his sudden stiffness that he'd spotted her. It was what she expected after yesterday, what she intended—to keep him at a distance. If he hated her, so much the better. At least then she wouldn't always be on the defensive, or feel the disconcerting intimacy of his gaze.

But again she felt an uncomfortable wave of guilt. Guilt that only increased when he looked straight at her and shook his head with a disapproving frown, and she realized that even after her dismissal of him yesterday, he was still concerned about the way her friendship with Jiméne appeared.

That surprised and confused her. Ana felt a deep, slow warmth that had nothing to do with the heat, and she looked away quickly, summoning indifference, pretending she didn't care.

But he was right, and she knew it. There was too much gossip on the ship.

"Please, Jiméne," she said, pulling away. "People will talk."

"Let them talk," he protested passionately. "I do not care."

"But I do." Ana moved so they weren't touching. "Not here."

"I see." Jiméne's eyes were dark. "Very well then,

cariña, I will do as you wish. Today I will go. Tomorrow it will not be so easy."

Ana watched Jiméne march away with a relieved regret. By tomorrow it wouldn't matter. The ship's gossip wouldn't matter once they reached Chagres. Chagres, the beginning of the journey. The excitement that surged through her made her forget Jiméne's anger. *The beginning.* At last. The ship was her escape, but once she set foot in Central America, she would truly feel everything was behind her.

Even New York. That night with Benjamin Whitehall had only been eight days ago, and yet it felt like another life, another time. Rosalie would have given up the search by now, Ana was sure. She was safe as long as she stayed out of New York, and since she'd intended to do that anyway, it was hardly an inconvenience.

Certainly there was no one she minded leaving behind. In the seedy quarter of the city called Five Points, friendships were temporary, usually ended by violence and death. Before long, even Rosalie would forget her, and with her memory would go Ana's life in the city. It would be as if Anastasia, alias the Duchess, had never existed.

The thought made her sad for only a moment. She would start over in San Francisco, create another identity, a woman more in control of her life than the Duchess had ever been. A woman who didn't need anyone.

"Everyone needs someone, Anastasia."

Ana closed her eyes. Her skin felt hot suddenly, she tried to swallow the dry, tight lump in her throat. She heard her mother's voice as clearly as if she were standing there. *"The only people to pity, my darling, are those who are alone."*

Ana had believed that once. Once, when the little shanty house had been full of light and hope and joy. When her mother had been beautiful, happy, *sane.*

Ana opened her eyes and looked down at her feet.

Forever ago. That fairy-tale life had turned into a horror story so long ago she wondered if the memories were really hers. She remembered an icy winter night, lugging home a bucket of precious water that was nearly frozen while Mama told the story of how she and Ana's father had first met, how they'd danced and whispered perfumed intimacies, how they'd counted the stars in the Duvants' garden while the musicians in the ballroom began the first strains of a waltz. *We knew we loved each other then. When he comes for us, darling—oh, you'll see what a fine dancer your father was!*

Ana clenched her jaw. As a child, she'd memorized the things Mama told her about her father. A fine dancer. A handsome man. A lover of fine horseflesh. She knew him—oh, yes, she knew him.

But he had never bothered to know her, and the older she got, the more she told herself she didn't care. As the years went on, and she watched her mother going slowly mad waiting for him, Ana realized she finally, truly *didn't* care, didn't give a damn about him at all.

That was when the loneliness started, the sense of being completely alone. Now the feeling never went away. She told herself it didn't matter. It was a small price to pay for guaranteeing she would never be like her mother. Loneliness, vulnerability, would never destroy her that way, and the bitter memory of what her mother had become kept Ana strong, kept her from depending on anyone, or caring too much. No one had ever made her feel differently.

By the time her mother died, Ana learned to feel nothing. Not even love. Only pity and the will to survive. Only that. Loneliness was easy to ignore when she thought of the alternative.

The thought swelled inside her, and Ana shivered, hugging herself as a sudden chill went through her, consuming her until she stood there shaking. Lonely, yes, she could be lonely. She had been for years, she was used to it. She understood it. In a way she even needed it.

But in the back of her mind, she heard the faint strains of a waltz, heard the laughter of two people standing in a garden, counting the stars.

And she couldn't stop shaking.

"Watch it!"

Jeb Wilson crashed into Cain, sending him stumbling over a trunk. With effort, he caught himself. His head pounded as he tried to move out of the way. He cracked his shin on the corner. "Damn!"

Jeb dropped his bags and mopped his brow sheepishly. "Sorry about that, D'Alessandro. Didn't see you there."

"Everyone's in a hurry," Cain said wryly, rubbing his shin as Jeb rushed past. He looked about the deck, strewn now with trunks, valises, and canvas bags, and piling higher with every passing minute. Passengers thronged the deck, chattering with excitement, their hurry to leave the anchored ship vibrating in the air.

In fact, Cain thought dryly, the only thing that kept everyone from rushing forward was the mile of water that stretched between them and the mouth of the Chagres River. And for some men, even that wouldn't remain a problem for long. If the canoes spreading from the shore didn't reach the *Delilah* soon, Cain fully expected to see them jumping into the shallow bay and swimming for shore.

He stared at the wild green mountains, letting his gaze travel from the plant-choked ravines to the old, brown battlements of San Lorenzo, the castle that guarded the point.

It was unlike anything he'd ever seen, foreign and primitive, and it only increased the trepidation he'd felt since they anchored outside of the narrow river mouth this morning.

The native canoes were swarming closer to the ship, moving so frenziedly he kept expecting them to crash into each other. Men crowded the rails, shouting, pushing, each one wanting to be first.

Yet Cain found the very idea of leaving the ship terrifying.

He stepped back, letting the others vie for his place, wishing he was drunk. He'd deliberately stopped drinking yesterday, wanting to be feeling well—or if not well, then at least sober—for their arrival in Chagres. As a result, he had a splitting headache, he was sweating profusely in the tropical heat, and his stomach lurched at every movement.

He blamed the Duchess for all of it.

Cain frowned sourly and sank onto a nearby trunk. It was all her fault. If she hadn't managed to make him feel slightly lower than a snake, he wouldn't be feeling this absurd urge to prove himself to her. If she hadn't made it so clear that he was somehow incapable of being a man —if not a human being—he would be too numb to care if he drowned falling out of one of those damn canoes.

She had this way with words . . . He winced, remembering how she'd told him that she expected Casteñeras to take care of everything. The Panamanian was younger than Cain by at least ten years, he'd bet his life on it. Jiméne was more a boy than a man, still caring more about polishing his boots than learning to survive, spending his life flirting with women instead of loving them.

In short, he was a gentleman. And around Casteñeras, Cain was all too aware of how he didn't measure up—at least in her eyes.

He sighed, raking his hand through his hair. The last few nights had hammered at his self-esteem. He'd buried himself in cards and conversation, trying to ignore the way Jiméne was always by the Duchess's side: solicitous, charming, entertaining. Christ, Cain hadn't even known she *had* the kind of bright, sincere smile she turned on the Panamanian.

And he told himself he didn't care. He wanted—God, how he wanted—to leave her to Jiméne, to go back to his existence of traveling aimlessly, trading medicine for drink. He wanted to be free to drown in the failure that had haunted him his entire life. He buried his face in his hands.

But there was that damned agreement. He'd said he would pose as her husband, and regardless of what she thought that meant, he knew part of the job was to keep her safe.

Because of that responsibility, he'd vowed to himself that, in spite of what she'd told him about Castañeras, he would take charge once they arrived in Chagres, he would prove to her that her money was well spent.

Footsteps echoed on the deck beside him, then stopped. Cain peered through his fingers at the pair of boots stopped before him. Shiny boots.

"¿Estás enfermo?"

Cain lifted his head. "Hello, Castañeras."

"You do not look well today, *amigo.*" Jiméne's eyes widened in mock concern as he leaned down to look closer into Cain's face.

"Thank you. I feel fine."

"Fine? *Perdón,* but I must disagree. Perhaps it would be best if Ana and I went on." Jiméne's dark eyes lit maliciously. "You could sleep, perhaps. We could meet you later—say, perhaps, in Gorgona?"

Cain smiled thinly. "Have a care, Castañeras."

"I am only concerned, *amigo!*"

"I am concerned too," Cain said. "Concerned that you might find yourself floating in the harbor." His gaze traveled pointedly over Jiméne's bright mustard coat. "I would hate to see your fine apparel ruined. Who knows where you could get another coat in this godforsaken place."

Jiméne's mustache twitched, his eyes narrowed. "I do not know why she wastes her time with you."

"Watch yourself," Cain warned. "I am her husband."

"So you say."

"So does she."

"I think," Jiméne said thoughtfully, "that it is you who should watch yourself, *amigo*. I will warn you now: Know I will do everything I can to see that she leaves you."

The warning was delivered with the force of certainty, and a stab of anger went through Cain. He suddenly ached for a drink so badly his hands trembled. But a loud noise at one side of the ship distracted him.

He followed Jiméne's gaze to the source of the sound.

"The bungos," Jiméne said tonelessly.

The natives had arrived, crowding the ship, colliding with each other, all shouting: *"¡Canoa! ¡Canoa!"* in their efforts to find the richest passengers. Trunks, valises, and bags were thrown haphazardly over the side, banging on heads and falling in the bay just as often as they landed in the canoes.

It was Cain's chance. His chance to go forward and prove how indispensable he could be. His chance to hire a bungo and load their things, to be ready when Ana was.

But he couldn't seem to rise from the trunk, and in the time it took him to realize that, Jiméne was already across the deck, shouting in Spanish. No doubt getting the best price as well, Cain thought grimly. The flask in his pocket grew heavier against his chest. It all seemed suddenly pointless—trying to be sober, to be indispensable. He could never compete with Jiméne, and she didn't want him to anyway.

"Damn, they're here sooner than I thought." Robert Jameson hurried on deck, pausing beside Cain. He held a half-empty bottle of rum, and Ana was close on his heels. Cain caught the distinct, sweet smell of the liquor, and his stomach lurched in longing.

A longing that became almost painful when he saw Robert tip the rum into his hands and splash it over his arms.

"What the hell are you doing?"

Robert looked at him distractedly. "Warding off the fever," he said. He handed the bottle back to Ana, who took it gingerly. Like Robert, she poured a small portion into her hands and splashed it on her face, careful not to wet her hair, before she handed it back.

It was more than he could take. No one except himself cared if he was sober—and now, after Jiméne's words, even he didn't care that much. The yearning was too strong to fight.

"Give me that." Cain snatched the bottle from Robert's grasp and tipped it to his mouth. The rum was sweet and warm, and he gulped it thirstily, feeling better immediately. He handed the bottle back to Robert and wiped his mouth with the back of his hand. "That's what you do with rum, Jameson. You *drink* it."

Behind Robert, Ana stopped. Her hands dropped to her sides, and she stared at him warily. "It doesn't stop the fever?"

Smiling, Cain shook his head. "No."

"What the hell do you know?" Robert demanded.

Ana wiped her face with her sleeve, her brown eyes glittering. "He's a *doctor,* Mr. Jameson." Her voice was heavy with accusing scorn, as if the word itself were blasphemy.

"A doctor?"

Cain shrugged. "Hard to believe, isn't it?"

"But you never said anything." Robert's face clouded. "Even when Bartlett had that fever."

"And have all of you begging for my services?" Cain laughed shortly. "Besides, Bartlett was only drunk, not sick."

"A doctor." Robert rubbed his chin, his eyes measuring. "Well, then. Perhaps you and Mrs. D'Alessandro would reconsider joining us? A doctor would be a good—"

"No," Ana said quickly, stepping forward. "We've made our plans already, Mr. Jameson." She sent a pointed glance to Cain. "And I would hate to add to your difficulties."

The words sent a shaft of resentment stabbing through him. The rum in Robert's hand seemed to glow. Cain struggled to speak lightly, nonchalantly. "As you can see, Jameson, my sweet wife has little regard for my talents. And in that, she is probably right."

She frowned. "That isn't what—"

"I have it!" Jiméne's shout interrupted her, and the three of them looked toward the wildly waving Panamanian. "Ana, come now, they are ready to take us!"

She licked her lips and looked at Cain. "Are you ready?"

"As ready as I'll ever be." Slowly Cain rose, looking around for their luggage. He spotted their two valises and his medical case, along with a large leather trunk covered with canvas at Jiméne's feet.

Ana was already halfway there, cutting through the crowd easily, hips swaying beneath the heavy wool skirt. There was actually a bounce to her step, Cain noticed. Since Jiméne had joined them, the panic he'd sensed the night they met had disappeared. Now she seemed eager —almost excited—to get on with the journey.

At first, he'd thought she relaxed because the threat of capture was gone. Now he wondered bitterly if it had more to do with meeting Castañeras.

Cain's temples throbbed, his feet felt like lead as he dragged himself across the deck. Sourly he watched Jiméne throw the first valise over the side. Christ, the man was efficient. Probably it was too much to hope that the luggage would land in the water.

The bag landed with a steady thud in the bottom of the canoe. Jiméne glanced over his shoulder.

"We have the bungo for the trip," he announced loudly, over the shouts of the others. "I have hired them to go downriver."

Very efficient. Cain nodded wryly. "Wonderful." He restrained the urge to send Jiméne flying over the side with the luggage. With his luck, Castañeras would probably land in the canoe. "It looks like you've taken care of everything," he said sarcastically.

Jiméne nodded. "Everything, *amigo.*" He smiled. His eyes lit with challenge. "Even *aguardiente* for you. José says he has enough to hold you to Panama City."

There was no doubt in Cain's mind that Jiméne hoped Cain would get drunk enough to leave Ana to the Panamanian. A thin smile curved his lips. No point in disappointing the man. *"Muchas gracias."*

"It is my pleasure."

"I'm sure it is."

Jiméne held out his hand to Ana. "This way, *cariña.*"

Cain stepped back, waiting while Ana moved through the gate, dodging those too impatient to wait. She settled herself in the boat gracefully, smoothing her skirts around her. Jiméne followed her quickly, shouting hasty orders to the burly boatman, motioning impatiently to Cain. The bungo began to slip away from the steamer; Cain nearly had to jump to make it.

He sat with a thud. The canoe rocked, and he glared at Jiméne.

The Panamanian smiled back. "Give the man a *riale,* D'Alessandro. I have told him you are the one with the money."

It was going to be, Cain thought, a very long trip.

Chapter 6

One look at the town, and Ana's excitement dissolved in dismay. Chagres was a cesspool. There was no hotel, nothing but two hundred or so open huts squatting on the mud flats. Naked children, pigs, and dogs ran through the hovels, scrambling up and down streets that had once been roughly paved and now were nothing more than ruts cut into the mud. Ruts filled with empty bottles and sewage that baked in the sun. The stench of it, mixed with the odor of pigs and stagnant water, hovered in the hot, humid air.

Ana tried not to breathe. She stared at the filthy village, at the buzzards that sat on the high, peaked roofs, watching lazily, waiting for something to die. The smell alone said they wouldn't have to wait long. Ana thought a lifetime in the slums of New York had prepared her for the sight of poverty and squalor, but Chagres was worse than anything she'd ever seen. Against the rich green of the jungle around it, it was almost obscene.

It was nothing like she'd imagined it, nothing like she'd expected. The shores of Panama seemed so promising from a distance. But this—this was not a place that promised fresh starts and new beginnings.

She turned to her partner, ignoring for the moment the piles of luggage on the muddy ground surrounding her. "When do we leave?"

D'Alessandro glanced at her, frowning as if her question had taken him by surprise. He shrugged and swiped his heavy hair back from his forehead. "Castañeras said they'll be ready to go by morning."

"By morning?" Ana asked incredulously. "So what do we do?"

"Do?" D'Alessandro looked at her blankly.

"Well, we can't stay here."

"Of course we can." He sat heavily on the lid of Jiméne's trunk and uncorked his flask. "We have no choice anyway. They'll leave when they're ready."

Ana glanced at the rows of canoes beached on the mud of the Chagres River shore. Their owners scurried around the open-air boats like ants, rethatching the canopies with split palmetto while vendors selling *aguardiente* harangued them from the shore. She pulled at the collar of her dress and wiped back a limp curl clinging to her cheek. It was hot. Hot, humid, lethargic. The breeze that had eased the heat on the steamer was absent here, even the heavy foliage of the jungle seemed to steam.

"We can't stay here," she repeated, frowning.

"I agree." Jiméne walked up, sticky, stagnant black mud clinging to his once-shiny boots. "I have been trying to convince José to go, but he will not until morning."

"It *is* late," D'Alessandro said.

Jiméne scowled. "During the rainy season, they travel often at night. It is not unusual."

D'Alessandro glanced idly at the line of bungos. "Oh? Then why is no one leaving?"

"They are lazy." Jiméne nearly spat the words.

Ana stepped forward. Her disappointment made her

irritable and edgy, and she wanted nothing more than to be in a bungo on its way downriver, feeling the breeze on her face again and retreating into the cool green of the jungle. The humidity here was oppressive, the village of Chagres stank, and D'Alessandro's reluctance to agree with her and Jiméne was annoying. In fact, it was more than annoying. It was infuriating.

"It's dangerous." D'Alessandro tipped back the flask and swallowed.

"Why do you say this?" Jiméne's dark brows came together, his mustache twitched. *"I* am the one who was born here, *amigo.* You know nothing of the jungle. Nothing!"

"Dangerous?" Ana pulled again at her collar. This damn corset was like being in an iron coffin. "What do you mean, dangerous?"

D'Alessandro regarded them both steadily. "Did you ask José why he wouldn't go on tonight, Castañeras? Why he won't go into the jungle after dark?"

"It is not yet after dark," Jiméne retorted. "He is afraid, that is all. He is not a man." He bit off a sound of frustration, turning on his heel. "Very well. José will not go, but there are others who will."

"Why the hell are you in such a hurry?"

D'Alessandro's comment stopped Jiméne. The Panamanian looked over his shoulder, and Ana saw anger and distress in his eyes before he turned again and marched off without answering.

"Something's bothering him," she said thoughtfully.

"He's probably afraid he'll get his coat dirty," D'Alessandro said.

Ana glared at him, trying vainly to quell her annoyance. "Why don't you stop being so disagreeable? Why shouldn't we leave today?"

"Because, Duchess, it's growing late. Traveling at night doesn't appeal to me."

"Afraid of the dark?"

"In an unknown place—a jungle?" D'Alessandro laughed shortly. "In a word, yes."

"Jiméne says it's safe."

"Jiméne is a fool." He shrugged. "If he wants to court death, let him."

His words sent a nagging doubt through her, and Ana squashed it ruthlessly. She had to remember whom she was listening to. A drunkard. There was no reason to pay attention to his misgivings. After all, Jiméne was the expert, and if he said they should go, she was more than willing to trust him—especially because she too wanted out of this hellhole. D'Alessandro's trepidation was no doubt a product of his drunken imaginings.

"He's just in a hurry," she said, brushing off D'Alessandro's worries. "You make too much of it."

"Maybe." He shrugged, taking another swig before he tucked the flask away. "So what's your hurry, Duchess? Why the rush to go on? So quick to be rid of me?"

She ignored his jibe, motioning to the village. "This is . . . I just want to get away from here."

"You're braver than I thought."

"There's no bravery involved," she snapped irritably. "I've two big strong men to protect me, don't I?"

"One anyway," he murmured.

"Don't insult Jiméne."

"I was talking about Jiméne."

His humor was almost more than she could bear. That was all she needed—a self-pitying drunkard. She shielded her eyes with her hand, looking toward Jiméne. He was talking with a burly boatman now, perhaps negotiating. With a sigh, she sank onto the trunk beside D'Alessandro.

"Relax, Duchess," he said.

"Relax?" Ana snorted, moving away from him so they weren't touching. She looked over her shoulder at the village. "God, what a pigsty."

"What were you expecting? A grand hotel?"

"A bed would have been nice." Ana had to admit that after spending eight days in a steamer hammock, she had looked forward to actually sleeping on a real mattress. No more swaying back and forth with the ship's motion, no more aching back or numb shoulders.

"This isn't going to be an easy trip," Cain said mildly.

"Really?" she said sarcastically.

D'Alessandro rested one booted foot on his knee and leaned forward, as if trying to focus on something just beyond his sight.

Ana swatted at the dragging feather on her hat and looked down at the black, slimy mud beneath her feet.

D'Alessandro shifted beside her, and Ana looked up. He was still staring at the opposite shore, silently assessing something. Frowning, she followed his glance.

And saw for the first time the beauty of the jungle.

She'd been so appalled by Chagres that she hadn't really noticed the wild opulence on the other shore of the broad, clear river. The high, steep hills sheltering the west bank were covered with orange and lemon trees, palms, banana, and plantain. Most of the plants she'd never seen before, never even imagined. Exotic orchids punctuated the green with vibrant color, and bright butterflies battled for attention. Quick, acrobatic buzzards circled through the palmettos and coconuts while multihued parrots screamed their disapproval.

"It reminds me of a fairy tale," she murmured without thinking.

D'Alessandro looked at her. "A fairy tale?"

She nodded, not taking her eyes from the jungle. "I had this book when I was young, a book of Russian stories with pictures. This reminds me of it."

"I didn't know Russia had jungles."

"I don't know that it does," she said. "But the pictures were so beautiful—" Ana stopped, suddenly realizing that she was talking to him, really talking. Telling him about a book she'd had when she was a child. Telling him about her life . . .

She stiffened, feeling strangely violated. She'd never spoken of even the most casual aspect of her life to anyone. Not in years. The more people knew about you, the more dangerous they were. And D'Alessandro was the most dangerous of all. He already knew too much about her, and here she was, volunteering information—again. Something about him made her forget she wanted to keep him firmly at arm's length.

Her hands clenched in her lap. That was something she *had* to remember.

"—so beautiful?" he prompted in the kind of tone that asked for an explanation. His eyes were dark and interested.

But she was not going to explain. Not anything, and the sooner he realized that, the better. Her life was her business, and she wanted to keep it that way. She turned away abruptly. "It was a book, that's all," she said. Her voice sounded stiff and unkind even to her. "Look, Jiméne's returning."

"So he is," D'Alessandro said quietly, his tone edged with censure.

She looked up, watching Jiméne. His dark face was split by a white-toothed smile. Ana felt D'Alessandro tense beside her.

"A knight in shining armor," he murmured under his breath.

The moment Jiméne was close enough to speak, Ana was on her feet. "Well?"

"We have a *cayuca,*" he said triumphantly. "The men are waiting for us now. I had to pay them more, of course—"

"Of course," D'Alessandro broke in.

Jiméne glared at him. "But they ask for only a moment. Then we will leave." He motioned towards the river. "Come with me now, eh? We must help load."

With his words, Ana's excitement came bounding back. They were leaving. Thank God. D'Alessandro lumbered to his feet and followed Jiméne down to their waiting bungo. Ana trailed behind, hiking up her heavy skirts so they didn't drag in the mud, waiting with bated excitement while the two of them worked with the canoe. Yes, everything was going to be fine now.

Jiméne and D'Alessandro slipped and slid as they pushed the twenty-five-foot bungo through the mud and shoal water to the bank. By the time they had the bungo readied and the luggage stowed, the late afternoon sun was starting to fade, though it was still brutally hot. Jiméne's bright coat was spotted with mud, and D'Alessandro was sopping wet. Gingerly Ana made her way to the boat, stopping just at the edge of the river.

D'Alessandro sat on the side of the bungo, his boots half submerged in the water. He barely spared her a glance as she neared. Instead he wiped his dripping forehead with his sleeve and turned to look at a sweaty, disheveled Jiméne.

"So now what, Castañeras?" he asked. "Where are these men you hired?"

Jiméne mopped his face with a delicate handkerchief. "They have gone to get supplies," he breathed. "They will return soon."

"Soon?"

"Yes, soon," Jiméne snapped. "Unless you do not want to eat, let them do as they will."

D'Alessandro looked up at the sky. "If they don't hurry, it'll be dark before they get back."

"So?" Jiméne shoved the handkerchief into his pocket angrily. "Then we will travel at night. It is done often during the rainy season."

"You said that before. I didn't know it was the rainy season."

Jiméne glared at D'Alessandro. "It is not."

D'Alessandro lifted his feet over the side of the boat,

easing backward until he was beneath the palmetto canopy. He propped one foot on the seat and leaned back. "*Querida,*" he called to her, patting the space beside him. "Come in out of the sun."

The offer was inviting. Sweat was gathering beneath the brim of her hat, and Ana felt the trickle of it down her spine. Shade would be worth anything, even sitting next to D'Alessandro. Nodding shortly, she lifted her skirts and took the few steps into the water.

Jiméne lunged forward, nearly losing his balance when the boat rocked at his sudden motion. He jumped over the side, and Ana winced as his splashing drenched her skirt.

"A gentleman," he said, never taking his eyes from D'Alessandro as he helped Ana into the bungo, "helps a lady."

"A gentleman," D'Alessandro pointed out, "probably sees that she's dry when she gets into the boat."

Ana put a hand to her temple and settled herself into the canoe, trying to ignore their bickering. She could take anything for a short while, as long as they got started quickly. "When did you say the men were returning, Jiméne?"

"They will hurry," he promised. "We paid them a fortune to be sure."

"Good." The shade felt better, but her hat was sweltering and she wanted nothing more than to fling it into the river. It and the corset had been a godsend leaving New York, but she knew already that wearing them for the rest of this journey would make it a living hell. Tonight, when they rested, she resolved to take the whalebone contraption off and leave it behind. The dress was big enough to wear without a corset, and there was no point in torturing herself.

And as for the hat . . . Ana pulled at the satin bows and tugged the stiff silk from her head, closing her eyes in relief as air touched her heavy hair. But the thick chignon was nearly as bad as the hat. Tendrils escaped, clinging to her neck and cheeks, and she felt for her gold comb, wondering if she had enough time to redo the heavy bun.

She sighed, turning slightly in the seat, and met D'Alessandro's gaze. He was staring at her, his dark eyes lit with amusement. Ana had the feeling he was laughing at her, and she snatched back her hand, burying it in her lap.

"Why don't you braid it?" he suggested.

"Braid it?"

"Seems to me it would help." He smiled. "But then, I guess it would be beneath you, wouldn't it? Only farm girls braid their hair."

His tone annoyed her—precisely because what he said was true. She would never have considered such a common style. Even when she was young, she never braided her hair. Her mother—

Ana swallowed, pushing away the thought before it could begin. "I don't know how to braid," she said finally.

His eyebrows rose in surprise. "No? I thought all little girls could braid."

"Apparently not."

"No, apparently not," he mimicked. He leaned back, never taking his eyes from her. "What kind of a little girl were you, Duchess, that you had a book of Russian fairy tales but you never learned to braid your hair?"

His question shocked her, and Ana felt a tight knot grow in her stomach.

"There they are!" Jiméne's sudden shout stopped her retort in her throat. He leapt to his feet, the bungo swayed at his quick movements. *"Dios, en el último minuto. Las bogas*—the boatmen."

Ana looked ashore. Two men walked toward the boat, their muscles straining beneath their coarse canvas shirts. Each wore a large-brimmed hat and carried bulging burlap sacks, though other than that they were very different. One was big, strong-looking and swarthy. The other was more wiry, and his deep brown skin was nearly the color of the river mud.

Once they grew close enough to hear, Jiméne shouted orders in rapid-fire Spanish. It didn't seem to move them at all. The bigger man looked at the other and shrugged.

"Poco tiempo," he said lazily. *"Poco tiempo."*

"What are they saying?" she asked.

D'Alessandro leaned close. "Castañeras is trying to get them to hurry," he translated in a low voice. "They're telling him they'll get moving in a little while."

"A little while?" Ana's protestations died as the two men approached the boat. With no thought to who sat inside, they shoved the burlap bags under the seat. Ana heard the unmistakable sound of clanking bottles.

D'Alessandro sat up a little straighter beside her.

Ana leaned forward until she could see Jiméne. "Jiméne, did these men bring bourbon?"

"Most probably it is brandy," Jiméne informed her. He moved about the bungo, shoving things out of the way in an obvious attempt to hurry the boatmen. "It is necessary for them, *cariña*. They will refuse to go without it."

Ana closed her eyes, taking a deep breath. Thank God. *Brandy*. Perhaps D'Alessandro would get so drunk he would pass out. The thought made her feel good for the first time in hours.

¡Ten piedad, piedad de mis penas!" The tenor and alto of the boatmen rose together. The sound echoed over the river and then disappeared, muffled by the dense, darkening jungle. Then they laughed uproariously, passing the brandy.

Ana watched sourly and then looked away. They had been like this for the last two hours of the journey, seemingly oblivious to the close, threatening beauty of the darkening jungle. The cries of monkeys and parrots were growing louder, but in spite of that, the jungle had an oppressive, silent feel. Rather like an animal stalking its prey, Ana thought uncomfortably. And it was stiflingly hot—the air was heavy and soft. The thick, cloying denseness pressed in on Ana, and she tightened her fingers on the side of the boat. The boatmen were so drunk she didn't trust either of them to navigate the river, which was a labyrinth of twists and turns. Islands formed suddenly in the center, strange whirlpools and eddies swirled around snags and quickly rising logs. And every now and then, one of those logs would bubble and raise its snout to take the form of an alligator.

Ana suddenly wished that she hadn't insisted on going forward tonight. The dirty huts of Chagres town seemed more appealing with every mile. But it was too late now. She'd made the decision, and there was nothing left to do but live with it. Ana straightened, lifting her chin determinedly.

"Decided something, have you, Duchess?" D'Alessandro asked.

Ana twisted to look at him. "What are you talking about?"

"You get that look," he explained. "The one that usually means you've decided something."

Ana ignored his irritatingly perceptive comment. Instead, she gave him her best disinterested stare. "Why don't you go to sleep? You look as if you could use it."

He glanced at Ambrosio, who poled smoothly and silently at the bow. "Yeah. Why don't you tell me a story? That should keep us entertained."

"Ask one of them." She gestured to Ruben, the boatman at the stern. "I'm sure they've plenty."

"Maybe." He shrugged. "I'd rather hear one of yours."

She turned away. "I don't know any."

"No? What about your Russian storybook?"

The words sliced through her. Ana fought the sudden lump in her throat. "I don't remember the stories."

"Just the pictures?"

"Yes." Damn him, anyway. As much as she could, Ana kept her memories sealed tight, refusing to even look at them herself. They were a vulnerability, a dangerous habit she had worked hard to forget.

And yet now, only a few simple words brought the memory back. Yes, she remembered the pictures, and the stories, and the way her mother had whispered the unfamiliar Russian names as if they were magic. As if they held some wonderful promise . . .

She tried to swallow the grief that welled up at the image, refusing to think of it, just as she'd refused to think of it for years. "If you want stories, I suggest you make them up yourself."

"But I—"

The bungo swerved suddenly, cutting D'Alessandro short, forcing them both to grab the sides for balance. Jiméne tumbled forward, and he scrambled back into his seat, his distracted look gone.

"*¿Qué hace?*" he shouted.

The boat scraped along the shore, branches from the overhanging trees clattered on the canopy, and vines trailed over Ana's arm. She shrank away from the side, staring at Ambrosio in confusion. The boatman's muscles strained with the pole. Then, suddenly, he dropped it and dove over the side into the dark water.

"Ambrosio!" D'Alessandro yelled, reaching for the pole. "*¿Qué hace?*"

The bungo shuddered to a stop. The current swirled around it, lapping against the plants dragging into the river. A few feet away Ana heard something slide into the water.

Her fingers clenched on the side of the boat. She

glanced up just in time to see Ambrosio break the surface, his dark hair streaming into his face.

He yelled something quickly in Spanish.

Jiméne blanched. *"Dios."*

Behind them, Ruben lurched to his feet. He chattered something to his partner, who answered just as quickly.

A shiver went up Ana's spine. She turned to D'Alessandro. "What is it? What is he saying?"

D'Alessandro's eyes were dark and unfathomable, his voice emotionless. "We've hit a snag. It's done some damage."

"Damage? What does that mean?"

"It means, Duchess, that until they fix it, we're stuck," he said, grabbing the abandoned brandy bottle from the floor and tipping it to his mouth. "Looks like you won't be getting a bed tonight after all."

Chapter 7

It took them half an hour to find the clearing that was only a few yards from shore. Apparently whoever created it had left only recently. Palmetto branches still lay severed and rotting on the ground, and the small firepit in the center had not yet been overgrown. Still, in the darkness it was a miracle they'd found it.

Ambrosio had lit a lantern, but the dim light only made the jungle at the perimeter of the clearing seem encroaching, silently malicious. Ana looked across the clearing at Jiméne. The others had gone to fix the boat —D'Alessandro with them—leaving Jiméne to protect her, though what there was to protect her from she didn't know.

Still, she was glad she wasn't alone. The unfamiliar jungle was unsettling, and, if nothing else, talking to Jiméne was a way to pass the time.

Near the perimeter, Jiméne lifted one of their supply bags and pawed through it. "There is plenty of food," he said. "You will have everything you need to cook dinner."

"Cook dinner?" Ana laughed shortly. "You may not want to eat when I'm through. I can't cook."

Jiméne stared at her as if she'd suddenly grown two heads. "You cannot cook?"

"No."

"But—but all women cook!"

"I don't."

"But—" Jiméne sank to the ground, the bags of food falling limply beside him. The bewilderment in his face was almost laughable. "I do not understand. How is this possible? You had servants, then?"

Ana restrained an urge to laugh sarcastically. "Servants? But of course we had servants, *monsieur.*"

Jiméne looked sheepish. "You tease me, *amiga.*"

"You are easy to tease," she said, kneeling beside him on the swampy loam.

"It is only that you surprised me. I have never met a woman who could not cook."

"Well, now you have." Ana reached for one of the bags laying beside him and weighed it in her hand. "What will you be making for dinner?"

His laugh sounded strangled, and Ana glanced at him in surprise.

"I must admit I cannot cook either, *cariña.*"

"You can't?"

Jiméne shook his head. "No. It was always my sisters who cooked. Or *mi madre.*" He grew suddenly quiet, his smile died, and Ana sensed distress. But before she could say anything, he forced a strained grin. "What about you, Ana? How is it you do not cook? Did not your mother teach you?"

"No, she didn't." Ana deflected the personal question with practiced ease. "Really, Jiméne, surely you know *something* about cooking? Didn't you ever watch your mother?"

Jiméne shrugged. "Once or twice, perhaps. Most of the time, I worked with *mi padre.* He was only *un labra-*

dor, a—a—" He scrambled for the word. "A farmer. We were poor. My brothers and I had to help . . ."

He chattered on, oblivious of Ana's silence as he moved about the clearing, lighting a damp, smoky fire and setting out a clay cooking jar.

Ana watched quietly while he clumsily prepared their meal, his talk fading to a meaningless buzz in her ears. It was so easy. It was always so easy. Men loved to hear themselves talk. She was skilled at getting them started, skilled at the subtle question, the turn in conversation, the interested murmurs. At Rosalie's, she'd often worked to keep them talking even as they thrust into her, because it hid the fact that she didn't move or respond at all.

There were some men who hadn't minded a still body, but others felt they were paying for her mind and emotions as well, and those were the men she hated most. So she let them talk, and ridiculed them silently, and let them leave thinking they knew her, when it was she who held their secrets and not the other way around.

Ana sighed. When she got to San Francisco, when she ran her own place, she would only take the ones who didn't talk. There, she would lay down the rules and make them understand they were paying only for her body, not her soul.

". . . but that is not my dream. I would like to be rich, to live in America and send money to them all, to not have to worry. It is hard, *cariña,* to be so far away, to worry so . . ." Jiméne talked on, gesturing in between his sloppy measuring of the rice.

Ana watched him. He was like the others, telling her his dreams as if she cared what they were, as if she had a stake in his life. She knew what would come next. They all expected it; one intimacy traded for another. A man would tell her his dreams and suddenly believe she shared them. Soon he would ask something of her—a question, a favor, it didn't matter. Soon he would be behaving as if she were a friend or a lover instead of a whore.

She waited for Jiméne to turn and look at her with those same, glowing eyes. The eyes that told her that, in his mind, they were already intimate. She prepared herself for it, letting her disdain build, knowing he would see it in her face when he turned to her. It was an old defense, one she had used a hundred times to dissuade men from getting too close. Disdain, mockery, ridicule—they all worked. They all made a man realize what a fool he'd made of himself. All made a man remember that she was only a whore, a woman whose time and body was for sale.

But Jiméne turned before she was ready, taking her hands in his before she could move.

"Ah, Ana, I will admit I want you, that I try to impress you. If you would let me, I would kill that *perro* who says he is your husband."

His brown eyes looked bottomless in the darkness, full of a passionate yearning that made Ana uncomfortable. They were the eyes she'd expected. The look that asked for intimacy—begged for it.

"Tell me the truth, *mi amiga hermosa*. Tell me he is not your husband. Tell me and I will take you away from this. I will take you to a place where we can make love in the sunshine . . ."

Ana pulled away, wrapping her hands in her skirt. "Don't be ridiculous, Jiméne."

She got to her feet, turning her back on him and walking to the opposite side of the fire. Then, gathering her rough skirts, she sank onto the dirt.

Their silence seemed to intensify the jungle's sounds: the soft pad of heavy animals over the swampy ground, the quiet splash of something sliding into the river. Monkeys chattered, the branches above their heads clattered and moved apart. The constant hum and clicking of insects rose from the shadows.

Across the fire, Jiméne stirred the rice in the earthenware pot sullenly, his eyes downcast. Ana wished suddenly that she hadn't hurt him. Jiméne was the closest thing to a friend she had on this trip. It was true he was like the other men she'd known, but that was exactly why he was no real threat.

Ana looked over at him, feeling a familiar regret. Over the years she had wanted friends, but she couldn't seem to let down the barrier protecting herself long enough to have them.

She often wondered if she would ever stop being afraid, wondered if she was even capable of having a friend. God knew she'd never been before. The fear that they would get too close paralyzed her, the memory of her mother froze her inside.

But Jiméne wasn't dangerous to her; she could easily keep him at bay if she wanted to. There was no chance he'd get too close; she had no fear that he knew something about her just by looking in her eyes.

Unlike D'Alessandro.

Ana closed her eyes, shivering slightly. No, Jiméne was nothing like D'Alessandro. She felt comfortable with Jiméne, and perhaps that was enough to start. Perhaps, if she really tried, she could make him the first real friend she'd ever had.

Ana took a deep breath. "Jiméne," she said softly.

He looked up, his hand stilled over the pot. *"¿Sí?"* His voice was wary.

"Tell me about your family."

"Why? You do not wish to hear."

"But I do," she insisted. "I really do."

But when he started to tell her, Ana's mind drifted far away.

After twenty minutes of toying with his bowl, Cain finally put it aside. He wasn't hungry anyway, but if he had been, the unpalatable stew Ana and Castañeras had concocted would have destroyed his appetite. Half-cooked rice floated in a tasteless, watery broth, while chunks of tough and slimy pork bobbed like rotten wood. The only decent thing was the coconut—thank God they hadn't had to cook it—and between gulps of brandy, he'd managed to get down a few bites of that, though it was the most he'd eaten since the one night he'd gorged himself on the ship, and now the chunks of coconut churned in his stomach uncomfortably.

He held the bottle of brandy to his lips and took a deep, comforting sip. His blood warmed, and his stomach immediately settled. In the last hours, with the aid of liquor, he'd managed to forget he'd ever seen the night jungle as threatening. Now it seemed to take on a comforting darkness, and he leaned back against the leaf-covered trunk and closed his eyes, listening to the sounds.

Jiméne's voice floated to him, the rapid Spanish syllables blending and shifting. With part of his mind, Cain understood the words; Jiméne was busy making plans for the morning. They'd be setting off early, with the sunrise, since the boat had needed only minimal repairs.

Jiméne, Ambrosio, and Ruben sat close together, talking so quickly it sounded almost like music. The only thing missing was the voice of a woman. Gentle, sweet, perhaps even singing . . .

Cain smiled and opened his eyes. There was the Duchess, of course. Not gentle, or even sweet, but there was a soft music in her voice that sometimes warmed the chill edge of her words. She was quiet now, just the way he liked her, and she sat across from him, carefully combing her hair with that gold comb she carried everywhere. Her eyes were hooded, the firelight cast reddish shadows on her hair, and the smoke softened her features so she almost looked as if she were smiling.

He knew *that* had to be an illusion, but Cain felt drawn to her all the same. She intrigued him, with her unassailable secrecy and her aristocratic demeanor. He'd watched her as they traveled the river, when she didn't know anyone was looking, watched her widening eyes and the way her lips parted in wonder. But there was always that edge—that wall that never came down.

Suddenly he had the urge to see if he could dent it, to see if he could make her smile, or laugh, or tell him anything about herself.

Jiméne and the others were so involved in their conversation they didn't even glance up as Cain lurched to his feet. Carefully, since the ground seemed to be coming up to meet him, he stepped to where she sat. She didn't look up, just kept combing her long, thick curls.

"Hello, D'Alessandro," she murmured softly.

"Hello."

She looked up, surveyed him coolly. "Did you want something?"

"Thought you might need some help," he said. "With your hair."

"Thank you, no, I don't."

"I could—" Cain took a deep breath. "I could braid it for you."

Her hands stilled, and when she looked at him, Cain thought he saw gentle mockery in her eyes. "I don't think so."

"No?" Cain smiled. He dropped down beside her, taking the comb from her stiff fingers. It glittered in the half light, the delicate scrollery and swirls reflecting the flame nearly as beautifully as her hair had. "Where did you get this? It's beautiful."

She licked her lips. For a moment, he thought she wasn't going to answer, but then, in a voice so quiet he barely heard it, she said, "It was my mother's."

"Was it?" He turned it over in his hand. "Looks Spanish."

"Spanish?" She looked up quickly, and he got the feeling he'd surprised her. "She told me it was Russian."

A small smile touched her lips. "But then, she told me everything was Russian."

"Like the storybook?"

She stiffened. Cain cursed himself for asking the question. He saw the shutters come down over her eyes.

"What about you, Mr. D'Alessandro? Did you have a favorite storybook as a child?"

The question startled him, and it took a moment for Cain to realize what she was doing. He'd heard it before, the whore's trick, the way of keeping men from encroaching on her privacy. The Duchess had learned it better than most. For a minute he'd almost believed she was interested, almost thought she wanted to know something about him as badly as he wanted to know something about her.

In fact, he still wasn't sure she wasn't interested. Cain stared at her, at the flickering of the firelight across her high cheekbones and smooth skin, at the tawny eyes that glinted gold in the darkness. She *was* beautiful. She'd probably been one of Rosalie's highest-paid girls, one of the most compelling and most skilled.

Most skilled. The words echoed in his brain. She was skilled enough to twist him up inside if he let her. He knew he should walk away from her now, away from her beauty and her tricks, and her icy stare. But he couldn't move.

Cain swallowed and took a deep breath. Not knowing what possessed him, except that in spite of his warnings, he didn't want to leave her, he held out the comb.

"Will you let me braid it?"

She bit her lip, looking uncertain, and then she nodded. "Yes, go ahead. If tomorrow is anything like today, it would be best."

The sorrow he heard in her voice made him smile. It was as if she regretting pinning up her hair more than she dreaded his touch. Cain waited while she turned her back to him and took a deep breath, as if steeling herself for some arduous pain.

Cain touched the comb to her hair. He felt her stiffen, but he didn't stop. Instead, he gathered the long tresses into his hands.

He wasn't sure what he'd been expecting, but it wasn't this. Not this erotic shudder that slid through him when he touched it. Her hair looked like she'd just been made love to. It was thick, tousled, tangled in beautiful heavy curls. Cain clenched his jaw, suppressing an urge to bury himself in it, tormenting himself with the thought of wrapping its thick softness around him.

Christ, he was crazy. He'd barely touched her, and now suddenly he wanted her so badly he could barely stand it. Not that it mattered. She had made it very clear that she was more than uninterested in him. And the last thing he wanted was for her to brand him even more of a fool than she already had. But it was also clear that if he didn't do something to take his mind off his desire, he would probably do something incredibly stupid. Like proposition her here, where the three Panamanians a few yards away would undoubtedly make him sorry to be alive if he so much as touched her—even if he was pretending to be her husband.

He glanced longingly at the brandy, and licked his lips, searching his mind for something to say as he began the braid.

"You looked lonely, sitting here," he said finally.

"Did I?" She turned her head. A brittle smile curved her full lips. "I assure you I'm not."

"Why not?" Cain gently tugged her head back around. His fingers moved skillfully through her hair. "So far away from home, with none of your friends—don't tell me you don't miss them."

She paused infintesimally. "No. I don't miss them."

"Not any of the other girls?" he teased.

"No."

"Not Rosalie?"

"Especially not her."

"What about Davey?"

She shrugged. "Davey was only around when he was paid."

He paused, then plunged ahead. "What about the man you killed? Do you—"

She tore away from him, twisting until her golden eyes fastened on his, yanking the braid from his hands so it flopped across her shoulders. "That is none of your business, Mr. D'Alessandro. I thought I made that clear that night at Davey's."

Her words sank into him like a stone. Cain's grin was tight and forced. "Sorry, *querida*. I don't remember much about that night."

"Oh, yes." She made a short sound of exasperation. "Well, that was the agreement."

Stop, he thought. *Walk away, leave her alone.* But he couldn't. He couldn't help himself. The drink—he prayed it was the drink—was affecting his mind. He leaned forward, unable to resist asking her, wanting to know something—anything—about her besides the fact that she'd read fairy tales as a child. "Did you tell me then what happened that night? Did you tell me why he put that mark on your cheek? Why you had to kill him?"

She turned away sharply. "No."

"Who was he?" he pushed. "Did you care about him? Did you—"

"Perhaps you didn't understand," she said in the coldest voice he'd ever heard. "I don't want you to know anything about me, Mr. D'Alessandro, and I don't want to know anything about you. I need your help now, and I'm willing to pay for it, but that's all I want from you." She took a deep breath. "To be blunt, I don't trust you. You drink too much, and I'm never sure what you're going to say. I don't like being surprised."

"I see." Cain felt cold, the warm balm of the night

was suddenly only dark and barren. He grabbed at the bottle and gulped thirstily at the brandy, but it didn't help, and when he saw the disgust in her glance, he lowered the bottle again. "No one's ever surprised you?"

"Not for a long time," she said, but he saw something in her eyes that told him she wasn't telling the whole truth. "People—especially men—do exactly what you expect them to."

"Perhaps you don't understand them as well as you think."

"No?" She raised a slender brow. "You think not? I assure you, there wasn't a man who came into Rosalie's who wasn't there for only one thing."

"Maybe their reasons for wanting a woman had nothing to do with—"

"Their reasons for coming in don't interest me." She laughed shortly, a bitter sound without humor. "I don't care why. As long as they paid for it, I gave them what they wanted."

Cain said nothing. He looked at Castañeras and the boatmen, wondering if they'd heard any of the conversation, but they were too engrossed in gaming to pay attention to what was happening only a few yards away.

It wouldn't matter if they did, he realized. There were a thousand questions burning on his tongue. Questions he could ask because he was buoyed by brandy and there was no place for her to run.

He stared off into the darkness. Conscious of the others for her sake, he kept his voice low. "Fine, you don't care about their reasons. What about yours? How did a girl like you end up in a brothel in Five Points?"

She was so quiet he turned to look at her, and was immediately sorry that he had. She stared at him with such contempt he felt as if she'd slapped him, and in that moment he felt innocent and naive as a young boy caught in the flush of first love. Christ, it was a stupid question, a clichéd question, but one, for some reason, he wanted answered badly enough to risk her disdain.

He fumbled for the words. "I—I know—"

"You don't know," she said, and her icy voice covered so much anger it shocked him. "Tell *me* something, Mr. D'Alessandro. How did you end up being such a drunkard?"

He recoiled, and she leaned close, so close he could smell the strangely citrusy scent of her hair. "What is it you really want to know, D'Alessandro? Do you wonder how I can bring myself to sell my body? How I can demean myself so much?" She got to her feet in a swish of wool, shaking her braid back, every move as controlled and elegant as a ice queen. "Let me enlighten you. It's not demeaning. Demeaning is working your fingers to the bone doing other people's laundry and still not having enough to eat, or stripping the clothes off the dead so you have something to wear. Demeaning is having to depend on somebody's mood when you're begging on the streets." She glared at him. "Does that explain it for you?"

He didn't look away. "I'm sorry."

Her stance was rigid, her fists clenched, but she didn't move. She took a deep breath and closed her eyes, and Cain watched her fingers uncurl. When she looked at him again, her eyes were strangely expressionless. "No, I'm sorry," she said slowly. "I'm sorry for losing—"

"Well, well, what have we here?"

The heavily accented voice boomed from the jungle surrounding them. Cain jerked upright so suddenly he nearly fell. Ana spun around. Castañeras and the boatmen were startled into silence.

The darkness seemed to part. Down the center of it walked a large man dressed in a pair of ragged, stained breeches and little else. His dark, greasy hair was slicked back from his broad forehead, and his mustache was so bushy it nearly hid his thin lips. His muscled vested chest ended at a broad belt. From that belt hung a huge knife, and a pistol glinted in his hand. Cain's blood ran cold.

"Dios." Jiméne's voice was a whisper.

The man turned to look at him, a wicked smile curving his lips. "Not God, *amigo.*" He waved his hand, and two other men materialized from the darkness. "But close. Meet my men, Ramon and Juan. My . . . angels. Lucifer's angels." He smiled and pointed his gun directly at Ana. "Welcome to hell, *chica.*"

Chapter 8

Ana stood in stunned amazement. She heard D'Alessandro climb slowly to his feet behind her.

"Pare!" The leader growled, raising the pistol. The cold smile never left his face. "Will you risk death to yourself or the lady?"

"We have nothing." D'Alessandro's voice seemed loud in her ear. He was standing so close she felt his heat. *"Nada."*

"That is for me to decide." The man nodded toward Ruben and Ambrosio. *"Muy bueno, amigos. Váyanse!"* Neither moved. *"¡Váyanse!"*

The boatmen were on their feet in a moment. They fled into the jungle, leaving behind only the sound of thrashing underbrush. Within minutes, the splash of the bungo sliding into the water and the lapping of paddles filled the darkness.

The boatmen were gone, along with all the luggage still in the boat. *"Yo creo que nos han engañado,"* Jiméne said slowly.

Their captor laughed. *"Sí, amigo.* You were duped.

Ambrosio and Ruben, they know to bring the miners here. To me." He poked a thumb at his broad chest. "And now I have you—and everything you have."

"Which is nothing." Jiméne rose, carefully, slowly. "There are others behind us. Richer—"

"Quiet!" the man bellowed. Once again he leveled his pistol at Ana. "Will I shoot her? Or will you cease this arguing?"

Ana's stomach tightened. She glanced at Jiméne, then at D'Alessandro. Both men were watching their attackers with intense concentration, though D'Alessandro was swaying, as if he couldn't really focus. Her heart sank. He'd been drinking, and he was probably useless. Everything depended on herself and Jiméne. Two against three, and they were at a distinct disadvantage, since their attackers were armed.

Jiméne held up his hands in surrender. "Take what we have, then. We want no trouble."

"But trouble is what you have, eh?" The big man smiled. He made a quick motion with the pistol. "Ramon, Juan—"

Something rustled in the darkness behind him. He turned, and in that split second, Jiméne lunged for the bag near the fire.

In the same moment, D'Alessandro pushed Ana with all his strength, sending her sprawling to the ground, out of the line of fire. "Stay there!" he shouted.

Before she could react, he was beyond her, moving in behind Jiméne as Ramon and Juan advanced.

"¡Pare!" The leader spun around, brandishing the pistol wildly now that his target was gone. Jiméne, his face was dark with rage, held a full brandy bottle in each hand.

Ramon lunged forward. Jiméne raised the bottle.

D'Alessandro turned to help Jiméne. Behind him, Juan pulled a long knife from his vest. The sight of it sent terror spinning through Ana.

"Cain!" she shouted. "Cain! Behind you—"

Wildly Cain twisted. Without looking behind him, Jiméne jerked back to attack, accidentally cracking a bottle against D'Alessandro's skull. Ana saw his surprise, and she watched helplessly as her partner crumpled, unconscious, to the ground.

"¡Dios!" Jimené's distress rang through the curse. He spun from D'Alessandro, fear glowing in his eyes as he faced their attackers.

Juan straightened, his gold tooth gleaming as he smiled. "One down," he said, turning, staring at her.

Ana scrambled to her feet. She had to get out of there. Had to run—

She was too late. Someone grabbed her wrist, yanking her to a stop.

"Not so fast, *chica.*"

It was the leader. Ana tried to wrench away, but he was too strong. He barely moved, and yet she found herself pulled back against his nearly naked chest, the barrel of a pistol shoved in her side.

"¡Pare!" He twisted around, taking her with him, until they were facing the battle in the middle of the clearing.

An unfair battle. Juan and Ramon surrounded Jiméne, and Ana looked just in time to see Ramon's fist thud into Jiméne's stomach. Jiméne's grunt of pain echoed in the clearing, the bottles fell to the ground and rolled out of reach.

"Stop!" the leader screeched, his voice deafening. The gun poked painfully into her waist; he held her so close she couldn't struggle. Juan stopped and turned, his knife gleaming dully in the dim light, but it was as if Ramon and Jiméne heard nothing.

Ana's heart pounded in her ears, desperation brought cold sweat to her skin. The leader held her so tightly she could do nothing but watch Ramon pound Jiméne, nothing but wait for them to finish him so they could take a turn at her.

The image pierced her mind with brutal clarity, adrenaline sped through her blood. Her instincts took over. Ana twisted in her captor's arms and slammed her knee into his groin. In the split second of his surprise, she jerked away, racing from the clearing without a backward glance.

She crashed into the underbrush, slipping and sliding over the moist ground, fighting the clawing vines and brambles as if they were enemies. She searched the darkness for someplace to hide, knowing she wouldn't be able to run far enough or fast enough to escape them. No, her only chance was to hide and wait it out and then continue on when it was over.

The image of Jiméne and D'Alessandro flashed through her mind, and Ana pushed it away. She didn't have time for them, she had no choice but to save her own life. Surely they would understand? D'Alessandro was already out, and Jiméne would never survive Juan and Ramon. They would *want* her to go on without them—

But she could not make it without them. The knowledge hit her like a blow, and Ana slowed, cursing herself. She needed at least one of them. She had no idea where to go, or what to do. Dammit, she had no choice but to go back and help.

Even as she thought it, she heard the thrashing of vegetation behind her. Desperately she surged forward. Something caught at her skirt, holding her back, and Ana vainly wrenched at the wool, trying to tear it loose—

"Be still, *puta.*" The whisk of drawn steel was in her ears; suddenly the deadly edge of a knife was pressed to her collar bone. "Be still or I will slit your throat."

Juan. Ana's heart fell into her stomach.

"That's better." The knife edge bit into her skin,

pressing her until she felt him against her back. His breath was hot and moist and garlicky on her ear. "I have her, Esteban!" he shouted. "I have—"

Ana jabbed her elbow into his gut, and he choked. The knife pressure lessened. She twisted, feeling the blade run along her throat, feeling the thin trickle of blood. It didn't matter. Nothing mattered except her chance to get away.

Using all the skills she'd mastered in the slums, Ana doubled her fist and aimed blindly in the darkness. She wanted Juan's groin, she got his stomach. His grunt of a curse brought a rush of breath on her face. Ana backed away, trying to dodge the branches in the darkness.

But they blocked her way, and Juan was barely slowed. He grabbed her arm, fingers biting into her tender flesh, and yanked her back.

"Puta," he said with a snarl. "You will pay for this, I promise it."

Ana tried vainly to escape. "Let me go!"

He wrapped his arm around her waist, holding her so tightly she couldn't breathe. The knife pressed to her throat again. "Do not worry, *gallita.*" He laughed. "Esteban, he will have plans for such as you."

Ana stiffened, remaining as motionless as possible as Juan dragged her backward to the clearing. The combination of his arm and her corset made her light-headed; the darkness seemed to be swimming around her. Determinedly she blinked, trying to focus, trying to breathe. She felt the warmth of her own blood trailing down her throat. With every movement, the point of the knife pricked her a little more, sending tiny stabs of pain into her neck.

There had to be a way out of this. But even if Jiméne *had* bested Ramon, there was still the leader, the man Juan had called Esteban. And as long as he held the pistol, they were severely unmatched.

The moment they got to the clearing, Ana knew it was

hopeless. Ramon and Jiméne still struggled in the dirt. The moment Esteban saw her, a nasty sneer broke over his face.

"Ramon!" he shouted.

Ramon's head came up, and Jiméne scrambled from beneath him. Taking advantage of Ramon's pause, he lunged.

"Do it, and the girl dies." Esteban's voice boomed through the trees.

Jiméne glanced up, saw her, and skidded to a stop. "Ana," he breathed. He was covered with dirt, the whites of his eyes widened in his muddy face. He glanced to Esteban. "Don't hurt her."

"We do not *want* to hurt her, *amigo.*" Esteban smiled. "All we want is *su dinero.*"

"Jiméne—" Ana gasped for enough breath to say his name. Juan jerked her head back so roughly she saw stars.

Esteban threw her a perfunctory glance. "Shut her up, Juan," he said. "Before I silence her permanently."

The blade pressed further into her throat.

"Please," she rasped. Her voice sounded harsh and frightened even to her own ears. "Please, take anything you want. Anything."

Esteban's eyes glittered. "Anything, eh?" He laughed. "Juan?"

Juan laughed as well. The odor of garlic and tobacco made Ana want to retch. The blade left her throat, and Ana watched in numb horror as he dragged it down her bodice, slicing a triangular tear in the fabric. "Whatever we want, *puta?*"

"Yes," she breathed. The knife glimmered in the darkness. Please God, she had to keep her head, had to think. She would do whatever she had to buy time. As long as they left her alive. God, that was all she wanted, to be alive . . .

"No." The voice came from behind them. Harsh, uncompromising, commanding. She felt Juan stiffen.

D'Alessandro.

Cain pressed the scalpel closer to the skin, until he felt Juan jump, and a drop of blood oozed from his neck. The knife thudded to the ground, but Juan didn't release his hold on Ana.

"Esteban," Juan said, warning and panic in his voice.

The leader turned. His eyes glittered. "Ah, you are clever. I had forgotten about you."

"Let her go," Cain said. "Or your man dies."

Esteban aimed the gun at Jiméne. "Then your friend dies."

"He is not my friend," Cain said, hoping he sounded as brutal and uncaring as Esteban did. "Shoot him if you like."

"Oh?" Esteban raised an eyebrow. Then, before Cain could say anything, the leader pulled the trigger. He heard the crack of a bullet cutting the darkness.

Along with Jiméne's yelp of pain.

"Jiméne!" Ana's scream pierced his brain. Cain clenched his jaw. Damn. He couldn't see, couldn't tell how badly Castañeras was hurt, or if he was hurt at all. His knees began to wobble, but Cain tried to ignore it.

"A neat trick," he said. With great care, Cain drew the scalpel along Juan's neck. He heard the thief's muffled curse, and, steeling himself, he cut a little deeper. "Let the girl go."

When Esteban said nothing, Cain looked at him. "Don't doubt me, *amigo*. He will die if you don't let us go."

There was a groan at the other side of the clearing. Esteban calmly pointed his gun once again in Jiméne's direction. "Perhaps you do not understand—"

It was as if Ana saw a chance and grabbed it. She jammed her elbow into Juan, knocking him into Cain, and Cain staggered backward as the full weight of the thief was suddenly on him. The scalpel slipped, Juan's scream filled his ears as the blade sliced into his neck, severing an artery. Juan collapsed, pinning Cain beneath him, and Cain's face and hands were suddenly covered with blood. Blood that was spurting, pumping from Juan's throat.

Cain struggled to push the body away, searching anxiously for Ana, but the whole clearing seemed to have erupted in chaos. He could see nothing, hear nothing but the report of the gun fired once, twice. Screaming echoed around his head, and he didn't know whether it came from Juan or from someone else.

Christ, what was going on? Cain gave one hefty shrug, throwing an already dead Juan to the side, pulling himself to his feet.

What he saw stopped him in his tracks. Ana stood alone in the clearing, the pistol dangling from her hands, Esteban in a crumpled heap at her feet. The other man, Ramon, was gone, but on the far side of the fire, Castañeras sat, holding his arm and groaning in pain.

"Ana?" Cain croaked. Slowly, as if in a daze, she turned, staring at him with eyes so lifeless it seemed to paralyze his soul. Cain swallowed.

"You saved us," she said. Her voice was hoarse, but he thought he heard something in her tone—a grudging respect, maybe, or even simple disbelief. She reached up and touched the bleeding scratch on her throat.

He stared at her and then glanced to the lifeless body at her feet. "What the hell happened?"

"She grabbed the gun, you stupid dog," Castañeras growled, staggering to his feet, gripping his arm. "What did you think to do, asking him to kill me?"

Relief ran through Cain's blood so potently he felt weightless. He couldn't help smiling. "I'm sorry he didn't kill you, you worthless swine."

Jiméne stared at him, and then grinned back. "He has

probably already done that," he said. "I doubt I will live until morning."

"We can only hope."

"Stop it. He saved us, Jiméne. You should at least thank him." Ana stepped forward, dropping the pistol.

She looked limp, almost shaken, and Cain watched in surprise as she turned to face him. Funny, if he hadn't known better, he would bet she was in shock, and ready to faint. But this was the Duchess. Somehow it was impossible to believe he was even seeing this, hard to believe she would allow such a weakness.

She motioned bonelessly to Jiméne. "Fix him," she murmured. "You know how."

Then she swayed, dignity and aristocratic bearing crumpling before Cain's disbelieving eyes. He rushed forward, catching her just before she hit the ground.

Chapter 9

Something was holding her so tightly she couldn't move. Something was *lifting* her—

Full consciousness hit Ana like a blow, and her eyes snapped open. She stared at the swarthy face bent over hers, seeing in a split second the concern in his eyes, and the fear.

Damn. D'Alessandro was carrying her, touching her. D'Alessandro was seeing her weak and helpless—again. She pushed futilely against his chest. "Put me down," she demanded.

"No."

"I said, put me down."

"I heard what you said. Christ, you just fainted."

"I didn't faint." Ana struggled, and his arms tightened around her. He was strong, she thought, strangely so for someone who had so recently been unconscious. But her sense of reassurance disappeared the moment she felt him trembling. She noticed the pallor of his skin beneath the dark streaks of Juan's blood. He was still drunk. For some inexplicable reason, the realization made her angry. Furious, in fact. "Damn it, D'Alessandro, put me down or—"

"Please do not fight." Jiméne's voice, weary and heavy with pain, came from a short distance away.

"There, you see?" D'Alessandro looked into her face, his eyes narrowed with censure. "If you'd relax long enough for me to dump you someplace, I could see to your friend over there."

"Kindly do not hurry," Jiméne said. "I am only dying."

"Unfortunately, I doubt that," D'Alessandro threw the words over his shoulder. He took a few steps and stopped, and Ana realized he was letting her drop—awkwardly. She slid down the length of his body until her feet touched the ground, one of his arms keeping her pinned close.

She felt the hard muscles of his lean frame, the heat of his skin, and for a moment, Ana felt slightly dizzy. She was still weak, she thought dazedly. Still confused.

With what force she could muster, she pushed away from him, and immediately lost her balance. She staggered backward, falling to her rump with a grunt of surprise.

"Christ," D'Alessandro muttered, squatting beside her. He reached out, and before Ana could protest, he had his hand on her forehead. He peered anxiously into her eyes. "I thought you said you were all right."

She wrenched away. "I *am* all right. I merely fell."

"Please, keep talking. I am only bleeding to death over here," Jiméne said. Ana glanced over at him. He was pale. One hand was clamped around his injured arm and the sleeve was red with blood.

"My God," she muttered. She turned to D'Alessandro, and saw a flash of what she thought was fear in his eyes, but before she could say anything he was moving away from her, toward the leather-bound case laying near the burlap bags.

"Thank God they left this," he said, snatching a bottle of brandy along with his case and the lantern, and moving back to them. "You'll need it."

"For what?" Jiméne sounded wary.

"For drinking," D'Alessandro twisted off the cork and took a deep swig. "Both of us, *amigo*. This isn't going to be pleasant."

"If you are involved," Jiméne said dryly, "I am not surprised."

D'Alessandro smiled and carefully laid his medicine kit and the bottle on the ground. He placed the lantern close.

"Have you ever seen a gunshot wound?" Jiméne asked hesitantly. "Or do you just guess?"

Ana swallowed and licked her lips. "He's a doctor, Jiméne."

If possible, Jiméne's face paled more. "A doctor? I did not know."

"It's not something we make public." D'Alessandro turned to Ana, lifting one dark brow. "Is it, *querida?*" When she didn't answer, he unbuckled the leather straps of his case and opened it.

Ana watched with fascinated revulsion as he took out the tools of his trade. The inside of the kit was roomy, despite its small size, with tiny compartments holding different bottles of medicines. He set aside a small, metal box perforated with holes—a leech box, Ana recognized with a shudder—and then lifted out the top layer, which was mainly medicines, and a small leather roll.

"You are really a doctor," Jiméne said, shaking his head in disbelief as D'Alessandro unrolled the leather to reveal a range of knives and instruments.

"I've been called that," D'Alessandro said casually. "And worse."

He seemed nonchalant, but Ana didn't miss the way he kept the brandy bottle close to him, or the quick, hurried sips he took before he handed it to Jiméne. Nor did she miss the way his fingers shook as they ran over the array of tools. He was taking such a long time, she thought maybe he was going to do nothing.

But then he reached for a pair of small, straight scissors. "Lie back, Castañeras," he said briefly. "I don't want you fainting on me."

"I am a man, not a—"

D'Alessandro pushed him back gently. "Take a drink," he instructed. "And lie back."

Jiméne did as D'Alessandro instructed, and Ana felt a strange tension build in her chest as she watched her partner cut through the dirty mustard yellow of Jiméne's frock coat and the once-white shirt below. The material fell away. Jiméne winced with pain as D'Alessandro picked at the wound with shaking fingers, clearing away the bits of cloth that stuck to the blood.

"Ana, come here," he commanded.

She looked up in surprise. "What for?"

"I need your help." He kept examining Jiméne's wound. Then, when she didn't move, he glanced at her questioningly. "Ana?"

Ana felt the revulsion uncoiling in her stomach, and she felt as if she had somehow frozen to the ground. "But I—"

"You'll be fine," he said. "Unless you plan on fainting again."

"I didn't faint. I fell," she said, hating the feeble sound of her own voice.

"Come here."

She saw Jiméne's face, almost colorless with shock and pain, and reluctantly she walked over to them. D'Alessandro motioned for her to kneel beside him.

She obeyed hesitantly, keeping distance between them, and folded her hands in her lap. "What should I do?"

"Hold the lantern," D'Alessandro said briefly. The fine sheen of perspiration that had broken out on his forehead gleamed in the lamplight, and his long hair fell into his face. He shook it aside impatiently, his full lips thin as he probed the wound. Ana shot a quick glance to Jiméne, who looked sick and ready to pass out. The brandy bottle lay abandoned by his side, and she reached for it with her other hand, holding it to his lips and forcing him to drink. Jiméne gulped quickly, gratefully, and slumped back again.

"Good," D'Alessandro said to Ana. To Jiméne, he added, "Pass out if you like, Castañeras. It'll ease the pain."

"You—" Jiméne took a deep breath and winced. "You . . . do . . . not . . . have . . . the . . . gentlest hands."

"No."

D'Alessandro's fingers were bloody. Ana's stomach flipped as she watched him dig into Jiméne's flesh, pushing aside the black powder-stained skin and ignoring the blood. D'Alessandro's brow was furrowed, and sweat had begun to drip in tiny rivulets from his temples. His hands shook so badly now Ana wondered if he would stay conscious long enough to finish the job.

D'Alessandro took a deep, steadying breath and sat back on his heels, wiping his forehead with the back of his sleeve. He nodded shortly to the bottle in her hand, and without a word, Ana handed it to him. He gulped furiously, so quickly brandy ran over his chin to drip on his shirt. When he handed it back, he seemed calmer, his hands were steadier.

"One more time, *amigo,*" he said, his deep voice shaking slightly.

Jiméne nodded, and D'Alessandro began to probe again. "Hold the lantern closer, Ana," he ordered. Ana reacted quickly, holding it so he could see, unable to take her own eyes from his bloodied fingers.

"Closer!"

His tone made her wince, the familiarity of its harshness slid over her skin. Ana's stomach knotted, her fingers tightened on the handle of the lantern. Jiméne coughed slightly. Ana jumped. This was all too familiar, and she was filled with such sick revulsion she glanced away from D'Alessandro's searching, focusing on Jiméne's face in an attempt to keep her nausea at bay. The Panamanian's eyes were closed, his breathing short and shallow.

Jiméne's body went limp; she heard a sigh of relief from D'Alessandro. He sat back on his heels, closing his eyes for a moment before he stared at the misshapen piece of metal in his fingers.

"That's the worst of it, *amigo,*" he said, tossing the piece away and wiping his bloody fingers on his frock coat. He reached in his kit for a pad of lint and some linen. "Get me some water, please."

Get me some water. The order was nothing new, the *please* faded off as if it had never been said. Ana swallowed, suddenly smelling the stifling scent of cigar smoke even though there was none in the clearing, suddenly hearing the coarse, demanding tones of the doctor who ministered to her dying mother.

She stiffened, unable to move, her nails biting into the palms of her hand as she stared at D'Alessandro. He glanced over at her, and instead of his dark brown eyes, she saw watery blue ones, bright with lecherous appreciation, promising hell . . .

"Ana? Get some water." D'Alessandro's gentle tones broke through the memory, and suddenly, it was gone. She took a deep breath, struggling to pull herself together. It was the attack that had unnerved her, she told herself. The attack, and watching D'Alessandro work. She was shaken, and on edge, and because of that she'd let her revulsion for doctors get the better of her. Because of it, she'd been weak enough to let the memory in.

D'Alessandro looked at her strangely, and Ana lifted her chin and got to her feet, avoiding his gaze.

She was trembling, and Ana clutched her skirt, trying to quell it. She glanced at the grisly bodies of Esteban and Juan, lying motionless only a few yards away, and her preoccupation with her old fear disappeared. How had she managed to forget? There was still Ramon, still the chance that he would come back. They weren't safe.

She grabbed the bucket of water and hurried back to the two huddled on the ground, nearly throwing the bucket down. Water sloshed out, wetting D'Alessandro's trouser leg, but he didn't seem to notice. He concentrated so intently on cutting bandages, she doubted he even noticed she was back. She stood stiffly beside him, waiting for him to finish so she could tell him they had to go, watching impatiently as he bathed Jiméne's wound with water and snipped away the frayed and blackened skin before he applied a wet dressing.

By the time he finished, Jiméne was mercifully unconscious. D'Alessandro tied off the bandage and sat back, swiping back his long hair. In the lantern's dim light, it pooled like shadow on his shoulders.

He took a deep breath and turned to look at her. "You all right?"

She nodded shortly. "How long before we can go?"

He shrugged and gestured at Jiméne with the bottle. "He'll be feverish by morning. Probably have some infection. It might be days before we should move him."

"Days?" Ana stared at him in horror. He was promising days—maybe even weeks—of danger. "That's impossible."

He threw her a quizzical glance. "Is it? Listen, Duchess, we joined Castañeras because you wanted it. We left Chagres because you wanted it. This time we're doing what I want."

Ana drew herself up. "You must have forgotten who hired you."

"I haven't forgotten. I also haven't forgotten what you hired me for: to get you to San Francisco in one piece."

"You've certainly done an admirable job thus far," she said sarcastically.

D'Alessandro glanced at the bodies lying in the clearing. "I haven't done so badly, and you know it." He sighed and stared off into the darkness. "Though I have to admit you're right, it's not safe here. There might be others with Ramon. Better leave in the morning."

His promise to leave filled Ana with relief, though she would have preferred to go now instead of waiting. But that was impossible, she knew. The jungle was dangerous in the daytime; at night they would never survive. Especially not with D'Alessandro drinking as if there were no tomorrow.

She looked pointedly at the bottle. "If we're leaving then, perhaps it would be best if you—"

His cold smile stopped her dead. "I always get a little shaky after I work, Duchess."

"And when you're not working?"

He looked at her. His eyes looked dead, somehow, as if he had some deep pain that he didn't allow himself to feel, as if looking at her made him angry enough to keep it at bay. His gaze suddenly made her feel colder than she'd ever felt before. And more afraid because his pain was too familiar. Too much like her own.

Ana bit her lip, clenching her hands into fists when she felt her fingers tremble. She turned to the fire. "Just be sure you're sober tomorrow, D'Alessandro," she said harshly. "Or I swear I'll leave you behind."

By the time the faint shafts of sunlight pierced the thick canopy of trees, Ana was short-tempered and tired. She had lain awake through the long night, haunted by the cacophony of jungle sounds, imagining the slightest noise or movement was Ramon returning. She was horrifyingly aware of the dead and rotting bodies nearby, even though she couldn't see them in the darkness. But every time she tried to sleep, the memory of the attack came back to her so clearly it was if it was happening all over again.

Ana saw them clearly enough in her mind: Juan motionless in a pool of blood, Esteban's chest blown open by the bullet she'd fired.

Her second murder. The words pierced her consciousness, even as Ana tried to ignore them. The second time she'd ended someone's life.

"Damn!" The sound of D'Alessandro's voice startled her and Ana's eyes jerked open. A low-hanging, miasmic fog filled the clearing, making D'Alessandro's legs look ghostly. But his jerky movements and bitten curses were anything but spiritual. He was applying blisters to Jiméne's wound, muttering obscenities as the Panamanian tossed restlessly beneath his hands.

Her panic returned full force. Jiméne was feverish, as D'Alessandro had predicted, and it was possible they wouldn't be able to leave. The thought sent an irrational and abominable rush of resentment through her, and Ana forced it away. Damn it, she didn't want Jiméne to die, but they had to go—the sooner the better.

And D'Alessandro wasn't helping. He was drunk, of course, in spite of her threats last night, and Ana tensed with displeasure. Damn, she wished she could do what she'd promised and leave him behind, but she and Jiméne needed him—and D'Alessandro knew it.

As calmly as she could, banking her irritation, Ana rose and sauntered over to him, wishing she could speed up the healing process.

"Shouldn't you be bleeding him?" she asked.

He glanced over his shoulder at her. "Good morning to you too." When she said nothing, he sighed and turned back to his patient. "I won't bleed him yet. Not unless the fever doesn't go down."

"I see." Ana watched skeptically for a few moments. Jiméne tossed his head back and forth, but he was weak enough that D'Alessandro's hand on his shoulder kept his body still. And that had to be weak, she mused, since D'Alessandro's movements were clumsy.

She leaned closer. "Maybe you should amputate."

D'Alessandro paled. "Didn't know you were a doctor."

"I'm not, but even I know it's what you people do. Isn't it?"

"Not me." He lifted the bottle to his mouth.

Her temper rose without warning. He was useless to her drunk. Useless and slow. Without thinking, Ana yanked the bottle away. Brandy spilled over his jaw and shirt, puddled on the ground. It took every ounce of strength she had to keep her voice even. "Listen to me, D'Alessandro. We need a plan."

He wiped the brandy from his face slowly and calmly, but Ana didn't miss the fury shining in his dark eyes. "A plan," he repeated deliberately. "Suppose you come up with that, Duchess. It's what you're best at."

His tone made her wince, Ana tried to forget the fact that, once again, D'Alessandro had made her lose her temper.

She'd think about that later, once they were gone from this hellhole. She glanced at the bodies of Esteban and Juan. In the fog, they were nearly hidden, but it didn't stop the buzzards from finding them. The birds' black shadows glided through the mist to tear noisily at the rotting flesh. She shivered with revulsion. "We should leave here now. You said it last night—Ramon might be back. Maybe there are others." She waited for his reaction, and when there wasn't one, she went on. "And much as I respect your . . . abilities . . . we've got to get Jiméne to some sort of civilization."

Slowly, methodically, D'Alessandro laid another hot compress on Jiméne's wound. The Panamanian jumped, though he remained unconscious. His muttering and thrashing increased.

D'Alessandro shook back his hair. He watched thoughtfully as his patient tossed and jerked.

He didn't look at her as he spoke. "And how d'you propose to do that?"

"You'll have to carry him."

He stared at her in disbelief.

Ana lifted her chin and took a deep breath, trying not to betray her anxiety. "We've got to get him to Gatún. Even if he wasn't sick, we're in danger here. You admitted it yourself."

D'Alessandro looked at Jiméne again. "Where's Gatún?"

"What?"

He crossed his arms, rubbing his lip with his thumb. "Where's Gatún?"

That silenced her. Ana stared at him. Where *was* Gatún? All she knew was that it was the first stop on the river route, yet she had no idea how far that was, or even where the settlement might be. Only Jiméne knew, and Jiméne was unconscious, perhaps too delirious to understand anything for days—even if he survived the fever.

She refused to think of Jiméne dying. He would get better, and everything would be fine. If he was lucky, he'd be unconscious until they got to Gatún.

Because they *would* get to Gatún. Her lips tightened with resolve. It didn't matter where the damn city was. They had to reach it, and soon, because she wanted out of this jungle, she wanted to be safely in San Francisco and away from Ramon's hunters and D'Alessandro. She would find the city because there was no other choice.

"I suppose we could just follow the river," she said finally.

"Just follow the river?"

"Unless you have a better idea."

D'Alessandro exhaled slowly, rising to his feet with a

motion that was fluid for a man who'd been so shaky only moments ago. "Fine," he said, walking to the fire.

Ana stared after him incredulously. "Fine?"

He glanced back at her, cocking a brow. "Is there something you didn't understand, Duchess? I said fine. Get him ready and let's get the hell out of here."

Relief slid over her, making Ana feel almost faint. She had no idea why he'd agreed, and she wasn't sure she really wanted to know. She spent no more time pondering it. He was doing what she wanted, that was all she cared about.

Ana paid little attention to D'Alessandro as she readied Jiméne for the journey, dressing him as warmly as she could in his torn and soiled frock coat and knotting one of their blankets around his shoulders even though it was sweltering. The humidity weighed on her like a stifling, damp canopy. She didn't remember it being this hot yesterday, or this humid, but they'd been on the river then. No doubt it was cooler there.

By the time Ana gathered the burlap bags together and slung them over her shoulder, her wool dress was wet with perspiration, and tendrils of hair clung to her face and neck. The fog had lifted, and it no longer concealed the bodies in the clearing, nor the buzzards that flapped raucously about. Their dizzying movements and harsh caws nauseated her, and she gulped for breath.

It didn't help. The air was so heavy it was difficult to breathe. It pressed down on her relentlessly, and she thought again about relinquishing the corset. It was impossible now; the knife rip Juan had made in her bodice was large and gaping, revealing the lower swell of a breast that was now safely covered by corset. She would have to mend it once she could get her hands on a needle and thread. It was too revealing, and the last thing she needed was the pointed stares it would draw. But now there wasn't time.

She glanced at D'Alessandro, who sat watching her.

His gaze had been on her the entire time she worked, and she had ignored it steadfastly, refusing to meet his eyes or even wonder why he watched her with such steady determination.

Now she ignored it again, along with the disquieting feeling it gave her, and went to stand beside Jiméne. She adjusted the burlap over her shoulder. "I'm ready."

"So I see." He got to his feet. The buzzards scattered at the movement, but he didn't even glance at them. "Then by all means, let's go."

Chapter 10

Ana pushed aside the vines and brambles in front of her, no longer feeling the raw, red cuts and scratches on her hands. Long ago, she had tied the burlap bags around her waist, and their contents banged against her legs, bruising her thighs and hips. The wool dress clung to the middle of her back, beneath her arms and between her breasts, stained and wet with sweat.

Push on, push on, push on. The words forced her onward even though she was exhausted. She couldn't get far enough away from the clearing.

Wiping at the hair that tangled around her neck and fell into her face, Ana tried again to banish her fear. Everything would be fine. She was in control now, she could get them to Gatún quickly—hopefully before nightfall. The anxiety she'd managed to control last night and this morning was just below the surface, struggling to erupt, and she wanted a private place to let it explode, a place where she could sit and shake silently. The closest place to do that was Gatún, and she was desperately afraid it wasn't close enough.

She would get them there by tonight if it took everything she had.

It just might do that, she thought, wiping her forehead, feeling grit roll beneath her hand. God, she was tired. So tired. And so damned hot . . . Ana clenched her jaw and glanced at the river curling at the bottom of the steep bank beside her. It tempted her, as it had for hours. But she knew that the moment she stepped toward it the howler monkeys would keen louder, and she would see the slow, unblinking eyes of alligators rising from the still water.

If she didn't know better, she would think they were deliberately following her, torturing her on purpose—

The palmettos thrashed behind her, she heard the slipping, sliding thud of a crash.

"Dammit!"

Ana stopped, clutching her waist, taking the chance to grab a breath. She didn't bother to look behind her. She would only see D'Alessandro stumbling, trying to right himself with a comatose Jiméne slung over his shoulders like a freshly killed deer.

She heard the *slip, crash, crunch* of D'Alessandro trying to right himself, the soft groan from Jiméne, and then the inevitable curse.

Ana sighed, once again moving forward. Her patience was stretched to the limit, and irrationally, she blamed D'Alessandro because it was taking so long. As much as she wanted to, she couldn't push him to go any faster. Drunk or not, with Jiméne on his shoulders, he simply could not do more than stagger along at a snail's pace.

Ana frowned with annoyance. Without D'Alessandro dragging behind her, she would probably be in Gatún by now—

Without him, she would probably be dead.

She refused to believe it. Yes, he'd saved their lives, but if it hadn't been for him, they wouldn't have been in the situation to begin with.

Another lie. D'Alessandro was the one who hadn't wanted to leave Chagres so late in the day. He'd been the one insisting it wasn't safe.

The knowledge galled her. He'd been right, and for the first time since she'd met him, she began to understand why Davey had recommended him for the job. D'Alessandro had survival instincts. As impossible as it seemed, she was beginning to believe he was much more capable of surviving in the jungle than she.

Ana lashed out at a vine, viciously pushing it aside. A sharp pain shot up her side, and Ana gasped and stopped short, trying to catch her breath. Her lungs felt strained, and she grasped onto a nearby palm as her head spun.

D'Alessandro stumbled to a stop behind her. "What's . . . wrong?"

"Nothing," she said. Ana forced herself to move forward, even though the sharp pain stabbed through her again, nearly choking her with its intensity. "Nothing."

She slowed her step infinitesimally, praying D'Alessandro wouldn't notice. The corset cut into her skin, constricting her lungs, and the air felt heavier and heavier. But gradually, step by step, her breathing grew more steady, the dizzy spells faded. She refused to say anything to him. It was one more weakness, and he'd already seen too many.

Behind her, another crash resounded through the brush, along with a bitten-off "Damn!" Ana paused and looked over her shoulder.

D'Alessandro shoved his hair out of his face with the back of his arm. He looked up hopefully. "Ready to stop?"

Ana frowned. "No."

"Listen, Duchess," he breathed. "It's time to stop. You're driving too hard—"

"We can't afford to stop," she said sharply. "What if Ramon's behind us? What if someone's after us?"

He shrugged. "They'll find us if they want to."

"And kill us," she said, turning around. "No thank you."

"Ramon ran off last night," he reminded her solemnly. "They've got a head start. If they haven't found us by now, they're not looking."

"I don't believe you."

"I don't give a damn what you believe. I need a rest."

"You'll have one, as soon as we reach Gatún." Ana tried to keep the desperation from her voice. She clamped her lips together tightly. Not here. Not yet. She could quietly fall apart in Gatún, when everyone was asleep—

Crash!

Ana jumped, spinning around, an angry insult dying on her lips when she saw the reason for this crash. D'Alessandro was on his knees, desperately grabbing at Jiméne, whose limp body was falling, tumbling through the underbrush, over the steep embankment toward the hungry, gurgling river.

The sound of his fall startled the alligators sunning themselves on the far shore, and Ana watched in horror as, one by one, they looked up while Jiméne rolled closer and closer.

His dim yellow coat flashed through the vines. Ana grabbed her skirts, nearly falling as she raced back along the makeshift trail. D'Alessandro was already on his feet, crashing and sliding down the slippery, plant-covered cliff, grabbing on to fallen trees for purchase, stumbling over vines.

He looked back just as Ana reached the edge. "Stay there!" he commanded.

She ignored him and stepped over the edge.

Her booted feet skidded on the trailing vegetation, and Ana went sliding. Roots, rocks, and sharp-edged branches clawed at her skin and dress. She flailed out, desperately reaching for something, anything to halt her downward spiral, but she was moving too fast. She couldn't stop.

Somewhere in the back of her mind, Ana heard D'Alessandro's shouts, but she couldn't understand the words. They didn't matter. It was all over, she was falling to her death. How did it feel to be eaten by an alligator—

"Aaagh!" She thudded to a stop, knocking the breath from her lungs. Ana lay there for a moment, coughing and choking, before she realized that she was lying in some kind of foul black mud, with her hand dangling in the water.

The river. She yanked her hand back and pushed herself away so quickly her head spun. Oh God, the river. Jiméne.

"Ana, dammit, come here!" D'Alessandro's voice was strained and urgent. "Now!"

Dimly she heard the sound of splashing. Ana forced herself to rise. The corset cut into her skin, dizziness made the world tilt in a strange kaleidoscope of color. She tried desperately to focus.

The splashing she heard was D'Alessandro. He was waist-deep in the river, grasping on to creepers that trailed in the water, desperately trying to keep his hold on Jiméne, whose head was barely above water, kept there only by D'Alessandro's arm. But not for much longer. Vines tangled around Jiméne's legs, holding him captive, pulling at him even as D'Alessandro worked to yank him ashore.

"My God," she breathed, panic and fear forcing her legs to move, forcing her forward even as the world threatened to turn upside down before her. Soon the alligators would see them. Already she saw them massing on the opposite shore. "Wait!" She pushed past an overturned ceiba tree, fighting to keep her footing on the slippery mud. "I'm coming!"

"Come faster, dammit!" D'Alessandro struggled to keep his hold on Jiméne. The cords in his wrist stood out as he grabbed on to an exposed snag for balance and tried to move backward.

Ana stumbled over a viney orchid and caught herself before she fell, trampling the pristine white flower into the mud beneath her feet. Her hair fell into her face, blinding her, and she pushed it aside, fighting to keep her skirts from tangling in the undergrowth.

"Ana!"

"I—am—here!" She was there in seconds, though it seemed like years, plunging through the trees, reaching D'Alessandro the very moment he called her name. Her head spun, her breath felt pulled from her lungs. D'Alessandro tried to move around. The veins at his temples stood out at the effort it took to drag Jiméne around with him. The arm that clutched the snag was so taut it looked like it might break.

"Try to . . . grab him." D'Alessandro pushed Jiméne forward. His limp body floated in the water, his dark hair like an inky stain around his head. His eyes were closed, and his face was so pale it looked nearly blue.

"Is he . . . ?"

"Just take him." D'Alessandro's words were bitten off, his breath rasped harshly from his throat.

Ana reached out, trying to grab Jiméne's arm, but the current pulled it away again. She stumbled forward, into the river. The warm water lapped against her ankles, poured into the tight lacing of her boots. Behind D'Alessandro, she heard a splash of water, saw an alligator slide into the river.

She reached again. Jiméne's hand floated only inches from her own. Looking up, she met D'Alessandro's eyes, saw the desperation there that matched her own.

"Again," he instructed tersely.

She reached, he pushed, and this time Jiméne's fingers brushed her hand. Ana grasped on to him with all her strength. Her arms felt ready to burst from their sockets as she fought the river current and the vines.

"I—can't—"

"Just hold him. I'm—letting go."

He dropped his hold. Ana struggled to keep her grip on Jiméne.

"Hold on."

D'Alessandro's words filled her with resolve. He swayed in the current, and she saw how much strength it was taking him to stay upright as the river surged around his waist. He dipped his hand in the water, she saw the glimmer of the scalpel blade. At the sound of another splash, he twisted around, and Ana caught the fear in his eyes as he saw the approaching alligator.

"Christ." He lunged forward, slicing the vines holding Jiméne and grappling with his limp body. D'Alessandro pushed, Ana pulled, and suddenly the current let go, and Ana fell backward, dragging Jiméne's weight with her.

"Hurry." D'Alessandro stumbled from the water, glancing back over his shoulder, and Ana followed his eyes. The river was swirling with alligators.

Desperately she clawed at Jiméne's coat, trying to pull his legs free of the water. Then D'Alessandro was there, pocketing his scalpel before he yanked Jiméne by the arm, bending and swinging the man over his shoulder.

She followed him up the embankment, her wet skirts wrapping around her legs, her own breathing as labored as his. Behind her, she heard the slopping of the alligators. The sound gave her renewed strength.

When they reached the top, she stumbled, falling to her face in the brambles. Ana lay there, stiff with fear and exhaustion. The world was black in front of her, with little shooting sparks of stars. Her ribs ached, her hands and arms stung, and the river water seeped into her skin.

It was a moment before she heard D'Alessandro's harsh breathing, a moment before she heard the thud of his body slumping to the ground and the second, softer thump of Jiméne's.

Ana rolled to her side, looking up into her partner's face. His swarthy skin was almost yellow, he looked ready to collapse, and yet there was something in his dark eyes when he looked at her, a compassion she'd never seen before.

Despite all her promises, despite her efforts to keep control, Ana began to shake. Desperately she tried to hold it back, clenching her fists in the dirt, turning her face into the ground and biting her lip. Relentlessly she clamped the panic down, forced it away.

Then the rain started.

Cain pushed wet hair back from his face and stared out at the river. The rain fell in sheets, steaming as it hit the jungle floor, making the twilight sky seem darker than it was. He watched the ivory-colored herons as they fished in the river, their black crests and head plumes dancing in the rain. Egrets and green parrots flew among the leaves, oblivious to the wet, and the bright red flowers adorning a nearby wild banana tree seemed to open up and welcome it.

In the jungle, the rain stopped nothing. Except Ana, apparently. Christ, was he glad it had finally stopped her.

He turned, glancing over his shoulder at Ana, who huddled in the corner of their makeshift shelter, staring wide-eyed at Jiméne. Her fingers were clenched in tight white fists, her shoulders and neck were so stiff it looked as if they were made of stone. She was holding something in, something so powerful she was terrified it might break loose, and Cain wondered what it was.

He forced himself not to care, just as he'd forced himself not to care the night before, after the attack. He wondered if he would ever learn, or if Ana was going to beat him into the ground the way his mother had—

Ana, he knew, would never let him get close enough, he was beginning to realize that now. The woman had built a wall around herself so thick no one could break through it.

A self-deprecating smile touched his lips. Or at least he couldn't. Hell, he didn't even want to try. Saviors—heroes—were for men like Jiméne. Men who wanted to fight relentless forces.

God knew, he'd had his fill of it.

Cain looked longingly at the wet burlap bags that held their supplies. They rested in the corner—right under a hole in the leafy canopy covering them. A steady stream of water flooded in, soaking everything inside.

It didn't matter, as long as the bottles were intact. Cain's fingers clenched, his mouth felt dry, and he fought the urge to grab one and twist it open. Even he knew better than to drink now. The Duchess was like a powder keg waiting to explode. The last thing he wanted was to ignite her.

He glanced over at her. She watched Jimené with a growing desperation that matched his own. Castañeras was still feverish, and with every step Cain took, the knowledge that the man would die grew like a cancer inside of him.

He was losing again. He looked down at his hands. They were shaking violently now. He couldn't control them or think clearly enough to make a decision about what to do next for Jimené, and he told himself he didn't care enough to try.

It was a lie and he knew it, but he was so tired of fighting. Tired of losing. There had been a time—not so long ago—when he thought, despite everything, he'd finally succeeded, finally made something of himself. But he hadn't. Not really.

The memory dipped inside him, harsh and unyielding,

and Cain closed his eyes and pushed it away. After John had died, the battle only began again, harder now, less easily fought, and he'd made the decision not to try anymore. There was nothing in life worth fighting the obstacles thrown in his path. Nothing worth having that hadn't already been taken from him.

He glanced again at the burlap bag, and then again at the Duchess. Her skin and dress were streaked with mud, the hair she took such pride in was tangled and loose, falling in her face. He remembered that he still held her precious comb in his pocket. Licking his lips, feeling nervous for no reason that he could say, Cain pulled it out.

"I imagine you want this back," he said.

She looked up at him, her golden eyes expressionless. "Thank you." She took it, holding it in her hand and then staring at Jiméne as if she'd already forgotten about it. "Is he going to be all right?"

Castañeras again. Cain felt an insane surge of jealousy, and he banished it. He'd known for a long time that she preferred Castañeras to him, and he told himself he didn't care. Hell, she was a whore, after all, and he was just tired and maudlin. Her affections didn't matter to him. Castañeras could have her—and good riddance.

He looked over at his patient. Since the dunking in the river, Jiméne had been still, the restless tossing that had made carrying him so difficult was gone. Just after the rain began, Cain had forced a weak Fowler's solution down Castañeras's throat, hoping the arsenic powder would help fight the fever, and followed it with laudanum for the pain.

"If he's not conscious by morning, I'll have to bleed him."

"Perhaps you should do it now."

Her concern was touching. It was all Cain could do to keep the sarcasm from his voice. "Don't worry, Duchess, I won't let him die."

Her eyes met his in an unrelenting stare. "I'm not worried that you'd do it deliberately."

He swallowed. Her words stabbed inside him, and Cain felt a sudden, overwhelming thirst. Instead, he summoned every ounce of his calm. "Is it all doctors you dislike, or just me?"

She looked taken aback, he noticed with satisfaction, and he thought he saw something like fear flit across her eyes—but only for a moment. Her fingers clenched the golden comb and she lifted her chin.

"I don't dislike you any more or less than the others," she answered brittlely, hurriedly glancing away.

"That's not an answer."

"It's the only answer you're going to get." She jerked around again to face him, and Cain saw the fury in her eyes, the rapid pulse in her throat. For a moment, she looked ready to say something else, and he steeled himself for her temper, but then she clenched her jaw tight and looked down at the comb in her hand. "My life is none of your business, D'Alessandro."

"I'm not asking for a life history, goddammit. I'm asking why you dislike doctors." He nearly winced at the raw sound of his voice.

"It . . . is . . . none . . . of . . . your . . . business." She spat each word, as if it took all her effort to force them from her mouth.

When he looked at her, her eyes were focused on Jiméne, but he didn't miss the slight trembling of her hands, nor the way her full lips were bloodless.

He swallowed, pretending her enmity didn't reach down into his very bones, didn't twist around that dark place already inside of him. Instead, he looked back out into the darkening jungle. The rain was a shadowed veil, he heard the spattering of drops on the leaves covering their shelter, heard the soft whispered rush of it falling through the trees.

"Go to sleep," he said quietly. "We've got a long day tomorrow."

"You go to sleep, D'Alessandro." Even now, there was no softness in her voice, no forgiveness. "Leave me alone. Just leave me alone."

He woke in the middle of the night to darkness and the sounds of the jungle, and it took him a moment to realize the rain had stopped. The chattering of monkeys and the far away roars of the jungle cats mixed with the hum and clatter of insects and Jiméne's quiet, even snores. The damp air brushed soft and cool over his skin.

Cain didn't move, was too comfortable to move. He'd been sleeping the sleep of the righteously exhausted for a change, and he had no idea what had awakened him.

He frowned, listening to the night, waiting.

And then he heard it. A subtle movement in the darkness, the choking breaths cut off before they could become sobs. Around him, the air seemed to shiver, as if someone was shaking . . .

"Ana?" he whispered. The sounds stopped. The air was suddenly still. "Ana? Are you awake?"

Silence. Cain tried to tell himself that she was asleep, that everything had been his imagination and nothing more, but he couldn't. Something was wrong, and despite himself, he felt an overwhelming urge to make it right.

He reached out. Her back was to him. She was only an arm's length away, and when he touched her shoulder, she stiffened almost imperceptively. But it was enough to let him know she was awake.

"Ana," he said softly.

"Leave me alone." Her voice was raw, and again she started shaking. Cain felt the rigid control of her muscles, the tension in her body.

"What's wrong?"

"Noth—" The word was broken by a choking breath, a sob stopped before it could begin. "Nothing."

She tried to shrug off his hand, but Cain curled his fingers around her shoulder. He heard it again, that pain that had been in her voice earlier, when she'd turned on him before Esteban and his men had entered the clearing. The pain that warned him away, that came from someplace so deep in her past he wondered if anyone but she knew it existed.

The pain that matched his own. God, how well he understood it. He knew what it was like to hide what you felt from people, hell, to hide it from yourself. He knew, and so when she began to shake harder, when he heard her shallow, ragged breaths, he couldn't stop himself from moving closer. Couldn't stop himself from pressing against her back and wrapping his arms around her. Couldn't stop himself from holding her as tightly as he could and burying his face in her hair.

She was like a piece of ice in his arms, but Cain pretended not to feel it. Instead, he closed his eyes and smelled the rainwater scent of her hair, letting her shaking move into his bones until he was shaking with her.

"Ah, *querida,*" he murmured. "I know. I know. I know."

He whispered the words over and over, pressing his lips against her skin, chanting them like some religious litany until they took on their own rhythm, became a lullaby. He rocked back and forth in time to the words, stroking her hair with one hand, holding her with the other. Waiting.

Finally she crumpled against him, trembling violently, her sobs cracking through clenched teeth. Her fingers curled around his, and she clung to his hand so tightly her nails dug into his palm.

He held her that way until the shaking stopped, until her breathing calmed. Held her until the dawn broke through the trees and she had fallen into an exhausted, dreamless sleep.

It wasn't until then that he realized she hadn't told him anything, or looked at him a single time.

He hadn't even dented the wall.

Chapter 11

She couldn't bring herself to look at him.

The memory of last night was blazoned into her brain, an incident so humiliating Ana was afraid she would remember it forever. He had seen her at her most vulnerable, had seen her helpless and shaking. She couldn't bear the thought that he knew how afraid she'd been, or how out of control.

Ana's breath caught in her throat. The muggy air was stifling, it pressed down on her, making it hard to inhale or even move. But she kept hacking violently and impatiently at the vines blocking her way. She felt like running, fast and far. Away from the hellish jungle and the lethal river, away from this damned farce of a journey that thwarted her every step. Away from D'Alessandro.

She heard him behind her, stumbling, cursing. The sound of his voice filled her with fear. Whenever she heard his deep baritone, she heard again the ceaseless lullaby that had calmed her the night before. *I know. I know. I know.* As if he somehow understood her fear. As if he shared it.

It had been a long time since anyone had cared enough to hold her. A very long time, and it startled her—frightened her—that it had felt so good, that his warmth had seeped into her very bones.

Speeding her step, Ana pushed herself to put distance between them, ignoring her shortness of breath. The panic she'd felt yesterday was nothing compared to this fierce, unrelenting fear. How had he done it? How had he managed to so insidiously pierce her defenses? She'd spent a lifetime guarding them, a lifetime keeping anyone from getting too close.

And now here he was, with his drunken ways and clumsy doctoring. D'Alessandro, who managed to find out more about her in a few days than anyone else had in years.

She stumbled over a loose root, and a sharp pain stabbed into her side, curled tightly around her lungs. Ana clutched her waist and bit off a curse.

"Ana? Y'all right?"

His voice echoed in her ears, curled warmly inside of her, and Ana winced, fighting it. She hated the way he said her name. All soft and drawn out, almost drawled. He said it the way her mother had said Anastasia, with rounded vowels and cultured *ah*s. The way it was supposed to be said.

She wished he was still calling her Duchess.

"I'm fine," she said, moving forward even more determinedly.

But she wasn't fine. She was tired and on edge. Her feet felt heavy; only sheer force of will kept her moving through the trees. The jungle felt oppressive, and Ana suddenly hated it more than she'd ever hated New York. Hated the beauty that hid such evil, hated the cloying opulence that made her feel helpless and small. Hated the way it fought her at every damned turn.

Vines grabbed at her shoulders, tangled in her hair, and Ana yanked them away, pushing on, fighting for breath and strength. She could hardly wait for this damn journey to end—

The pain stabbing through her was so sharp, Ana doubled over, grabbing her side. Her ears rang, the howling monkeys echoed in her brain. She couldn't breathe; it felt as if her lungs were held by a tight iron band. Frantically she grabbed at her collar.

She was dimly aware of D'Alessandro crashing around beside her, and she thought she heard him asking questions, but the pain kept her from answering. She couldn't get enough air. God, where was the air? It felt as if something had sucked it all away.

Ana watched through a haze as he dropped Jiméne and lunged at her, grabbing at her bodice, her throat. His voice was loud in her ears, like an echo in an empty room. The world was spinning, yet D'Alessandro didn't seem to care. He was ripping at her dress, pulling it off, and Ana didn't have the strength to keep it on. Violently he spun her around. She felt his fingers at her back, forcing her up when all she wanted to do was bend over and try to breathe.

Suddenly she could. The pain disappeared, and Ana gasped as air filled her lungs. She gulped deeply, tears stinging the corners of her eyes. The dizziness left, but her legs still felt like jelly, and if it hadn't been for D'Alessandro's steady hands on her arms, she would have fallen to the ground.

But she could breathe.

"Christ." D'Alessandro's voice was raw. He dropped his hands. "Christ."

Ana straightened, realizing that her dress was down around her waist, and her corset was loose. Carefully holding the garment to her, she turned to face him.

He looked shaken and unsteady. He took a deep breath, dragging his hand through his dark hair.

"Take it off," he said.

Ana stared at him disbelievingly. "Excuse me?"

"Take off the damn corset."

"But—but the tear—"

"To hell with the tear. You can't breathe with the damn thing on. Take it off."

His words severed the iron control she'd had on her anger, and it surged through her. Anger at all his questions, anger at the fact that he'd been right when she was wrong. Anger because of last night. This time, she was too tired to control it. "You have no right to tell me—"

He moved until he was merely inches from her. In the hot, still air, she smelled the brandy on his breath, the musky scent of his sweat. His eyes were dark, cold stones in his face, and it was all Ana could do to keep from backing away.

"Listen to me, *Duchess,*" he said with a snarl. "If you don't take the damn thing off, I'll do it for you." He grabbed her shoulder.

Ana wrenched away. "Let go of me, you bastard," she spat. "Just because you touched me last night doesn't mean—"

Awareness dawned in his dark eyes. "So that's it. Last night." His coldness disappeared, a small smile tugged at his lips. "What's wrong, Duchess? What is it that bothers you most about last night? The fact that I touched you? Or the fact that you slept willingly in my arms?"

He turned away, not waiting for her answer, moving back to Jiméne while she stood there, motionless. The realization came with sickening speed: He was right. She *had* slept willingly in his arms. More than that. She had *needed* his comfort.

Need was something she had never allowed herself to feel before. Loneliness, yes. But never the kind of fierce, unrelenting need that made her curl against someone, craving a touch. All this time she had been fooling herself, telling herself she was afraid because he saw through her, because he knew so much about her.

The truth was that she was afraid because she felt herself needing him.

A lump filled her throat until Ana could scarcely breathe. God, it couldn't be happening. She knew what need did to a person, how it snuck inside and took over a life, how it molded and twisted and broke will and turned strength into weakness. It was insidious, and inescapable once it started, and long ago she had vowed never to succumb to it, never to depend on anyone. Never to become the insane shell her mother had become.

And now here she was, turning to a drunkard, for God's sake. Turning to a man she should be running from.

She should leave. Run. Fast and far away, until D'Alessandro was only a dim and unpleasant memory. And she should do it now, before it was too late.

What she needed was a plan. Ana turned her back to him and unlaced her corset completely, drawing it off and pulling the wool gown back on over her naked skin. The plan grew in her mind quickly, so full blown she wondered why she hadn't thought of it earlier. Once they reached Gatún, she would steal her ticket back from him and go on alone. There would be other groups resting there; perhaps she could even find the men from the ship and join up with them for the rest of the journey. And as for her promise not to leave D'Alessandro, well, promises were made to be broken. After all, she'd made that one under false pretenses—to a drunken, helpless man who was very different from the one who had saved her life and ministered to Jiméne. A man she hadn't expected to have the intelligence or will to make such an assault on her senses. He didn't need her, the way he'd claimed, and she most certainly didn't need him.

She knew exactly how she'd do it. There would undoubtedly be enough liquor in Gatún to get him good and drunk. The only thing she had to do was wait. Once he was snoring contentedly, she would simply steal her ticket and go on.

The thought brought a niggling sense of wrongness and betrayal, but Ana pushed it away. She had no choice. He'd given her no choice. She owed him nothing, after all. Nothing but the money to get back home. In Gatún, she was sure he could find someone willing to take him back to Chagres.

"Ana—"

His voice cut into her thoughts, and Ana felt the flush of guilt work its way over her skin before she managed to gain control. She refused to look at him, but continued fumbling with the buttons on her dress. "What?"

"Bring me my—"

The sound of shouting on the river quieted them both. Ana glanced down at the water, eyes fastened on the bend hidden by undergrowth and trees, wondering if she'd imagined it.

D'Alessandro looked at her. "Did you hear . . . ?"

It came again. Laughter this time, words spoken in rapid Spanish. She heard the sound of paddles in the current, saw the tip of the bungo as it eased into sight.

"Thank God," she breathed. She almost slid over the edge in her haste to get closer. "Hello!" She lifted her arms, waving, trying to be heard above the noise of the jungle. "Please! Please, hello!"

The boatman in the front of the bungo looked up, his paddle stilled. In that moment, Ana felt D'Alessandro beside her. He put his hands to his mouth and called out something in Spanish.

The man sitting in the boat yelled something back. From where she stood, Ana thought he looked like a native. He wore the same kind of clothing the men in Chagres town had worn—a straight, hip-length shirt made of coarse, painted cloth, and trousers cut off at the knees. His face was shadowed by a large, broad-brimmed hat.

She turned to D'Alessandro, her distress momentarily forgotten. "What did he say?"

"He's coming up." He didn't look at her, merely watched as the boatman poled the bungo to the shore. "He's going to a village a bit farther downriver, but he says they'll take us as far as Gatún."

"They'll take us—" Ana felt relief rush through her, so intense it nearly left her weak. They would get to Gatún. She hadn't realized how frightened she was that they would remain lost in the jungle forever until now. This man was the answer to a prayer. She watched as he gathered his things and started up the steep bank, then she turned back to the burlap bags and quickly slung them again over her shoulder. "At least we can get Jimené to a village. Maybe there will be someone there who can help."

"Yeah." His voice was low, so low Ana turned to look at him.

He was staring at Jimené thoughtfully. In that moment, D'Alessandro looked so pale, so weak, she couldn't believe he was the same man who had held her last night, the same man who had walked miles with Jimené slung over his shoulders.

She turned away. She didn't have time to worry about him, even if she wanted to. They would be in Gatún soon. She could put her plan into action. Before long, she would be on her way. Without him. It seemed almost too good to be true.

"He's a *curandero.*" D'Alessandro's words were slow and heavy.

Ana frowned, glancing back over her shoulder. "A *curandero*? What's that?"

"A doctor," he said quietly. "Folk doctor. From the village of Dos Hermanos."

"A folk doctor." Ana looked down the bank, at the man fighting his way through the underbrush. She let the bags slip slowly to the ground. "Did you tell him about Jimené?"

"No."

"Why not? Maybe he can help."

"I don't need help."

His steady words made her angry, the quiet struggle in them reminded her of last night. *I know. I know. I know.* Her fingernails dug into the palm of her hand. The memory brought back her uncertainty, and she felt it again—that need. That damnable need. Fear of it coiled inside her, making it suddenly hard to move or breathe. Because of it, she did the most hurtful thing she could think of.

She laughed. "Oh no?" She motioned to Jimené. "Pardon me for disagreeing, but it seems you *do* need him. Jimené's no better than he was before. Maybe *this* doctor knows what he's doing."

If possible, he turned even paler than before. He looked away.

She waited for something. Some biting comment, some nasty jibe, and when it didn't come, she felt suddenly mean and spiteful. She shouldn't have said those things, she thought, and for a moment, she wished she could take the words back, but then the *curandero* eased up the final yards of the bank, and his fluent Spanish filled the air.

He watched from the other side of the campfire. Watched the medicine man bend over Jimené, murmuring prayer songs in a high, singsong voice, forcing tamarind water down his throat and then praying again. Voodoo medicine, Cain thought, but he said nothing, and he didn't interrupt.

He should be glad Alejo had come along, he told himself. At least now he wouldn't bear the entire responsibility for Jimené's death. Because the Panamanian would die, he had no doubt of it. The last miles, since the dip in the river, Jimené's breathing had been raspy and broken, rattling in his chest.

Cain had listened to it until he thought he might go mad.

Yes, he was glad the *curandero* had happened along. Glad that he no longer had to fight his fear or feel that hopeless, restless desperation that had dogged him since Jimené became unconscious.

Her laughter still rang in his ears, jeering and horrible, echoing in his brain, impossible to forget or deny. It joined those other voices, the ones that told him he was useless as a doctor. The ones that second-guessed him and tormented him. The demons that brought back the memories of a blood-soaked room and a rasping voice. *You're a doctor, Cain. I trust you, trust you, trust you . . .*

Ah, Jesus, if only he had been worth trusting. If only he hadn't taken that final, senseless risk.

But you did take it. You weren't much of a doctor after all, were you? John Matson's most promising apprentice turned out to be nothing. Less than nothing.

Why had he thought it would ever be different? His mother had told him—dozens of times—what a failure he was. But he'd refused to believe her then. It wasn't until later—years later, that he'd realized how right she was . . .

Hell, he couldn't even cure a damn fever. He'd been fooling no one with his potions and his knowledge. Not himself, and not her. He stole a glance at Ana, who sat ramrod-straight against a nearby ceiba. Especially not her.

"He's no better than he was before." "Maybe this doctor knows what he's doing." She hadn't said it, but the implication was there: *"Because you don't. You can't heal him."* Her eyes burned through him, and he remembered her fear last night, remembered the strength of that damn wall.

You can't even soothe a woman in the dead of night. How the hell did you expect to heal the sick?

Ah, God, he didn't want to fight anymore, he thought again. He glanced at the burlap bags, laying abandoned near the fire, and tried to summon the strength to go over to them. But then he saw her again, saw the stiffness of her spine and her unwavering gaze on Alejo, and Cain knew he wouldn't get up. Not just now, not when the thought of her contempt left him feeling weak and hopelessly inept. Not until later, when she was sleeping, when she wouldn't be able to see his desperation—or the relief the brandy brought him.

"He is growing cooler, I think." The sound of Alejo's quiet Spanish made Cain straighten. "I believe the gods have answered my prayers."

"I do not feel so well." Jimené's voice was soft, barely audible.

Alejo looked up. "He is awake," he said softly.

Across the way, Ana leapt to her feet. "What did you say?" The hope in her voice made Cain recoil. "Is he awake? Is the fever broken?"

Alejo nodded shortly. "The gods have been kind," he said, glancing at Cain. "He is well."

Spoken with the certainty of a man sure of heaven's goodwill, Cain thought sourly. He struggled to his feet. "Thank you," he answered, in Spanish. "We are grateful for your help."

Jimené opened his eyes, staring into Alejo's face. "Who are you?"

Ana laughed, relief exploding in the sound. "He is the man who saved your life, Jimené," she said, kneeling beside him. She looked up at Alejo as he drew away, and the gratitude lighting her face was almost painful to see. "Thank you."

"Ahhh!" Jimené tossed his good arm over his eyes. "I feel trampled."

"You were shot," she said. "Don't you remember?"

"Sí." Jimené lowered his arm and struggled to one elbow. The blood drained from his face at the movement, and he fell back again, but his expression remained stern. *"Sí,* I remember. *Bastardos.* We must kill them."

Cain moved closer. "We did already. Most of them, anyway. And as soon as you can hold a gun again, *amigo,* I'll be the first to send you after the last one."

Jimené scowled, looking doubly fierce with the dark circles beneath his eyes marking his fever-pale skin. "He is mine."

"As you wish." Cain squatted beside him. "How do you feel?"

"As if I have been dropped off a cliff." He scowled at Cain's snorted laughter. "What is it? Why do you laugh?"

"He laughs because he's a buffoon." Ana's sharp voice evaporated Cain's humor. "He's been carrying you most of the way. No wonder you're sore."

"Carrying me? Like a babe?"

"More like a very heavy dog." Cain reached for Jimené's arm. "I should check that wrapping, *amigo,* just to make sure the wound hasn't—"

Ana's involuntary movement stopped him before he touched the bandage. Cain glanced at her, curious, and what he saw in her eyes sent despair spiraling into his gut, brought his hands back to his sides and made the longing explode in his brain.

She didn't want him to touch Jimené. Didn't trust him.

Do you blame her?

He drew away, hands shaking, denial surging through his body. *You're a fool,* the voice said in his head. *She has never trusted you, and you know it.* And he had known it. He remembered her words outside of Chagres, when she'd simply told him she trusted Jimené more than him. Heard her words again only hours ago, when she laughed at him for saying he didn't need Alejo's help.

But this further, tangible proof of her distrust devastated him. Before it had only been in her eyes, in words he could easily believe were lies. Her unconscious gesture now was more than all that. Before her distrust had been almost deliberate. Now it was real. Real, and painful.

With it came the realization that she was right not to trust him. With Jimené's life or hers. *Jesus, I don't even trust myself.* He hadn't cured Jimené. Alejo had done that. Prayers and tamarind had done more than Cain's knowledge had done, more than all those years of learning, all the sacrifice.

The demons were there again, mocking him. He was a hopeless excuse for a doctor. A failure. *Nothing. Less than nothing* . . .

Cain stumbled away, moving to the burlap bag across the fire, to the bottles he knew were within. Any self-control he'd had disappeared, melted away as though it had never been. He no longer cared about the contempt in her eyes. No longer cared because he shared it, had always shared it. He grabbed a bottle, twisted off the cork, and gulped the raw, fiery *aguardiente,* gasping with relief at the burn in his chest.

And he knew before he started that it wouldn't make anything different. Wouldn't change the way she felt about him or how he felt about himself. There wasn't enough liquor in the world to do that.

But he was willing to try to make it enough. More than willing.

"Do you try to kill me?" Jiméne asked irritably. He turned his head away, grabbing at the spoon Ana held while a chunk of pork slid greasily down his chin. He wiped it away irritably. "I can do it."

"Fine." Ana dropped the spoon into his lap and

pushed back her rickety stool. "You're the one who asked for help, Jiméne. Don't scream for me when it doesn't work the way you wish."

"Of course." He was immediately contrite. "Please forgive me, *cariña,* it is just that—" He paused, then motioned at the bowl of pork stew in his lap. It was cold and congealed now, a layer of thick yellow fat on the surface. "It is just that I cannot eat this slop."

"It's all there is," Ana said simply. She pulled the stool close to his hammock again, brushing aside the thick braid that lopped forward at her movement. "Eat it. You need the strength."

He nodded, his mouth curving in a dour grin before he picked up the spoon again with his good hand and took a bite. For a moment, Ana watched him, making sure he could handle the job himself before she looked away. Right into D'Alessandro's back.

Ana scowled. Her partner sat at a table at the side of the crowded one-room hut, surrounded by other men. They were playing monte and drinking, and talking loudly. But mostly drinking. She watched as D'Alessandro tipped back his head and gulped at a bottle of *aguarediente.* He was oblivious to everything: to the mean, dirty hut where they'd paid to stay, to the blasted heat and the odor of sweat and pork clinging to the walls. All he cared about was drinking and gambling away her gold coins.

Since they'd arrived in Gatún and Alejo had moved on, D'Alessandro had even forgotten Jimené. It was true that the Panamanian had made a remarkable recovery—the only real sign of his fever was the sling wrapped around his arm—but short of dosing him lightly with laudanum and some other kind of powder, D'Alessandro had done nothing more to make sure Jiméne was healing.

His biggest concern, she remembered, was finding another bottle.

Well, he'd found it easily, and his actions only strengthened her resolve. The moment she could, she was leaving. All that remained was to steal the ticket from D'Alessandro, which would be easy once he was asleep. Actually, as drunk as he was, she could probably do it while he was awake without his feeling a thing. Then, once the ticket was in her hands, she would grab Jiméne and go.

In fact, the one hitch to her plan so far was Jimené. She hadn't told him what she planned, though the idea to take him had occurred to her when the *curandero* healed him so quickly. Why should she go on with strangers when she could take Jimené? She didn't need to scour Gatún for a partner to replace D'Alessandro. She already *had* another partner. That was, she did if he was well enough to walk.

She still had to get Jiméne to agree to leave with her, but Ana didn't doubt his answer. In spite of their new-found bantering, he and D'Alessandro still disliked each other. And Jiméne claimed often enough that he loved her. Now it was time for him to prove he meant it.

She swallowed, and turned again to watch Jiméne eat. The nauseating stew was almost gone, and he was starting to look a little green. Which was hardly surprising, considering she'd barely managed to choke down a few mouthfuls herself.

"Full?" she asked.

Jiméne nodded, pushing the bowl away. "*Sí,* take it." Then, when Ana lowered it to the floor, he smiled weakly. "*Gracias, cariña.* I apologize for my temper. I am—I am not myself."

"Your arm hurts?"

He hesitated slightly. "*Sí.* It hurts. Perhaps you should call D'Alessandro?"

"I doubt he can spare the time." As if to punctuate her comment, the laughter at the table grew. She threw them a bitter glance. "You'll have to wait until he's out of brandy."

"Ah." Jiméne was quiet. He stared at his fingers thoughtfully. "He has been like this for a long time?"

"Since I've known him."

"He has never been better?"

"He's getting worse." Ana bit off the words, surprised at the extent of her rising anger. Dammit, D'Alessandro didn't matter to her. His drinking made no difference anymore. She was leaving. Putting him behind her as a bad wager and a worse memory. She forced her voice to stay calm and even. Now was the time to ask Jiméne to go along. Now that he'd seen firsthand what a liability D'Alessandro was. "In fact, I—"

"¡Dios!" A loud voice boomed from the table, followed by hysterical laughter. *"¡Creo que Pedro está traqueado!"*

"¡Sí!"

Jiméne chuckled. "It is not only Pedro who is drunk," he said in a low voice. "They are all drunk."

"Jiméne—"

"Perhaps D'Alessandro is winning, eh? Then *he* could pay for this hovel."

"Yes, of course. Now—"

"Or even the boat ride to Gorgona. I have heard—"

"Jiméne!" She snapped, so intently he nearly jumped from his hammock. When he turned to look at her, his brown eyes wide, she took a deep breath, forcing calm. "Jiméne," she said slowly. "I have something important to ask you."

"Of course, *cariña,*" he said, suddenly serious. "Whatever you wish, you have if it is in my power to give you."

"I need your help." Ana didn't take her eyes from his face. "I need to leave."

"Leave?" Jiméne looked puzzled. "But we will leave, as soon as D'Alessandro hires another bungo."

"You don't understand," she said firmly. "I want to leave without him."

"Without . . . ? Without D'Alessandro? But he is your husband!"

"Oh, for God's sake, don't be a fool!" Her voice was sharp, sharper than she'd intended. "He isn't my husband and you know it. You've known it since the beginning."

"But—but you insisted."

"I was lying!"

Jiméne stared at her skeptically. "You said he was your husband. Now you say he is not?"

"Because he isn't. He never was. I hired him, Jiméne. I hired him to pose as my husband for the trip to San Francisco. I thought that way I'd be less conspicuous, that it would be easier to travel." Ana spoke quickly. "He's a drunkard, that's all. Not my husband. Not anything to me."

"I see." He looked thoughtful. "And now you want to leave him?"

She nodded eagerly. "He's slowing me down, Jiméne. He's spending all my money. I have no other choice but to leave him behind."

He didn't look at her, merely rubbed his chin. "What is it you wish me to do?"

Victory sped through her. It was all she could do to keep from laughing in triumph. "Come with me. I need a partner, someone I can trust. I can't go on alone. You say you care about me, Jiméne. Show me that's true. Show me you care enough to leave with me."

"Cariña." He choked the word as if tortured by it.

Ana reached out and caressed his hand. "Jiméne, please."

"Ah, *cariña."* Jiméne shook his head sadly. "I cannot. I cannot."

Ana snatched her hand back and stared at him disbelievingly. "What?"

"I cannot." Jiméne couldn't even look at her. Instead, he focused on the notched pole leading to the sleeping loft above. Misery lined his face, but Ana felt no sympathy at all.

"What do you mean, you cannot?"

"Mi madre is ill, *cariña.* I must go home. But even if I could, I would not help you with this. D'Alessandro saved my life."

"He certainly did not," Ana said, surprised. "If not for Alejo—"

"A witch doctor," Jimené said simply, brushing away her comment. "They do the same for everyone—tamarind water and prayer. It is doctoring for fools. No, it is D'Alessandro who saved my poor life. I am certain of this. I will not repay him by leaving him behind. I cannot. He needs our help."

"Our help?" Confusion made her tone sharp. "What does that mean?"

Jiméne pursed his lips thoughtfully. "I am not sure I can explain it to you, *cariña,* but you must trust me in this. It is better for you—for all of us—to stay with D'Alessandro."

"How can you say that?" It took every ounce of control she had to keep from stomping away in frustration. She had lost. Jiméne had refused to help her. In all her planning, this was the one thing she had not expected. "He's a drunkard, Jiméne. If nothing else, he'll make trouble."

"He saved my life," he said simply.

She opened her mouth to argue, but his unwavering confidence defeated her. Ana glanced again at D'Alessandro's broad back. In her mind, she heard again the words he'd thrown at her in the middle of the jungle. *What is it that bothers you most about last night? The fact that I touched you? Or the fact that you slept willingly in my arms?*

Panic sped through her. It didn't matter what Jiméne said. She *had* to leave. D'Alessandro was too dangerous. She would go on alone if there was no other way. And she would go tonight.

Chapter 12

Ana lay stiff and silent on the stinking hammock. The hut shook with snoring as loud as the shouts that had filled it less than an hour before. Near the dying fire, two dogs scratched constantly.

From somewhere far away came the faint sound of a jaguar's roar, quickly followed by the laughter of men drinking in a neighboring hovel, and Ana shuddered. Once she stole the ticket from D'Alessandro, she planned to go there, where the men were still awake and drunk enough to think taking on a female companion might have its advantages. If she had to, she would prove just how many advantages there were.

She clenched her fists at the thought. She hated to be forced to trade her favors for permission to join, but there might not be any other choice. After all, her plan to pick and choose her customers was for San Francisco, not for the journey there. For now, she would do what she had to.

If that meant leaving Jiméne behind, so be it. Ana closed her eyes briefly, pushing away sadness. She had not expected Jiméne's refusal, nor had she expected her sorrowful reaction to it. She had not wanted to say good-bye so soon, but there was no help for it. If his ties to D'Alessandro were stronger than his ties to her, there was nothing she could do except go ahead without him.

She glanced over at the shape that was D'Alessandro, sprawled on the hide-covered bamboo floor. His chest heaved slowly, deeply, a snore rattled from his open mouth. Ana frowned. She had watched him this evening, getting rapidly and completely drunk. So drunk, she thought with disgust, that even the fleas jumping all over the floor didn't stir him.

But for once, his drunkenness didn't fill her with dismay. It would make it easier to steal the tickets. Ana slowly, carefully worked her way out of the hammock. One of the dogs by the fire rose, watching her expectantly with big brown eyes while the other gnawed at a flea bite on its tail. She ignored them, stepping carefully over one sprawled body and then another, holding her breath every time the cane creaked beneath her weight.

"Aaaah."

She froze, her heart racing. Slowly she looked over her shoulder at the man who'd made the noise. He turned over, disturbed by the dog, who had decided to rub its back on the bottom of his low-hanging hammock. Ana breathed a sigh of relief as the snores began again. She waited, paralyzed until the animal lay down, resting its head on its paws.

D'Alessandro was only a few feet away, and Ana skillfully skirted the other shadows until she stood beside him. She hadn't imagined his deep sleep, she noted with satisfaction. His body didn't even twitch in dreams. The moonlight slanting against his cheekbones made him look pale and slightly sinister, the dark hair framing his face blended into the shadows so it seemed as if his face were disembodied, glowing. Somehow threatening . . .

Ana pushed the notion away. Asleep, he was no more

threatening than a newborn babe. Drunk, even less so. It was only her imagination. All she had to do was lean down, reach into his open frock coat, and find the pocket with the tickets. An easy matter, really. So simple the most inexperienced pickpocket could do it.

So why was she standing here, staring at him as if frozen by a witch's curse? Why did that strange fear send her heart pounding loudly in her ears?

Because she was a fool, Ana told herself firmly. There wouldn't be a better time. As quietly as she could, she knelt beside him. Slowly, licking her lips with nervousness, she reached out and touched the worn lapel of his coat, carefully—oh so carefully—pulling it aside—

His hand snaked out, clamping tightly around her wrist. Ana choked back a scream and tried to yank her hand back. But his grip was too tight, his fingers cut into the tendons of her wrist, bringing tears of pain.

His eyes snapped open. To her surprise, Ana saw clarity and sharpness in his gaze. He said nothing, releasing her wrist with lethal suddenness. Then, before she could escape, he grabbed her again, his arm like an iron bar across her back, holding her prisoner against his chest.

"Well, well, if it isn't m'little partner," he whispered. She heard the slur of drink in his voice even though it wasn't in his eyes. "Miss m'arms tonight?"

She tried to pull away, but his arm kept her in place with a strength she didn't expect. His fingers tangled in her hair, holding her still.

"Let me go."

"A'right," he said agreeably, though his hold didn't lessen. "First tell me why y'were going through m'pockets. Looking for something?"

"No."

"Don't lie t' me, Ana."

If possible, his voice was smoother at a whisper. The *ahs* of her name rolled off his tongue to shiver down her spine. Ana was uncomfortably aware of the heat of his body through their clothes, aware of the way her breasts pressed into him. He smelled like brandy and river water and sweat, and the combination was strangely familiar and reassuring. But it was his gaze that affected her the most. He looked at her in a lazy, half-lidded way that stabbed right through her, as if he tried to fathom the secrets in her eyes. As if she held the key to some locked door . . .

Ana closed her eyes against the onslaught of emotions his gaze roused.

"Well?"

Ana twisted, wincing as his fingers tightened on her hair. "Dammit, let go of me!" She pushed at his chest, digging her fingernails into the skin at his throat. "Let go of me."

"Christ!" he cursed softly, rolling.

Ana found herself suddenly pinned beneath him, star ing up into his face. His hair fell forward, shadowing his expression, but the moonlight slanting through the hut's open door accentuated the full curve of his smile.

"Well, Ana?" he said again. "Tell me what y'want, unless you're looking to spend the night this way."

"I can promise you'll get no satisfaction from it," she said as coolly as she could.

"Now there you're wrong," he said. He looped a strand of her hair around his finger and stared at it. "Just holding y'is all the satisfaction I need."

Damn him, he knew just what to say, how to make her the most uncomfortable. She twisted her head, looking away from him, trying to ignore the press of his hips against hers, trying not to see his steady stare.

He laughed softly, his brandy-scented breath fanning her face. "So if it's not me, y'want, Duchess, what is it? Not money, since y'hold it all. Not my clothes, you've got your own. So it must be—" He stopped short, Ana looked at him just in time to see his eyes widen in surprise. "Christ. The tickets. Y'want the tickets."

Ana's lips thinned. "You've been nothing but trouble," she said, too furious at her failure to care about saving his feelings. "I'm severing our deal right now. Forget about helping me, or saving me, or pretending to be my husband. From now on, I travel alone."

Cain was too stunned to do anything but stare at her. She wanted the tickets. Wanted to leave him behind while she gallivanted off to San Francisco by herself. In spite of her cruelty over the *curandero* a few days ago, the knowledge brought with it a fierce and unrelenting panic. The fear of his blackouts came rushing back. He could not be alone—not here in the jungle—not left to the mercy of *aguardiente* and memories. But she meant to leave him just the same. Christ, if he hadn't been used to sleeping outside and alone, used to waking at the slightest movement, she would have stolen the tickets without a word. She would be gone.

In spite of her promise.

She glared at him defiantly, her eyes dark holes in the moonlight, her hair tangled around her face. Her full lips were sculpted by the shadows into a thin, forbidding line. She meant it, he knew. Meant every word. The realization made him fully sober in an instant. Sober and angry.

"You promised," he said quietly. He realized too late how stupid it sounded, and winced.

She laughed in his face. "Promised? What does that matter?"

He stared at her unbelievingly, feeling a sense of loss so great it surprised him. He had overestimated her again. Hell, she was nothing but a whore on the run from the law. On the banks of the Chagres, she'd proven that she had no compassion and little faith. Why did it surprise him to learn she had no honor either?

She twisted uncomfortably beneath him, turning her face away. "Don't look at me like that."

"Like what?"

"As if I've disappointed you."

"You have."

She made a soft sound of impatience. "You can't be that naive, D'Alessandro. You don't need me, you never did. I thought you'd be happy to be rid of me."

He tried hard to keep disappointment from coloring his voice. "I fulfilled my part of the bargain, Duchess," he said softly. "The least you can do is fulfill yours."

Her eyes narrowed, she moved again beneath his hips. "I've given you everything I said I would. Money, drink—"

"Y'promised to stay with me."

She closed her eyes briefly, heaving a deep sigh, and he felt her relax. When she opened her eyes again, she was smiling a soft, provocative smile. "What is it you really want, D'Alessandro? You said you needed me. Maybe it's only that you want me."

Her smile broadened, and Cain stiffened, suddenly realizing where her words were leading. She was trying to trade her favors for her freedom—the thought plunged him into a new kind of hell. God knew, he'd always wanted her, and now here she was, offering herself to him, and he realized he didn't want her like this. Not as part of a bargain. His stomach knotted as if he'd been punched hard and the rest of him went numb. Cold sweat broke out on his forehead even though the room was stiflingly warm.

She wiggled again between his legs, and somehow that made the tear in her bodice gape wider over her breast, revealing more of the soft swell. "Give me the ticket, D'Alessandro, and I'm yours for the night. To do whatever you want with."

He swallowed, feeling the blood drain from his face. His voice was embarrassingly husky and raw. "No."

"No?" She lifted a brow, her voice edged with derision. "What are you afraid of? Is there some strange liking you have? Don't worry, D'Alessandro, I've accommodated them all—"

He got to his feet so quickly she stared at him in surprise. Cain raked his hand through his hair, his fingers trembling.

Ana sat up, shaking back her hair, a frown contorting her features. "Am I that repulsive to you?"

"No." He shook his head. "God, no."

"Then I don't understand."

"No deals," he said roughly, struggling to keep from revealing just how disconcerted he was. "You made a promise, Duchess. I won't let you out of it so easily."

She got to her feet, brushing off her skirt, her eyes puzzled. "I don't understand you. Knowing I don't want to be here, why do you want me to stay?"

He said nothing for a moment, seeing curiosity in eyes that had so recently held scorn—hell, that always held scorn. She didn't like him and never had, and he knew it would probably never change. But, in spite of everything, there was something about her he recognized, something in her that matched what was in him, and it was the belief it was there that he couldn't turn away from, that he couldn't let escape. He took a deep breath. "You tell me, Duchess. Why is it you want so badly to go?" he asked finally.

She jumped a little, and he saw fear flit through her eyes. Lifting her skirts, she brushed by him. "Damn you," she said, so quietly he wasn't sure he'd heard it.

He watched her make her way across the floor, across the sleeping bodies until she reached her hammock. She didn't look at him again as she sank down into it.

The voices from the neighboring huts seemed to grow louder in his ears, a beckoning call that moved him almost against his will past the sleeping men on the floor, toward the moonlight slanting in the open doorway. He had to leave, had to get out of this cabin before she made him insane, before he had time to think about the fact that he wanted her almost badly enough to go over to that hammock right now and trade the ticket for her body.

But if he did that, he'd be alone, without her, without anyone, and he was desperate enough—and afraid enough—to do whatever he had to to make sure that didn't happen. He could bear it all as long as she stayed with him. He could bear the fact that she felt nothing but contempt for him, that she was so frantic to leave she would steal the ticket without a word.

Bitterness rose in his throat. Even a whore could barely stand the sight of him. Then he remembered. She wanted Castañeras, and it wasn't surprising that she should pick the steady, handsome Panamanian over a drunken doctor. Not surprising at all.

The thought sent a strange ache into his heart, and Cain tried to banish it. It didn't matter. *She* didn't matter. The Duchess was unattainable, which was just as well, since he didn't have the strength to fight for her.

Not for her, not for anything.

They left Gatún the next morning, and though the sun had barely risen in the sky, it was already hot. The rain of yesterday steamed up from the jungle floor to form a stinking fog. It hovered over the ground, hiding the river and making everything seem muffled and quiet.

Ana stared straight ahead, watching the passing shadows in the mist and the swirling eddies created in the fog when the boatmen plunged their poles through it. The monkeys were still mercifully quiet, but the insects were rampant, and they were eating her alive.

A swarm of tiny bugs whirled around her and disappeared, and Ana irritably swatted at her neck. She felt dirty and sweaty and terrible; the heat pressed down heavily, and beneath the damp wool dress her skin itched as if it were on fire. Every strand of hair sticking to her face and neck was torturous. She dipped one of Jiméne's handkerchiefs into the river repeatedly, swathing her sticky skin with the relatively cool river water.

"How much farther to Gorgona?" she asked no one in particular, dragging the wet cloth over her throat, wishing she could unbutton more than one or two buttons to let the air touch her skin.

In the bow, Jiméne twisted to see her. He smiled, his white teeth flashing, and she forced herself not to grimace. He was in a charitable mood; he thought he talked her out of her plan to steal the tickets and leave. He didn't know that D'Alessandro had thwarted her, leaving her trapped and helpless—proving her theory that God didn't wait for a person to die before he plunged them into hell.

"A small distance only," Jiméne reassured her. He bit off a piece of the strongly flavored sausage that was the universal food of the boatmen and glanced at the man in the bow. *"Quantos leguas a Gorgona?"* When the boatman shrugged, Jiméne looked at her again. "He does not know."

"He doesn't know," she mimicked, too uncomfortable to care any longer about her temper. "He's probably made this trip a hundred times."

In the stern, D'Alessandro snorted in amusement. Ana glared at him. He sprawled indolently, sucking away at a bottle of *aguardiente.* God, she was tired of that sight. Tired of that and tired of D'Alessandro's strange nobility. He wasn't like other men. She remembered being relieved by his refusal to take sex as payment when she first met him, but now she felt only frustration. Frustration and an odd disappointment.

After he left the hut last night, she tossed and turned for hours, churning with anger. She couldn't believe he'd thrown her offer back in her face, that he retreated as if he couldn't bear the touch of her. She couldn't believe she misjudged him so completely that she'd failed to steal the tickets and make her escape.

But mostly, she couldn't believe the quiet little nudge of curiosity she'd felt when she decided to bargain with him.

Curiosity she was sure she'd imagined. D'Alessandro was handsome enough, but his drinking made him unattractive, and the fact that he was a doctor repulsed her. More than that, he was dangerous. Dangerous because even as he'd refused her last night, she thought he might have accepted if she'd offered something more.

That was the problem with him. He was like those other men—the ones she couldn't abide. The ones who were never satisfied with what she was willing to offer—her body and nothing else.

She sat back, forcing D'Alessandro from her mind, listening to the gentle splash of the river against the boat. The lulling *dip slosh* of the poles moving through the water and the soft, humid heat made her lids heavy, and Ana closed her eyes and leaned back on the side of the bungo, letting exhaustion from the sleepless night creep over her. *Dip slosh, dip slosh* . . . The rhythm chimed in her ears, soothed her muscles. *Dip slosh, dip slosh, dip* . . .

She stared at the line of drops falling from the ceiling. They echoed hollowly, plopping one by one into the half-full bucket beneath the hole in the peeling plaster ceiling. Rats rustled in the dark corners, looking for something to eat, and she let them stay, too tired to kick them out, too dispirited to move. Her mother's coughs rattled like dry wood, a death knell that rang in her ears.

When she heard the sharp rapping on the door, she jumped, even though she'd been waiting for it, and rose wearily from the chair, her feet feeling hobbled by chains as she went to the door and let him in.

He looked the same as he always did. For some reason, she'd been hoping he would look different, but that was only wishful thinking. He stood on the doorstep, a sickening grin on his face, watching her with those hungry, bloodshot eyes. Pushing his way past her, he dropped his heavy bag on the floor and grabbed her arms as if afraid she would escape.

"I'm glad you've come around, Anastasia," he said, still grinning that horrible, leering grin. "You won't regret it—"

"I already do."

His smile died for only a second. His gaze swept the sparsely furnished room, focusing on the rude bed in the corner spread with the grayish-white ruffled quilt her father had sent her when she was just a child. From the other room came her mother's hacking cough.

"Anastasia? Anastasia? Is that Dr. Reynolds?"

"Yes, Mama," she answered dully.

"I'll be in in a moment, Katherine," Dr. Reynolds called. He raised a dirty gray brow at Ana. "Now, my dear, time to pay the bills . . ."

She retreated, dragging herself back to the bed, feeling his hot, stinking breath on her face. She stopped when the backs of her knees slapped against the bedstand, and swallowed, waiting. There was still time. Still time for him to say it was all a mistake, that he wouldn't exact this price from her, but she knew the moment he touched her shoulder that she'd been waiting in vain. He pushed her. She fell sprawling to the bed, and then he was on top of her, tearing at her bodice, pulling her skirt up around her waist, fumbling with his trousers.

He panted, writhing in impatience as he forced her legs apart. Ana said nothing and did nothing, merely lay there motionlessly, staring at the peeling ceiling, listening to the drip and the rats.

When he thrust into her, she bit her lip to keep from crying out, trying to divorce her mind from her body, trying not to feel his heavy stomach on hers, or his raw, painful thrusting. The sound of the leak—dip slosh, dip slosh—was heavy and echoing in her ears, blending with Reynolds's obscene gasps. She concentrated on the rhythm and blocked out the feel of his hands kneading her breasts and the stench of his breath.

It was over in moments. Reynolds heaved himself off her, a smug, satisfied smile on his face, and buttoned his trousers. "You did very well, Anastasia," he congratulated her—as if she'd just won a prize. "Very well."

And then he was gone, leaving her lying on the bed while he visited her mother.

Her whole body ached, and she was freezing, but Ana clenched her jaw and refused to feel it. She pushed down her skirts, rising from the bed. But when she leaned down to straighten the covers, she saw the dark red spot of blood, marring the white quilt, growing and growing until it filled her gaze—

Crash!

Ana's eyes snapped open, the dream fled. She stared wildly about her, taking in the darkening air, the wild activity on the boat. The crash—where had the crash come from?

Crack!

"La borrasca!" the boatman in the bow shouted over his shoulder, signaling something to D'Alessandro, who ducked under the shelter beside her, fumbling beneath the seat. Behind her, Jiméne grabbed a paddle, with his good arm frantically trying to help the other man steer against the wildly rising current.

"What's going on?" she shouted.

D'Alessandro looked up. "A storm," he yelled, but the wind whipped the sound away, and she only saw him mouth the words.

The moment he said it, the sky opened up. Torrents of rain roared through the trees, sounded like a stampede on the leaves. The earth seemed to tremble beneath them. D'Alessandro shoved something at her hurriedly, leaving the shelter of the canopy. He joined the boatman at the bow and Ana looked down at what he'd given her. It was a folded square of India rubber cloth.

India rubber to keep her dry while he and the others worked desperately to keep the boat righted in the storm. The simple gesture of concern was made worse by the fact that D'Alessandro was still obviously drunk. Now he swayed and slipped in the bow, more a hindrance than a help—but helpful enough to make sure she was all right before he aided the others.

Ana slowly unfolded the square and wrapped the stinking cloth around her shoulders, huddling beneath it. The rain poured in sheets, graying everything in front of her, making the men swim like unfocused blobs of color before her eyes. The red sash around the boatman's waist was the brightest of all, and glowing, just as the blood had in her dream.

The memory came flooding back to her then, and Ana shuddered and pulled the cloth closer. She'd thought the dream was lost, finally. It had been years since she'd had it. Years since she'd allowed herself to remember. Now, as always, it left a stale, sick feeling in the pit of her stomach, and she struggled to clear her mind, to forget.

But it wouldn't go away this time. It sat there like a vulture in the back of her brain, waiting, watching. Reminding her again of what a trick life had played on her, letting her believe—at least for a little while—that there had been a time when she was innocent and trusting. A time when the future had stretched uncertain and promising before her.

She stared at D'Alessandro's broad back, and was surprised when he suddenly turned to stare at her through the rain, his dark hair plastered over his head and dripping into his face, his eyes intense and knowing. And with that look, she knew what it was that brought the dream back.

D'Alessandro. His disappointment at her attempt to leave him behind had made her feel worthless. The promise she'd made to him had been more important than she understood, and that realization confused her.

She didn't understand that kind of honor. Didn't know how to be the kind of friend whose word could be trusted.

The knowledge filled her with a sense of loss, as if she'd hurt someone she didn't want to hurt.

As if she'd once again traded a bright future for hell.

Chapter 13

The drums had been beating since they'd arrived in Gorgona. The slow, steady *boom boom boom,* as regular as the ringing of churchbells, echoed through the make-shift town, bouncing off the green mountains surrounding the broad savannah. Every *boom* added another layer of excitement, and the *aguardiente* vendors wandering the streets wore broad, satisfied smiles. The Americans had come, and tonight the *alcalde* had decided to hold a *fandango* in celebration. Anticipation of the dance vibrated in the air.

Ana smiled at the thought and dished some kind of savory meat pie onto her plate beside a stringy mule steak. It was completely a coincidence that they'd arrived on the steep banks of Gorgona at the same time as a large group of other Americans, but she was more than willing to join the natives in celebrating. They were only halfway to Panama City, but every step had been a challenge. If nothing else, a *fandango* would give her the chance to relax.

She wished her mind would relax as well. It had been

a day and a half since she'd tried to steal the tickets from D'Alessandro, but she could not forget the look in his eyes. All during the long, silent boat trip from Gatún to Gorgona, she remembered.

She glanced across the large, crowded room of the Hotel Française, involuntarily searching for him. He was easy to find. He'd been in the same spot since they arrived, sitting with a group of men in a pose that was becoming all too familiar—cards in one hand, *aguardiente* in the other. He laughed at something someone had said, his white teeth flashing in his face, and gulped at the bottle. He was very, very drunk.

It was hardly new, though he was drunker now than he'd been since the night she met him. He'd at least been in control of himself before. But since the *curanderos* had cured Jimené, that control had slipped, and it had only grown worse since Gatún. That morning he'd nearly put a hole in the bungo by falling into the canopy poles, and he'd fallen into the river when they left the boat. It wasn't like him.

She couldn't help but think it had something to do with her attempt to steal the tickets.

Ana watched the brandy course over his jaw, down the tanned skin of his throat to disappear into the curls of chest hair peeking through his open collar. Long ago, he had taken off his frock coat and wadded it into a ball, jamming it into one of the bags along with his medical case. Now he wore only the mud-streaked, limp white shirt and his brocaded vest, which was so stained with dirt and blood she couldn't remember what color it had been. He was a mess.

The men around him were cramming food into their mouths as they played, while D'Alessandro steadily drank. He never ate, she realized suddenly. She didn't think she had ever seen him chew a thing. No, there was that one time on the ship, she remembered. One of their last meals, he'd eaten so much she thought he would be sick. But she hadn't seen him eat much of anything before or since. No wonder he was so lean, with that haunted, undernourished look in his face. Why hadn't she ever noticed it before?

"What do you stare at?" Jiméne walked back to their table with a jug of wine. He sat down, a knowing glance lighting his eyes as he looked in the direction she'd been staring. "Ah. *Su esposo.*"

"What did you say?"

"D'Alessandro." Jiméne poured wine into her cup and then his. He nodded toward her plate. "Do you like the iguana pie?"

"I was not staring at him."

"Of course not," Jiméne said soothingly.

"I wasn't." Ana took a biteful of food, chewing angrily for a moment until Jiméne's question registered. She swallowed quickly, nearly choking. "Iguana pie?"

"It is a specialty," he said, a smile curving his lips. "It is delicious, no?"

"No." Ana put down her fork firmly and gulped the rough, vinegary wine. "I'm not hungry, really."

"Of course you are not. You are worried, as I am."

"Worried about what?"

"About your husband, of course. You do not listen, *cariña,*" he admonished. "We were speaking of D'Alessandro."

"I see." Ana watched Jiméne take an enthusiastic bite of the iguana pie. Her stomach flipped, and she looked away. Her gaze touched on her partner just as he took a huge gulp from the bottle. She clenched her fists in her lap. "Unfortunately, this time you're wrong, Jiméne. I'm not worried about him. He can do as he likes."

"But the drinking—"

"—isn't going to change."

"You do not try."

"I don't have to." Ana said, forcing away her guilt.

"It's his choice to drink. If he wanted to stop, he could."

"Ah." Jiméne leaned his elbow on the table. *"La vista del amo engorde el caballo."*

"I don't speak Spanish."

"It is an old saying: The sight of the master fattens the horse."

"How beautiful." Sarcasm made her voice harsh. Ana tried to curb her impatience. "I don't like puzzles, Jiméne. What are you trying to say?"

"Only that he would stop for you, if you tried to help him."

Ana stared at him in disbelief. "Don't be ridiculous. He's a drunkard, and he likes being that way. Why would he stop for me?"

Jiméne shrugged. "He loves you."

Ana exhaled in exasperation. "You're the one who's been drinking too much wine. He is not my husband, Jiméne. He cares nothing for me. Just as I care nothing for him."

"As you say." Jiméne leaned back in his chair, smiling enigmatically. "But his drinking, it must be hard for you, *sí*? Even if it is as you say, and he is not *su esposo*, then he is no good to you drunk."

Ana looked at him warily. A slow trickle of dread crept up her spine. Jiméne was building up to something, and she had the distinct feeling she wouldn't like what he was going to say. Especially if it had something to do with D'Alessandro being sober.

The very thought made her shudder. D'Alessandro sober. D'Alessandro knowing what he was doing. D'Alessandro without the handicap of too much liquor.

Who knew what he would be capable of then? She had the distinct feeling that once he was sober, that veil over his eyes would float away, and she would see—really see—what was inside of him. She would know what he felt and she would be incapable of keeping him at bay with a glance of disgust or a derisive comment.

Sober, she would not be able to control him at all.

Ana dug her nails into the palm of her hand to stop her sudden trembling. No, a sober D'Alessandro was something she had to prevent at all costs. It was already hard enough to resist his determination to get to know her. She was too tired, too vulnerable to fight him the way she should, the way she would have in New York. Here, in the draining, primitive jungle, she was terribly afraid she wouldn't be able to fight him at all.

"He's fine the way he is," she told Jiméne defensively, wincing at the tremulousness in her voice. "He saved our lives drunk."

"He could do more sober." Jiméne leaned forward, his expression oddly intense. "He would be a good doctor."

His earnestness made her nervous. Ana licked her lips. "It doesn't matter, Jiméne, he won't stop."

"Many years ago, the man who lived next door to *mi madre* drank too much *aguardiente.* He beat his wife every night. She grew tired of it. One day she tied him to a tree."

Dread grew, filling her heart, her throat. Ana's voice was a whisper. "A tree?"

Jiméne nodded somberly. "She left him there for three days. Then she let him go. After that, no *aguardiente.*"

Ana struggled for an excuse. "But that—that's cruel."

Jiméne shrugged. "It worked. It will work for D'Alessandro too."

"I can't—I can't allow it. No. I—forbid it."

He looked at her thoughtfully, and Ana had the uncomfortable feeling that he saw her fear and condemned her for it. But all he said was "As you wish, Ana. I will not do it then, until you agree. But I will ask you to think on it."

"I will." Ana rose from the table so quickly she nearly tipped over her stool. Anxiously she snatched her skirts out of the way. "I will, I promise."

She turned on her heel, fleeing the dirty, flea-bitten hotel before he could call her back.

The colors swirled and danced before his eyes, dipping and blending together in one long swash of pink and white and black. Bemused, Cain leaned back on the adobe wall of the *alcalde*'s ballroom, trying to focus while the entire world tilted around him. Under the haze of drink, everyone looked beautiful and elegant. The flowers in the women's dark hair flashed in bright spots of color before his eyes, and the men in their white shirts and somber colored frock coats were a stark, graceful contrast.

Music swelled around him, filling his mind, encompassing his whole body in a cocoon of the rich, woody tones of guitars and violins. And all the time, in the fields outside the house, the drums vibrated. He felt their heavy booming in his bones; it sang through his blood like wine, heating him until he had only one thought.

Ana. He searched for her, letting the need to see her well up inside him uncontrollably. He couldn't find her. In fact, couldn't really focus on anyone. They were all shifting colors and high, laughing voices. It took all his concentration to keep the ceiling and the floor in the right place.

He was as drunk as he could remember being in a long time. It felt as if someone had laid a heavy, warm blanket over his senses—soothing and stifling at the same time. Everything was in a fog. Motion, sound, touch . . . Except for those drums. The constant *boom boom boom* was a pinpoint of sobriety; it sent a flush of heat coursing through his body. He concentrated on it, letting it pound in his brain. Christ, it felt as if his very skin were pulsing in rhythm.

Where was Ana? He had to tell her about this, show her . . . Cain pushed away from the wall. The world swayed. He struggled to maintain his balance and failed. His shoulder thudded back against the wall, hard enough that he thought he should feel something, though he didn't. He frowned, trying to catch hold of a thought that was just beyond his reach. Oh, yes. Ana. He needed to find her—

Though exactly why he needed to find her, he couldn't remember. Maybe just to look at her. To watch her when she didn't know he was watching her. To see the shimmering of her hair in the moonlight and the soft smile that touched her lips when Jiméne told an amusing story. To hear, once again, that soft gasp of surprise when he touched her skin.

She was on his mind constantly. He couldn't drink enough to forget about her. Nothing erased the memory of her scorn when she stopped him from tending to Jimené's wound. Nothing took away that calculating look on her face as she'd squirmed beneath him, bartering her body for freedom.

Cain closed his eyes, groaning softly at the memory. He wanted to let her go, he really did. He wanted her to walk away and leave him alone, leave him if not exactly whole, then at least the way he'd been before she walked into his life. But it was too late for that, and he knew it. She would haunt him forever with her cold eyes and heart, with the knowledge that beneath her icy shell, waiting for him to break through, was something they both needed.

Ah, but he didn't have the strength, had never had the strength. She would walk away in San Francisco, if she didn't before then, and he would be left alone with the knowledge that they could have saved each other if only he'd been strong enough.

No, he couldn't drink enough to forget that, though he'd forgotten other things. Like leaving Gatún. The last thing he remembered was fleeing Ana and the hut for the party next door. From then on, everything was blank, filled with cold black terror. But he couldn't concentrate long enough to remember how he'd gotten here to Gorgona, and actually, he didn't really want to try. Didn't want to find out that no amount of effort would bring the memory back.

The music stopped. Cain opened his eyes, wishing he had the balance to make it over to the refreshment table on the far side of the room, feeling a tiny edge on his drunkenness and needing to blur it again. Badly. Before he could do anything about it, he caught a movement beside him, a flash of deep pink. No, not pink. Rose. Rose wool.

Ana.

He turned, meaning to say something to her, but then he saw her back was to him. She was talking to someone, someone who was in fuzzy blocks of black and white and peach. A man. Cain heard a deep chuckle, her answering laughter, and his heart sank into his stomach. For a moment, he wanted to hear that laughter again so badly he almost cried. Christ, why had she never laughed like that with him?

"—then I will leave you to your husband, *Señora* D'Alessandro." The man bowed deeply before her. "It was a pleasure dancing with you."

She inclined her head. "And with you, sir."

Those soft, cultured tones startled Cain. Each time he heard her politeness, her well-bred courtesy, it shocked him. He wondered again where she'd learned it. Wondered how a whore had become a whore. Wished she trusted him enough to tell him.

She turned to face him. Cain struggled to focus, concentrating on her golden eyes until they settled into clarity. Then he noticed that she had done her best to look respectable for the party. Though the wool dress was stained and filthy, she had sewn shut the tear beneath her breast. The collar was buttoned up to her throat, where it hadn't been since they'd started the trip, hiding the soft apricot skin he knew was beneath. The severity of the fashion was in direct contrast to the other women there, whose smooth olive shoulders flashed bare and unadorned above their low-necked dresses, but it made her look elegant and refined.

Or maybe it was just the way she held herself. Straight backed, head high. She'd piled all that beautiful mahogany hair in a knot at the back of her head and fastened a bright pink orchid at one ear. Like a duchess, he thought, smiling.

"What are you laughing at?" she asked sharply, all the softness gone from her voice.

The music started again, the drums shortly after, thrumming through his blood, making him so hungry all he could do was stare at her.

She turned away in disgust. "God, you're drunk."

" 'Fraid so."

She moved as if to walk away, and he reached out to grab her, suddenly panicked. She stopped, looking at him with a question in her eyes.

"Ana, don't go," he said, ashamed at how hoarse his voice sounded. His control was gone. The liquor had taken it all away, and somehow that gave him more freedom than he ever thought he had. "Dance with me."

She looked surprised. And afraid. "You're too drunk to dance."

"No. I'm not."

Her eyes met his, her jaw clenched. He heard her uncertain breathing even through the music. Knowing he was asking to be hurt, but unable to stop himself, Cain held out his hand.

"I'm not," he said again.

She looked around the room, and then she sighed in resignation. "Very well," she said, in tight, sharp tones. "One dance."

Cain stared at her in disbelief. He hadn't expected her acquiescence, hadn't even known how much he wanted it until she agreed. But in spite of her agreement, she didn't take his outstretched hand, and finally Cain dropped it.

Frowning, she sent him a pointed glance. "Well?"

Well? It dawned on him suddenly that she was waiting for him to lead the way out onto the floor. He pushed himself away from the wall, lost his balance, and promptly fell back again.

"You're too drunk," she said.

"No."

But of course he was. He knew he was too drunk to even walk, but the need to touch her, to look at her, was too great for him to back down from the challenge. Clumsily he moved from the wall and stumbled out onto the floor, pushing past dancers to an empty space on the floor. The music was a waltz; he vaguely remembered the steps from a time long ago, but the dim memory, combined with the drink, made him awkward, and when Ana finally came into the circle of his arms he tripped over her feet.

Frigidly she moved away, standing there in the middle of the floor with the other dancers swirling around them. Cain thought he saw a flush moving over her skin, but in the dim candlelight it was hard to see. What wasn't hard to see was the icy anger in her eyes.

He reached out, she jerked away. "Don't touch me."

"Ana, I—"

"Don't call me that." She swallowed, her shoulders went rigid as she backed off the floor.

He wished he could let her go, wanted to just let her run from the house and leave him there, drunk and bereft and alone. But he couldn't. Outside, the drumbeats grew louder. Blood pounded in his ears. He closed his eyes, trying to think, to concentrate, and when he opened them again, she was staring at him warily, with something that looked like panic.

Boom boom boom. Christ, the drums were loud. *Boom boom boom.* He knew the natives were outside, dancing their own dances while the *alcalde* and his guests moved to the sedate and sentimental rhythms of the waltz. Hot, pounding dances of joy and celebration. Dances of abandonment.

Dances he wanted Ana to see.

"Come with me." He didn't wait for her permission, merely grabbed her hand and pulled her stiffly behind him as he wavered through the crowd. He was distinctly aware of the fact that she could pull away from him easily—he was too drunk to stop her—but she didn't. She stumbled along behind him as he wove his way through the blurs of color, the laughter, the voices, and pulled her out into the moonlit night.

The smells seemed especially rich and pungent tonight. The sickly sweet perfume of orchids filled the air, along with the heavy scents of smoke and roasted pork and sweat. Warm breezes caressed Cain's skin, fluttered his hair back from his face. He tightened his fingers around Ana's hand, not turning to look at her, moving inexorably toward the sound of the drums.

Then he stopped. There, in a large, grassy clearing, the natives danced in the moonlight. They formed a circle, moving in a slow, lazy shuffle to the rhythm pounded by two men on cocoa-tree drums. A small Spanish guitar wound sweet and soulful through the beats, casting a melody that pulled at Cain's heart and yanked at his soul.

The women danced, their thin cotton chemises sliding sinuously against their hips and breasts, their dark hair loose and falling over their faces. Necklaces fashioned of gaudy, bright colored ribbons and beads bounced around their necks, flowers fell from their hair.

"Ña, ña, ña," they sang in a strange nasal monotone.

Twisting, shuffling, the moonlight falling over their bodies in cold shadows.

The drumbeats grew louder, more potent, and the women danced faster, moving their hips in a primitive, erotic rhythm. *"Ña, ña, ña."*

"My God." Her voice, a mere whisper of sound behind him, cut through the spell.

Cain turned, unable to keep the smile from spreading across his face. "Dance with me?"

She didn't answer. Instead, she pulled her hand away and crossed her arms over her chest, staring at the dancers as if he didn't exist. No, he thought, more as if she didn't want him to exist. More as if she was consciously shutting him out, putting up the wall.

He didn't want her to do it this time. Without thinking, suddenly desperate to keep her icy disdain at bay, Cain twisted around, grabbing her arms, pulling her close. "Don't do it, Duchess," he pleaded. "Let me in. Please, let me in—"

She stared at him. In the moonlight he saw the fear in her gaze, the panic. It felt like a knife blade between his ribs. Frantically she twisted in his arms, yanking away so violently her hair tumbled to her shoulders. The orchid behind her ear fell to the ground.

"What do you want from me?" Her voice was thin, shaking. He heard her bewilderment and panic. "What do you want?"

But before he could answer, she spun away, racing across the grass until she was nothing but a speck of bright shadow in the moonlight.

She lay awake. It was very late, but she couldn't sleep. The music had faded long ago, but it still rang in her mind. Tormenting her. Reminding her. She couldn't believe what he had done, wouldn't believe it. Even when her arms felt hot where he'd touched her, even when she saw again the painful need in his eyes, she refused to believe it had happened. His voice twisted in her mind. *"Please, let me in. Let me in. Let me in . . .* And with it came the sound of the drums. The hungry, thrumming drums that sent her blood racing . . . God, she thought she would go insane with it.

It seemed suddenly horribly ludicrous that she had ever thought him safe. But then again, had she? All she remembered was thinking he was dangerous, knowing she needed to stay far away from his penetrating eyes and his questions.

She'd thought keeping him drunk would keep him away, but now Ana knew she'd only been lying to herself. Since their journey started, he had come closer and closer, threatening to smash the wall she'd built around herself. With every touch, with every word, he cracked it a little more.

The images rushed through her mind: D'Alessandro combing her hair with gentle hands, D'Alessandro saving her from Esteban and Juan, D'Alessandro holding her while she shook through the night. Damn, she *should* have run away in Gatún and left him the damn tickets. She'd known then how dangerous he was to her.

But she thought she could control him, and now she realized she couldn't. Drunk or not, he would keep pushing her, gradually breaking through her emotions until she was vulnerable. Until she cared about him.

In fact, the drunkenness made him worse. It made him brave. Brave enough to ask her to dance. Brave enough to say the words *"Let me in. Let me in. Let me in. Let me—"*

Ana shook her head frantically, trying to purge the echo from her mind. She had to do something, anything . . .

Jiméne's suggestion crashed into her thoughts, and Ana grabbed hold of it like a bright, shining beacon. There was no other choice, really. Even if it didn't work, even if sober he was no better than he was drunk, at least

Jiméne's plan would give her a few days to grab control, to mend the hole D'Alessandro had put in her emotions.

Determined, she rose from her hammock and moved through the darkness and the other sleeping bodies. As quietly as she could, she shoved aside the canvas sheet that separated the men from the few women and stood there, her eyes searching the darkness for Jiméne's familiar form. She spotted him in moments and made her way to him, kneeling beside him to shake his shoulder.

"Jiméne," she whispered, bending closer. "Jiméne, wake up."

He stirred, groaning. Then, when he realized who she was, he sat up so quickly he nearly smacked into her. "Ana?" His voice was groggy with sleep and surprise. "What do you—"

"Shhh." Ana licked her lips. She wished she could push aside the edge of desperation dogging her, but she couldn't. She heard it in her own voice, along with the panic she couldn't shake. "Jiméne, I've changed my mind. Let's do it."

"Do it?" He blinked and rubbed his eyes. "You do not mean—?"

"Yes." She nodded. "We'll do as you said and tie him to a tree."

"Oh. D'Alessandro."

Ana frowned at his disappointment. "You've changed your mind?"

"No, no, I—" He took a deep breath. "I am sleepy, *cariña,* that is all."

"Then we can?"

"Of course." He nodded. "I am glad, very glad you have changed your mind. Tomorrow, then."

Ana nodded, scooting away and rising. "Good." She wanted to sound glad, but the word came out so weak and thin that Jiméne stared at her.

"What is it, Ana?" he asked, suddenly wide awake. "What is it that made you change your mind?"

"Nothing," she said, stepping back. "Nothing at all. It's better for him, as you said. Much better."

She moved away before he could ask any other questions, before he could see how vulnerable she felt, and alone. And lonely. God, so lonely.

Chapter 14

She came to him that morning. She was part of a dream where they were at his father's house in New Orleans, just outside the big iron gates that separated the house from the road. The gates were open, as they'd never been in reality, and together they looked at the long expanse of grass and trees, smelled the sweet perfume of wisteria.

A door opened in the wall of the house—a door where there'd never been one before—and his mother stepped out. Aging but still blond and beautiful, leading one of her many young lovers, flashing challenge to him with her eyes. The world gave way beneath his feet and rolled, twisting and turning until he couldn't find his balance. He grabbed for the gate and suddenly it was gone. Everything was gone, whisking past him in bright rainbows of color, untouchable, unreachable. Unstoppable.

Then, suddenly, Ana was there, reaching out to him, a steady vision in a world gone horribly awry. He grabbed for her hand, but she was just beyond his reach, and the harder he tried, the farther away she went—

"D'Alessandro."

The whisper cut through his consciousness. The dream fled. He squeezed his eyes shut.

"D'Alessandro." Ana touched him, pressing his shoulder, gently shaking him. His stomach twisted, pain pounded into his brain, slicing through the vague fuzziness.

"Wake up." Her voice was insistent this time. No more gentleness, simply hard-edged impatience and . . . and something else he couldn't quite identify. Regret?

He rolled onto his side, dislodging her hand, reaching automatically for his flask. He had the cork out and gulped it in one fluid, practiced movement. The raw rum burned down his throat, settling like a soothing balm on his stomach. He didn't want to open his eyes. Even though he was still slightly drunk, he wasn't drunk enough, and until he got to that point, he knew his head would throb.

Before he even finished drinking, she pulled the flask from his hand, and his eyes snapped open. Light pierced his brain and he groaned, shutting them quickly again and then barely cracking them to see her.

"Good. You're awake." Her face looked harder than usual, her eyes emotionless. She had been leaning over him, but now she backed away as if touching him was more than she could bear. "Come with me. Jiméne's waiting."

"Waiting?" Cain struggled to one elbow. The hammock tilted sickeningly beneath him. "Waiting for what?"

"For us." She started to walk away, then stopped. "It's time to get started. Hurry. We've got to leave right away." Her voice sounded stiff, strangely so.

Cain frowned. "Is something wrong?"

"Don't be absurd." She looked at him over her shoulder; for a moment he thought he saw distress in her eyes.

Cain stiffened. Last night. Christ, again there was a black hole, a nothingness where memory should be. He remembered getting ready to go to the *fandango*, but not leaving, not anything after that. He swallowed, his mouth dry, and reached again for the flask, but it was in her hand.

"Duchess," he croaked. Clumsily he tried to sit up. The room spun and he closed his eyes, rubbing his temples. "I'm sorry. I'm sorry."

"For what?"

"For last night. For whatever I did."

"You don't remember." Her voice held vindication, a relieved satisfaction that was so strange he stared at her. The hardness of her face had relaxed, and in that moment he knew that he *had* done something, something he never would have dared sober—though it was true it had been so long since he was sober he couldn't honestly remember what he would have dared.

"No. But whatever it was, I'm sorry."

"So am I." The words were soft, so much he barely heard them, and she walked stiffly to the door. "Hurry."

So am I. Confusion rattled through him, bringing with it an intense distress. Christ, what had he done? He didn't want to ask, didn't want to reveal the depth of his drunkenness, but his need to know made cold sweat break out over his skin, made him long for drink so badly he didn't know if he could move without it.

But he did move. As quickly as he could, he climbed from the hammock and hurried after her. He felt unsteady; his knees sagged, his head pounded. Once or twice he tripped over the poor souls who had the misfortune to sleep on the floor. But finally he made it. Blinking, he stepped from the Hotel Française into the blindingly bright Gorgona sunshine.

She walked quickly ahead of him, and Cain followed, feeling as if he were running some sort of gauntlet. Natives ran back and forth over the dusty street, chasing squawking chickens, squealing hogs, and naked children. Macaws and buzzards screeched above his head, slashing across his vision in streaks of color. He stumbled over rocks and nearly fell when a dog dodged in front of him, but Ana didn't even turn around or lessen her step.

They headed away from the Chagres, and for a moment Cain wondered why, until he remembered that from this point on they no longer followed the river. Mules. Something about mules. He wracked his brain, trying to remember what it was Ana had said. Something about hiring mules to take them through the jungle to Panama City.

Cain's stomach turned. Christ, mules. He wondered if he could even stay aboard one, much less ride it the entire way to Panama City. "Duchess! You didn't forget *aguardiente,* did you?"

"Forget?" Ana turned, frowning. "No, I didn't forget."

They were at the edge of the village now, and suddenly Ana stopped. Castañeras was there, waiting beside a tree. At his feet were a huge coil of rope and a clay jug. Cain frowned. Where were their supplies? The mules? Where the hell was his flask?

"Buenos días, amigo." Castañeras stood there, obscenely cheerful. *"Como estas?"*

"I feel like hell," Cain croaked.

"You look like hell."

"Are we waitin' for something?"

The quick look Ana threw Jiméne made him nervous. "No," she said softly.

There was something strange about all this, but Cain couldn't put his finger on it. Hell, couldn't put his finger on anything, the world was twisting so much before his eyes. "Where's m'flask?"

"Ana has it." Castañeras reassured him, holding out his hand. "Do you need my help, *amigo?*"

"No. No." Cain shook his head, sending blinding, painful flashes of light through his skull. Unsteadily he pushed his hand through his hair and pressed on his temples, trying to ease the pain. "Let's go."

"Would you like breakfast first?"

Cain's stomach lurched. "You must be joking."

Jiméne smiled. *"Sí."*

No one moved. Trepidation trickled up Cain's spine. "Aren't there—aren't there supposed to be mules?"

Ana swallowed, avoiding his gaze, and looked pleadingly at Jiméne.

Cain's wariness increased. He glanced at Jiméne. "What's going on?"

Jiméne motioned limply to the tree. "If you will just sit down—"

"Hell, no, I won't sit down. What's going on?" He glared at Ana.

This time she looked at him calmly. "Sit down, Cain."

It was the *Cain* that did it. He couldn't remember her ever using his name before—at least not with such gentle deliberateness. It took the muscle away from him, turned his bones to liquid. Something serious was happening here, something that filled him with dread. He sank down onto the ground, leaning against the tree, and took a deep breath, waiting for their explanations, watching while Castañeras grabbed the coil of rope resting on the ground.

"You understand," Jiméne began, "we do not have a choice in this." He walked behind the tree, and Cain twisted around to see.

Ana knelt in front of him. He turned to look at her, the lump in his stomach growing when he realized she wasn't going to say a word. She simply sat there, her hands convulsively tightening on her heavy wool skirt, her eyes downcast as if she couldn't bring herself to look at him. He was so busy trying to figure her out that he barely noticed when the rope dropped into his lap.

It wasn't until it tightened across his chest that he began to struggle.

"Christ! What the hell are you doing?" He looked up at Ana in disbelief. She looked anywhere but at him, and Cain felt a tightening in his chest, a strange terror that made him still. "What is it, Ana?" he asked quietly. "What's going on here?"

"We have had too much of your drinking," Jiméne answered quickly. "This is the only way we could think of to end it."

"To end it?" Cain tried to concentrate, but the words were too unbelievable. He stared at Ana. "Is this true, Ana?" Then, when she looked again at her knotted hands. "Damn it, is it true?"

His anger seemed to affect her. She looked up, and Cain's heart sank when he saw the cold mask of her face, the emptiness in her eyes. "I'm sorry, D'Alessandro," she said slowly. "Believe me, I *am* sorry."

But he didn't believe anything anymore, not her words or the regret he thought he heard in them. She thought she was sorry now—she would be sorrier when he was sober—when she learned what he had known for years. There was nothing redeemable in his character, nothing worth saving. This was all such a waste of time.

And again, he would be the one to suffer for it.

He shook so hard he couldn't see, so hard the sweat running from his temples dashed over his cheeks and into his mouth, leaving him with a greater thirst than before—a great, yawning thirst that threatened to suck him dry. But he couldn't drink. He'd tried the water in the clay pot next to him, and it only made him sick. Christ, the very thought of it sent his stomach spinning. He needed a *drink*, dammit. Something. Anything.

Cain swallowed and glanced at Ana. She stood a short

distance away, her back to him, staring back at town. She wouldn't get anything for him; he knew she wouldn't because he'd already tried. Need boiled up inside of him so strongly he thought he might die if he didn't have a sip—just a sip. Just enough to settle his stomach and his vision. Just enough to make this terrible shaking go away.

"Duchess," he croaked. She didn't turn around. He tried to swallow the hard lump in his throat, then tried again. "Ana—"

"It's for your own good," she said softly, without looking at him.

Cain licked his lips. They felt dry and swollen. "Ana, I swear to you—anything y'want. Anything. I'll—" He struggled, trying to control the growing fog in his mind. "I'll pay you—"

"With what?" she asked. "You don't have any money."

"I'll find some."

Silence. Cain clenched his fists, struggling once again against the ropes looped around his wrists, wishing he could stand long enough to try the ones at his ankles. Dizzily he wondered where Jiméne had learned to tie knots. The man had him leashed out like an animal. He could move about five feet from the tree in only one direction—if he found the strength to move at all.

He yanked against the bindings. They didn't budge and the effort only made him sweat more. He shook so badly he couldn't think. Desperately he looked again at Ana. "Tell me what y'want—anything y'want." He lowered his voice cajolingly. "Please, Ana. God, please."

"I don't want anything." She turned, staring at him with the most emotionless eyes he'd ever seen. Her arms were crossed tightly over her chest.

"Please—" Inspiration flashed through him. The burning thirst was so overwhelming he didn't care what he had to do to make it go away. "I'll give y'what you want. I'll leave. Y'can have the tickets." She hesitated, and sensing victory, he pressed on. "The tickets, the money, everything. Y'can go on, forget about me." Desperation was so sharp in his mouth he could taste it. "Please. Please."

"No." She shook her head slightly. "It's better this way."

"For who?" His temper broke, frustration made his voice sharp. "Goddammit, who asked you to help? Who told you I *wanted* it better?"

"Cain—"

"Get me a fucking drink!"

"No!" She stepped toward him, her own eyes flashing. "No."

Cain wrenched against the ropes. The rough hemp cut into his skin, but he barely felt it. Sweat coursed down his cheeks, he was so tense with frustration he wanted to cry, the gnawing ache inside him was unbearable. Damn her. *Damn her damn her damn her.* He struggled to contain his anger. "All right, Duchess," he said slowly, every word bitten off. "Get me a drink before I tell everyone in this goddamned city just what you are—a murdering whore."

"You want a drink?" She stepped forward, barely beyond his reach, and dipped the ladle into the clay pot. "Here's a drink." She shoved it at him, into his chest. Cain lashed out. His fingers curled around her wrist. The ladle fell, drenching him with water.

"That's not what I want and y'know it." He tried to yank her closer, but he was too weak. Without effort, she pulled away.

"Sobriety would do you good," she said shortly, in that cold, emotionless voice he hated.

He hated it more now than he ever had. "Who made you God?" he sneered.

"Today, Jiméne did," she retorted sharply.

"Where the hell is that bastard?"

"Back at the hotel—away from your foul mouth and your nasty temper. I wish I was with him."

"I'll bet y'do." He glared at her. Pure fury flooded him—fury at everything—her, Jiméne, his own weakness —coursed through him. "Why don't y'just go to him, Duchess? You've been hot after him for weeks, anyway—"

"Don't," she said, and the cracking in her icy voice surprised him so much he quieted. "Don't make me—don't."

"Then get me a drink."

She shook her head.

Cain squeezed his eyes shut. The fog spread in his brain, his teeth chattered. His throat seemed to have closed up on him. The need swelled again inside of him, taking over, becoming him. He was burning, shaking . . . *Please God, don't let this be happening to me,* he begged silently. *Please* . . . But when he stopped praying he was still there, tied to a tree and humiliatingly sick and afraid.

"Please, Ana." He spoke in a whisper that took all the strength he had. "Please, just one drink."

"I'm sorry." She touched him then, suddenly, softly, her fingers warm against his cheek, but not warm enough to erase the all-encompassing need.

"Please, you—don't know." He begged helplessly now, unable to stop, wanting to cry with frustration and fear. It felt as if his insides were twisting up, ready to erupt through his skin . . . "I need it. I need it, please . . ."

Then her hand was gone, and when he opened his eyes again, so was she.

He was dying. Cain stared blankly into the night, seeing the huddled figures of Ana and Jiméne a short distance beyond. They had wanted to kill him from the beginning, he knew that now. Why hadn't he seen it?

Why hadn't he realized that all the time they were plotting against him, waiting for the right moment?

Christ, he was thirsty. And hot. He pulled again at his shirt, trying to open it, forgetting that he'd long since unfastened it completely. He could no longer feel the breeze against his skin. Couldn't feel anything except for heat and thirst. Couldn't even feel the shaking, though he knew he was shaking because earlier he'd seen his hands in the dim twilight.

Why the hell were they trying to kill him? What had he done? What couldn't he remember?

He couldn't sleep because of the shaking. Or was it because his eyes wouldn't close? His eyes were swollen open, everything was swollen. He thought maybe he could close them if he reached up and flipped them down. But he couldn't lift his hand. It was too heavy, and besides, he was trembling so much he would probably put out his eye—

"Rafael."

He started, jerking upright and staring wildly into the darkness. The voice was inhuman, eerie, hauntingly familiar. It echoed through the night, seemed to become part of the trees.

"Rafael."

The shadow at the edge of his vision moved, and Cain was struck with such cold terror his shaking stopped. No. No, it couldn't be. He wouldn't *let* it be. Desperately he tried to raise his hand, to stop it, but the shadow kept moving, not pausing, closer and closer and closer.

"Rafael."

"Don't call me that." Cain's breath came harsh and fast. He couldn't get enough air. "Father, don't call me that." He wanted to scream *Go away!* wanted to run, to escape, to hide, but the ropes cut into his skin, holding him fast, keeping him prisoner. Desperately he yanked away, tried to stand and run. The loop around his ankle caught, and he fell, slamming face-first into the ground.

Frantically he got to his knees, spitting dirt. The shadow came closer. A hand reached from the folds of the dark cloak. Long fingers, one crowned with a large gold signet ring, reached for his. Cain tried to crawl away. The ropes stretched taut, his fingers clawed uselessly.

Wild terror made him almost sick. He cringed, unable to move, too afraid to stay. "No." He finally squeezed out a sound. A gutless whimper, like that of a child. "No, please go away. Don't punish me. I'll be good. I—I promise I'll be good. I'll pray. Please—I'll pray."

"Come with me, Rafael."

Cain collapsed. Tears started at the corners of his eyes, and he fought them back. Weakness. Christ, not weakness. Not now. The tears coursed down his cheeks. Fear clenched his stomach. "Go away." Damn them. Damn them for tying him here, for making him a prisoner. Damn them—

"Crying, my son?" The hood of the cloak fell back. Bones shimmered in the moonlight. Bones half covered by peeling, rotting flesh, with hollow sockets for eyes. But it wasn't his father. Not anymore. The skeleton pitched forward with an unbalanced, one-legged gait . . .

His scream of horror caught in his throat. He couldn't move, was paralyzed with dread and terror. He cowered against the tree, whimpering like a frightened animal.

"Do I frighten you, Cain?" John Matson's rotting face cracked in a wretched, hideous grin. He laughed, and flesh fell away in sickening patches. "Afraid of hell? You cannot escape it, my friend." Long fingers reached for him. Closer. Closer. "You cannot escape me—"

The fingers touched his shoulder, and Cain exploded.

"Ana!" His scream tore through the night, startling the animals into silence. Ana snapped awake, looking around wildly, throwing off the blanket she had wrapped around her shoulders. Beside her, Jiméne jumped to his feet, sputtering in Spanish.

Hastily she lit the lamp. The area glowed with dim light, enough to see D'Alessandro struggling against his ropes, convulsing against the tree.

"My God." She turned to Jiméne, fear coiling in her stomach. "Is this . . . normal?"

He nodded, settling back down, wrapping himself back in his own blanket. *"Sí.* There is nothing we can do."

Nothing they could do. Ana swallowed, staring at D'Alessandro, twisting and turning, jerking as if trying to get away from something. Sweat glistened on his skin, the cords of his throat were hard ridges, his dark hair trailed and stuck to his face.

Nothing they could do. She licked her lips and looked at Jiméne, who watched grimly. "But I—"

"Aaaaaah!" D'Alessandro's scream made them both jump. "No! No! Stay away!"

Without letting herself think, Ana ran to Cain. At her approach, he jerked so suddenly his head cracked against the tree.

"Cain," she whispered. She touched his arm, he lurched away from her touch. For the first time, she saw that his eyes were wide open. Wide and unseeing, staring past her to some horror in the darkness, something he tried to escape even as he called her name.

"Keep away from me." He scrambled backward, rigid against the tree, his whole body shaking from effort. "Stay away from me, John, goddammit. Stay away from me!"

"Jiméne!" Ana shouted over her shoulder. "Jiméne, something's wrong!"

"Not Rafael." D'Alessandro's head twitched from side to side. "Rafael—"

"Jiméne!"

"Christ. John—no!" Cain's shout was so loud it echoed through the shadows. She saw terror and hopelessness, mindless, excruciating fear.

"Jiméne!"

"I am here." Jiméne stood beside her, holding the ladle in his hand. "Stand back, Ana."

"But—"

"Stand back."

She stepped away, and Jiméne flung the water into Cain's face. D'Alessandro stiffened, frozen into place, and then he sputtered and choked. His body sagged, the shaking gone, and for a moment he was completely still.

They had done this to him. For a moment, Ana was so shaken by remorse and shame she couldn't think. They had done this to him. They had made him this. Her reasons for doing it now seemed unspeakably cruel, achingly selfish. She had done it because she was afraid of him, because she had not been able to face the fact that she was beginning to care about him.

She stared at his face, remembering how warm and comforting his body had felt wrapped around hers, and she suddenly felt tired and old.

Jiméne stepped away. "He will be fine, *cariña,*" he said softly. "Trust me."

The moment he said the words, D'Alessandro shivered, his whole body convulsed in final, hopeless surrender. Then he began to sob. Hoarse, terrible sounds, as if torn from his soul. Though his eyes were closed, tears streamed from them, racing down his cheeks, shining in the lamplight.

He sobbed, and she wanted to sob with him. She couldn't bear it; her whole heart felt leaden and heavy in her chest. Her reasons for staying away from him faded then. Without thinking, without knowing anything at all except that she wanted to comfort him, had to comfort him, she pulled him down beside her, wrapping her arms around him until his sobs shook her body, until she felt his hot tears on her throat.

"I'm here, Cain," she whispered. "I'm here, with you. I'm not going away." She said the words over and over again, until his sobs stopped and his arms tightened around her, holding her so close the ropes at his wrists cut into her skin.

It wasn't until then that she wondered if it was for Cain she said the words.

Or herself.

Ana and Jiméne took turns watching him. Jiméne would go into town to get food and water and sleep while she took care of D'Alessandro, and she would sleep while Jiméne watched.

Except that she didn't really sleep. She couldn't. In the last four days, she hadn't done more than take short, restless naps. Naps full of dreams and memories, naps so disconcerting that she kept herself awake, too afraid to sleep, staring at the shadows and listening to D'Alessandro's hoarse, grating cries.

This was her fault. All her fault. Ana wished now that she hadn't gone to the damn *fandango*, wished she hadn't let him touch her, or let the pleading in his eyes convince her that it might be all right to dance with him, just once. She wished he hadn't taken her outside into the erotic moonlight.

But most of all, she wished she hadn't agreed with Jiméne to force him into sobriety.

Because he still hadn't stopped tossing and turning. He didn't stop screaming. It looked as if he were awake all the time, awake and wide-eyed, though his gaze was blank, as if he were watching things she couldn't even imagine. By the way he was screaming, they were very dark things indeed.

Ana closed her eyes, resting her chin on her raised knees. She felt old and tired, and more alone than she could ever remember feeling. There was a dull throb of regret deep in her heart. She wouldn't have done this to him if she had known what he would go through, but the thought didn't make her feel any better—especially because she wondered if it was really true. She remembered how frightened she'd been that night, how panicked when she ran to Jiméne, and she wondered if knowing the price D'Alessandro would pay to become sober would have changed her decision.

Probably not.

She never would have guessed she would feel such regret, or such a need to make this all up to him. The last few days tormented her with images: D'Alessandro warning her that the men were talking about her and Jiméne, D'Alessandro rushing to her aid when she'd fainted in the jungle, D'Alessandro handing her a blanket of India rubber to protect her from the rain. A hundred little kindnesses, and she had repaid him by trusting a folk doctor over him and trying to steal the tickets, by tying him to a tree and watching him suffer.

Something had to be missing inside of her. Something important. Something she didn't understand. She had always wanted a friend, but now it occurred to her that maybe the reason she had none was because she couldn't be a friend back. She was too afraid of revealing something that could be used as a weapon against her, too afraid of being indebted.

More than that, she was desperately afraid that she had learned so well how to survive on her own, she had no honor left, and no understanding of what a promise really meant. She'd had to learn to be selfish, had learned the hard way that honor could be anything you made it, that the only dignity was in surviving.

Ana glanced over at D'Alessandro, who was sleeping fitfully, his body jerking, his skin bathed in sweat. She wondered what made him what he was. He was alone, like she was. He had survived too. But there was a sad integrity about him, the sense that there were things he would not do, principles he would not sacrifice.

Unlike her.

Loneliness swept over her, so intense she hugged her knees tightly, digging her fingers into her skin until it hurt. She had wanted to make Jiméne her friend, but she had made the decision based on how easy it was to manipulate him. And even then, she had the feeling that though she and Jiméne were companionable, it was D'Alessandro who had truly become Jiméne's friend over the past days, not her. Jiméne wanted Cain sober because he would be healthier that way. She wanted him sober because she was afraid for herself. She had never once thought about how it would help him. Hardly what a friend would do.

She wondered that Cain talked to her at all. Ana closed her eyes, fighting sadness. Once again, she was on the outside looking in, just as she'd always been. Excluded. Alone. And it was all her own fault. All her own—

"Ana." He groaned her name, it sounded dredged up from his very soul. "Ana—"

She was on her feet in a moment, racing the short distance between them, falling to her knees at his side.

"Save me," he mumbled, tossing his head from side to side. His hair whipped into his face, clung to his skin, his mouth. His fingers curled. "Get him away from me. Christ! Christ, get him away . . ."

Her heart rose to her throat. Ana reached out, touching his shoulder gently. He reacted as if she'd hit him, jerking away, eyes wide open and black with fever and delusion. "Don't touch me! Get him away! Get him away!" He clawed at his skin, scrambling with his feet, pushing against the tree. "Ana!"

"I'm here, I'm here."

"Ana!" His voice broke. "Please God, help me. Help me . . ."

Desperately Ana grabbed his hands, pulling them away from his eyes, not knowing what else to do, how to calm him. "Shhh. I'm here. Shhh." She smoothed his hair away from his face, dragging it out of his mouth, running her hands along his slick, hot skin. "Cain. Cain, I'm sorry. I'm so sorry."

He stared at her, but she saw with a sinking heart that he wasn't really seeing her, though her touch seemed to calm him. She heard the whimper from his throat, and then he closed his eyes, breathing raggedly, and sagged into her arms, his face against her breasts.

His weight was heavy and solid, and Ana stared at his dark head for a moment while the memories came flooding back. Memories of holding her mother in her arms, just this way. Memories of stroking her and rocking her frail body. Memories of being needed.

Being needed. She was good at that anyway. She could comfort him, if nothing else. Especially now, when his disconcerting gaze demanded nothing of her. Yes, she knew how to be needed.

The thought sent a warm, soft feeling coursing through her, something she hadn't felt in a long time. It surprised her, just as it surprised her how badly she wanted to help him. He had called her name, asked for *her,* though she hardly deserved such trust. But he called for her help, not Jiméne's.

The loneliness inside her eased slightly, and Ana curved her arms around him. She felt his tighten around her waist, felt his hands dig into her skin as if he was afraid she was leaving him.

Behind her, she heard the sound of footsteps on the grass, and she turned her head to see Jiméne standing there, a jug of water in his hand.

"Cariña," he said softly. "Should I take over now? Would you like to sleep?"

D'Alessandro moaned. She felt the vibration of the sound deep in her chest, in her heart, and she shook her head. "No," she whispered, trying to ignore the trembling in her voice. "No. He—he called for me."

"He called for you."

"Yes. Yes, he did."

"I see." Jiméne studied her for so long Ana turned her head away, not looking at him as he moved back to the fire, and she heard the thunking of the water jug on the ground, his heavy sigh as he followed it.

Uncomfortably, she wondered what he'd seen, and why she heard that curious tone in his voice, but then D'Alessandro moved in her arms again, and she held him tight and rocked back and forth in time to the breeze singing through the trees, in time to the humming insects, forgetting Jiméne as she tried to remember a lullaby.

Chapter 15

He felt like hell. Cain wasn't sure he'd really known the definition of the word before now. His head throbbed—a low, dull ache at the back of his skull. His stomach was sore, his mouth dry, and his skin felt as if tiny bugs with sticky feet crawled all over him. His hands were still shaking—or, if they weren't, they felt as if they were.

But mostly he felt hollow, like a reed with all the pith blown out. As if just opening his eyes would be an effort. So for a moment, he didn't open them. He sat there, with his head against the rough bark of a tree, and remembered with painful clarity why he was here and what had happened. Or at least, he remembered most of it. Some of it was foggy and hard to focus on, and Cain had the feeling that was exactly how he wanted it to stay. The last hours had been the worst nightmare of his life. Even worse than his childhood, and God knew that was bad.

The thought made him smile, and the movement cracked his lips painfully. He tried to swallow, but his throat felt raw and strained, and there was no saliva to swallow with. What he needed was a drink. Bourbon, straight and slightly warm from the sun. The thought of it sent a pleasurable heat through his veins and his thirst intensified until his mouth was watering. Yes, bourbon. Smooth, amber bourbon . . .

Slow suicide.

The words plunged through him, an echo of thoughts he'd had before. Slow suicide. He remembered—or thought he did—a long time ago, when he'd vowed to stop drinking, when he felt guilty and ashamed and miserable in the morning after he'd broken the vow. God, how long ago that was. Now, in the morning, he felt afraid, mostly. Afraid of the fact that he couldn't get through a day without a drink, or two, or ten. Afraid of his loss of control and the horrible, terrifying loss of memory. But he no longer promised himself to stop. That strength had disappeared, along with any good thought he'd ever had about himself.

Slow suicide. Funny, how the words were so clear—almost blindingly brilliant in his mind. Funny, too, how divorced he felt from them. As if they were about someone else. As if he no longer cared enough to do anything about them.

That was true enough. He no longer cared. He was a miserable excuse for a human being—all it took was the memory of John Matson's death to remind him of that, even if his father's punishments and his mother's scorn hadn't already battered his self-esteem.

Slow suicide. Hell, it was either that or kill himself quickly, and Cain had long ago faced the fact that he didn't have the kind of courage it took to end his life. At least not so blatantly.

"Are you awake?" Ana's soft voice cut through his thoughts, and Cain opened his eyes, closing them again quickly as the morning light speared through his brain.

"I don't know," he croaked.

"You are awake." Relief colored her tone, he heard the swish of her skirts as she knelt beside him. "Thank God."

That startled him. Cain peered at her through slitted eyes. Her expression was worried and concerned, and though that too was surprising, what wasn't surprising was that she knelt just beyond his reach, and she looked wary, ready to fly at the slightest provocation.

No wonder, he thought wryly. He vaguely remembered his hallucinations—and the fact that her face had gone in and out of his delirium.

He closed his eyes again wearily. "Did I hurt you?"

"No." She didn't pretend to misunderstand. "No, you didn't. You gave Jiméne a black eye, though."

Cain smiled. "No doubt he deserved it. I suppose he's mad because I spoiled his good looks?"

"He'll get over it." Amusement filled her voice. "How do you feel?"

"Thirsty."

"Oh." There was movement beside him; Cain heard the dripping of liquid on the grassy ground. "Here."

"Not for water," he said shortly.

"Oh." He heard her disappointment and the soft thud of the ladle dropping. "You want a drink."

"Bourbon, if you have it." The very word made him swallow with painful longing. "Though I suppose *aguardiente* will do."

"Jiméne said—he said you wouldn't want it any longer."

"He was wrong."

"He had hoped . . ." She trailed off. Cain could almost hear the nervous clenching of her hands on her skirt. "You haven't had a drink in six days."

His eyes flew open in surprise. The sunlight exploded in his brain, and he tented his hand over his eyes long enough to look at her. Six days. He would have said one day, maybe. Two at the most. But not six days. Christ, not *six.* But then he saw the anxiety in her eyes. "You're telling the truth," he said flatly.

She nodded, and he noticed how tired she looked. There were circles marring the peachy skin beneath her eyes, her hair escaped her braid to blow across her face and curl in thin strands over her shoulders. The collar of her dress was unbuttoned, and her skin looked dull, streaked with dirt and blood.

"You've been here the whole time?" he asked.

"I couldn't very well stay in the village alone," she explained unemotionally. "And one of us had to stay with you. Jiméne—Jiméne was here too."

"Until I hit him."

"Even after you hit him." She smiled, and the soft warmth of it spiraled through him, easing the sharp edge of thirst until Cain had enough strength to smile back.

"So now he's left you alone with the beast."

She hesitated, started to say something and then changed her mind. "Do you remember much of it?"

"Some." He shrugged. The movement sent pain shooting into his skull. "Not six days' worth. I imagine it was bad." He put a hand to his temples. The rope around his wrist pulled painfully, and Cain looked down at it, seeing the rubbed raw skin and the blood marking the rags someone had tied around the rope for comfort. "Christ."

She had the grace to look chagrined. "Something had to be done."

"Apparently you thought so," he said, anger rising through his headache. "Too bad it didn't work quite the way you wanted it to."

"You've stopped drinking."

"The hell I have."

"Jiméne says—"

"Fuck Jiméne."

"So you won't try," she said in that cold, cultured tone. "Destroy yourself, then."

Her words crushed his anger; Cain suddenly felt hatefully, uncontrollably ashamed. *Destroy yourself, then.* But it wasn't as easy as that. He had no will to stop. Not anymore. He no longer knew how to control the need that even now held him captive. He wanted a drink—the words were capitalized in his mind—bold and undeniable. Inescapable.

He groaned, burying his face in his hands and wishing this was all a bad dream.

Time to make a choice. The sentence came full blown in his mind and he wanted to push it away, wanted so badly not to have to decide he could almost taste it. To stop drinking meant to fight, meant he had to find something in himself he liked enough to want to fight for. But there was nothing. Nothing . . .

"Amigo!" Castañeras's voice was so cheerful Cain wished he had a gun. "You are awake!"

He lifted his face from his hands and looked up. *"Buenos días, hijo de la perra."*

Jiméne flushed. He dropped the bag he was carrying beside Ana. "I was afraid you would not take this well."

"Take it well?" Cain held out his wrists. "I can't imagine why you thought I wouldn't. Why not just kill me? It'd be quicker."

"But then you would not be alive, *sí?"* Jiméne smiled. "I have brought food."

The thought made Cain's stomach flip. He leaned his head against the tree. "I can't remember the last time I ate something."

"Yesterday," Ana informed him, searching through the bag. "Or at least you tried to."

"I'm not hungry."

"It does not matter. You will eat." Jiméne said. "As I had to when I was ill. Pork stew and iguana pie—they are lifesavers, *sí?"*

Cain's stomach rose to his throat.

Ana glanced at him. "Be kind, Jiméne. He looks green."

"I was green when you gave it to me. The grease, *amigo,* it will be good for—"

Cain heaved, twisting to the side and vomiting up the liquid in his stomach. His hands shook, he was too weak to even hold himself up as he choked and sputtered. But his stomach lurched even after there was nothing left inside of it.

Ana was at his side in an instant, smoothing his hair out of his face, supporting him. He recognized the feel of her hands on his brow, and even through his sickness, the memory came wavering back, thin and cloudy, but there nonetheless. Ana, touching his face with her cool hands, making the all-too-vivid dreams flee for a few moments. Ana, singing mindless, calming lullabies.

The memory surprised him. He had not imagined she had such compassion, or even that she cared enough about him to help. Had she done it through the entire six days? Or just once?

It didn't matter suddenly; he didn't care whether she'd held him for a minute or an hour. All that mattered was that she *had* held him, that for a little while, anyway, she had cared about him.

Destroy yourself, then. He heard again the cool anger of her words, and for the first time recognized them for what they were. Concern. Not contempt. Concern.

The thought was startling. Frantically Cain twisted in her arms, jerking around so he could look into her face, and what he saw there both terrified and exhilirated him. It *was* caring, and concern, but . . .

But he had wanted badly to see concern in other people's eyes before, had fooled himself into thinking other people cared. Never before had he wanted it as badly as he did in that moment. He didn't trust himself any longer to know what he saw, so when she reached again to push the hair back from his face, he grabbed her wrist.

His hand was shaking. She could have escaped his grip easily, but she didn't. She looked at him. Slowly, warily, but she *did* look at him, and Cain's heart jumped in his chest.

"Duchess," he said roughly. "Duchess, do you care what happens to me?"

She didn't smile, didn't move. But she didn't pull away, either. "Call me Ana," she said gently.

It was barely eight o'clock the next morning when Jiméne came back from the hotel, five recalcitrant mules in tow. With them was the animals' taciturn master, José. The muleteer's only greeting to Ana had been the twitching of his heavy mustache, and then he and Jiméne left again for supplies, leaving her alone with a sick, shaking D'Alessandro.

Ana glanced at her partner. He was tugging at the pile of newly purchased saddlebags, sweating profusely, looking distressingly pale. Guilt washed over her, and Ana's throat tightened.

Before she knew it, she was walking across the grass toward him. He didn't look up until she was barely a few feet away, and then he straightened, bracing his hand on a nearby tree to keep from falling. His shirt was loose, and it hung open, revealing his chest. The dark curls covering his skin didn't hide the accentuated ridges of his ribs, and his broad, high cheekbones highlighted the gauntness of his face. He was much too thin.

She bit her lip and moved forward. "Are you all right?"

"That seems to be the question of the day," he answered in that deep baritone, still husky from all the screaming he'd done in his delirium. "Yeah, I'm all right." He moved away from the tree and rubbed the back of his neck. The sleeves of his shirt fell back, revealing the raw, red welts around his wrists.

Shame dropped into her stomach. "I—I wish we hadn't had to do that."

He followed her gaze. "Ana, let's not talk about it now," he said. She heard the struggle in his voice, a hungry pain that pierced through her. His hands began to tremble, and he dropped them again. "I don't want to think about it. I—I can't think about it."

"You seem much better this morning."

He laughed shortly, bitterly. "Do I? I don't feel any better. To tell you the truth, if Jiméne hadn't been walking beside me on the way into town earlier, I'd have dodged into one of those taverns without a second thought." He paused and looked away from her as if seeing something else entirely. "Do you know how many empty bottles are lying in the road from here to the village? Two hundred and six." He exhaled slowly. "Two hundred and six."

"You could control it if you wanted to." Her voice sounded cold, and she winced.

D'Alessandro looked at her. "You sound like a friend of mine."

"A friend? Is his name John? Or Rafael?"

It was a casual question, a way to take the uncomfortable vulnerability from his eyes. But he jerked as if she'd slapped him. His mouth tightened, his eyes blazed. "Where did you hear those names?" he demanded.

"You said them in your fever." Ana frowned. "Why? Who are they?"

"No one."

His distress made her curious. Something was bothering him, something important, and suddenly she wanted badly enough to know what it was that she forgot he might ask a question in return. She stepped closer. "Obviously they were men who tormented you."

He stepped away. "It's none of your business."

"You sound like me now." She tried to inject a lighter

tone in her voice, to tease him, and he stared at her as if she'd just reminded him of something important.

"That's a good idea, Duchess," he said slowly. His mouth curved in a mocking smile. "Tit for tat. You tell me a secret and I'll tell you one of mine."

Ana stiffened. This was not what she'd intended. Her mouth felt dry. "I don't—"

"I didn't think so," he said, an edge of satisfaction in his voice. He turned, lifting the saddlebags with effort, and started to walk away.

She stared at his retreating back, feeling foolish and angry. Her heart raced in her chest, the hot flush of embarrassment crept up her throat. He had turned the tables so neatly, had thrown her own reticence back in her face, making it look strangely like selfishness.

After nights of listening to him scream, struggling with her guilt, she knew it *was* selfishness. She had always worked to keep her real self hidden, had avoided questions and turned the tables as well as D'Alessandro just had. *"What do you do for a living, sir?" "Do you have a sweetheart back home?"* The questions flew through her mind. She'd done it with Jiméne, with dozens of others. She had asked and never even listened to the answers. All she wanted was for them to know nothing about her.

What did she have as a result? Nothing. No friends, nothing. The same loneliness that assailed her the other night came back with a vengeance. With it came the memory of D'Alessandro calling for her, needing her . . .

After six days of holding him in her arms and comforting him, after six days of feeling needed, Ana couldn't stand his contempt, and she knew that was what she'd see if she kept her distance.

The thought paralyzed her. This was her chance. Her chance to pay him back for everything, her chance to be a friend. This once, she thought, this once she could lower the wall a little bit. After all, friendship wasn't the same thing as love, with its frightening vulnerability. And after being on the inside, even briefly, she didn't want to go back to before. Couldn't stand to go back.

Her voice tightened in desperation. "I—I had a cat once."

He turned, grinning weakly. "Not good enough. I had a dog."

What else could she say? There was nothing else, nothing that didn't make her weak with fear. He watched her still, waiting, and before she knew it, Ana blurted, "My father was Russian. He was—he was a baron. My mother waited for him to come to us her whole life, and he never did."

She froze, stunned at her admission, waiting for his answer, waiting for the words that would hurt her, that would curl around her and cut her apart.

The words didn't come. He looked at her thoughtfully for a moment, and then he smiled; a soft, slight smile filled more with self-deprecation than derision. "I'm Rafael," he said. "Rafael is my name."

"Your name? But—what do you mean, your name? Your name is Cain," she blurted.

He ran his hand through his hair and took a deep breath. "That's right," he said softly. "Cain Rafael D'Alessandro."

Ana stared at him, confused. "I don't understand. Why were you screaming your own name? And who is John?"

"How did you become a whore?"

His response was so quick it unnerved her. Involuntarily Ana stepped back, trying to hide the uncontrollable panic his words sent rushing over her. It was no longer easy. She felt suddenly out of her realm. There were some things it was better if friends never knew.

She foundered for something, some little secret, something that wouldn't matter if he knew, but there was nothing. Nothing she could think of that would leave her safe.

Frantically she tried to think, needing more desperately than she wanted to show him how willing she was to be friends. But she was too afraid. She needed more time. Maybe there would never be enough time—

"Well?" He was standing there, watching her, and she refused to look at him, knowing she'd see that disappointment in his eyes. Sad disappointment—oh, God, she didn't want to face it.

But she couldn't give him what he wanted either. Ana lifted her chin and looked at the road—anywhere but at him. "That's enough for now, D'Alessandro," she said, wiping her hands on her skirt. Her voice shook, and she tried unsuccessfully to control it. "I've got better things to do than play confession."

He didn't say anything as she walked away, and it wasn't until she was halfway to the road that Ana realized she was waiting for him to call her back.

He watched her walk away, as unable to take his eyes from her as he was to call out her name and stop her. Her hips swayed beneath the rose wool skirt, the material flapped around her legs, and her thick mahogany braid slapped between her shoulder blades. Everything about her was angry. Angry and disappointed, and he wondered why. Was it because he hadn't told her who Rafael was? Or because he had?

The whole conversation left him feeling confused and unbalanced. He had expected her to walk away from him the moment he'd proposed they trade secrets. That she hadn't was a surprise. What was more surprising was the fact that she'd revealed something about her life. Granted, it hadn't been much, but it hinted at a pain that left him curious—and unprepared.

She had changed a little. Sometime in the last six days,

something about her had eased, loosened, *something.* She was wary, yes, but she was also . . . receptive.

The idea was heady, intriguing. It caught him off guard, and because of it, he'd answered her question. *Who was Rafael?* Himself, yes, but there was so much more to it than that. So much more.

The thought brought faint memories that hovered like apparitions in his mind. His father screaming, his mother answering back with a screech of her own. *"Cain!" "Rafael!" "Cain!" "Rafael!"* And then, a stronger memory. John Matson's soft, quiet voice. *"Call yourself whatever you want. The name doesn't matter. It says nothing about who you are. The only thing that matters is your future here as a doctor . . ."* God, the thought of it made him sick inside.

Pain rushed through him and reflexively, he reached into the pocket of a frock coat he no longer wore, searching blindly for the flask. His hand brushed limply against his chest, and he stared at his empty fingers for a moment, confused, until he remembered that he no longer had a flask, or a bottle, or any kind of liquor at all.

Shaken, he sat down, staring at the saddlebags. No liquor. Hopeless frustration rose in his chest, constricting his breathing. Numbly he reached out and fumbled with the leather straps. Maybe he was wrong. Maybe there was a bottle inside, hidden away . . .

He knew there wasn't, but he couldn't stop his fingers from grabbing the straps, couldn't stop them from trembling as he tried to loosen the leather fastenings. Cain clenched his jaw and tried to focus. Sweat broke out on his forehead, trickled from his temples. His fingers blurred before him, nausea roiled in his stomach, and he took a deep breath, closing his eyes and resting his head in his hands.

The longing wasn't any better. In the two days since he'd been lucid, it had gotten worse. The scent of bourbon taunted him in his imagination; he knew its smooth, sweet taste and the burning warmth of it sliding down his throat. He wanted it so badly he could cry—hell, last night he *had* cried—useless, burning tears that dried on his fever-hot skin and made him thirstier than ever.

Cain squeezed his eyes shut, tried to think of something, anything. Ana's confession, the cool river, the sweet scent of orchids. But all those visions wavered flimsily, too elusive to be distractions, and all he could think about was the splash of bourbon into a glass, the feel of it sliding down his throat, warming his stomach . . .

If he didn't have a drink, he would go mad.

Hastily Cain climbed to his feet, choking back the bile rising in his throat, and stumbled toward the mule waiting a short distance away. The animal turned to look at him with liquid brown, unblinking eyes the color of whiskey. Cain swallowed. He needed a distraction. Any distraction. Desperately he looked at the mule, at the bulging saddlebags, and latched on to the first thing that came into his mind.

The saddlebags needed to be put on the mule. Yes, that was it. The saddlebags. Carefully Cain reached for them, nearly losing his balance when he picked them up and slung them over his shoulder. Carefully he walked toward the mule, leaned forward slightly, and tried to throw them onto her.

The mule sidestepped, the bags missed by inches. They clunked to the ground. Cain glared at the animal and grabbed for the bags again. He stepped closer, measuring the distance, his eyes narrowing, focusing. One at a time, step by step—

"Señor."

He was concentrating so intently on his job, he didn't really hear the voice at first.

"Señor."

Someone touched him. Cain twisted around, startled, dropping the bags. They thudded onto his foot, and he crashed backward, into the mule. But this time the animal stood still, and Cain braced his hand on its withers, trembling as he gained purchase, and stared at the man standing in front of him. The man was a native, short and wizened, wearing a gaily embroidered *montuno* that almost completely covered his shortened trousers. The straw hat on his head was bent and stained, and over his back hung a burlap bag that clanked at his every movement.

A familiar clanking, Cain thought. Very familiar. His stomach clenched. *"Sí?"*

"Aguardiente de venta?" the man asked, gesturing to his bag. *"Compre usted?"*

Would he like to buy some aguardiente? The world tilted beneath Cain's feet, he felt light headed. This man was an answer to a prayer. Cain resisted the urge to reach out and touch him to see if he was a hallucination.

Careful, he had to be very careful. What if it *was* delirium? Christ, he couldn't stand it if it was only a dream. Cain licked his lips, raked back his hair. *"Aguardiente?"* he asked slowly. *"Esta de vente?"*

"Sí, estoy de vente." The man looked at Cain as if he were mad. Well, perhaps he was, in a way.

"Then yes, I'd like some—*sí, sí.*" His hands shook. The old man stepped back, waiting, and Cain bent over, fumbling impatiently with the saddlebags, burrowing for his last gold coins. There were one or two, he knew, surely that was enough.

He nearly shouted with joy when he found one, abandoned at the bottom of the bag. His fingers curled around it and he pulled it out with a flourish. The sunlight sparkled on it. The old man smiled and reached into his bag—

Then Ana laughed. She was far enough away where she couldn't see a thing, but that clear, cool laugh rang out, spiraling through Cain, landing with a thud against his solar plexus.

The gold coin dropped from his fingers, plopped on the grass, and rolled at his feet. His eyes watered, his throat constricted, and all he could hear were her words from two days ago. *Destroy yourself, then.*

His whole body was so taut he felt he might snap. Before he could stop himself, before he even had time to think about what he was doing, Cain turned to the old man, who watched him in confusion.

"No." Cain licked his lips and shook his head. "No. *No compro. Nada más.*"

Ah, hell, what was he doing? What was he doing—

For the life of him, he couldn't change the words or reach out and motion for the liquor seller to stay. The old man nodded and walked away, and Cain watched the vendor go, unable to believe what he had just done, unable to believe that he was watching his salvation walk away, *listening* to it clank away from him.

He looked over his shoulder at Ana, who motioned impatiently at the muleteer. She hadn't even noticed. He doubted she had even seen the liquor salesman, much less his sacrifice. *You are a fool, Cain D'Alessandro.* His own condemnation echoed in his head.

It was that laugh, that goddamned laugh. Hell, the woman had the timing of a saint. What had made her decide to laugh right then, *right that second*? If she hadn't, he would have a bottle in his hand right now.

She would never know how much it cost him to refuse the liquor. And she wouldn't care. Not really. Even today, every word he'd coaxed out of her had been an effort. He would never get past that wall, he knew it, and yet here he was, trying to impress her. Christ, it was enough to make him want to throw himself over a cliff right now, to end the humiliation before it started.

Cain pushed his hair out of his face, wiped the sweat from his forehead with the back of his sleeve. He wished the damn liquor seller would come back, so he could buy a bottle and forget that he'd ever tried to make a hero of himself. He couldn't sustain this—didn't want to. Sooner or later, he would have another drink because he didn't want to stop. Sooner or later, he would disappoint Ana and Jiméne and get soused again. Sooner or later, he would fail.

Deep inside, he knew he wouldn't even be able to survive *this* trial. He was fooling no one—least of all himself—by pretending that leaving one bottle behind was even a step toward giving up drinking. He wasn't strong enough. He would never be strong enough. If there was one thing the last three years of drinking had taught him, it was that he hadn't the will to resist, or the desire to.

Cain took a deep, steadying breath. He was going to have to do something about this wretched desire for Ana—and soon. Before it completely destroyed him. Before he kept making these insanely impulsive decisions guaranteed to make him look as ridiculous as possible.

But even as he thought it, he found himself watching her laugh at something the muleteer said, watching the simple, sexy way she pushed back loose tendrils of her hair and the way her small breasts jiggled gently when she walked. Cain's loins tightened, and he closed his eyes, trying to choke back the twin desires for her and whiskey. Damn, it was going to be a long—

"Jiméne!" Her voice rang out, and Cain's eyes snapped open in time to see Castañeras approach. He was talking with a stranger in low, quick tones that stopped the moment Ana's voice reverberated into the street. But Cain didn't miss the frustrated impatience on Jiméne's face, or the startled realization in his eyes—as if he'd forgotten where he was and whom he was with. Nor did Cain miss Jiméne's quick calculation, the way he turned to his friend and spoke a few hurried words before he waved to Ana.

The man he was with nodded and hurried away, and Jiméne walked over to Ana and smiled a too-bright smile of greeting. Cain waited as the two of them walked his way.

"We are ready, then?" Jiméne asked when they were close enough. He motioned to his sling with his good hand. "Forgive me for not helping, but—"

Cain crossed his arms over his chest, his own obsessions forgotten in his sudden curiosity. "Who was your friend, *amigo?*"

Jiméne threw him a strange, preoccupied look. "A friend, that is all. Are we ready to go?"

"In just a moment," Ana answered. She motioned back to the muleteer. "José says I should have some trousers. I was just getting ready to go into town—"

"You do not need those." Jiméne cut her off sharply. He nodded shortly to Cain. "Are you ready, *amigo?* If you are, let us go. Let us not stand around all day."

He marched off, toward his mule, the tails of his blue coat flapping behind him.

Ana stared after him, a puzzled expression on her face. "What's wrong with him?"

Cain shrugged, trying to pass Jiméne's strange behavior off as unimportant, though he was equally disturbed. "Maybe he just had a fight with his friend," he said. "Who knows? With him, it could be anything."

She sent him a brief, sideways look. "It doesn't bother you?"

"Everything about him bothers me." Cain snorted. He glanced at Jiméne, who was already mounted and staring at them impatiently. "But it looks like we'd better do what he says," he said dryly. "Before he trots off without us."

Chapter 16

They had been traveling for only six hours, but it seemed like years. By the time José finally called a halt to camp for the night, Ana's legs were numb. In fact, her whole body was numb from the waist down, though in a way she was grateful for that. At least she couldn't feel the wet itch of her filthy, sodden wool skirt. It draped over her thighs and fell from her half-revealed legs to drag in muddy, heavy folds across the mule's sides.

Once again, as she had several times during this journey, Ana cursed Jiméne for being in such a hurry to go. José had been right—she needed trousers. Her stockings were torn and filthy, her boots filled with mud, and the only dress she owned was ruined.

If she hadn't been so sore from the mule's uneven, jarring gait, Ana would have jumped from the saddle and confronted Jiméne about his inconsideration. But all she could do was sit there, too tired to get off or do more than stare helplessly in his direction. She could barely see him anyway. The twilight-gloom of the daytime jungle had deepened now with evening. Ana looked up at the woven canopy of tree branches high above her, not for the first time noticing that the sounds—except for insects—had faded. The raucous screams of the parrots and macaws had stopped and the monkeys were quiet. It would only last a short while, she knew. The jungle was in transition. Before long, the far more frightening sounds of night would begin.

She wanted to be asleep when that happened. Actually, she wanted to be asleep now, but she was too wet and uncomfortable and hungry to give in completely to her exhaustion.

Ana closed her eyes. Her arms were sore from holding on to the saddle pommel through the radical descents and rises of the mountainous trail. The narrow, steep passages cut into the soft rock by hundreds of sharp mule hooves were like tunnels—muggy and dark, overhung by thick forest, draped with moss and ferns. There were times when the path had been barely wide enough for the mule, and Ana had been forced to put her feet on the animal's neck in order to keep her legs from being torn off by the walls of the *callejons,* as Jiméne called them. Mud was everywhere—in the narrow gulleys, in the three-foot-deep hoofprints the mule stepped into with perfect precision, everywhere.

The thought that they would have to do it again tomorrow was exhausting.

"Planning on staying there all night?" D'Alessandro's voice was low and soft behind her, heavy with weariness. "I doubt the mule would get much rest that way."

Ana forced herself to look around, to speak even though the sound of his voice brought an uncomfortable lump to her throat. "I don't think I can move."

"I know. Neither can I." In the near darkness, D'Alessandro looked white—a pale face topped with black hair that nearly disappeared in shadow. His fingers clenched the pommel of his high Spanish saddle convulsively. He glanced towards Jiméne and José, who were already off their mounts. José was quickly unloading saddlebags. A wry, tired smile twisted his lips. "I'm surprised he let us stop."

Ana nodded. Jiméne had barely spoken two words since they'd left Gorgona that morning. He had ridden ahead, his shoulders stiff beneath the blue superfine coat in spite of the sling, forcing José to a faster pace as if something were chasing him. After the first hour, Ana had been too miserable to care, but now she felt a faint trickle of worry. "I wonder what's wrong."

"Who knows?" D'Alessandro shrugged. "Probably just a headache. Maybe a little *señorita* turned him down."

"Do you two plan to sit there all night?" Jiméne snapped, looking over his shoulder.

"It speaks," D'Alessandro said in a low voice.

Ana chuckled. "Be kind," she admonished.

D'Alessandro threw her a look. "I am always kind." He took a deep breath and tried to dismount, but the moment he did, he fell back against the animal, his face whitening, his mouth drawing up in a tight line. "Christ." He groaned. He shook so badly he could barely hold onto the mule's neck. "Ah, Christ."

Guilt raced through her. Ana swallowed, feeling suddenly, overpoweringly concerned. He was so obviously sick—

"Wait." She responded before she could think, ignoring her own numbness as she shoved the sodden folds of her skirt out of her way and slid from the saddle. Her knees buckled for just a moment, blood flooded into her limbs in painful pins and needles.

As quickly as she could, she went to him, stumbling over the skirt tangling in her legs, nearly falling against his animal. Carefully Ana braced her hand on the mule's neck and looked up at D'Alessandro.

He looked ill. His eyes were closed, and his hair hung in his face, clinging to his pale skin like inky shadows.

His breathing came harsh and uneven, and the fingers clenched around the saddlehorn trembled.

She moved closer. "Let me help you down."

His eyes opened and he inhaled slowly.

"D'Alessandro, you have the food in your bags!" Jiméne yelled, his voice rife with irritation. "Hurry!"

D'Alessandro gave a short, breathless snort of a laugh. "Damn, he's annoying."

She held out her hand. "Let me help you."

"Yeah." He licked his lips, struggled to lift his head. "Christ, Duchess, I feel like hell."

"I'm not surprised." She grasped his arm, steadying him while he half slid, half fell down the mule's side. The animal sidestepped anxiously, D'Alessandro crashed into her arms. She staggered back, catching herself, holding him upright.

He struggled for balance, his hands hard and heavy on her shoulders. Laughing slightly, he pushed shakily away. "Sorry," he breathed. Wearily he rubbed the back of his neck as if the action somehow steadied him. "Usually I'm at my best in a woman's arms."

His words sent an odd shiver rushing through her. "Have you—have you eaten today at all?"

"D'Alessandro!" Jiméne nearly screeched.

D'Alessandro glared in Jiméne's direction. "In a minute, you impatient bastard!" He looked back at Ana.

His glance was so unfocused it unnerved her. Ana took a step backward. She nodded toward the saddlebags. "You'd better get those to him before he decides to carve into José."

He nodded and turned to the mule. Ana went hesitantly to her own mount. The mule needed to be unloaded, and she should help the others set up camp. But she suddenly couldn't take her eyes off D'Alessandro's unsteady movements. He could barely stand, and the fingers fumbling with the straps were clumsy and slow.

Every now and then, he rested his forehead on the mule's heaving sides, gathering strength.

Worry surged through her, climbed into her throat until just watching him made it hard to breathe. His helplessness, his need, tormented her. Called to her.

She'd felt nothing like it since her mother died.

D'Alessandro moved from the mule, and Ana watched him stumble through the half darkness. He walked slowly, every now and then misjudging the distance to the ground and putting one foot down too hard. When he finally got to where Jiméne and José were preparing camp, D'Alessandro shrugged the bags off his shoulders and fell against a tree, sliding limply to its base.

Ana tightened her fingers on the saddle and turned away.

By the time the men had a fire going, and the smell of hot, thick coffee floated through their tiny camp, D'Alessandro was nearly unconscious. He still slumped against the tree, his chin resting on his chest, arms crossed. His soft, quiet breathing filled the shadows behind Ana, mixing with the crackling snap of the fire. In the darkness, they were comforting sounds.

It was truly dark now, the kind of heavy dark that existed only in the jungle—dense and shadowy, filled with sound and movement. After two weeks, Ana still didn't like it, but at least she was used to it. And she felt safe tonight, with quiet, serious José keeping watch at the edge of the camp, arms akimbo, and D'Alessandro's even snores familiar and soothing.

Ana stared into the fire, watching the steam from the rice stew lift the lid off the pot. Her stomach growled at the fragrant, spicy scent of rice and sausage. She was starving, so hungry it kept her eyes from slamming shut in exhaustion.

She glanced at Jiméne. His back was to her, his movements faintly illuminated as he fumbled impatiently through his saddlebags.

"Jiméne?" she ventured. When he said nothing, she tried again. "Jiméne, is it ready to eat now?"

He looked over his shoulder at her, the faint strain of irritation on his face. "How would I know? I am no cook."

José pivoted on his heel. His heavy mustache dipped in a frown. *"Sí, señora,* you eat." He moved over to the fire himself, squatting beside it and lifting the lid off the pot. The camp filled with the mouth-watering smell.

Ana's stomach growled again. She reached for the pile of tin bowls sitting nearby and held them out.

"You can eat later, José." Jiméne shoved the saddlebags aside with a grunt of displeasure. He took the two steps to the fire and stood there, his one good hand planted firmly on his hip. "You have much to do now. We will leave before sunrise."

"Before sunrise?" Ana stared at him in surprise. The path had been treacherous in the daytime. At night, it would be impossible. "You must be joking."

"I assure you, I am not joking." Jiméne said firmly. He spat a virulent stream of Spanish at José.

Usually calm, easygoing José spat something back. He rose from the fire, clanking the lid on the pot, nearly stepping on the bowls before he strode away.

Ana stared at Jiméne in surprise. "What did you say to him?"

He glared after José. "Nothing. He is a lazy, stupid—"

"What the hell is your problem, Castañeras?" D'Alessandro's voice came out of the darkness, weary and annoyed.

Ana started. She swiveled around. "You're awake."

He cracked open an eye. "You have a remarkably firm grasp of the obvious, Duchess." He glanced at Jiméne. "What is it, *amigo,* José do something to bother you?"

"He is a lazy—"

"So you said. You've been an ass all day. What's wrong?"

Jiméne hesitated. "There is nothing wrong."

"You *are* acting differently," Ana said.

"You two, you know nothing—nothing!" Angrily Jiméne threw up his hand, spinning on his heel. Ana watched until the darkness swallowed him up, hearing his rapid pace to the mules.

She turned to D'Alessandro. The firelight glowed on his skin, turning it a pale apricot—the most color she'd seen on his face in days. His eyes sparkled in the firelight.

"Just tired," he repeated thoughtfully. "I don't believe him. Do you?"

"I don't know." Ana shrugged. She lifted the lid off the pot. The steam burned her face, formed instant tiny curls at her forehead. She reached for a bowl. "I know *I'm* tired. And hungry. You must be too. You haven't eaten all day." She ladled out the hot stew, carefully holding the tin bowl with the edge of her skirt. She held it out to him. "Here. Your dinner."

"I'm not hungry."

She knelt beside him. "You need to eat." She shoved the bowl at him, nudging it against his chest until he took it from her. Then she laughed, shortly, nervously. "Listen to me. I sound like your mother."

He stiffened. "Somebody's mother, maybe. Not mine."

"She didn't care whether you ate or not?" she teased.

"She didn't care whether I lived or not." His voice was light, but Ana didn't miss the underlying pain.

Curiosity burned like a white-hot flame inside her. Ana bit her lip. She wanted to know, but she knew if she asked, he would expect a secret in return. *And you can't do it. You know you can't.*

The thought mocked her, tormented her, and Ana

looked away, staring into the dark jungle. "Eat your dinner," she choked.

He leaned his head back on the tree and closed his eyes, pushing away the bowl of stew. "Christ, I don't need food. I need someone to talk to me, Ana. Just talk to me."

Fear and longing made her stomach tight. Ana couldn't keep the wariness from her tone. "Talk about what?"

"Ah—anything. Anything." He sighed. "Can you sing?"

She stared at him, taken aback. "Can I sing? No."

"Just 'no'? Not 'I can, but not very well,' or 'I'm completely tone deaf, D'Alessandro, don't be a fool'?" he mimicked her perfectly, Ana heard the familiar condescension in his voice. "Just 'no'? Didn't you ever sing when you were a child?"

"Did you?"

He lifted a brow and smiled wickedly. "In the church choir."

"You were in a choir? How did that happen?"

He shook his finger at her, scolding. "Uh-uh, Duchess. Tit for tat."

Ana stiffened. *Tit for tat.* Like choosing weapons for a duel. But his eyes were on her, urging her on, demanding— She swallowed. "I didn't sing much as a child." She hoped it would be enough, but he said nothing, waiting, and impulsively, she said, "My mother had a beautiful voice. But I—I don't sing."

"You sang lullabies for me."

A hot flush moved over her skin. Ana glanced away, feeling uncomfortably naked. "I didn't know you heard."

"I did." A husky admission, oddly vulnerable. "You have a pretty voice, Ana."

She couldn't help smiling; his words took away her

discomfort. Ana looked back at him. "Not as pretty as my mother's."

He shrugged. "Prettier than my voice."

"You sang in a choir."

"For about one day." He grinned. "I threw off the others so badly, they kicked me out."

Ana laughed in spite of herself. "You cheated. Tit for tat, indeed. That's hardly a secret."

"A secret?" He looked at her questioningly. "Is that what we were doing, Ana? Telling secrets? I thought we were just talking."

Heat worked its way over her face. There it was again, the slight chastising, the assumption that she should have known something she didn't know, should have been something she could never be . . .

Ana swallowed. "Don't mock me, D'Alessandro."

"I'm not mocking you." His voice was very quiet, the firelight made his face eerily somber. "You know I wouldn't do that."

No, he wouldn't. She knew that even before he said it. He wasn't like she was. Wasn't cold and pragmatic and removed. Suddenly what had once seemed to be virtues were vices instead. A lump rose in her throat, made it impossible to speak even if she'd known what to say. Ana twisted her hands in her skirt, staring down at her fingers, trying to think of something, anything to fill the silence—

"I keep thinking of that Russian storybook you told me about," he said gently. "The one with all the pretty pictures?"

She looked up, relief flooding over her. Relief and obligation. "Yes?"

"And I was wondering." He ran a hand through his hair, leaned his head back on the tree. "I was wondering if you remember any of them—the stories, I mean."

Ana stared at him, hands stilled, trying to figure out

where this was leading. "Some. I remember some of them."

"Think you could tell me one?"

"I'm not a storyteller."

He smiled wanly. "You can't sing, you can't tell stories—what *can* you do, Duchess?"

I can be a whore. The thought flashed through her mind before she could stop it. Ana looked away, feeling suddenly ashamed of a profession she'd accepted long ago. Ashamed and somehow lacking. "I wish you wouldn't call me that," she said.

"Call you what?"

"Duchess." She waved her hand, dismissing it. "I hate it. I've always hated it."

"Ana." His voice was so quiet she had to strain to hear it. "I feel like hell. Tell me a story."

She hesitated. His eyes were closed now, his mouth pinched and tight, his breathing shallow. She looked at the bowl of stew, sitting untouched beside him. "You should eat, you know."

"I should be dead now, by all rights," he replied hoarsely. "Eating won't help."

"It might," she urged.

"The only thing that will help is a soft pillow and a glass of bourbon," he said. "I guess since I don't have one, I might as well get the other."

Before she could protest, he moved, swiveling lying down, until his dark head rested in her lap. She felt the heavy, pressing warmth through the damp wool—a center of heat that spread upward into her hips, into her belly. Ana stared at him, frozen in place, unsure what to do, what to say. Her voice felt strangled in her throat. "What—are—you—doing?"

"Finding a soft pillow."

"But I—"

"I need comfort, Ana. Comfort me."

Touch him now, she thought, *before he moves away, before you're on the outside again.*

She stared down into his face, seeing the shadow of his lashes on his cheeks, the high, broad cheekbones chiseled by darkness, the fullness of his mouth. His hair fell in a heavy swathe over his forehead, and she lifted her hand, meaning to smooth it away.

She stopped just in time. Her hand hovered over his face, and she clenched her fingers, trying to force herself to move, to leave—to go to her bedroll and curl inside and forget he'd ever asked this of her, this display of caring she didn't know how to give.

She yanked her hand back. He grabbed her wrist, stilling it, and when she looked down at him in surprise, he was staring up at her, his dark eyes glinting, bottomless shadows in the firelight. Then slowly, easily, he brought her hand down to his face, laying it against his cheek so her clenched fingers curled against his skin. Equally slowly, he pressed his thumb beneath her fingers, forcing them to open, to lie flat.

Ana felt strangled, her limbs like stone. She stared at her hand, white and pale against his face, and it felt disembodied, not a part of her at all. Except it *was* hers, she knew it was because the warmth of his skin burned, the rough stubble of his beard rasped against her fingers.

"It's easy," he whispered, his hoarse baritone moving over her like honey, soothing her nerves. "Just move it like this." He took her hand, stroking it along his cheek, over his forehead, through his hair. "If you tell me a story, I'm sure you'll even forget you're doing it."

"D'Alessandro—"

"Shhh. The story, Ana."

He let go of her hand. But surprisingly, it kept moving. Clumsily, jerkily, but moving all the same, smoothing back his hair, threading through it.

"I remember one story," she choked. It didn't even

sound like her voice, it came from so far away. "It was my favorite once."

"How old were you then?"

She laughed nervously. "Six maybe. Or seven." Her hand kept stroking. His hair felt like satin. Heavy, dark satin, winding through her fingers like shadows through moonbeams. The fire crackled, the light wandered over his face, highlighting his eyes, his cheekbones, his lips. Showing the trembling of his hands resting on his chest.

Warmth wound through her, spiraling until it became the smile tugging at the corners of her mouth, a smile she couldn't stop, or help. "Once upon a time," she began slowly, "there was a man named Ilia Muromec, and he was a hero in the city of Kiev . . ."

Chapter 17

They were on their way at sunrise. By noon they'd left the most mountainous part of the trail, entering wider, shallower valleys and wide open savannahs. Solitary ranches dotted the trail at intervals, but they were little more than momentary rest stations, ill-equipped to handle the groups of Americans heading to Panama City. Mostly, all they could supply was a cup of scalding black coffee, but it was enough. The hot weather and the frequent, torrential rainstorms sapped Ana's strength and took away her appetite. Hours ago she had resigned herself to bumping along on the mule's back, so sore that every moment she swore she couldn't stand it any longer.

But she stood it. She stood it because she was too tired to get off. The beginning of this journey had been hard, but it hadn't really seemed like a *journey* until now, when there was nothing but this monotonous riding, and the dark jungle pressing in all around.

Ana pulled at her wool collar, wishing she could unbutton a few more buttons, desperate to be cool. But she'd already revealed too much of her cleavage, and though at the best of times that hardly worried her, with D'Alessandro now so—unpredictable—showing more flesh made her nervous.

Involuntarily she remembered last night, and the memory brought with it a soft, warm satisfaction that she couldn't ignore, didn't want to ignore. She hadn't failed last night; the knowledge made her feel good, so good it made her fear seem inconsequential. It was a small victory, one she still couldn't quite believe. He had asked her for comfort and she had given it to him, wanted to give it. He hadn't been disappointed, and she hadn't failed.

She was surprised at how happy the thought made her. She had touched him, and though she'd been afraid, in the end it had been all right. In the end, he hadn't asked any more of her than she'd been willing to give. He'd fallen asleep in her lap, and it felt so good to have him there she hadn't wanted to wake him. This morning, his smile made her forget her initial nervousness.

The mule stumbled over a rock, lurching sideways, and Ana gritted her teeth as pain shot up her legs, into her buttocks. Thoughts of her partner flew from her mind. For the hundredth time, she thought about walking, and for the hundredth time, she remembered the Indian baggage carriers they'd passed. She was lucky; at least she had a mule to ride. The slender natives walked to Panama City, bent under the weight of the trunks and bags slung between the poles they carried, trudging over the rough terrain. She'd felt sorry for them until Jiméne informed her dryly that they were paid very well for their services, and that when the load became too much for them, they merely left it behind.

They were the only words he'd spoken besides "Hurry up" and "You are too slow." Ana knew that even if she did decide to walk, Jiméne would never allow it. She would slow them down far too much.

Grimly she remembered that she had been the one in a hurry when they'd first started the trek across the isthmus. She'd no doubt been as obnoxious as Jiméne, ordering all speed in spite of danger. She remembered Esteban's attack, and clenched her hand around the pommel of the saddle. For her, the lesson to slow down had been hard won. She wondered if she would end up paying for Jiméne's obsession as well.

She stared ahead. Jiméne was right behind José, so close the nose of his mule nudged the backside of the muleteer's. At the start of the high ravines only wide enough for one mule, Jiméne had waited impatiently while José called out a warning to riders on the other side, looking for all the world as if he wanted to take the risk and charge ahead.

"Let's stop." D'Alessandro's voice was so low behind her, she barely heard it. For a moment, she wondered if she even had. Then it came again, louder. "Let's stop."

She twisted in her saddle. He looked terrible. White and shaking, both hands clenched around the saddlehorn. She twisted back again. "Jiméne!" she called out. "We need to stop!"

He didn't even turn around. "No."

"Dammit, Castañeras, if you don't— Damn."

Ana looked over her shoulder. D'Alessandro was clinging to the saddle, nearly sliding off his mount. "Jiméne, wait!" She was off her mule in seconds, helping D'Alessandro down. He fell to the ground with a thud and she knelt beside him. "Are you all right?"

"I feel great," he said sarcastically. He struggled to one elbow and then sat up, shakily brushing the dust from his shirt, concentrating on the simple motion as if it took all his strength. "Ana, I'm sorry, but I need to rest."

"Then we'll rest," she said simply. She got to her feet,

placing her hands on her hips, her eyes narrowing angrily as she watched Jiméne slowly moving away. "Jiméne!" she shouted, wincing at the high-pitched sound of her voice. "Damn you, stop!"

He slowed, looked back over his shoulder, and yanked on the reins. "What are you doing?" he called back. "Come along, you will slow—"

"D'Alessandro can't go on," she cut him off abruptly.

"Can't go—" Jiméne's jaw clenched. He turned to José, muttered a few impatient words, and then dismounted. His step was stiff and angry as he moved to where they stood. Brushing past Ana, he went to D'Alessandro and stood over him. *"Como te sientes?"*

"I feel weak," D'Alessandro replied, raking a hand through his hair. "Not just weak, actually, Castañeras. Sick."

"I do not believe this," Jiméne snapped, absently rubbing his injured arm. "You are worse than a child. A week without drink—"

"Nine days," D'Alessandro corrected.

"Whatever. We cannot stop for you."

Slowly, carefully, D'Alessandro grasped on to the mule, pulling himself up bit by bit until he stood, one hand resting on the saddle. "I need to stop," he said, every word careful, heavy with anger. "Go on without me, if you must, but I'm not getting back on that mule. Not now."

Jiméne expelled his breath in a tight, impatient rush of sound. His eyes narrowed. "I thought—if you were sober—you would be a good doctor. A man, not a child."

D'Alessandro stiffened. "You—"

"Enough of this." Ana took a deep breath, stepping between them. She turned to Jiméne. "Surely stopping for the rest of the day will hurt nothing. We have three weeks until the steamer arrives in Panama City. There's plenty of time."

"You know nothing." Jiméne's jaw clenched.

"I know you've been unbearable since Gorgona." She touched his arm. "Jiméne, what's wrong?"

"Nothing is wrong." He wrenched away. "Nothing." He turned to D'Alessandro, motioning angrily. "Him. He is too weak, useless."

"Thank you," D'Alessandro murmured.

Ana threw him a warning glance and turned back to Jiméne. "That's not the reason you're so upset, is it?"

"It is exactly the reason," Jiméne contradicted. "I—" Rubbing his forehead, he turned away, staring at the jungle. Then he turned back, his face a study in indecision. His voice was hoarse with misery. "Ah—I have no choice. I need your help."

"Our help?"

"Well . . ." Jiméne looked sheepish. He pointed to D'Alessandro. "His help."

"You have a funny way of showing it," D'Alessandro said.

"I know. I am *el tonto*—the fool. But I did not know what else to do. You are not well, *amigo.*"

"No kidding."

"And I thought you would be well. I thought you would be ready."

"Ready?" Ana frowned, suspicion rising in her mind. "Ready for what?"

Jiméne looked up, down, anywhere but at her. "I must have a doctor."

"You're sick?" D'Alessandro asked.

Jiméne shook his head. "Not me, no. *Mi madre.*" He sighed and leaned against Ana's mule. "In Gorgona, I saw a friend—Diego Villenueve. He has just come from home, and he tells me she is ill—*mi madre.* The *curanderos* say it is *el pasmo.* The fever. But I do not believe them." He snorted in derision. "They are fakes, folk doctors who treat with juice and prayer. They know nothing of medicine and they save no one. Not me—not her."

He looked back at D'Alessandro, who watched with serious eyes, arms folded over his chest. "Diego says they are worried—they think she is not long for this world. It is time for a real doctor, I fear."

"And you think I can help?" D'Alessandro asked.

Jiméne looked at him somberly, speculatively. When he spoke, it was as if the words pained him immeasurably. "I do not know, *amigo*. You saved my life, but it is in spite of yourself, I think. I am not sure—" The words came out in a rush. "I do not know if I can trust you with *mi madre*. I hoped, if you were sober, then *sí*, maybe you could help. Now I do not know."

There was a long silence. Jiméne stared at his feet. Ana looked at D'Alessandro. His expression was closed, his gaze focused on something in the distance, something hidden in the lush, tangled foliage beyond. Her chest tightened, there was a strange squeezing in her throat and a burning behind her eyes.

"I don't know if I can do it either, *amigo,*" he said quietly, without looking at either of them. "But I'm willing to try, if you want me to. And I won't be upset if you'd rather I didn't."

"You will stay sober until we get there?" Jiméne asked.

D'Alessandro nodded. The muscle in his jaw jumped. "Yes."

"Then I would be honored if you would try." Jiméne turned to José and spoke quickly in Spanish. Then he looked at Ana. "We will rest for now, then. But we must leave early. It is another two days away."

Ana swallowed thickly. "Of course."

Jiméne marched off, and she turned to D'Alessandro, meaning to say something to him, to try to ease the bite of Jiméne's words, but he was already walking toward the jungle, and she still didn't have the slightest idea of what to say.

Yards from the path, Cain stood motionless, listening. No footsteps came hurrying after him, no voices echoed soft and muffled through the vegetation. It was quiet. Well, not quiet. The jungle was never quiet. But there were no human sounds at all, and he closed his eyes and took a deep breath and reveled in it.

Christ, it felt good to just stand here, to inhale the humid, fecund scent of plant life and the sweet perfume of flowers. The warm, wet air caressed his skin, too heavy to dry the sweat clinging to his temples, too heavy even to breathe. His heart thudded in his chest. It felt as if he'd just run miles instead of only walked a short distance, and he was exhausted, drained of everything. Drained of even the ability to feel pain.

It had been three years since he'd practiced medicine sober. Three years of fighting the demons that jumped at him from his patients' eyes, three years of trying to drown the memory of John Matson in bourbon. He thought—if nothing else—he'd at least grown used to his own fears, used to the smell of blood and death and the constant shadow of uncertainty.

But the drink had only numbed him. It hadn't removed his terror. It was still there, brought to life by Jiméne's words, only now it was worse than ever. Now he didn't know how to fight it. He'd promised not to drink, but the thought of making a diagnosis sober made him weak. And horribly, deeply afraid.

Because you can't do it. You'll fail. You always fail.

"I trust you, Cain. I trust you . . ."

Cain squeezed his eyes shut, forcing away the images, reaching instinctively for the flask that was no longer there. But the memory wouldn't leave him this time—actually, it had never left at all, had merely been clouded by drink. Now, without the bourbon, it bombarded him. In his mind he felt John's blood, heavy and wet on his hands, heard the ragged sawing of bone and the rasp of breathing. In his mind, he felt the sticky gel of an isinglass dressing and smelled the stench of putrefaction.

There hadn't been any screaming then. Not a sound. But, ah, God, how he heard the screaming now.

Christ, he had failed so often. So often. And now here was Jiméne, asking for help, offering the same trust that had killed John Matson, and all Cain could think was that he should say no. Should turn around and ride away to Panama City. He was so afraid to face that failure again when he could see it clearly. Much better to be drunk and unfocused and alone. The way he'd always been—

"D'Alessandro?"

He heard her voice before he heard the swish of her skirts against the ferns. It cut through him, running roughshod over his thoughts, banishing everything until he was so focused on her he practically felt her skin beneath his hands.

"D'Alessandro?" She stopped just behind him, just beyond his reach.

That's right, be careful, he thought. He wondered what her reaction would be if she knew how often he'd dreamed about her during the uncomfortable ride; dreamed about the touch of her hands, caressing her, kissing her—doing more than that.

"Are you all right?" She sounded uncertain, hesitant. Strangely breathless.

He turned around, smiling slightly. "I'm all right."

"Oh. Good. Well, I—" She half turned. "I guess I'll leave you alone then."

"Don't go." He spoke before he thought, and squeezed his eyes shut, waiting for her refusal. When she said nothing, the relief spilling through him was nearly more than he could bear. He leaned his head back, staring at the leafy canopy above their heads. "A few days ago, you asked me who John was. He was—John Matson was a doctor at Massachusetts General. I apprenticed under him." He paused, closing his eyes at the memory. "John became . . . more than a father to me. I studied under him for three years. Then there was a carriage accident—nothing serious, just a cut on his leg. But it . . . it got worse. He wasn't much of a patient. By the time he stopped working long enough to see to it, the leg had festered, there was gangrene. We had to amputate." He laughed shortly, bitterly. "That is, I had to amputate."

"What happened?"

Ana's voice sounded vague and far away, barely intruding upon the memory that was as clear and distinct as the day it had happened. He pulled the emotion from his voice, spoke as flatly as he could, meaning to shock her with a callousness he didn't feel. "I made a mistake. He died."

He waited for Ana's response, waited for the horror in her voice, the inevitable platitudes. An "It was an accident," or "You couldn't have meant to"—the same things he'd told himself and didn't believe. But she was quiet. So quiet, for so long, that Cain opened his eyes.

"I—I wish Jiméne hadn't said those things," she said softly. "I'm sorry he did."

"But you don't think he's wrong."

"I think you think he's right." She smiled dryly, raising a finely arched brow. "My opinion doesn't matter."

"It does to me."

"It shouldn't. It shouldn't matter what other people think of you."

She looked so positive, fiercely so, as if it was the one thing she believed with all her heart. Cain's self-pity vanished. Now, instead, he felt strangely sorry for her. "No?" he whispered. "What a sad, cold world it's been for you, *querida,* if you believe that."

She seemed to melt before his eyes. "Where I come from, not caring means you survive."

He took a step toward her. "Tell me about where you come from then, Ana."

She looked like a rabbit caught in a trap, wide-eyed and ready to run. He'd temporarily forgotten that this was a woman who would always be wary, a woman who needed to be handled gingerly. But he didn't have the energy to do that right now. He wanted her to be like other women, suddenly, to chatter on about inconsequential things like hats and the weather. To be like his aunts—women who had been known to spend entire days commenting on a single needlepoint stitch.

But Ana would never be like those women. She would never be like any woman, and for a moment, he hated that about her, because he *needed* someone to talk. Just talk. Someone to fill his ears with stories and distractions. Someone who made him forget about bourbon and Jiméne and imminent failure.

She licked her lips, her hands twisted in her skirt. "There's nothing to tell."

"Nothing?" Cain frowned. "I don't believe you. Where did you live?"

She threw him a glance laden with sarcasm. "You know where I lived. In Madam Rosalie's Home for Women."

"Did you like it there?"

"It was one of the best houses in the city. I was lucky to be there."

"That's not what I asked you."

"Yes, it is." She frowned, her brown eyes lit with confusion. "You asked me if I liked it there."

"You didn't answer me."

"But I did. I told you—"

"Did you *like* it there, Ana?" He watched her, feeling a strange tension build in his chest as he waited for her answer. He could almost see the wheels turning in her mind, the agile way she searched for an impartial answer to his personal question. He wasn't sure what he would do if she answered him that way, didn't know whether he would shake her or walk away—or even why he wanted so desperately to know about her.

"I don't understand," she said finally, her voice colored with anxiety. "I don't know what you want."

"It's a yes-or-no question," he answered tightly. "Did you like it there or not? How goddamned hard is it to answer? 'Yes, I liked it' or 'No, I didn't.' Christ, Ana, what the hell is wrong with you? Why won't you talk to me?"

She backed away. "I'm trying to."

"The hell you are."

He heard the tightness in her voice, saw the beginning bricks of the wall, and Cain ached with frustration. In that moment, he knew he could never break through the wall she'd spent years building. He was too weak, too tired. Hell, it was all he could do to keep himself sane. He'd been wrong, thinking she could save him, thinking she needed him as much as he needed her. Maybe it had only been what he wanted to see. Maybe it had only been the drink talking.

Abruptly he sighed, shoving his hand through his hair, feeling old and exhausted and sicker than he'd felt even a few minutes before. "Jiméne's waiting," he said wearily, moving past her, back toward the road. "Let's go."

He was several feet away from her before he realized she hadn't moved. Frowning, he turned on his heel, meaning to tell her impatiently to hurry, but the look on her face stopped him.

There it was again, that angry desperation, the fear that made her sherry-colored eyes seem large and golden. "What is it?" he whispered. "What's wrong?"

"There's nothing wrong," she said finally. "You're right, let's go. Jiméne's waiting."

Later that night, he was sitting by the fire, staring at the play of light and shadow across his legs, wishing he were far away from her. Wishing he were still in New York, in a little tavern called Cavey Davey's, watching the buxom waitresses slosh beer across the patrons, with nothing more to worry about than where his next bottle was coming from.

He heard her footsteps behind him, heard the flapping of her wet skirt against her legs, and he didn't turn around. But she stopped, and he felt her waiting. He didn't want to acknowledge her, but she stood there silently, and he had the uncomfortable impression that she would wait there until he did.

So he twisted to look at her. Her eyes were spitting fire, her face was hard and tight, her shoulders stiff.

"I didn't like living at Rose's," she said quickly, as if trying to get the words out before she changed her mind. "She didn't like me and I liked her less, and every day I was there, I wanted to be somewhere else."

Then, before he could answer, she spun on her heel and marched away.

Chapter 18

"—Jiméne! Jiméne!" The shout exploded from the *quincha,* startling the pigs and chickens in the front yard into a screeching, scrambling frenzy. The old mongrel dog curled by the door staggered to his feet, hurrying away on stiff legs, ears flopping.

A wide smile stretched across Jiméne's face. He was off his mule in a trice, running pell-mell across the grass toward the house like a small boy.

Just in the nick of time, Ana thought, watching his dark-haired brothers and sisters stream from the door. Waving, shrieking, laughing, and crying—they made so much noise it sounded like a crowd instead of only six people. A small boy attached himself to Jiméne's legs, the adults talked over each other in an attempt to be heard. And all the while, Jiméne laughed and hugged and cried. Their joy was palpable—it filled the air around Ana and made her smile.

D'Alessandro rode up beside her, pulling his mule to a halt and staring at Jiméne's family with a bemused expression. "It must be nice to have people miss you so much," he said softly.

Ana nodded. "I suppose so." *Yes, it must be nice.* It had been a long time since anyone had missed her that much. Ana saw the warmth in Jiméne's eyes as he looked down at his nephew, and she saw the sparkling, dimply smile he got in return. Once upon a time, she remembered, her mother had looked at her that way.

For a moment, sadness threatened to overtake her, and Ana fought it. There wasn't time to think about that now, even if she wanted to. Family, warmth, love—those were things she had never expected to find again. She had long ago decided she didn't want them.

She glanced at one of the women surrounding Jiméne—his sister, by the looks of her. She cradled a baby in her arms, and her brown eyes were wet with tears. That especially was something Ana didn't miss. The pain that came from loving someone, the vulnerability that made a person cry even when they were happiest. Strangely, the thought made her sadder than before, and Ana suddenly didn't want to get off her mule and go over to them. She was a stranger; someone who couldn't share their joy. Someone who didn't even understand it—

D'Alessandro slid from his mule and turned to her. "Ready to face the circus?"

She licked her lips, a tight knot of nervousness in her chest. "I'm not sure I'll ever be ready."

"Just pretend you're in the salon at Madam Rosalie's," he said in a low voice, a half smile tugging at his lips. "I'll bet there wasn't a man there you were afraid to meet."

"It's not the same," Ana said tightly.

"Meeting people is always the same," he said. "Mind your manners and smile. You can do that. I've seen you."

"Ana! D'Alessandro!" With perfect timing, Jiméne

turned, motioning for them to join him. "Come and meet *mi familia!*"

D'Alessandro offered her his hand. He raised a challenging dark brow. "Well?"

She pushed aside the dirty folds of her skirt and laid her hand in his. His fingers curled warmly around hers, and she felt shivery suddenly.

"Ana! D'Alessandro! Hurry!" Jiméne's smile grew wider. Clumsily he lifted the small child tugging on his leg, hugging him as close as he could without dislodging the sling. "Come now—I would like you to meet them all."

D'Alessandro strode forward easily, and Ana hurried to catch up to him, stumbling over her sodden skirts. She looked up, catching the gaze of the sister with the baby. The woman's smile was gone; she was quietly assessing. Ana paused, suddenly aware of her filthy clothes and her mud-streaked skin. Her hair was curling over her shoulders, her braid nothing more than a few strands twisted together. She must look like a miserable wretch of a human being. Not a lady, certainly.

But Ana took a deep breath, straightening her shoulders, raising her chin. D'Alessandro was right, she could do this. She was the Duchess, the whore with manners so excruciatingly polite even the other girls had often wondered if she was nobility. That, at least, she thought wryly, she could thank her mother for.

"Ah, here we are," Jiméne said as they approached the group. "Ana, D'Alessandro, may I present my brothers and sisters." Then, as the child in his arms squirmed, he laughed. "And my niece and nephew. That is Serafina with the baby Melia, then Dolores, Amado and Juan Domingo—Serafina's husband. And this"—he jiggled his nephew—"is Enzo."

He went on, introducing them to his family in a rapid spate of Spanish, and Ana tried to match the names with the faces. Serafina was the most beautiful of the sisters, though Dolores was pretty in a bright, round-cheeked way. Tall Amado was a younger version of Jiméne, and Serafina's husband, Juan Domingo, was the masculine counterpart to her dark beauty. All in all, a handsome family, and when D'Alessandro said something to them in Spanish, their laughter was a booming echo of Jiméne's.

"What did you say?" she asked softly.

D'Alessandro shrugged. "I thanked them for having us. My Spanish must be a little rusty."

"No, no," Jiméne protested. "They did not expect it, that is all." He said something to his brothers and sisters, and they nodded soberly. "I have told them D'Alessandro is the skilled doctor come to cure Mama," he informed Ana. He motioned to his sling. "They trust him because they know he saved my life."

She threw a quick glance at D'Alessandro. Some expression she couldn't interpret passed across his eyes and then disappeared. He looked as if he hadn't even heard.

In unspoken agreement, Jimené's family began to walk back to the house. Dolores took the squirming Enzo from Jiméne, walking just in front with Amado while Serafina, the baby, and Juan went hurrying ahead.

Jiméne watched them go, a thoughtful look on his face. "Juan has done a good job while I was gone."

Ana followed his gaze to the *quincha*. Jiméne said the farm was a small one, but the native house was one of the bigger and sturdier ones she'd seen. Three small huts attached to the main rectangular building, and their cane-and-twig walls were well kept, smooth with clay. The high, conical roof showed no holes in its palmetto thatch. An outdoor kitchen was just off to the left, and the pots and jugs stacked to one side were clean and unbroken, the patch of dirt separating it from the house well swept and void of animals.

"And Amado too," Jiméne went on distractedly. "He has grown. The last time I saw him, he was"—he leveled his hand at his waist—"this high." His glance followed his brother across the dirt yard. "He is no longer a boy, eh? More a man. Sixteen now." He paused.

"You were gone a long time," she said because it was all she could think of.

Jiméne smiled dryly. *"Sí,* too long. I thought I would not come back. I thought I would stay in New York and make my fortune. But now I think perhaps it is not for me. I would worry too much." He took a deep breath, and turned to D'Alessandro. Jiméne's brow furrowed, he lowered his voice. "Dolores says *mi madre* is no better, *amigo.* I am sorry, but you could perhaps look at her now?"

D'Alessandro's lips tightened, he paled slightly. "Yes, of course." He motioned to the mule. "I'll need to get my case—"

"Amado!" Jiméne called. His younger brother spun around, and Jiméne rattled off a command. Within seconds, Amado was running toward D'Alessandro's mule.

They walked across the ring of dirt edging the house into the bustling *quincha.* Dolores was in the corner, trying to interest small Enzo in a game. In a hammock nearby, baby Melia gurgled incessantly while Serafina leaned over the fire, stirring something in a big clay pot.

The room was redolent with the smell of savory stew, smoke, and sweat. Ana stood aside to make room for D'Alessandro and Jiméne to pass through, waiting for her eyes to become accustomed to the dim light after the blinding sun. The inside was like every other native house she'd seen, with little furniture besides a table and bench, and a cane ceiling forming an attic with a notched pole serving as a ladder. The smells were the same, the sights. The only thing that was different was the noise, and the warmth that seemed to emanate from the very walls.

"Dónde esta?" Jiméne asked tersely.

Serafina turned from the fire, nodding her dark head

in the direction of a curtained doorway off the back of the main room. *"Esta allí—en su cuarto."*

"Ah." Jiméne's mouth tightened. He looked expectantly at D'Alessandro.

As did Ana. Her partner looked taut. His jaw was tight, a tiny muscle bunched in his jaw, and his fingers clenched and unclenched.

Serafina plunked a stack of bowls onto the table, along with a blue pitcher. Drops of red wine splattered from its lip onto the wood.

"I must talk to Serafina a moment," Jiméne said quickly, his face suddenly white. He motioned to the doorway. "Please, D'Alessandro, if you would go—"

D'Alessandro nodded, his gaze fastened on the pitcher, on the spilling wine. Ana could read the yearning in his eyes, saw the burning hope.

She touched his arm, and he looked at her as if he'd forgotten she was there. He was as strained as she'd ever seen him.

He nodded shortly, distractedly, and started to walk across the bamboo-matted floor to Jiméne's mother's room. Ana watched him, feeling the heaviness in her stomach grow with every step. She wanted to curse Serafina for putting out the wine, even though Jiméne's sister could know nothing of D'Alessandro's struggle. Though Ana knew Jiméne would make sure there was no trace of the wine when D'Alessandro returned, she also knew that D'Alessandro wouldn't forget it was there. By the look on his face, it was already tormenting him.

Behind her, Jiméne jabbered to his sister. The baby gurgled, and Enzo laughed—a shrill, innocently happy laugh. But Ana couldn't take her eyes off D'Alessandro's slow, even walk. Once he was at the doorway, he stopped and looked in, and then he pushed aside the curtain and leaned heavily against the jamb, the pain in his expression so pronounced his profile looked sharp and harsh.

Her heart ached, her chest felt so tight she couldn't breathe. She had an unexpected, absurd urge to break into tears, to rush over and take him in her arms, to ease the pain since she couldn't erase it. To do *something*.

She stared at him, realizing suddenly that she was afraid for him, afraid that he would live up to his prediction and fail, afraid that he would care too much. She wished she could protect him from that, wished she could show him how people lived in Five Points, how pretending you didn't care kept you alive, how loud bravado was more effective than miserable tears.

But she couldn't. He was nothing like her. The misery on his face was there for anyone to see. It wouldn't inspire confidence, only doubt, and Ana knew that if Jiméne's family saw him like that, they would question Jiméne's judgment, question D'Alessandro's skill. They would see only a doctor too uncertain to begin.

What she saw was a man who believed he murdered someone he loved. A man desperately afraid he might do it again.

Ana picked up her skirts and walked to where he stood, staring into the darkened room. Quickly, quietly, she touched his clenched hand. He looked down at her, startled, and that second was all she needed. His hand loosened, she slid her fingers between his.

"So, Doctor," she said with forced brightness, squeezing his hand. "Tell me how you treat a fever."

Cain stared at her, stunned at the warm, sweet feel of her hand in his. It was as if she understood, as if she *knew* . . . But that was impossible, wasn't it? *Wasn't it?*

"I—" His words caught in his throat, he looked at her helplessly.

"You healed Jiméne, didn't you?" Her voice was infinitely soft. "You can heal her too."

"I didn't heal him. You know that."

She looked stricken for a moment, and then she shook her head. "I was wrong to say those things before."

"You don't need to—"

"Yes, I do," she said quickly. "Those doctors did nothing but pray. Jimené was right. *You* saved his life."

Her words held the quiet, clean heat of conviction—honest conviction, he was sure, and that was even more shocking than the slender fingers curled around his. He didn't understand, it was too foreign to understand, and he started to move away from her.

Then she squeezed his hand again, and Cain forgot that he didn't understand her, forgot the sight of the wine staining the tabletop like blood. He even forgot the fear that the woman lying motionless in the dark, stifling room had roused in him.

"Aquí!" Amado raced into the house, holding out the medical case, and with him came all the attention in the room. Cain felt the pressure of several sets of eyes. He swallowed nervously as he took the case from the boy and thanked him.

Ana stepped back, starting to take her hand away, but Cain grasped it tightly. "Don't," he said, feeling as if he walked on the edge of a dark and dangerous cliff. "Don't go."

"But I—" She tensed.

"I need your help," he said. It was the truth, anyway, he did need her help. But not for doctoring. Not for anything but keeping away the fear. She was the only thing keeping him from turning away from the illness and death in the room. The only thing keeping him from drowning his fear in drink.

The darkness in the tiny room was cloying, the air thick with the odor of sickness and musk and smoke, sharp with the acidic scent of tamarind. Jiméne's mother was a mound of shadow in the corner, her ragged breathing rattled through the still darkness.

Cain felt Ana's hand slipping from his, and he let it go, telling himself that he couldn't diagnose Jiméne's mother while clinging to Ana's hand like a child. Still, his fingers were suddenly ice cold. He clenched the case closer to his body and glanced over his shoulder at Ana.

Jiméne was suddenly in the opening. "Mama," he breathed. He shot a glance at Cain.

"I need a light." Cain's voice sounded rough and uneven. Jiméne dashed from the doorway and was back again in seconds with a lamp. Quickly he lit it, setting it on the bamboo table beside the bed. The small room was instantly illuminated.

Señora Castañeras lay on a high pallet, covered only with a thin, multicolored blanket, a lump with a thin black braid trailing from the covers. The light danced over her body, flickered on the cane walls, and sent shadows into the darkened corners, and Cain swallowed, feeling trapped. Jiméne was watching him expectantly, and Ana had drawn away into the corner. There but not there. He remembered suddenly her strange aversion to doctors, and wondered that she'd stayed at all.

He wanted to run from this room, grab the wine and hide in the jungle, but he knew already that Jiméne would have hidden the liquor well, and there was no escaping anyway. He had promised to help—he had to at least try, even though the thought of trying made that deep, hopeless darkness in the pit of his stomach swell.

Cain ran a hand through his hair and moved to the short stool beside the bed. His medical case was hard and reassuring in his hand, the brass tacks warm against his skin. *It's all right,* he told himself, sitting heavily. *Everything will be fine.* He stole a glance at Ana. Her arms were crossed over her chest, she looked stiff and unyielding. But she caught his gaze and smiled—a small reassuring smile that made him feel if not confident, then at least capable.

He took a deep breath, fighting the urge for drink,

and touched the woman's shoulder. *"Señora,* he whispered. *"Señora Castañeras, despertese."*

She shrugged off his hand, moaning, and Jiméne was instantly at her side. "Call her *Doña* Melia," he said quickly. "It is what she prefers." Then, before Cain could oblige, Jiméne leaned over his mother. "Mama," he said anxiously. "Mama, *esta Jiméne. Jiméne—estoy di regreso.* Mama."

The woman's eyes flickered open, she rolled onto her back, blinking in the dim light. "Jiméne? Jiméne, *mi hijo?"*

"Sí, Mama." Jiméne grabbed her hand, holding it to his lips. *"Sí, Mama, su hijo."*

Cain waited while Jiméne explained to his mother that he'd brought a doctor to look at her. Jiméne's mother's eyes were glazed, her breathing shallow, and when Cain touched her shoulder, her skin was hot and dry. Jiméne was right, it was *el pasmo,* a fever, and curing fevers was an elusive business.

Too elusive. Cain remembered attending lectures on the subject at Massachusetts General. No one really knew much about fevers, where they came from, why they went away. His own experience had taught him that people either got better or they died, and nothing he did made much difference.

His mouth was dry. He would give anything for a drink.

Jiméne finished talking and sat back on his heels, looking at Cain worriedly, waiting. There was no more time to delay; Cain set aside his case and leaned forward. In Spanish, he told *Doña* Melia to sit up, and his voice was harsh and strained. Weakly she did as she was told, turning her back to him. His hands were trembling again as he laid his fingers against her body and began the sharp, pounding movements of percussion.

He was acutely aware of Jiméne's eyes following his every movement, but Cain said nothing, merely kept pounding, listening for the dull thud that warned him of liquid in her organs. He heard it, just as he thought he would—a solid, resistant sound where her lungs were.

Cain sat back, reaching for his case. "What have they been giving her?" he asked.

Jiméne hesitated. "Tamarind water and sour orange rind with cinnamon."

"I suppose that can't hurt," Cain said, though he had no idea if it would or not. He unbuckled the straps of his case, willing his fingers to stop shaking, and lifted out the layer of instruments. The perforated tin box of leeches he set carefully aside, hoping that the animals were still alive after the wretched journey and his worse care. He reached for his lancet and bleeding cups, and then, finally, for the small vial of quinine salts.

"Get me some water, Jiméne. And sugar if you have it," he directed. Then, when Jiméne left the room, he smiled into the frightened eyes of the sick woman in front of him. *"Acuéstate, Doña* Melia," he said gently, pushing her back again. She lay back obediently. In the lamplight, her eyes looked large and liquid, the flesh around her face loose from weight loss. She must have been an attractive woman when she was young, Cain thought. But now she looked only sick, the dark circles beneath her eyes accentuated by shadow.

She responded to his smile, as he knew she would. They all did, even those—and there were many—who regarded all doctors as quacks. Sickness had a way of making everyone helpless, of reducing everyone to blind hope and supplication. Even doctors. Especially doctors . . .

Cain banished the thought and tried to concentrate on his patient. She made no sound as he lifted her chemise and brought the blankets up to cover her nakedness, leaving only her stomach bare. Jiméne came back into the room, his eyes wordlessly searching Cain's as he handed over a jug of water and a lump of raw brown sugar.

"I'm going to bleed her," Cain explained briefly, mixing a small bit of sugar and water in a cup and setting it aside. He reached into his case and pulled out a piece of linen, and then dropped some of the sugar water onto *Señora* Castañeras's abdomen. Finally he took the tin leech box and opened it carefully.

They were still inside, rearing up on their tails when he took the lid off, still lively despite the jouncing they'd taken. He hated the sight of them; much of the time Cain ignored them simply because he wanted them to die, to relieve himself of the slimy feel of them, the parasitic plumpness. This time was no different. Painstakingly he lifted them into the linen, suppressing his shudder as he placed them on *Doña* Melia's stomach while Jiméne explained to her what was happening. Cain watched her eyes close as the bloodsuckers grabbed for the sugar water and latched on to her skin.

Behind him, he heard Ana's gasp. Cain lifted a bleeding cup from his case, squeezing the vulcanized rubber bulb at the top of it as a test. He heard the quick gasp of suction, then the release, and he took a deep breath. His fingers were trembling, and when he grabbed the lancet and took the *señora*'s arm, he closed his eyes for a moment to steady himself. It took every ounce of control he had to keep from reaching for the flask he knew was no longer there, and when he opened his eyes again and stared at the veins pulsing just below her dry, heated skin, he suddenly couldn't remember how to cut her. The lancet lay folded in his hand and he couldn't remember, didn't know what to do, needed a drink . . .

"Ana," he gasped. "Ana, come here."

"What is it?" Jiméne jerked to look at him. "What is wrong?"

"Nothing," Cain shook his head. "Nothing. Ana?"

"I'm right here." Her hand was on his shoulder,

steadying, warm, and suddenly the amnesia passed, his trembling quieted.

Cain swallowed and opened the lancet. He felt Ana's fingers dig into his shoulder, and he knew what this was costing her, how much his work filled her with revulsion. He had a fleeting urge to turn to her, to ask her again why she hated doctors, but *Señora* Castañeras's arm pulsed beneath his hand, and he knew he didn't have time for those questions. But later, perhaps, later, when this was all over and he could sit and look at Ana's glorious hair and those sherry-colored eyes, and ask questions over a glass of rough red wine.

The thought gave him strength. Cain cut.

Chapter 19

He shook all through dinner. Cain curled his hand around a cup of coffee, his jaw clenching as he thought of the hidden wine. There was no sign of it. Everyone at the table drank water or goat's milk as if they were the drinks of choice, though he knew it wasn't true, knew Jimené had ordered Serafina to put the wine away. It didn't help. Every gulp reminded him of wine, and that tortured him like nothing else he could have imagined.

So he tried to forget about it, to enjoy the spicy stew of chicken, yams, plantain, and rice called *sancoche* and listen to the conversation. But he had no appetite; even the juicy oranges and bananas Serafina brought out for dessert didn't tempt him. Nothing did. He felt tired and dispirited, remembering Jiméne's mother lying sick and weak in the bedroom, now dosed with a draft of quinine and opium for pain. Cain was deeply aware that he had no idea what was causing her illness, or even what to do about it except bleed and dose her until either the fever or the medicine killed her.

It was a familiar feeling, too familiar, and Cain had

never felt it as sharply as he did now. But that was mostly because every other time he'd gotten roaring drunk, and that had always blurred the edges, made him forget.

He glanced again at Jiméne. It wasn't an option for him now, unfortunately. At least not until Jiméne went to bed.

The thought made him smile.

"Ah, now he is laughing!" Dolores smiled back, chattering in Spanish. "You looked so dour, *Señor* D'Alessandro, I was afraid for a moment."

"There's no need to be afraid," he reassured her. "Your mother will be fine." Empty words. Useless words. They fell off his tongue easily, by rote. "Worrying won't make her better."

"I haven't worried since you walked into the house," Dolores confided simply. "A real doctor, finally. It was the medicine men who were killing her, I know it."

"I doubt that," he said.

"You do not know them," she insisted. She touched Serafina's arm. "Is it not so, sister? Those old folk doctors come in here, they do some dances, they pray—for what, we do not know. Then they leave her with nothing but useless potions. She has drunk so much tamarind water I am surprised she has not turned into one!"

Serafina smiled slightly. "You exaggerate, Dolores, as usual, but she is right about one thing, *señor*. We are glad you have come."

"I hope I can help." There was nothing else to say but that, and it was true, at least.

"Enough of this talk," Jiméne broke in. "Mama will get better under D'Alessandro's expert hands, and we will all laugh about our worry. Now, tell me, Juan, what has happened while I have been gone?"

Juan launched into a narrative about the work done on the farm, how their neighbor, *Señor* Gonzalez, had been killed earlier that year by the bite of the poisonous fer-de-lance snake, and about the scorpion little Enzo had killed last week with his bare hands. Cain sat back, folding his arms across his chest while he listened.

He looked around him, at the rapt and smiling faces of Jiméne's family, and warmth seeped into the dark, empty space inside him. Fer-de-lances, scorpions, alligators . . . These people faced death every day, and it brought them closer together, made them the kind of family he had always longed for.

But then, he supposed they had loved each other from the beginning. There had never been betrayal and lies and infidelities, never the kind of fierce hatred that ate away at a person's soul.

He glanced at Serafina, who constantly rocked the baby she held in her arms. Her eyes were warm as she watched her husband, every now and then her teeth flashed in laughter, every few moments she leaned down to kiss the soft, downy curls on Melia's head. The sight filled Cain with a painful yearning. Christ, how he had wanted that as a child. Unconditional love, the forgiving touch of a mother's hand. He wanted to feel warm arms around him, wanted to be safe and warm and loved.

It surprised him, how much the thought still haunted him. He'd thought he had long ago forgotten that desire, killed it with whiskey. But it was still there, buried beneath years of pain and neglect. Still there, but different, because now he no longer thought of being the child, but of being the father . . .

Shaking, he lifted the coffee cup to his lips and drank the lukewarm liquid, nearly choking when his tongue realized it wasn't bourbon. Hell, it was absurd that he was thinking of this again, thinking of it now. There were no children in his future. No dancing, bright-eyed daughters, no love, no nothing. He'd grown used to it, and just because now there was a reason to think differently—

He tried to halt the thought before he could finish it,

but it went on, fading into his brain. *Just because now there was Ana.*

No, there wasn't Ana, he told himself. *You just need her now because she makes you forget the drink. But that will fade, and she'll leave.* Yes, she would leave. Just because she'd begun to tell him little things about her life, just because she'd seen his fear and given him the strength to go into *Doña* Melia's room didn't mean she cared about him. Probably she just wanted to get this over with quickly so she could get to San Francisco. So she could refuse him when he stood in line with all the other men willing to pay an ounce of gold for her services.

His fingers curled around the coffee cup so tightly it felt like the pottery might crack in his grip. It didn't matter. In San Francisco, there would be taverns and hotels. Safe places. Places where a lapse of memory or unconsciousness would be less dangerous. He could go back to his old life then. He wouldn't need her, she could do as she liked. But even as he told himself that, he felt a sharp, aching pain in the pit of his stomach, a loss so intense he couldn't bear to think about it.

So he didn't. He sat back, forcing himself to release his hold on the coffee cup, forcing himself to listen to Juan's stories, Serafina's laughter, and Jiméne's ridiculous jokes. Forcing himself not to look at Ana, though he hadn't really looked at her all night, hadn't heard her voice—

Because they were all speaking in Spanish. The realization plunged into him; Cain felt himself go stupidly pale. They had been speaking in Spanish all night. She couldn't understand them, couldn't understand a damn word.

He jerked around to look at her. She was near the end of the table, on the same side, alienated not only by language but by distance. Her shoulders were erect, but her head was bowed, and she listlessly dragged her spoon through her half-eaten *sancoche*. Her hair curled over her shoulders and down her back, wisping into her face in thin tendrils that she didn't bother to push away.

She looked tired, he thought, though it could have been simply that she was bored, and even from where he sat, he felt the cold, rigid wall surrounding her, protecting her. *Exiling her*.

The words pounded through him, and he tried not to hear. But he couldn't stop them. The sight of her sitting there, alone amid a tableful of people, made him sick with dismay. It was her choice, he knew it was. Knew that distance was what she preferred. So why was it he had the sense that she was hurting, that this time the wall was simply a response to being ignored?

Because she'd been letting it down, little by little, and he'd become used to that, he told himself. The thought of the Duchess hurting was a contradiction—

Except she wasn't the Duchess anymore, and he couldn't stand the idea that she would ever be that way again. Cain didn't stop to wonder why, didn't think at all. Before he knew what he was doing, he leaned over to Amado, who sat next to him, and whispered: "Trade places with my wife, Amado, will you? She doesn't understand Spanish. I can translate for her."

Amado scurried to his feet, his eyes wide with horror. "She does not? But of course I will trade places, *señor*. Of course!"

The boy's sudden movement made Ana look up, her forehead wrinkled in consternation. When Amado held out his chair for her, motioning for her to take it, her gaze shot to Cain's.

"It is not necessary," she said softly.

"Yes it is, *querida*," he answered her. "Take the chair."

She didn't argue. She looked at Amado, and then at Cain again, and then she rose regally, moving to Amado's seat and arranging her filthy skirts around her as if they were fine lace and she were the Queen of England. For a moment, Cain thought she didn't understand. For a moment, he thought she would sit beside him, still cold and distant. But she slid a sideways glance at him, and her mouth curved in a quiet, grateful smile.

Tit for tat, he thought, and began to translate.

It was late when Ana finally looked again at the notched pole leading to loft bedroom. She was exhausted. The day had been long, and emotionally draining, and she had wanted to go to bed the same time Cain had—at least two hours ago. But she couldn't bring herself to climb that pole with him, couldn't make herself face the night ahead with enough equanimity to join him while they were both awake and waiting for sleep.

Because they were sharing a bed, as they hadn't done the entire journey. She had protested earlier, before dinner, when Jiméne told her that Serafina had moved herself and Juan in with Amado and Enzo, leaving the loft bedroom free for Ana and Cain to share. But he had only smiled and said: "My family will think it strange that you travel with two single men, *cariña.* Better for them to believe you and D'Alessandro are married."

She knew he was right, but she wished he wasn't. Ana told herself it wouldn't be any different than the nights before, when she'd held Cain all through his delirium, or when he'd fallen asleep with his head in her lap. She told herself it would be the same.

But it wouldn't be, she knew it. He was sober now, and no longer as sick. And she was afraid of what he would ask her for in the dark loneliness of nighttime. Afraid of what she would want to give him.

So she'd waited, shaking her head when D'Alessandro told her he was going to bed, telling him she wasn't tired, that she preferred to sit and listen to their stories. Stories they both knew she couldn't understand.

Now, everyone was fading. The children had long ago gone to bed, Amado with them, and one by one the adults had left until only she and Jiméne were awake, listening to Juan's guitar.

Juan put aside the instrument and stretched, yawning.

Jiméne stood up. "I think it is time to go to bed, eh, *cariña?*"

She swallowed. "Yes. Of course."

"Then I will wish you *buenas noches.*"

"Buenas noches." Juan nodded.

Ana got to her feet. She glanced up at the loft, offering a silent prayer that D'Alessandro was asleep, and gathered her skirts to climb the notched pole.

Please, please, please be asleep, she hoped. The pole was securely attached to the loft floor, but even so, it thudded against the bamboo with every step. By the time she reached the top, Ana was sure D'Alessandro would be wide awake, but as she stuck her head through the square opening, she heard only his soft, even breathing.

She stifled a sigh of relief and stood there for a moment, letting her eyes grow accustomed to the pitch-black darkness before she pulled herself over the edge and made her way past deep-shadowed baskets full of rice, beans, and dried pork to the wide pallet that served as their bed. She thought she heard a change in his breathing then, and she stopped short, but he only started to snore.

Carefully she sat on the edge of the bed, the palmetto leaf mattress rustled softly beneath her weight. Slowly, silently, she fumbled with her boots, pulling them off, biting her lip to keep from crying out when one of her broken fingernails caught.

D'Alessandro was still snoring. Ana pushed back the thin blanket and lay down. It was too hot, and the wool of her dress itched painfully. Not for the first time, she wished she had a chemise underneath. She hated sleeping bundled in the stinking, dirty wool. Tonight it was worse than ever. The skirt bunched around her knees, and she didn't dare tug it down for fear the movement would wake him. She lay stiffly, arms at her sides, willing herself to relax—

"Where have you been?"

She jumped, nearly falling from the pallet. "You're awake!"

"Yes."

Damn! Her pulse raced. Through the confusion came a queer thrill of—of anticipation. Ana turned away from him, onto her side, trying to calm her pounding heart. "I—I'm sorry. I didn't mean to wake you."

"You didn't."

"No, of course not," she snapped. "You always snore when you're awake."

"Like this, you mean?" His deep voice lowered, rasped into the same snore she'd heard minutes before. "Like that?"

She heard the laughter in his voice, and Ana flushed. "You were only pretending."

"Once again, *querida,* you stun me with your perceptiveness."

"Why?"

"Why?" he repeated. He moved on the mattress, turning on his side. She felt the warmth of his body barely touching her back. "Would you have come up if you'd known I was awake?"

"Of course," she lied. "Why wouldn't I?"

"I don't know." He sounded thoughtful. "I thought maybe you wouldn't. Maybe I was wrong."

Ana struggled to keep her voice even. "You looked tired. You've a lot of work tomorrow, you should get some sleep."

"Yes."

She felt his hand on her hair, winding a tendril around his finger. Ana tensed. "What are you doing?" she whispered.

"Touching you. Is that all right?"

"No." She felt breathless, shaky, frightened. "No."

He was silent for a moment, so quiet she heard their breathing in the darkness, thought she heard the pounding of his heart, though it was probably only hers. He was so close she felt his heat, smelled the bitter quinine and orange still clinging to him, the soft musk of his skin.

He didn't stop stroking her hair. When he finally spoke, his voice was so quiet she barely heard it. "Thank you."

"For what?"

"I know you hated being in that room."

That room. *Doña* Melia's room. Ana waited for the inevitable question, the one he'd asked her already, the one she hadn't answered. *Why do you hate doctors?* But it didn't come, and she twisted away from him again, staring into the darkness beyond the pallet, her stomach in knots.

"Yes . . . well . . ." She inhaled deeply. "I couldn't let them see you like that. You don't always hide your emotions very well."

"Unlike you," he said dryly.

She caught her breath. "I told you—"

"Yes, I know." He touched her hair again, spinning his fingers through the strands, and she froze. "Ah, Ana, too bad. You've beaten the smile right out of yourself."

She felt strangely offended—absurdly hurt. Ana rolled onto her back, oddly surprised to find him so close, levered up on one elbow, the black shadow of his hair falling forward. She inched away. "I smile," she said tightly.

"Not for me, you don't. I don't think I've ever seen you smile at me. Not a real one, anyway."

"That's ridiculous." She frowned. "I *do* smile when you're around."

"If Jiméne's there," he agreed. "Or one of the boatmen, or José—even the *alcalde* at Gorgona got more smiles than I do, and you barely knew him."

"That's not true."

"I think you protest too much, *querida,*" he said. His voice grew lighter. "I've wondered why it seems to be only me. I thought maybe it was because I remind you of the men at Rosalie's. But if you didn't smile at them, I doubt you'd get much business. So maybe it's that I *don't* remind you of them—"

"Be quiet." Ana sounded more cross than she intended. This was what she'd been afraid of tonight. His damn perceptiveness, the way he seemed to see inside her. "I wish you'd really been asleep."

"No, you don't," he said reasonably. "You just would have gone to bed disappointed."

"That's not true." But it was. *It was.*

"Liar." Softly. So softly she barely heard it.

Ana swallowed, wishing she could see his expression, wondering if the tenderness in his voice was reflected on his face and hating herself for wanting it there. She wanted to tell him to go away, to leave her alone, but she was afraid if she said the words, he would do what she asked, and she suddenly realized she would hate that more.

He reached down, touching her cheek, moving aside her hair. When she flinched, he drew away. His sigh was heavy in the darkness.

"Ana," he said, and she heard the need in his voice, the pain. "Smile for me."

"I don't feel much like smiling."

"But I want you to," he urged. "Do what I want for once, Ana. Smile."

Ana bit her lip. There was a vulnerability in his voice that made her more afraid than ever. Smile, he'd said, but she didn't think she *could* smile, she felt so unsettled. But she also sensed he needed it from her tonight.

It was one thing she could do for him, and in the darkness, he couldn't see anyway. "Very well. I'm smiling."

Silence. Ana closed her eyes, trying to restrain a sigh of relief. He believed her.

"I can't see your face," he said suddenly. "*Are* you smiling?"

"Yes. Yes, I'm smiling."

"Describe it to me."

"What?" Ana pushed herself up on her elbows. "Do what?"

"Describe it to me," he said calmly. "I can't see, so you'll have to tell me. You can do that, can't you? It's not too hard?"

"No, of course not."

"Then go on." He leaned back. "Describe it."

"Well." Ana paused. She felt unbelievingly stupid. Describing a smile. She took a deep breath. "My mouth is curving upward."

"Are there dimples?"

"Dimples?" Ana frowned. She couldn't remember, did she have dimples or not? Experimentally she tried smiling. It felt stiff, false, painted on like a clown's, but obediently, she felt along her cheeks. "No," she said finally. "No dimples."

"Is your mouth open or closed?"

"Well—closed."

"Oh." He sounded disappointed. "What about your lower lip?"

"What about it?"

"Sometimes it's crooked when you laugh. Is it now?"

Her lower lip? Ana stared at his shadow, stunned. A flutter of discomfort went through her. He had noticed her lower lip, knew it was crooked when she laughed.

"Well?" he urged.

Ana pushed away her unease, forced her lips into a broader curve and tentatively touched her mouth. "No," she said uncertainly. "It doesn't feel crooked."

"You must not be doing it right."

"Of course I'm doing it right," she objected. "It's my smile, I should know if it's right or not."

"If you were doing it right your lip would be crooked, and your mouth would be open. And there's this funny way you bring your tongue up so it's just against the bottom of your teeth—"

Her discomfort returned, stronger than before. "If you know it so well, you certainly don't need my description." Her voice sounded hoarse.

"If you were doing it right, I wouldn't have to tell you."

"Oh, for God's sake," she said. She stared at his reclining shadow. "This is ridiculous."

"Not to me," he said. He edged closer, his voice dipped, deepened. "I need you to smile now, Ana. Please. Please just—just smile for me."

She wanted to swallow, but she couldn't, her mouth was too dry. He was close, so close. Too close, and she had to do something, anything to keep him from creeping forward.

Frantically Ana scooted to the edge of the pallet. She pasted on another smile, touched the top of her lip with her fingertip. "My upper lip is thin and it curves at the edges," she said breathlessly, hating the tremor she heard in the words.

"Better."

"My cheeks are puffy."

"No dimples?"

"I already told you there were none."

"You might have been lying. You were lying about the smile."

"I was *not.*"

"You were too."

It was then that she realized all remnants of pain were gone from his tone. His words were light, gently mocking. There was laughter in his voice, and Ana stared at him, her discomfort turning to puzzlement. He was teasing her, she was sure. Teasing. No one had ever teased her before, or at least she didn't think they had. She wasn't even sure if that's what he was doing now. Tentatively she tested him. "Really, D'Alessandro—please. I'm tired. My head aches. Let's just go to sleep."

He shook his head, a shiver of movement in the darkness. "No excuses. If you'd only done what I asked you at the beginning, we wouldn't have this problem."

Yes, teasing. Ana felt suddenly safe, relaxed. "There is no problem. I can describe my own smile."

"You haven't done it correctly yet," he pointed out.

"You think you can do it better?"

"Probably." He sat up, leaning forward before she even discerned his movement. Suddenly his fingers were on her lips, forcing the corners of her mouth upward. "There. Like that."

She was so startled she forgot she was uncomfortable, forgot his touch was something to avoid. No one had ever touched her like that. No one—

"My, you feel ferocious," he teased. He tugged gently at her mouth.

Ana felt something churn inside her, a tickle in her stomach, a warmth deep, deep inside her, filling the hollow spot. With it came an unexpected, unasked-for delight. She tried to hold it back, but it exploded through her until she couldn't control it any longer.

She choked. His fingers dropped, and she jerked away, gasping. She clapped her hand over her mouth to stop it. It wouldn't stop. It wouldn't—

Ana snickered. "This . . . isn't . . . a smile," she denied, though it was. It was. She was smiling like a fool, wide-mouthed, choking, *laughing*. "It isn't a smile."

He laughed—a pure, unadulterated shout of pleasure. "Yes, it is. A real smile, Ana. Now describe it for me."

Chapter 20

The next morning, Ana sat at the table watching Dolores strip the peel from plantains with quick, economical movements. The fruit mounded in a terra-cotta bowl, waiting for Serafina to slice and fry it. Right now, the older woman knelt by the fire, holding back her long dark hair with her hand as she fried the fish for breakfast. The fragrance of it filled the *quincha,* making Ana's mouth water and her stomach growl.

She watched them both, working away, and wished she knew how to break the uncomfortable silence. The same tension that had enveloped her last night at dinner stole over her, making her tight and rigid. Except this was worse. Then, at least, she had been able to smile at their laughter, to feel the joy they took in each other. And once D'Alessandro had insisted she sit next to him so he could translate, she had actually felt like a part of things.

Now she only felt useless, and she had the unwelcome thought that Dolores and Serafina were silent because they didn't want to insult her by talking when she couldn't understand.

Ana sighed, looking at the open doorway. The sun slanted in across the floor, the banana trees at the perimeter of the house waved their broad leaves in the slight breeze. She wondered if perhaps it would be better to go outside, to disappear into the underbrush. At least that way, the others would be comfortable, and she wouldn't feel like such a burden.

Ana glanced at *Doña* Melia's room. He was in there now, with Jiméne, trying different methods, bleeding her again—the thought made Ana's stomach turn. He hadn't asked for her help today, and she told herself she didn't care, that she wasn't disappointed. She hated being in that room, watching the red blood swirl into the glass dome, or the fat leeches, drunk and satiated, fall from *Doña* Melia's stomach. It reminded Ana too much of her own mother, of the constant nostrums and prodding, of Dr. Reynolds's fat body crushing her own . . .

She winced, pushing away the thought, and desperately grabbed at the bowl of peeled plantains. Dolores looked up, frowning, and Ana felt herself flush. She took one of the fruits into her hand and pantomimed the motion of slicing.

"Help?" she asked. "Can I help?"

Dolores's frown disappeared, a bright smile rounded her cheeks. She handed Ana the knife, nodding encouragingly. *"Sí, sí. Rebane. Ralo—muy ralo."* The girl held her fingers apart slightly.

Ana stared, then smiled when she finally understood. *Cut them thinly.* Of course. She slid the knife into the soft fruit, then held up a slice for inspection. Dolores nodded her approval, and Ana felt a surprisingly sharp sense of satisfaction.

"Pescado." Dolores pointed to Serafina. *"Pescado."*

Ana followed the direction of her finger, looking at

Serafina, the fire, the skillet. She frowned, shaking her head. "I don't understand."

"Pescado." Dolores raised two fingers to her mouth, pantomimed chewing. Then, when Ana still frowned, she put her hands together, making an undulating, serpentine motion. Something that looked like a snake, only surely they weren't eating snake. They were eating fish—

"Fish," Ana exclaimed. *"Pescado,* fish." She pointed to the skillet, then imitated Dolores's motions until the other girl laughed.

"Sí," Dolores said. "Feesh—*pescado."*

"And this?" Ana asked, patting the table. "The table?"

Dolores paused only a moment. *"La tabla,"* she said, her dark eyes sparkling. She pointed to the clay bowl. *"El cuenco."* Then to the knife in Ana's hands: *"El trinchante."*

Ana laughed, holding up her hands. "Wait, stop—" Carefully, watching for Dolores's approval, she tried the words. *"El cuenco, el trinchante."*

"¡Sí, sí!" Dolores nodded excitedly. She patted her chair. *"La silla."*

At the fire, Serafina looked over her shoulder. She said something to Dolores, and though Ana didn't understand the words, she understood the slight censure in Serafina's tone. Something was wrong. She had done something Serafina didn't approve of, and the thought sent a wave of disappointment crashing through her.

She felt instantly chastened, like a small child who had wanted something too badly and been rebuffed. Ana looked down at the knife in her hands, slowly dragging it through the plantain, forcing herself to concentrate on the thinness of the slice.

"Perdón." Dolores said. Ana looked up. The girl wore an expression of contrition. *"Enseño muy rapidó."*

Ana looked at her blankly.

Dolores took a deep breath and tried again. She pointed to her chest, then quickly, one after the other, to the table, the bowl, the knife. *"Muy rapidó,"* she said again, repeating the motions. *"Muy rapidó."*

Finally, Ana understood—or thought she did. Too fast. Serafina had only told Dolores she was teaching too fast. It wasn't scolding, nothing was wrong. Ana smiled.

Dolores grinned and patted the table again. *"La tabla."*

"La tabla," Ana repeated. "The table."

Dolores nodded. "The table," she tried. Her try at English was so heavily accented, it was all Ana could do to keep from laughing, though she imagined she sounded as bad.

Dolores pointed to the bowl. *"El cuenco."*

"The bowl?" Ana tapped the side of the earthenware. *"El cuenco?"*

Dolores laughed. *"Sí, sí, el cuenco. Muy bueno, amiga, muy bueno."*

Those words Ana understood.

By the time D'Alessandro and Jiméne came out from *Señora* Castañeras's room, Ana and Dolores were laughing uproariously while Serafina was attempting to pantomime something that looked suspiciously like washing her hair. Though Ana couldn't be sure. In the last hour, she had guessed that sewing a dress was plucking a chicken, and cooking tortillas had become ironing.

She was no closer to knowing Spanish than she had been at the start, but it didn't matter. It amazed Ana how much she and Jiméne's sisters could communicate just by sign language, and the reticence that kept her silent this morning disappeared. Serafina and Dolores's laughter at her meager attempts was kind, not mean-spirited. Even Amado joined in at one point, before he left to feed the livestock, and Juan Domingo smiled softly when he walked through the room to go outside.

So she felt warm and happy when Jiméne and D'Alessandro came into the main room. She smiled up at them. *"Buenos días, amigos."*

Dolores laughed and clapped her hands. *"Muy bueno, muy bueno!"*

Jiméne flashed her a smile. "Ah, *cariña, mi hermana* is right. You do very well."

"I've had good teachers," she said. "How is your mother?"

Jiméne glanced at D'Alessandro and sobered immediately. "She will get better, I know it."

Ana looked at her partner. D'Alessandro said nothing, but he looked pale and drawn, and his dark hair was tousled and limp where he'd raked his hand through it—many times, it seemed. His arms were crossed over his chest, his fingers white-knuckled on his elbows, as if only that kept him from shaking.

"Do you have some water?" he asked quietly.

Jiméne nodded, pointing to the door. "Outside, there is some cool water in a jug." Then, as D'Alessandro strode across the floor to the doorway: "Watch for snakes, *amigo*—they like the cold—"

D'Alessandro disappeared outside. Ana shot a glance to Jiméne. "Is he all right?"

Jiméne shrugged. "Who knows with him? I cannot tell." He acted nonchalant, but she saw the worry in his eyes. "You will check on him, *cariña?"*

She got to her feet, instant concern banishing the light laughter of the morning. She pretended casual efficiency, though her stomach knotted and her throat felt tight. "Of course," she said, going to the door. "Of course."

The sun hit her full in the face as she walked outside, and Ana stood there for a moment, blinking and trying to find him in the bright sunshine. In the near distance she heard Amado and Juan shouting orders to each other over the lowing of cattle, and closer to the house howler monkeys filled the air with unearthly yowling. She batted at a cloud of insects and squinted into the light.

But she saw D'Alessandro nowhere. For a moment, she wondered if maybe he had simply disappeared, walked off into the jungle to wander the isthmus like a lost soul. It seemed entirely too possible, and Ana stood there, staring into the jungle, trying to decide if she should follow him.

Then she heard the splashing at the side of the *quincha*. Relief made her light-headed, and she rounded the corner, prepared to confront him, to tell him whatever he wanted to know, prepared to answer any question he might throw at her.

What she was not prepared for was his nakedness.

Ana stopped short, her breath catching in her throat. He had taken off his shirt, and his back was to her as he leaned over the water jug. He lifted the ladle, dipping his head and pouring water over his hair, his neck, his shoulders. Thick strands of hair curled against his skin, shimmered in the sunlight, and droplets spun down the olive skin of his back.

For a moment, she was incapable of moving. She watched the simple grace of his movements, the way he dropped the ladle and cupped water in his hands, splashing it over his face, his chest. Her stomach tightened, her entire body tensed. Then, suddenly, he straightened, throwing back his head so water sprayed from his hair in a sparkling rainbow, and opened his eyes, staring at the bright blue sky for one second before he turned and looked at her.

His eyes widened slightly in surprise, and he wiped at his face with the back of his arm and reached for the shirt he'd left hanging on a splintered piece of cane.

"Sorry," he said tightly, shrugging into it, though he left it unfastened, hanging open so she could see the dark wet curls covering his chest. "I didn't know you were there."

Water dripped from his hair onto his shoulders, making the worn material of his shirt nearly translucent. With effort, Ana drew her gaze to his face.

She clutched her skirt, feeling the reassuring roughness of wool between her fingers, and swallowed. "Is she going to be all right?"

"I don't know." He shrugged. He seemed oblivious of her discomfort, and for that Ana was grateful. He laughed shortly, bitterly. "I'm no better than one of their *curanderos.* For all I know, tamarind water *is* the best cure."

"You don't believe that."

"Don't I?" He raised a dark brow. "I don't know what I believe anymore, Ana. Sometimes—" He looked away, swallowing. "I believe I could actually be killing her. For all I know, the medicine is useless. Sometimes I think it's all up to the patient, whether they want to live or die. Nothing I do makes any difference."

"You cured Jiméne," she reminded him softly.

He threw her an inscrutible look. "Maybe. Or maybe Jiméne's just too damn stubborn to die." He rubbed his face with his hands, then dragged them through his hair. "Ah, Christ, Ana, I can't do this. I can't do this."

"Of course you can," she said, taking a step closer. "Jiméne believes you can, they all believe you can."

He stared at her, and the pain filling his eyes sliced into her heart, made her feel heavy and lost and alone. She hated it, that abandoned expression in his face, that raw anguish. But mostly she hated that he was hurting, and that she could do nothing about it. How could a person not believe in himself? In the end, that was all anyone had. Even when she had nothing else to believe in, Ana had always trusted herself. Had always believed in herself.

But D'Alessandro—Cain—believed in nothing.

"What about you?" he asked hoarsely. "What about you, Ana? Do you believe I can?"

She nodded shortly. "Yes."

That was all, just *yes,* but he squeezed his eyes shut, clenching his fingers at his sides. "I need a drink."

"You can do it without a drink."

"What makes you so sure?" He opened his eyes and stepped forward threateningly, his wet hair flapping forward into his face, his shirttails flying back. "What makes you so sure?"

"I—" Ana moved back, bracing her hand on the wall. Her good intentions fled. This was not a man she knew, this dangerously frightened man. She saw all his rough edges then, and she wanted suddenly to run. The conversation had grown too deep, she was afraid of what she saw in him, of his pain and her own response to it. Afraid of what she'd felt when she came around the corner and first seen him undressed. But for once there was another fear, a deeper one. She was afraid to run, as much as she wanted to. This time it was more important to stay.

She took a deep breath, stepping forward again, straightening her shoulders. "It doesn't matter, what happened with John. It was a long time ago. It's right now that matters—and right now people trust you. They believe in you. The liquor is only false courage, nothing more."

He exhaled sharply. "I don't give a damn if it's false or not," he said with a snarl, frustration ringing in his words. "Dammit, I need a drink!" He grabbed the ladle, throwing it with all his strength. It cracked against the wall, thudded to the ground and bounced, stopping at Ana's feet.

She gasped, stunned by the unexpectedness of his anger. For a moment she stared at the ladle, sure she hadn't really seen him throw it, and then she looked back up at Cain. His gaze was riveted to the ladle, and she saw the surprise in his eyes, and beyond it the fear and pain.

"Ana." He looked at her, his voice harsh and raw, his face white. "Ana, I'm sorry. I didn't—I can't . . . Christ. I'm sorry."

She didn't know what to say, so she said nothing. She stood there, feeling unsure, feeling his need and wanting to help him, wanting to put her arms around him and hold him tightly, to tell him everything would be all right even if she didn't really believe it. He *needed* her to tell him that, but she couldn't move, couldn't bring herself to touch him.

Ana swallowed and clutched her skirt. "I don't know how to help you, Cain," she said finally. "I want to help you, but I don't know how. Tell me how."

He said nothing. She saw the frustration in his face, the fear, yet he said nothing.

Then she remembered. *Comfort me,* he'd said once, and she had done it. Touched him and soothed him. She stepped forward, holding out her hand, and when he made no move to take it, she took a deep breath and kept going, walking into his arms, sliding her hands around his back, pulling him to her. For a moment he stiffened, and she waited for his rejection.

But it didn't happen. Instead, he grabbed her, pressing her face against his shoulder, holding her so tightly she couldn't move, couldn't breathe. She heard the tears in his voice, and desperation. "I don't know what to do. Christ, I'm afraid. I'm so afraid. I can't make it go away. I can't."

She felt his breath on her cheek as he buried his face in her hair, felt the warmth of his hands against her back. He held her as if afraid she would break loose and run away, and Ana was surprised to realize that she didn't want to do that at all. She closed her eyes, wanting to feel his arms even tighter around her, smelling the warm, clean muskiness of his skin. *Hold me,* she thought.

The words spiraled in her mind, growing and growing until she heard nothing else, thought nothing else. *Hold me, hold me, hold me.* She wanted it so badly. So badly.

Too badly. Gently Ana pulled away, stepping back until Cain's hands fell from her arms and he stood there, watching her, waiting.

She knew she should feel fear. She didn't. Only a fierce, unrelenting joy. Only a wish that she had stayed in his arms, a faint regret that she hadn't. The emotions startled her. Her fingers shook as she pushed back a tendril of loose hair. "Are you—are you all right now?" she asked softly, wincing at the banal question.

He smiled. "No."

"Better?"

"Better."

"Well, we—we should get back inside. They're waiting for us." Ana turned on her heel, looking back over her shoulder at him, feeling strangely awkward, strangely joyous—God, she wasn't sure how she felt, except that she didn't want to leave him standing there alone. "They're waiting."

"Then we should go." He buttoned his shirt and stepped toward her.

Together, silently, they walked back to the *quincha* door. Just before they went in, Cain grabbed her arm, stopping her, and when Ana looked back at him, he touched her cheek. Gently, softly. "Thank you," he said.

"You're welcome," she answered, and smiled to herself as she ducked her head and went inside.

Doña Melia was not improving.

Cain watched her anxiously, every two hours giving her another draft of the quinine and opium. That morning he'd added a few grains of tartar emetic as well, hoping the medicine would break the fever. His own desperation was rising, and Jiméne's constant surveilliance didn't help. It only made Cain's hands shake more, and muddied his thinking. It only increased his longing for whiskey.

Jiméne believes you can. They all believe you can. Ana's words from yesterday tormented him. Cain closed his eyes, remembered the feel of her in his arms, the softness of her hair against his face. *I believe you can.*

He didn't know what he would have done if she hadn't said the words. But Ana's quiet conviction had cut through his fear, gave him strength where he had none. *I believe you can.* Just those words, and he had started to believe. Maybe he could do it.

Even now he felt the raw terror of hope, the same terror that made him lose his temper—as if flinging that hope away would make him forget it existed, give him back the Cain D'Alessandro that was familiar: bitter, afraid, useless. The Cain he believed himself to be.

But it was hard to find that man now. Looking into Ana's face, into those golden eyes, made it difficult to keep believing in the old Cain. She refused to see he was a failure, and that surprised him. Pleased him. Frightened him.

He curled his hands into fists, remembering his despair and frustration, and the way she seemed to see it. Her touch had startled him. He expected her to run, to draw back into herself the way she always did. To put up the wall.

But there had been no wall, just as there hadn't been the night before, when she'd relaxed enough to understand that he needed to laugh, to forget. He didn't know what to think about that, and he decided it didn't matter. Since he stopped drinking, he no longer trusted himself even to know what he was feeling, or what was real and what was pure frustration. He only knew that Ana steadied him, that when she was around he felt as if there was something to grab on to, something stable and safe.

Doña Melia stirred restlessly, murmuring in her sleep,

and Cain let his thoughts wander, laying his hand on her forehead to calm her. Her skin was still hot and dry. He glanced at the leech box on the bamboo table, scattered among his vials and instruments, and then at the cups, crusted with blood from the last time he'd bled her.

"Will you bleed her again?" Jiméne's voice came from the doorway, and Cain turned to look at him.

"I think so."

"You have not said—" Jiméne broke off, gazing at his mother with his heart in his eyes. "You have not said what you think, whether she will die."

"Jiméne—" Cain was too worn to be anything but honest with him. "I don't know. I hope not, but I don't know."

"Perhaps we should call in the *curanderos* again, eh?" It was a lame joke, the smile on Jiméne's face held more pain than humor. "They will pray a little, sing a little. Perhaps you should sing."

"I don't suppose 'Oh Susannah' has any special healing powers," Cain said dryly.

"I do not think so," Jiméne said gravely. "It is not even a very good song."

"No."

"No."

They sat there, staring at Jiméne's mother, silent. Outside, a macaw screamed and flew close to the wall, the flapping of its wings loud in the tiny room. As if in response, Enzo shrieked in the main room, his childish footsteps pounded past the opening, innocent laughter bubbling in his wake.

"Ten piedad," Jiméne began softly, his thin voice wavering with the melancholy tune. *"Ten piedad, piedad de mis penas."*

Cain joined in. *"Ten piedad, piedad de mi amor . . ."*

Their voices rose, filling the room, reverberating off the solid cane walls as they sang the sad ballad the boatmen had chanted in Chagres. *Have pity on my sufferings, have pity on my love . . .* It was a song about love lost, and yet it seemed appropriate somehow, the drawling final syllables of each line oddly stirring, full of melodramatic longing. The kind of melody God would like, Cain thought. If God listened . . .

"You are probably killing her with that song," Serafina said in Spanish from the doorway, her beautiful face wrinkled in a frown. "She always hated it, Jiméne, and the two of you sound like fighting cats. Let her rest, for God's sake, and come eat your breakfast." She turned, disappearing back to the main room.

Jiméne looked chagrined. "She is right, *mi hermana.* I had forgot. You will bleed her now, *amigo?*"

Cain picked up the cups and his lancet and nodded.

Chapter 21

Hours later, he thought that the song might have helped as much as anything.

Alone in the room with *Doña* Melia, he stood listening to the fading sounds of the jungle twilight outside. Insects buzzed and chirped beyond the walls, cattle lowed. Closer than that, voices and laughter from the next room faded in and out; he heard the clank of pottery, clinking glass.

Cain squeezed his eyes tight, trying to ignore the sound and the thoughts that came with it. *Not yet,* he told himself, *you don't need the drink yet* . . .

He opened his eyes, forcing himself to concentrate on the woman in front of him. She was finally still. The feverish nightmares must have abated. Perhaps the opium was helping after all. Or perhaps not. Maybe she was only exhausted. He racked his brain for something else to do, something else to try. A doctor at Massachusetts General had once suggested arsenious acid if quinine failed to work. Tomorrow, if she wasn't any better, he would try that. And if that didn't work . . . If that didn't work, he had no other ideas.

Doña Melia sighed, and Cain felt like sighing with her as he once again picked up the leech box. Water sloshed from the perforations, wetting his fingers, and he turned to the table with a frown, grabbing the cotton towel and wiping the stinking liquid from his skin. Christ, he hated those things.

"Jiméne?"

The soft voice startled him so much he nearly dropped the box. Cain swiveled to the doorway. No one was there.

"Jiméne? *¿Mi hijo?*"

My son. It was *Doña* Melia who had spoken. Cain glanced at his patient, sure he was wrong, that it couldn't be her. But her eyes were open, she squinted at him, trying to see him clearly in the lamplight.

"Jiméne?"

"No," Cain said, gaping at her incredulously. "No, *Doña* Melia. *Estoy Cain D'Alessandro, el doctor.*"

She looked at him, then beyond him, and that was when he realized she was delirious. He'd been wrong about the nightmares fading. If possible, it was worse. She had mistaken him for Jiméne. The delirium had increased. Hope fled, leaving behind a dull, throbbing desperation. He touched her cheek and jerked his hand away quickly, disbelievingly. Her skin was cool, damp with sweat. He blinked, staring at her. He had to be imagining it—it was only because he wanted to feel coolness so badly . . .

She clutched his hand, pulling it back to her face. "Send my son to me," she said, the Spanish words soft, barely understandable. "Or was I dreaming he was here?"

"No, you weren't dreaming," he said. Though surely *he* was. Surely he'd fallen asleep. He would wake up soon and find this was all a dream . . .

Carefully he laid his hand again on her head, her cheek, the curve of her neck. No, he wasn't dreaming. He wasn't imagining it. Her fever had broken. At long last, it had broken, and Cain fought the overwhelming urge to fall to his knees and thank God. He couldn't believe it, wouldn't believe it. Christ, he didn't want to hope this much for something.

But he couldn't push it away this time. This victory was so unexpected he couldn't quite believe it was real. Half of him wanted to shout and dance and sing with relief while the other half wanted to keep it secret until he could be sure—until someone told him it was all right, that *Doña* Melia was well and it was all due to him.

The family had to be told, he reminded himself. Even if it was a false alarm, they had to be told. He forced his voice through the lump of relief in his throat. "Jiméne—the others—they're waiting for you to get well, to call for them . . . Let me get them for you."

He nearly fell over the stool as he backed away from the bed, stumbling to the doorway of the room. Bracing a hand on the door jamb, he leaned forward, unable to keep the smile from his face.

They sat around the table, passing bowls of food. He'd forgotten it was dinnertime, though Serafina had called him, and they were all eating and laughing and talking. Even Ana.

She looked up and saw him. He thought he saw happiness in her eyes. Happiness, and welcome—

Jiméne spun in his chair, throwing down his tortilla and rising when he saw who Ana was staring at. His eyes were black with fear. *"Dios,"* he whispered. "Is she—"

Cain shook his head. "No, it's not that," he assured Jiméne. "No, it's—her fever's broken. It's broken and she's asking for everyone."

Jiméne's mouth fell open. "This is—you are sure?"

"I'm sure."

"This is not just a—a rest?"

Cain's smile died; he tried to suppress the weariness in his voice. "I don't know, Jiméne. Fevers are . . . Well, no one really understands them. It might come back." He paused. "But I think it won't."

Jiméne closed his eyes. *"Gracias a Dios,"* he said briefly before he turned to his brothers and sisters and translated Cain's news.

Their reactions were instantaneous. Dolores jumped to her feet, clapping her hands in joy, Amado shouted, and Juan took Serafina into his arms for a smiling, grateful hug.

Only Ana remained sitting. Cain felt her gaze on him, and he looked up, catching her eye. A tentative smile touched her lips—the smile he'd been waiting for, as small as it was, and joy rushed through him. He wanted to touch her, to hug her the way Juan embraced Serafina. She was as responsible for this as he was—more so, since she'd given him the strength to go on. And right now he needed to feel her arms around him, to hear her soft "I told you so," her reassurance that everything would be all right, the fever wouldn't return.

He'd barely taken two steps toward her when Jiméne's family crowded around him, pulling him from the doorway while they asked questions, called him a miracle worker. Dolores kissed him and Serafina hugged him, and Juan's handshake was warm and grateful.

"Yes, yes, you're welcome," he found himself saying over and over. "You should go in to see her, she's asking for you . . ."

Jiméne clapped his arm around Cain's shoulders. *"Amigo,* you are truly a savior. Perhaps we will build a shrine to you, eh?"

"A simple thank-you would be fine," Cain said dryly.

"Then thank you—*gracias*—from the bottom of my heart." Jiméne bowed. "I am in your debt, *amigo."*

"Wonderful. Now, if you would let me—"

"A celebration!" Jiméne shouted. "That is what we must have—a celebration! A quiet one of course, so Mama may sleep—" He glanced up sharply as Amado pushed through the doorway. "Do not rush her, Amado! One at a time, please!" He looked back at Cain. "Now, what would you like?"

Ana. The thought rushed through him. Cain looked over at her again, wanting to touch her so badly he felt physical pain. She was watching them, toying with her spoon, and when she caught his eye she pushed back her chair, rose from the table. Cain felt desperate to get away, to get to her, to touch her.

"Excuse me, Jiméne," he said, starting to brush past Jiméne's hand. "Ana!"

She stopped, glancing over her shoulder.

"You are the wisest, best doctor I have ever known!" Dolores barreled from her mother's room, throwing her arms around his neck, pressing him into the wall as she hugged him. Cain reached up, trying to disentangle himself, but she only squeezed him tighter. "Mama is well, and a thousand thank-yous cannot express my joy."

"A party," Jiméne said again. "Do you not think so, Dolores? Where is Juan's guitar?"

Cain looked over Dolores's dark head. Ana stood there, staring at him, hesitating until Dolores dropped her arms and stepped aside. But before he could move, Serafina was in her place, hugging him, kissing him. Ana turned away, and Cain had to restrain himself from throwing Serafina aside and chasing after Ana as she moved to the door.

But he couldn't move. Serafina was whispering tearful thank-yous in his ear, and he was sure Ana wouldn't wait, sure he would have to stand there and watch helplessly as she walked out the door.

Desperately he nodded at Serafina, murmuring words

he didn't remember, as gently as he could pushing her away, breaking past her.

Just as he cleared the circle of family, he looked up, and relief burst through him so intensely his knees were weak. Ana was there, standing only a few feet away from him, waiting with a smile on her face and joy in her eyes.

Behind him, he heard the first strummings of Juan's guitar. He held out his hand. *"Voy baylár con usted, mi corazón,"* he said.

She laughed then, all open-mouthed and crooked-lipped, the smile he loved. "What does that mean?"

"It means: I am going to dance with you," *my heart.* But he didn't say the last words, couldn't say them, because he didn't want her to run. It would kill him to see her run.

"Don't I have a choice?" she asked.

His gut seized, Cain looked at her helplessly. He couldn't bear it if she refused him. Not now. *Please God, not now.* "Of course," he said rawly. "Of course."

Her smiled widened, she took his hand. "Then I would love to dance with you, Doctor."

His warm fingers curled around hers tightly, as if he was afraid she would change her mind and run away. Ana squeezed his fingers reassuringly, following him willingly as he pulled her with him to the middle of the *quincha.* Juan was seated at the table, his nimble fingers moving over the strings of the guitar, filling the room with its warm, woody tones.

From the corner of her eye, Ana saw Jiméne bow to Dolores and grab her hand. In moments, brother and sister were sweeping across the floor, twirling and tapping in a vibrant, laughing dance that Ana had never seen before while the others clapped and stomped in time to the music.

Cain stopped, turning to look at her, and the smile in his eyes was so blindingly bright it burst through Ana, sending a shiver of pure happiness running down her spine. It occurred to her that she liked seeing him this way, liked his swelling confidence, as fragile and uncertain as it was. She had never seen him like this, and he wore his newfound pride well, much better than he'd worn hopeless defeat.

But it was a little frightening too, seeing such confidence in his eyes. In a way, this was more dangerous than ever, much more threatening.

The thought had no place here, not now. She wanted to celebrate with him, wanted to make this night as perfect for him as she could. God, after all his struggle, it was so good to see him smile.

"Ready?" he asked.

She nodded, grabbing her skirt and holding it out from her legs. "Ready."

He swallowed—a little nervously, she thought. "It's been a long time since I danced," he said.

"Not so long."

He lifted a questioning brow.

"At Gorgona," she explained. "You danced there—or tried to."

Something dark and unreadable crossed his gaze, his smile wavered. "Oh. I—I don't remember."

Of course. Of course he wouldn't remember. Ana cursed herself inwardly, wishing she'd thought not to bring it up. For some reason, it hurt her—physically hurt her—to see that flash of fear on his face.

So she stepped forward, into his arms, and took his other hand, placing it firmly at her waist. "It doesn't matter," she said matter-of-factly. "It was a long time ago. Now, shall we dance?"

His smile steadied. Together they took the first, tentative steps. Ana hadn't danced in months, not since Rosalie's Christmas dance, but she felt as if it had been much longer. They took it slowly, out of rhythm with Juan's playing. One two three. One two three. She heard the count in her ears, followed Cain's unsure steps. *One two three.*

"I told you, it's been a long time," he said, laughter in his voice.

Ana smiled up at him. "You're a fine dancer."

"Liar." He chuckled. His brown eyes were warm, his fingers tightened around hers. "But thank you."

His words ran over her like honey, and Ana looked down at her feet. A simple thank-you, but it made her feel warm and good and needed. It was funny how Cain could put more meaning and emotion into his words than anyone she had ever known. It was what had always frightened her about him, that honesty.

But she didn't feel frightened now.

The tempo increased, the music swelled around them, and she felt him gain confidence, heard the vibration of his laughter in his chest as he swirled her into the dance, forgetting the careful counting, even forgetting the steps as he moved her around the floor. She let go of her skirt, and it swirled around his legs, making him stumble. They were moving so fast she felt dizzy. His hair whipped her face, and her straggling braid slapped against his shoulder.

Ana wanted to laugh out loud. How long it had been since she'd felt such simple pleasure, taken such simple pleasure? Too long. Much too long. The last time she had danced like this was with her mother, when she was just a child, and there had been nothing dark and horrible and sick in the world. She had laughed then, Ana remembered. Laughed and danced and thought the world would always be like that.

It wasn't, she knew that now, but Ana suddenly wondered if she had made a mistake by throwing away other things with her hope. Things like uncomplicated, heart-soaring joy. Things like laughter that lifted the shadows and friendship to push away the fear.

She had missed those things, and it had taken Cain to

bring them back to her. It had taken Cain to fill the hollow spot inside her, to make the loneliness go away.

As the music swirled around them, Ana had an overwhelming urge to move closer, to press against him the way she had yesterday, to feel again the wiry curls beneath the worn linen of his shirt, to feel his too-long hair brush against her cheek, her throat. His scent filled her nostrils: bitter quinine, acidic tamarind, and his own warm muskiness.

She closed her eyes briefly, swallowing, suddenly hot and flushed and a little bit faint.

The music stopped, and Ana felt a strange, lingering disappointment when Cain stopped as well. He dropped his hand, released hers. There was a sudden chill where his touch had been, a tiny shiver.

But except for that, he didn't move away. He stood close, so close she saw the pulse in his strong throat, the flutter of the curls at his open collar from her breath.

"Thank you," he said slowly. "For the dance. And for everything else."

"I—" She didn't know what to say. Ana looked up at him, trying to steady the trembling in her fingers, the quick, loud pounding of her heart. The room spun around her. "I—you're welcome."

His eyes were dark. There was some emotion in them, something she couldn't name, something uncertain and yearning. It pulled at her, pierced her heart and her stomach, made her feel warm and shaky.

He swallowed, took a half step forward. "Ana—"

"Ana!" Jiméne came rushing up, his face lit with happiness, flushed with excitement. "Juan is about to start another dance." He flashed a glance to Cain. "This one is mine, *amigo.*"

Cain stepped back again. His eyes were shielded. "Of course."

Ana felt a stab of regret. But before she could object, Jiméne was pulling her back to the middle of the room, the music started, and she was whirling across the floor, trying desperately to keep up with Jiméne's long, erratic steps.

She looked for Cain. He leaned against the wall, arms crossed over his chest, and his eyes were trained on her. Soft brown eyes, watching her spin across the floor, watching her laugh at Jiméne's bad jokes. Never letting her out of his sight.

The thought heated her. Suddenly her palms felt moist and hot and her throat breathlessly tight. Ana forced her gaze from Cain, focused on the motion of her feet. Jiméne was not a good dancer, and he stumbled over her toes, laughing as he did so, his enthusiasm making up for his clumsiness.

"I am as bad as the ox, eh?" he joked.

Ana smiled. "Worse than an ox, Jiméne. Much worse."

"I fear dancing is not one of the skills I was taught."

"You didn't dance in New York? I'm surprised you were invited to any parties."

Jiméne raised a brow, his mouth quirking in a grin. "All the mamas in New York believed I was injured in the war," he confided. "In my foot."

Ana laughed, and Jiméne swung her around in greater and greater arcs. The room flashed by her, she felt strangely light-headed.

"Wait, Jiméne—" She gripped his hand, wishing the room would stop spinning.

He slowed immediately, staring down into her face. "*Cariña,* you look hot. Would you care for some wine?"

"Wine? No. No." Ana shook her head, trying to clear away the sudden fogginess. "I'm fine. We were just going too fast, that's all."

"I think perhaps you should sit down, *amiga.*"

The music slowed, and Ana felt herself being pulled toward the table. Truthfully, something to drink sounded wonderful. But not wine. After all, Cain was still here, still awake, and she didn't want to tempt him. She looked over her shoulder, searching for him, but he was no longer against the wall. Or maybe he was, but her eyes were so unfocused she couldn't see. And now her head was pounding, just a bit, behind her eyes.

"My, that dancing—" She touched her forehead, blinking at the brightness of the room. "I must have been more tired than I thought."

"Of course." Jiméne's brows came together in a frown. "Just sit down, *cariña,* and I will get you something to drink. Then we will fetch D'Alessandro."

"Cain." She nodded. "Yes, do that, won't you, Jiméne?"

She sank down onto the bench with relief.

He wanted to kiss her. Cain watched her in Jiméne's arms, watched her hair flying behind her, the dark brown touched with red-gold light from the lamp. She laughed, unreservedly, sincerely, and the sound made him feel strangely weak and out of control. Christ, he loved that sound, he could spend the rest of his life listening to it, seeing the quick flash of humor in her tawny eyes, the flirtatious lift of her shoulder.

Yes, he wanted to kiss her, to make love to her. The memory of the other night came rushing back, the soft heaviness of her hair in his fingers, the warmth of her skin, her scent.

Cain's stomach clenched painfully. He closed his eyes for a moment, swallowing back the desire, wishing his emotions weren't so damned raw. Hell, all she had to do was *look* at him and he was hard, and it had been so damned long since anything like that had happened he wasn't sure what to do about it.

He wondered if he was imagining her melting toward him, if her smile really was warmer, if he was really seeing the flash of desire in her eyes.

And then she looked up, caught his gaze across the

room, and he saw the warm flush move over her skin, her sparkling smile before Jiméne swept her away again.

He was not imagining it. The knowledge brought heat curling into his stomach, his loins. It was all he could do to keep himself from rushing up to them and grabbing her from Jiméne's arms, pulling her outside into the soft moonlight so he could touch her the way he wanted to, feel the soft heaviness of her breasts and hear the startled intake of her breath.

Christ, he was out of control. Cain took a deep breath, leaned his head back against the wall, trying to concentrate on the conversations around him, trying not to think about her pink cheeks and the breathlessness of her laughter.

The music slowed, and he looked up, watching in surprise as Jiméne guided Ana back to the bench. She clung to him, her fingers tight around his arm, her eyes bright, and Cain felt a sudden, irrational stab of jealousy. Jealousy that had him walking across the room before he had time to think about it.

Jiméne bent over Ana, a concerned look on his face. He glanced up at Cain's approach. "Ah, there you are, *amigo*. Ana is not feeling well."

"Not feeling well?" Cain frowned and looked at her, his desire forgotten in sudden concern. "You said nothing of it before."

She waved Jiméne back. "I've told him it's nothing. Just a headache. I'm sure it's just the excitement—"

"You feel warm to me, *cariña,*" Jiméne disagreed.

She laughed quietly, but when she pushed back a loose tendril of hair, her hands shook slightly. "I'm fine. Just tired."

Cain felt the first edge of uneasiness.

"She had the headache," Jiméne said, straightening. "Go ahead, Doctor, give her a cure."

Cain eyed her closely. "Would you like something, Ana?"

"No, thank you." She shuddered, smiling weakly. "I'm fine. Only a little tired. I—I'm not used to dancing."

She still looked flushed, perhaps too flushed. And her shining eyes, maybe they were too bright. Cain sat beside her, putting his hand to her forehead. "You do feel warm," he said.

"You see? I told you, *cariña,* you are not well."

Cain leaned closer. "How do you feel?"

She looked at him, her eyes searching his face, and he felt her hesitate, as if loath to tell him anything at all. Cain's gut tightened, but he didn't move away. "Well?" he urged.

"I feel . . . shivery," she said with a deep breath. "And warm. Yes, I do feel . . . warm."

"Some fresh air, D'Alessandro?" Jiméne asked.

Fresh air. Cain nodded. He rose and offered her his hand. "Come on, *querida,* Jiméne's right. You could probably use some air."

She put her hand in his, let him pull her to her feet. She stumbled slightly, falling forward, bracing her hands on his chest before she pulled away again. She smiled shyly and gracefully tucked an errant curl behind her ear. "Maybe you're right. Some fresh air would do me—" She tripped again when he started to walk, clenching her fingers on his sleeve. "Sorry. This is . . . strange."

An alarm went off in his brain. Cain gripped her hand. "Strange?"

She didn't shrug him off. In fact, she grasped his hand as if she needed the support and closed her eyes. "My head is pounding. But I felt . . . fine. I felt fine earlier."

"But warm."

She licked her lips hesitantly. "Yes. I felt warm."

"And now? Besides your head, how do you feel?"

"Maybe a little dizzy."

Fear made a tight knot in his chest. He grabbed her

shoulders, turned her to face him. "Ana. Ana, listen to me." He gave her a little shake, forcing open her eyes, which had fluttered shut. "Ana—are you thirsty?"

She pulled away weakly. "Well, yes. Yes, I am, now that you mention it." She glanced at the water jug sitting near the front door, and started toward it, stumbling a little, tossing back her hair. "I'll be right back," she called over her shoulder. "I'll just get something to drin—"

She fell forward, catching herself on the table, sinking down onto the bench. "My God," she choked. "I feel terrible. Pounding—this—this pounding."

In that moment, Cain's joy was gone, relief fled. She had the fever. He had plunged back into the nightmare.

Chapter 22

She fought him when he tried to lift her into his arms, but when he finally did, she barely uttered a sound of protest, and her body was limp and heavy. It was all the proof Cain needed.

Juan came hurrying over. "What is it?" He spoke rapidly, in Spanish. "What is wrong with Ana?"

"The fever." The words felt forced from Cain's throat. Just the thought of it filled him with terror. He looked down at Ana's face. Her eyes were closed, she was half conscious, pushing fretfully at the strands of hair trailing over her face. The red flush on her cheeks was the only color to her skin.

"The fever?" Jiméne frowned. "Surely you are wrong, *amigo*. Moments ago she was fine. It is only just the headache."

"As it was with Mama," Juan broke in quietly. "You were not here, Jiméne, but it was the same with her. One moment she was fine, the next . . ." He shrugged.

"But—but I cannot believe—"

"Don't believe another time, Jiméne," Cain advised

grimly. He glanced at the thin pole ladder to the loft. "Just tell me where I can put her. The loft is out of the question."

Juan pointed to a doorway close to the front of the room. "There," he said. "Serafina and I will move back upstairs. Enzo and Amado will be with Jiméne."

"I'm sorry."

Juan shook his head. "You are welcome to anything of ours, *amigo*. For what you did for Mama, we are in your debt."

Cain didn't argue. His strength was not back completely, and he was quickly finding Ana's delicate frame a solid one. His arms ached. He went through the doorway, brushing past hammocks to the roughly made bedstand in the corner.

"My head hurts," Ana murmured, lolling her head against his shoulder. "Pounding."

Cain laid her on the bed, then looked at Jiméne, who stood in the doorway. "Get my case," he ordered shortly, turning back to Ana, laying his hand against her cheek. She was hot, damned hot. How the hell had it sneaked up on her so quickly? He tried to remember if she'd said anything, done anything to show the onset of fever, but there was nothing. Nothing. Christ, what kind of a doctor was he that he hadn't been able to see it coming?

A bad doctor . . .

Ana moved beneath his hand, her eyes fluttered open. "Cain," she murmured sleepily, looking up at him. "It's too hot." She pulled at her collar, trying for a moment to loosen the buttons until her hand fell limply against her breast. "Open a window, please."

He touched her forehead. Her eyes fell shut again. Gently he smoothed tendrils of her dark hair from her face, traced her jaw to the jet buttons at her throat. One by one, he unfastened them, peeling back the sweat-soaked wool. He paused just before her breasts when he noticed she wore no chemise. Of course, he'd forgotten he had thrown away her corset. There was nothing but wool next to her skin—

"Here." Jiméne sounded breathless. He handed Cain his medical case. "I gathered up what was in Mama's room. It is all there."

"Thank you."

"This is—" Jiméne paused, as if gathering strength. "This is the same fever, *sí?*"

Cain couldn't look at him. He clutched the case in his hands. "I think so."

"What will you do?"

Cain shrugged. His hands were trembling as he flipped open the case and stared down into it, seeing the leech box, the glass cups, the lancet, and below that all the medicines. He knew them by heart, knew what they did, and it was never any guarantee. Slowly, forcing every move, he drew out the bottle of quinine salts.

"Jiméne," he said quietly, "will you get some water, please?"

He heard Jiméne walk away, and Cain curled his fingers around the bottle, trying to calm his shaking. It didn't help, and he finally put the medicine aside, and his case, and reached for the woven blanket folded on the end of the bed. Quietly he shook it out and laid it over her.

She became restless almost immediately, shoving at the blanket, trying to roll out from beneath it. He tucked it around her shoulders and unbuttoned the rest of her gown, hiding her nakedness from himself and anyone else, working beneath the covers until he had drawn the wool down to her waist. Carefully, trying not to touch her skin, he slid it from her hips, pulled it from beneath the blanket and let the dress fall in a heap on the floor.

Cain closed his eyes briefly in relief, opening them to find she'd relaxed marginally. One slender pale arm trailed from beneath the blanket. Her long, heavy hair was caught beneath her head, trapping her, and gently Cain lifted her shoulders, pulling the loosened braid aside, letting the rich mahogany length of it fall over the side of the bed.

He couldn't take his eyes off her. Her full mouth moved slightly, as if she were talking in dreams, her eyelids fluttered, and her fingers clenched. She looked as if she were only sleeping, but Cain knew better. Soon this fitful, dreaming state would give way to delirium, and after that, to motionless, deathlike sleep. It was the stage he dreaded most, the stage that kept him constantly at the bedside, watching, waiting for the slightest breath, gulping wine to ease the worry.

Cain swallowed, burying the craving, turning away. Sometimes it never got to that stage. Sometimes patients died long before that.

But she wouldn't. He murmured the words to himself, as if giving them sound would make it real. She wouldn't die. He wouldn't let her. He could be wrong, after all. This might be nothing but a minor illness, something soon over.

He tried to make his mind believe it. But the words were only words, and as he stared down at Ana's fevered face he had a strong urge to hold her so closely death wouldn't dare take her away.

Already Cain felt it, that sharp, aching concern that made him watch her every breath, stare at her flushed face for any signs of life. The worry was so intense he felt sick and nauseated.

He had a yearning for whiskey so strong it nearly left him faint. It was all he could do to push it aside long enough to reach for the quinine. His fingers trembled as he pulled out the glass stopper. It slipped from his grasp and bounced on the bamboo-matted floor, rolling out of his reach. Shaking, he set the bottle down.

"Here is the water." Jiméne hurried into the room,

stopping with a frown—so quickly water splashed from the jug he held. "What is the matter, D'Alessandro? You look lost."

Cain took a deep breath, raking his hand through his hair. "I'm all right."

"Good. That is good." Jiméne didn't look quite convinced. He stepped farther into the room, setting the jug at Cain's feet before he glanced at the bed. "It is hard to believe, eh? That she was fine only moments ago."

"Juan says the fever hits fast."

"Yes. Juan says that." Jiméne nodded soberly. "What do you say?"

Cain shot Jiméne an irritated glance, trying to hide the fear his words roused.

Jiméne ignored the look, crossing his arms over his chest. "Will you bleed her?"

"No, not at first," Cain said softly. "Maybe later, if the fever doesn't break."

"You bled Mama."

"Your mother had been ill for days," Cain snapped. "Ana may not be so sick."

"Of course," Jiméne said quietly. "Of course you are right. She will probably be better tomorrow."

"Probably."

Jiméne hesitated. "Do you need my help, *amigo?*"

"No." Cain spoke quickly. The last thing he wanted was for Jiméne to go, but he couldn't bear the thought of Castañeras watching him shake, couldn't stand the weakness. No, better if he was alone here. Better if no one saw how frightened he was. What was it Ana had said the other night? *"You don't always hide your emotions very well."* No, he didn't. Perhaps she was right. Perhaps it was time he tried.

He looked at Jiméne. "No," he said again, "I don't need your help."

"Fine then." Jiméne nodded. "I will be near if you need me."

"Good." Cain turned his back, listening to Jiméne's footsteps going to the door. "Oh, Castañeras—"

"Yes?"

Cain still didn't look at him. "Maybe—could you ask Serafina to make up some tamarind water?"

There was silence. Cain glanced over his shoulder. Jiméne stood in the doorway, one hand on the frame, his face suddenly white and strained, his brown eyes large.

"Of course," he said quickly, ducking his head, turning away. "Of course."

Ana drifted in and out of dreams. Burning hot, elusive dreams that wavered before her eyes and disappeared. First she was with her mother—or no, it wasn't her mother, but Rosalie. Scolding, condemning. There was blood all over the floor. Ana was slipping in it, falling, trying to escape, desperate to escape. They were after her; she was so frightened she felt the splintery rope of the hangman's noose around her throat, tightening, tightening . . .

Then there were smooth, cool hands on her forehead, stroking back her hair, taking away the heat and the feel of the noose. Comforting, soft. Like her mother's hands but not like them. Bigger, gentler. Better. A man's hands. Benjamin Whitehall's hands. His face was suddenly in front of her, leering, his eyes sharp with anticipation. She heard the slash of the whip, felt it across her cheek. Sharp, intense pain whipped through her. Ana jerked away, but the hands wouldn't let her escape. They were holding her prisoner, trapping her. Stroking her.

Soothing her.

She faded back into nothingness.

He hadn't left her bedside in forty-eight hours. The others had come and gone, bringing him food he couldn't eat, refilling the water jug so he could keep mixing the potion of quinine and sugar and mint. He'd changed her blankets four times, since she often violently refused to drink the mixture, and even after he forced it down her throat she vomited it up again. Across the back of his chair hung a chemise Serafina had brought for Ana to wear, but he hadn't put it on her yet, preferring to wait until she was calm enough to keep the medicine down.

She was a little calmer now, he thought. Or maybe it was just his imagination, since he wanted so badly for it to be true. He'd started adding opium to the medicine, hoping it would settle her stomach, or at least bring her dreamless sleep. Not for the first time, Cain wondered what she dreamed about. What caused her convulsive tossing and turning and why she sometimes threw off his hands with a cry of fear.

Again he wished he knew something about her. Something more than the fact that she was a whore who killed a man. He wished he knew why she hated doctors and who she really was besides the illegitimate daughter of a Russian nobleman. Christ, he didn't even know her last name.

Cain pried his gaze away, trying not to hear her labored breathing. He didn't know anything about her. Not who she was or what she felt. Nothing. She might die tomorrow, and he would have nothing left of her except a gold Spanish comb that she thought was Russian. Nothing except that and the longing for her that he suspected would never go away.

And the guilt. Oh, yes, he would have that too. He wondered if he could survive it this time.

"D'Alessandro?"

Jiméne's soft voice broke into Cain's thoughts. He swiveled on his stool, blinking to focus. But his eyes were too bleary. He rubbed them with his fingers.

"Yes?"

"It is late. Time for you to sleep."

"Sleep?" Cain snapped awake. "No, I'm fine. I can't leave."

"I will keep watch for a while," Jiméne said. "Tell me what to do."

"I can't tell you what to do." Cain shook his head. He motioned to the table. "There's too much. I can't leave."

"It is not a matter of *can't,* my friend." Jiméne moved closer, kneeling beside him. "You *will* sleep—I will ask for Juan's help to make sure if I must. You can do her no good this way."

The cold bite of fear gnawed into Cain's stomach. "You don't understand. I can't leave her. What if she wakes? What if the fever gets worse?"

"Then I will call you," Jiméne said calmly. "You must sleep, or you will be no good to her."

"Thanks, but—"

"You are not the only one who cares for her, *amigo.*" Jiméne's voice was infinitely soft.

The words defeated Cain. He nodded slowly and rose from the stool. "Wake me in an hour," he said, moving to the strung hammock in the corner of the room. "One hour."

"One hour," Jiméne repeated solemnly.

For four days, Cain watched her because he could do nothing else. He sat there, watching, and knowing the quinine wasn't helping, and he was going to have to cut her slice into that lovely, peachy skin and watch her blood boil up into a glass cup. Put slimy, stinking leeches on her stomach and watch them sink their nasty little teeth into her and grow fat.

He knew it, had known for the last several hours that he had no other choice. He'd already waited too long, hoping against hope that the medicine would save her, hoping God wouldn't force him to go through with the farce of failing. But no, he wanted her to live too badly, he should have expected the punishment of watching her die.

Because he *was* watching it. Her breathing was shallow, her lips parched. There hadn't even been delirium, nothing but this calm acceptance of the fever. Nothing but motionless, comalike sleep.

He swallowed, pulling the lancet off the table, thinking again of wine, wishing he had a glass to steady his hands. He wanted it. He wanted it so much he could barely think, and he picked up the glass cups and tried to focus on them in an attempt to alleviate the hunger. They were still stained with *Doña* Melia's blood, and he tried to think of Jiméne's mother strong enough now to talk with her children a few hours each day, tried to take comfort from it. She had survived.

And he didn't know why. *He didn't know why.* The lack of knowledge tormented him, kept him awake. If only he could remember what he'd done, if only he knew if it had been his efforts, and not the *curanderos'*, that had made her well, that had cured Jimené . . .

He opened his eyes and unfolded the lancet, staring at it for a moment, watching the lamplight glint on the metal. It was already late; everyone else in the house was asleep. He had deliberately waited until now to do this—it was going to take all his concentration, every ounce of his strength. What he didn't want were questions and concerns. What he didn't want was kindness.

Swallowing, he lifted her arm from where it lay over her chest, stretching it out before him. He saw her pulse beneath the skin, eyed the perfect place to make the incision. His fingers tightened on her wrist and he licked his lips.

Then he cut. A small cut, but he felt dizzy when it turned into a line of red, and then a drop. Quickly, with trembling fingers, he turned the cup over it and squeezed the rubber ball. Quickly, efficiently. As he'd done it hundreds of times before.

The vacuum brought her blood swirling up into the small glass dome, washing away the stain of *Doña* Melia's, making his stomach clench. Cain reached for the box of leeches.

He felt nauseated, frightened. His hands shook as he lifted off the lid, the bile rose in his throat when the wormlike creatures lifted their heads, on the scent. He knew exactly what to do with them, where to place them on her smooth, flat stomach. Six leeches if American, only three if they were Spanish or Swedish. He wasn't sure which these were. How long had he kept them anyway? How many people had they helped him kill?

The thought brought with it a craving for drink so intense Cain had to clench his fists to keep from giving in to it. Deep red wine, or bourbon . . . Anything to bring that soothing, warm sense of confidence. Ah, Christ, he needed it now. Especially now. His mouth was dry, and his head spun. His fingers curled around the box. One of the leeches moved toward his hand, touching his skin. Cain squeezed his eyes shut and then looked again at her, at the soft shadow of lashes against her cheek, her partly opened mouth. *Please God,* he prayed. *Give me strength.*

He prayed, though he expected nothing. God had abandoned him long ago. If his mother were to be believed, it had happened at his birth. Abandoned by both God and mother during a painful delivery amid a lightning storm. Prophetic. His mother had even given him a special name to mark the occasion: Cain. The biblical bad seed. The murderer.

At least he and Ana had something in common. They were both murderers. Cain squeezed his eyes tight, trying to control the relentless fear welling up in him. God had no mercy for murderers, or at least that's what he'd heard. *Please, let it not be true,* he prayed. *Be merciful to her. Take me if you want, but be merciful to her.*

Cain opened his eyes and stared at the ceiling, watching the tiny gnats dart from the shadows. If the truth were told, he wasn't sure he even believed in God anyway. At least not in a benevolent God. No, the God he knew would not only take Ana's life, but make him responsible for it.

And you would be responsible. It would be your fault this time too. The voice was there again, insinuating itself into his brain, soft and feminine and beguiling, like an old friend—comforting and frightening at the same time.

His strength to resist it was gone. Without drink, without Ana, he was nothing. He had no will. The voice filled his mind, grew until it was all he heard, all he knew. *You can't do it. You don't have the skill. You'll fail because you always fail.*

Cain clenched his fists, trying to fight the voice. But it was too strong. He'd listened to it for a lifetime, heard it in the soft whispers of his mother and his father's thunder, and then again later—much later—in the quiet, reassuring voice of John Matson. *I trust you, Cain.*

The words were so simple. So easy. *I trust you, Cain.* The only words he'd ever heard that didn't tell him he was nothing, would always be nothing. The only words that made him believe in himself.

But in the end, they had been the worst words of all.

He heard a whimper in the darkness and started before he realized it was his. "No," he whispered. "No—"

But it was too late. The condemning voices were already in his head, whirling around, faint echoes of a past he didn't want to remember. With them came the visions. John Matson's confident smile even through the excruciating pain, the faith in his words. *"You can . . . do this, Cain, you know you . . . can. We . . . studied this. Remember? Just pretend . . . just pretend I'm that soldier . . . from a few weeks ago. Just . . . another patient."*

Cain closed his eyes.

"Do it quickly—one rapid . . . one rapid cut. Put your . . . hand below . . . Where the hell is that assistant? God . . ."

He could smell it now, the scent of ether and blood and the stench of infection. Could feel the heaviness of the knife in his hand. The knowledge swam in his head. Secure the patient, work quickly, use the right knife—not too broad a blade. Cut from the in'ner side outward, ready the saw . . .

Christ, he wanted it out of his head forever.

"John . . . John, listen to me. I can't do it. Not without an assistant. I can't do it. Christ, the ether isn't even working—"

"I . . . can't feel a thing. Hurry now."

"I don't remember—"

"You do remember. There's no one else, and you're a . . . doctor, Cain. I trust you. Believe me, I trust you . . ."

Cain shoved his hands against his ears, trying to drown out the voices. But the memories came back any way. The dim light shining in his eyes, blinding him, making the sweat break out on his forehead even though the room was frigidly cold. The burning taste of the bourbon he and John traded back and forth, because the ether wasn't strong enough, could never be strong enough. John's wrists straining against the cords that secured him to the bed. The stain of infection moving through veins that were bright red beneath his skin.

"Do it, Cain! Dammit, do it now!"

And he had. He'd cut into the leg, his hands shaking, the sweat dripping into his eyes so he could barely see. The blood had coursed over his hands, blinding him further, forcing him to cut by feel, making his fingers slip on the saw handle when he set it to the bone. Blood dripping on the rough pieces of cording used to tie off the arteries, making them so slippery he could barely feel to fasten the knots. Ah, God, there was so much blood. So much . . .

Too much.

It pooled on the floor, puddles of it soaking into the gore-polished wood, dripping from the table. And he couldn't stop it, didn't know why there was so much, couldn't think as John Matson's life ebbed away beneath his eyes. He could do nothing except watch the only man he'd ever loved, his only real family, bleed to death.

And it was his fault. It wasn't until later, when John lay still and silent, that Cain found an extra piece of cording on the floor.

There were supposed to be no extra pieces.

The panic washed over him again, just as it had three years ago. Panic and horror and self-recrimination.

If only he'd checked the lengths of cord before he bound the wound . . .

If only he'd trusted his instincts and waited another hour for the assistant . . .

If only . . .

"I trust you."

The voice tormented him, frightened him. It was in his dreams, keeping him from sleep. It was in the eyes of his patients, in their pleadings, reminding him, making his hands shaky and condemning his ineptitude.

It was then he realized he'd become just what his parents had told him he'd become: a failure. The only thing he'd done right was live up to their low expectations. Instead of healing, he destroyed. Instead of success, he had endless failure. And when he finally had enough, when he wanted to die so badly he could taste it, he couldn't even kill himself. Christ, he'd even failed at that, simple as it was.

And now he was failing again. Cain looked down into Ana's face, feeling desperation claw up his throat at the sound of her shallow breathing, her restless murmuring. He remembered the first time he saw her, walking into

Cavey Davey's with a bloodied gown and an air of pride. He remembered thinking that they needed each other, that he could somehow help her.

She'd helped him instead, of course. With her soft sincerity, she gave him strength he never expected to feel again. He had learned to rely on her, and he'd waited, knowing there would come a time when she would need him just as badly. Knowing he could wait patiently until that time.

That time was here. And he was failing.

He swallowed, suddenly horribly, terribly thirsty. He needed bourbon now. Especially now. She was going to die, and there was nothing he could do. He couldn't face the thought of a world without her in it. Even if she left him once she was well, even if he never saw her again, he would know she was somewhere, and that would be good enough. He was willing for it to be good enough, if God would only let her live.

Because *he* couldn't save her. He was too damned afraid, more afraid than he'd ever been. Because this time, he knew he couldn't drown the memory of her in bourbon. No, God—he couldn't live without her, didn't want to. He wanted her to live, dammit, because he wanted to be with her. He wanted to take care of her, make love to her, love her—

Love her.

Cain started as the realization washed over him. He felt the blood leave his face.

He was in love with Ana. He was in love with her, and she was dying, and he was sitting there watching her die. Watching her . . .

You are killing her. The voice pierced his skull, loud and undeniable.

Cain stared down at the leech box in his hand, unable to tear his eyes away. The voice echoed in his head, tormenting him, swirling round and round until it was all he heard. *You are killing her. You are killing her . . .*

"Damn you, no!" He lurched to his feet, hurling the leeches as hard as he could. The box slammed against the wall, sending water, pewter, and leeches flying, spattering, spewing across the floor, dripping down the cane walls. The liquid splashed onto him, spitting into his face, beading on his skin. The stench welled up in the room, overpowering the scent of quinine and tamarind.

Cain couldn't move. He stood there, staring at the mess, feeling the temper and desperation well up inside of him, unavoidable, inescapable. He glanced at Ana, motionless and colorless on the bed.

He *was* killing her. He didn't have the knowledge, or the skill, and even if he did it wouldn't matter. Hell, he didn't even know what kind of leeches he had—what kind of doctor was he?

The thirst rose in him, consuming him. He thought of the warmth of bourbon and the sweetness of rum, of rough wine and rougher *aguardiente*. But mostly he thought of how good it would be to be numb. He couldn't just sit here and watch her die. It was too much to ask, goddammit. Too much.

He looked at her pale face, then looked at the red blood, almost black in the dim lamplight, whirling into the cup. With a muttered curse, Cain slapped the cup off her arm. It bounced to the floor, blood splashing up to spatter on her arm, on the blanket. But Cain didn't stay to see it land. He was already on his way to the dining room.

To wine and oblivion.

Chapter 23

The *quincha* was dark. Everyone else had gone to bed hours ago. The warm darkness seemed empty; it sharpened his need, accentuated his hunger. He was alone and heartsick, and the feeling was achingly, hauntingly familiar.

He swallowed when he looked at the shadowed table. Moonlight slatted through the loose cane door, over the table, falling on the clay jug sitting there, making it glow and beckon. Jiméne had stopped hiding the wine now, and the evidence of his trust made Cain hesitate as he strode across the floor. But only for a moment, and then it was soon forgotten. Everything was forgotten except for the glowing jug, the scent of wine that seemed to float on the air, dizzying him.

Don't do this, he thought. *You can be strong. You can be strong.* But then the other voice whispered, and it was soft, bewitching. *One drink,* it said. *Just one, and then you can go back, then you can bear it.*

It wasn't much of a struggle. Cain knew he was going to take the drink, and the thought filled him with a sense of impending catastrophe even as it soothed him. But it didn't matter. Nothing mattered except easing the trapped, helpless feeling. Ana was dying, and he was sick of lying to himself, sick of trying to be something he wasn't. He wasn't strong, he wasn't good, and probably —probably she didn't give a damn about him anyway.

He sank onto the bench, gripping the handle of the jug and pulling it toward him. *One drink. Just one drink.*

The sharp, acidic scent wafted to his nostrils. His stomach clenched; the longing was fierce and undeniable. The wine called to him, it held him prisoner, and suddenly this was all that was important, just this sweet, fiery numbness and the warm curl of liquor in his belly, just doing whatever it took to stop the voices.

He brought the jug to his lips, threw back his head, and gulped the liquor until it ran over his chin and spilled from his jaw to his shirt. The taste of it, the smell of it, the heat of it took over his senses, and his tongue and his throat and his stomach burned with the fire of salvation.

Cain pulled the jug away, wiping his mouth with the back of his hand, closing his eyes as the longing intensified. One drink—he would never be able to stop with one drink, and suddenly he knew it. It fed the fire but it didn't soothe it, it only made him ache for more and more, for oblivion and sweet, gentle numbness.

The need was stronger than his self-disgust, more demanding than remorse. *You need this,* the voice inside him said, and Cain believed it, suddenly believed it with all his soul. He was sliding out of control and he didn't care. He would never be like other men, who relaxed with a drink in a club after a long day. For him, it was the lifeblood of his existence. Without it, he was nothing.

Slow suicide. He heard the words in his mind and ignored them and the fear they caused. Slow suicide—why not? He had nothing to live for anyway. If Ana died, the guilt alone would kill him. Why not start now?

Why not?

Cain lifted the jug to his lips and drank.

The moonlight reached across the floor in pale fingers, moving with every breeze rattling the door. Cain watched them, for a moment imagining they were the fingers of God, and he drew his feet back from them, afraid to be touched.

The thought brought a crooked smile to his lips. He closed his eyes, brought the cup to his mouth, and took a deep, long drink of wine. It eased the tension in his chest, brought him the familiar, numbing relief. It had always done that—he remembered dinners with his parents, listening to their vehement arguing, feeling the tightness grow around his heart, cramping his stomach so he couldn't eat. The wine had tasted good then too, felt good, *was* good.

He drained the cup. He often wished he had found the sanctity of wine at a much younger age. Maybe then there would be no memories at all. God knew he did his best to forget them now. But by the time he found drink it was too late. Wine only deadened, it didn't erase the memories. Sometimes, the more he drank, the more they bedeviled him. Those times had always been the worst. It was those times that sent him drinking to oblivion.

Cain brought the cup to his mouth so hard it slammed against his teeth, and he choked the liquor down. His stomach clenched, he felt unexpectedly nauseated. He laid his head in his arms, keeping his hold on the jug. Too much. He'd had too much and he'd drunk barely anything. Surely he'd drunk more wine than this before? He couldn't remember—all he knew was that he should stop and go to sleep. But he couldn't bring himself to put down the jug, or rise and stumble to bed. The only thing to do was drink more and more, to drink until he was dead—ah, Christ, that sounded good now. Perhaps he and Ana could meet in hell. After all, they were both murderers.

"D'Alessandro."

Cain raised his head, blinking. The moonlight was brighter now. Pale and almost violet, filling the room.

"D'Alessandro."

There was a touch on his shoulder. Someone shook him. Cain lifted his hand to rub his eyes, knocking over the cup so wine spilled over the edge of the table. He felt the wetness in his lap, but he couldn't find the energy to do anything about it. Hell, it was bright. He'd never seen a moon so bright. He blinked again, squinting until he made out the form of the tall, shadowed figure beside him. His father. Fear and tension stiffened his spine, he felt instantly wary.

"Father?" His voice sounded hoarse, there was a sick lump in his throat.

The figure moved into the light. "No, *amigo,* it is me. It is only Jiméne."

Relief washed over Cain. He dropped his head into his arms again. "Go away, Jiméne. Let me be. Iss too late for you t'be up."

Jiméne laughed shortly. "Late? No, not late. Too early perhaps." He touched Cain's shoulder again. "How long have you been here, my friend?"

Cain didn't bother to lift his head. "Few minutes."

"A few minutes? I do not think so."

Cain felt the jug lifted from his hands. The bench shuddered as Jiméne sat beside him.

"I do not think so," Jiméne repeated. "It is dawn, *amigo.*"

Dawn? Cain sat up, so quickly his head spun and his stomach lurched. He struggled to control it, and squinted at the door. Sunlight, not moonlight—how had he thought it was moonlight? "Christ."

"How long have you been here?"

Cain swallowed. His head pounded. He looked at the jug in Jiméne's hands and wanted more with an urgency that surprised him. "Give m'that."

Jiméne lifted the jug away, setting it on the floor, out of sight. "No more," he said soberly. "You are very drunk."

Cain didn't have the strength to fight. "Y'should be used to it by now."

"You promised to stop—"

"Until y'r mother was well." The room spun and Cain closed his eyes. "I did."

"What about Ana?"

The sound of her name sent pain stabbing through him. He had forgotten. For a moment, he'd forgotten, and the reminder brought the bleakness back, a desolation so intense he felt sick. His voice, when he could speak, was a whisper. "She's dying."

"And you are letting her die?"

"Lettin' her?" Cain looked up, wishing he could control the pain he heard in his own words. "Lettin' her? I can't stop it!"

"Ah." Jiméne nodded. His mouth pursed, he looked thoughtful. "You kept *mi madre* alive, and me."

"No."

"Then who did?"

Cain shrugged. His chest felt tight, his eyes burned. "A miracle."

"A miracle?" Jiméne looked surprised. "You are a god, then? I did not know. Perhaps I *should* build a shrine to you."

"Let m'have the jug."

"Amigo, I must tell you that I cannot go through another time as Gorgona. Not without Ana. She is the one who stayed with you. She helped you, not I." Jiméne sighed dramatically. "And if she dies, I cannot

allow you to drink again. It is too much trouble to get you sober."

Cain frowned. There was something in Jiméne's words, something important, but it dashed just beyond his grasp and he abandoned the struggle to figure it out. "Give m'the jug."

Jiméne ignored him, leaning on the table, shaking his dark head. "When I was very young, there was a *señorita*. I was in love with her, and when she came to love me too, I was happy. But then New York called, and I loved it more and left her behind."

Cain exhaled in exasperation and laid his head again in the crook of his arms. "Lovely."

"There were other *señoritas,* of course."

"Hmmmm."

"And then, one day, on board a ship, I saw a beautiful woman. Her hair, it had the fire of the sunset, her eyes like gold. I was in love. Forever, I believed."

Cain wondered if there was some way to throw Jiméne to the floor and grab the wine without waking up the entire house.

"Forever." Jiméne paused as if waiting for a response.

Cain struggled to remember what it was Castañeras had been talking about. Some woman. Forever. Ah, yes, forever. He turned his head slightly to look at Jiméne. "What happened?"

"She fell in love with another man."

"Sorry."

"She fell in love with you, my friend."

Cain blinked, confused. Had he missed something? He tried to focus through his drunken haze, to make sense of Jiméne's story. "What the hell are y'talking 'bout?"

"Do you not know?" Jiméne asked softly.

The tale came back to Cain then. Hair with the fire of sunset. Golden eyes. Meeting on a ship. Jiméne was talking about Ana. Ana in love. With him. The idea was ludicrous, exhilirating, and painful all at the same time. He sat up. Too quickly. The world spun, he swayed, and he grasped the edge of the table with a gasp, catching himself just before he fell.

He tried to force coherence, formed his words carefully. "We aren't—she's not m'wife."

"I know this."

"She's going to leave me in San Fra—Francisco."

"I do not think so."

"Damn you, Castañe—" Cain took a deep breath. "She's a—" He started to say "whore," but something stopped him. She would hate for Jiméne to know. She would hate it, and so he couldn't do it, but more than that, he realized he didn't think of her that way any longer. He couldn't remember if he ever had.

"I have long ago forgotten my threat, *amigo,*" Jiméne went on. "I am no longer going to steal her away."

"I know."

"She loves you," Jiméne said implacably. "And I think you love her, *amigo.*"

Hell, yes, he loved her.

"I am not a doctor. I cannot help her. You can." Jiméne picked up the jug, setting it on the table, directly in front of Cain. "If you do not, she will certainly die. And then you will die, because you love her. Or you will go on, without her forever. It is not much of a choice, eh?" He shook his head, slowly rising from the bench. "Enzo will be up in two hours, and then Serafina. I am going back to bed."

Cain listened to the creaking of bamboo as Jiméne walked off until he could no longer hear footsteps. The house seemed eerily quiet, though birds were calling to each other outside. Sun slanted across the floor, across his arm, lit the jug in front of him.

Cain stared at it, unable to tear his eyes away, feeling the insatiable monster growing inside him. He wanted to reach for it, but the echo of Jiméne's words filled the room.

But Jiméne doesn't know you, the voice inside him argued. He loved Ana, yes, but love couldn't save her. *He* couldn't save her. *Because you are nothing.*

He brought the cup to his mouth, frowning when he noticed it was empty, and turned back to the table. He leaned the jug over the cup. Wine poured in, splashing over the side to dribble on the table, staining his fingers —the same way the leech liquid had, he thought. For a moment, he thought it *was* the leeches, and he shuddered, looking for a towel to wipe it off. The movement made his hands more unsteady. He glanced down to find the cup was too full. He slammed the jug down, leaning over to suck the wine from the rim so he could lift it.

Suddenly he got a horrible, aching vision of himself. For a moment it was as if he were standing back, watching his body. He saw himself straighten, wiping his chin with the back of his sleeve, throwing back his head. He saw the shaking of his own hands and the desperate, pained look in his eyes.

False courage, Ana called it, and he thought suddenly it wasn't even that. Courage had left him so long ago he couldn't remember what it felt like. It had gone and left him with such unrelenting bleakness he thought it would never go away. Left him with a fear he fed every time he opened a bottle.

The thought was crystal clear, and Cain strained to channel his thoughts so it made sense. He had the feeling he was on the brink of some great discovery, some inner truth that would change his life forever. But it drifted away, wavered out of sight before he could reach out to grab it.

He buried his face in his hands, wishing she was here to talk to, wishing he could tell her what he was thinking and hear her calm voice soothing him. *I believe in you.*

How simple those words had seemed, how deceptively wise. How foolish he'd been to believe them, to think things had changed. Christ, nothing ever changed. He would never change. He would go on and on like this, fighting the craving, needing the drink and the dark, deep fear that came with it. Nothing anyone could do would make it go away.

Cain felt the tears seep from his eyes, trailing over his cheeks to the corners of his mouth, the saltiness mixing with the taste of wine. He imagined she was sitting beside him. In his mind he felt her warmth and smelled her citrusy scent. In his mind, her hair was loose and long and thick, and strands brushed against his shoulder and stayed there, webbing over his shirt. In his mind, she touched him, and he felt again the soothing touch of her hands, heard the soft croon of her lullaby: *"When you wake, you shall find all the pretty little horses. Blacks and bays, dapples and grays, go to sleep, little baby."*

She wasn't beside him, he knew it, yet his vision was so strong he was surprised when he dropped his hands and there was nothing but sunlight there. He longed to touch her, wished for her steady strength, her conviction. What he would give to hear her words now. *I believe you can.* What he would give to believe it himself.

He *had* believed it for a while, that was the hell of it. He'd felt himself getting stronger every hour, every day, and he realized now that it was the thought of her that had given him the courage. The thought that she cared about him, that she believed in him, that she needed him.

Yes, that thought had always been there, the knowledge that she needed him, if for no other reason than to make her smile in the middle of the night. Without him, she would always be hard, cold, unforgiving, because no one would care to change it as much as he did. She would never know the joy of laughing, loving, hurting. She would never know any of it.

He could teach her those things, he knew he could. He cared enough for both of them. He could save Ana, and in the process, save himself, because he needed her just as badly.

But she was going to die. There would be nothing for him. No redemption. No love. No pain. Nothing but desolation. Empty, lonely desolation like the last years had been. Moving from place to place, waking in strange streets and strange beds. Remembering nothing. Not good times. Not bad. Nothing.

He couldn't do it. Not anymore. Not since he'd heard her laugh and listened to her description of a smile in the darkness. Not since he'd looked into her sherry-colored eyes and felt hope for the second time in his life. He heard Jiméne's voice again in his mind: *"She fell in love with you."*

Cain almost hated to remember it, hated his hope that it was true. But what if it was true? *What if it was?*

The thought grew inside him, a beacon in his desperation. He wondered suddenly if maybe John's confidence in him hadn't been misplaced. He'd been a good doctor once—hadn't he? *I believe you can.* He heard her voice, felt her strength, and suddenly the past lost its hold on him, and he wanted nothing more than to prove she was right, that he was worth believing in. He wanted to prove it to her, prove it to himself.

It was a foreign feeling, not entirely pleasant, but better than his fear. Cain looked down at the cup in his hands, at the swirling red liquid. He smelled its tempting scent, thought again of what it would taste like, what it would feel like. And for the first time since he could remember, he shoved it away.

He shook when he pushed from the table. The world spun, his knees sagged, his head shrieked with pain. But he got to his feet and stumbled to the doorway of her room. He stood there, slumped against the door frame, staring at the mess he'd left hours ago. The puddle of leech water had stained the bamboo matting, the stench hovered in the air with that of quinine and tamarind and vomit. On the floor, the leeches were plump little shadows. The bleeding cup lay abandoned, a little blood still pooling inside, the rest spattered across the floor, the bed, her skin.

Finally he looked at her. The blanket was tangled now around her legs, leaving the long, pale whiteness of them exposed. Her hair fell like a curtain over the side of the bed, her mouth was open, and her chest rose and fell with shallow, uneven breaths.

Cain felt again the terrible despair, the empty hopelessness. But he made himself think about how it would be when she was better. How they would smile and laugh and talk. How he would touch her. He took a deep breath and stepped inside.

Then he knelt to pick up the leeches.

She woke to find him sound asleep. He sat on the stool, his dark head buried in his arms, his breathing deep and exhausted and even. It reminded her of the first time she'd seen him, passed out on the table at Cavey Davey's, and the memory made her smile.

How long ago it seemed. That night was hazy in her mind now. She remembered running and being cold. Remembered being frightened. But mostly what she remembered was the way D'Alessandro had paused outside his boardinghouse room and looked at her. What had he said then? *"I'm afraid of the dark. Will you stay,* querida*? Chase away the demons for me?"*

She wanted to reach out and touch him, but she was so tired, too tired. Ana tried to summon her voice. Her throat was dry and tight, but she forced the sound out, and was surprised to hear a thin, rasping noise. "Cain?"

He stirred. The lamplight flickered.

"Cain?"

He jerked upright, looking wildly around. "Jiméne?"

he croaked. He ran a hand over his eyes, shaking back his hair. "Christ, what a nightmare."

"Dreaming of demons?" she asked softly.

He looked so surprised she wanted to laugh. He frowned at her, and then held the lamp higher. The light hurt her dry, swollen eyes, and she made a sound of protest and tried to wave it away.

"Ana?" he asked.

She heard the disbelief in his tone, and something else too. Something familiar. A laziness, a slur— She shook it away, confused. No, he was just tired, not drunk. He didn't drink anymore—or had that just been a dream?

He looked tired. She squinted up at him, seeing the pale gauntness of his face, the smudges of shadow beneath his eyes. In his hand, the lamp shivered, and she thought for a moment that it was because it took all his strength to hold it. He used to tremble that way—

She closed her eyes. "I'm so tired."

"Go to sleep then," he said gently.

He touched her face, smoothed back her hair, and Ana recognized the touch. They were the hands from her dreams. His hands had soothed her to sleep, taken away the heat. He had taken away her demons, and she wondered why the thought didn't make her afraid.

But she was too tired to think about it now. Now all she wanted was to go back to sleep, to feel his wonderful hands on her skin and drift back into the comforting darkness.

"Go to sleep, *querida,*" he said again, and instinctively she obeyed him, letting her body relax, letting his hands take her into quiet, calming places.

She was almost asleep when she heard it: a soft, almost inaudible sob, whispered words. "Thank God," the voice said. *"Thank God, thank God, thank God"* . . .

A dream, she thought, and fell asleep to the lullaby of his prayers.

Chapter 24

"—Enzo falls off the cow, and when Juan and I go to him, he says, 'But Papa, she is my mule! Look, I am just like a miner!' "

Ana laughed weakly. "I don't think Americans are a very good influence on Enzo, Jiméne."

Jiméne smiled and sat on the stool beside the bed. "It is good for him. When he is old enough, I will send him to New York."

"So he turns out like you, of course," Ana said, eyeing Jiméne's brilliant green coat.

"Exactly so." He nodded, brushing lint off his sleeve before he moved closer. "Ah, *cariña,* it is good to see you smile. We were so worried—all of us."

Ana plucked at the ribbon drawstring of her borrowed chemise. "There was no need, I wasn't that sick."

"Who told you that?" Jiméne frowned. "You were nearly as sick as Mama. D'Alessandro—he was very worried."

The sound of his name sent a tremor through Ana,

her heartbeat sped. "He was? I—I didn't know. I haven't seen him."

"You have not seen him because he sleeps—at last." Jiméne shook his head in disgust. "Why he believes a man so tired can help I do not know."

Ana frowned, confused. "I don't understand."

"He would not sleep the entire time you were ill, *cariña*. Serafina could not even make him eat—"

"He didn't sleep?"

"No. Not for four days." Jiméne picked up a vial from the table, turning it in his hands thoughtfully. "He was afraid you would die."

Ana stared at him. Her whole body felt tight and strange. She had wondered why she had not seen Cain yet today. This morning she'd tried to keep awake while they all trudged into her room: Serafina and Dolores, Juan, Amado, and even little Enzo. But Cain did not come, and as the morning went on, her disappointment grew. Every time she saw a figure in the doorway, she caught her breath until she realized it wasn't he. With every passing moment, the vague sense of hurt enveloping her sharpened. He hadn't come, and she didn't know why, and she started to think that maybe it hadn't been his voice she heard in her dreams, or his hands whose touch she remembered. She started to believe that maybe he didn't care about her at all.

And now Jiméne was telling her that Cain had stayed awake for four days, tending her, afraid she would die. Warmth stole over her at the idea, and Ana got a sudden, clear vision of him sitting beside her, holding her hand so tightly it went numb. She wondered if it had really happened, or if it was just an illusion.

"So he's just . . . sleeping?" she whispered.

Jiméne nodded. "Like the dead, *cariña*. And there is something else, something I think you must know." He looked away from her inquiring gaze as if it made him uncomfortable. "He will probably look sick when you see him."

Her heart skipped a beat. "The fever?"

"No, no," Jiméne touched her hand reassuringly. "Not that. It is just—last night, he was very drunk."

Drunk. Ana closed her eyes and leaned back on the thin pillow. She knew him too well now to think he'd just been drinking aimlessly. For Cain, it was a way to ease pain—she understood that now, since he'd told her about John Matson—and Ana's whole body ached at the thought that he'd been alone and hurting. She swallowed, wishing with all her heart that she had been there to help him. He needed her, and she hadn't been there. She hadn't been there.

"You must understand," Jiméne continued on quickly. "He was afraid you would die, Ana, and he—he did not think he could—"

"I understand," she said softly, opening her eyes. "You don't need to explain."

"You must not hate him for it."

"I don't hate him." She looked at Jiméne in surprise. "How could you think that?"

"Think what?"

They both turned at the sound of the voice. D'Alessandro stood in the doorway, a tired grin on his face, and Ana felt suddenly light-headed. A warm, tingly feeling raced through her, and she smiled foolishly, absurdly glad to see him. "Cain."

"Morning," he said, sauntering into the room. "Or is it afternoon?"

"Afternoon," Jiméne informed him, rising from the stool. "You slept a long time."

"Yeah. Well, I was tired." He shoved a hand through his hair and looked at Ana. "You were quite a trial, *querida.*"

"I have told her already," Jiméne said in a low voice, stepping back.

"Oh?" Cain took the stool, sinking heavily onto it. "Told her what?"

"Jiméne was just telling me that you were drinking again," Ana said quietly.

Cain stiffened. He reached for a vial of powder and threw an irritated glance at Jiméne, but when he looked back at Ana, his eyes were shuttered.

Ana cursed herself. It had been the wrong thing to say, but she couldn't help herself. He needed her, and here she was, helpless and in bed, letting him and everyone else wait on her. She felt again the rough, sweet worry that had haunted her since Gorgona, the overwhelming urge to soothe him. So she touched his hand, drawing away quickly when he jumped. "I'm sorry I couldn't help," she said.

He smiled at that. "You did."

"But I was delirious—"

"You helped," he said simply. He poured a bit of water into a cup and tapped a few grains of powder into it. "Now, *querida,* though I like you worrying about me, it's not important now. What is important is how you feel."

Better now, she wanted to say. *Since you're here, I feel better.* But the feeling was still too private, too strange. "I'm fine."

"She is hardly fine." Jiméne spoke quickly, with dramatic somberness. "You are still very sick, Ana. You must take care. You have just escaped death—"

Cain swiveled on the stool. "Don't you have something to do, Castañeras? Some cow to bother or something?"

"No." Jiméne's smile was broad. "I am here to assist you, *amigo.*"

"I don't need your assistance."

"But after last night, you still look weak—"

Cain jerked his head at the door. "I think I hear Serafina calling."

"She is not—"

"Out, Jiméne. Let me tend my patient in peace." When Jiméne's mouth set stubbornly, Cain pointed. "I'll call if I need you."

"Very well. I will go, D'Alessandro, but only because I do not care to spend time with you in this mood." Jiméne pushed past Cain and leaned over the bed, taking Ana's hand to press it against his lips. "You will call if you need me?"

"Yes, Jiméne." She nodded.

"Then good-bye." He shot a chastising look at Cain. "Do not tire her out, *amigo*—"

"Good-bye, Castañeras." Cain waited until Jiméne left the room, and then he turned back to Ana, pressing a cup into her hand. "Here. Drink this."

"What is it?"

"A precaution," he said. He smiled at her, and it accentuated the dark shadows beneath his eyes and the gauntness of his face. "You're still not well. I don't want to risk another fever."

She looked down into the cup. "Is Jiméne's mother drinking this?"

"Yes, she's drinking it. I stopped in to check on her before I came here."

"Perhaps you should be watching after her," she said slowly. "I feel fine, and she was much sicker than I was."

"She's also had four days on you. She's much better today." He nudged the cup with his finger. "Drink it, Ana."

Obediently she held the cup to her lips and took a tentative sip. It was bitter, and she grimaced and put it down again. "This is vile."

"It saved your life. Or at least I think it did," he said wryly. He wrapped his hand around hers, forcing the cup to her mouth. "If you don't drink it, I'll open your mouth and pour it down myself."

She gulped the liquid and pushed his hand away. "That's enough. I'm fine."

"You just spent four days in a fever."

"I've been sicker than this." She pushed at the blankets, making to rise. "Don't worry about me. *Doña* Melia needs you more, I'm sure."

He pulled the blankets back up and gently pressed her back. "Ana—"

"You're the one who's not well," she pointed out. "You look terrible. You should be in bed."

"Christ, you're a rotten patient." He laughed. "Listen to you."

She folded her arms over her chest. "I can take care of myself. I always have."

He squeezed her hand and brought it to his mouth, grazing his lips across her knuckles—a light touch that made her strangely dizzy. Then he looked down at her fingers and sighed. "Maybe you don't need me to take care of you, Ana," he said. "But I need to. I want to. Trust me with this. Please, I—I need you to trust me."

The words and the obvious effort it took him to say them stole her strength. Relief washed over her in such strong waves she felt faint. He needed her. For the moment that eclipsed everything else, for the moment she actually believed that she was helping him by allowing him to take care of her, that he needed her far more than she needed him.

Yes, for a moment, she believed it. And because she believed it, she smiled back at him and nodded. "Of course," she said graciously. "Of course I trust you."

She saw the relief sweeping through his dark eyes, and that and his broad smile made her weak with pleasure.

"Good. I'll try not to disappoint you."

"I doubt you will." She tried to match his light tone. "After all, if Jiméne is to be believed, you saved my life."

"They're out there building a shrine to me now."

"Oh? Saint Cain—isn't that rather blasphemous?"

He dropped her hand and looked away, capping vials and moving things on the tabletop. "You've been talking to my father, I see."

"He thought you were a saint?"

He glanced at her, pausing a moment before he answered. "Hardly."

"He couldn't have thought you were a devil child or he wouldn't have put you in the choir."

"Not even to save my soul?"

Ana laughed. "Is it so black he thought a choir would help?"

"I think by then he was just taking precautions." Cain smiled back at her. His eyes widened, he lowered his voice melodramatically. "He wouldn't even say my name, you know. Afraid it would let the devil in."

Ana stared at him. "So he called you Rafael instead."

"How bright you are, *querida.*" He touched her shoulder, urging her forward, and then he stepped around the bed until he was behind her, pushing aside her hair. "Yes. He called me Rafael."

Ana frowned, feeling the hard tapping of his fingers on her back, the softness of his hair brushing her shoulder as he leaned close enough to hear. "He must have been a very religious man."

He made a noise of agreement.

"And your mother? Was she religious too?"

He backed away. "Why so curious?" He was still behind her. He touched her hair—gently, tentatively, and then his fingers glided down the length of it to her waist.

The touch was electrifying, so much so Ana stiffened, startled. A warm tingling web spun through her, and her skin felt suddenly sensitive and burning. "I—I just wondered."

He coiled a strand of hair around his finger, tugging gently, and Ana wished suddenly that she could see his face. But he didn't move, just kept his fingers spinning, playing.

"No," he said finally. "My mother wasn't religious. She named me Cain because it punished my father. No other reason than that."

His voice sounded distant and impersonal. But she heard the pain behind it, and recognized it because it was so familiar—so much like her own. She knew that solid, impersonal wall, the pretense that nothing touched it, that nothing hurt.

So she didn't pretend it wasn't there, couldn't ignore it. Ana looked over her shoulder, but she still couldn't see his face. "I'm sorry," she said.

"Are you?" He leaned closer again, she felt the warmth of his body against her back. "You don't need to be. It was a long time ago."

"Are they still alive?"

"No. No, my father died four years ago. My mother long before that. Thank God."

The hatred vibrating in his voice surprised her. It was the first time she'd ever heard it. She had seen him drowning in self-pity whenever he was drunk, had seen him miserable with self-recrimination and guilt.

But she had never heard anger, and the sound of it now made her strangely glad. It made him seem stronger somehow, made her wonder if perhaps it hadn't been the drink that ruined him, but his own hatred. She knew how insidious it was, how crippling it could be. God knew she'd fought it her entire life. Cain had given it control, had let all that anger and hatred destroy him. Until this moment, she'd never seen him fight back.

She liked seeing him fight now.

Ana was quiet for a moment, letting the new feeling overwhelm her. His fingers moved on her hair, caressing, smoothing. Even though she couldn't see him, she knew the tense way he was standing, the thoughtful look on his face, the slight purse of his full mouth. She knew the way his heavy lashes rested on his cheeks as he watched her hair fall through his fingers. Her awareness of him went clear into her bones.

And suddenly she understood how he had known exactly what her smile looked like.

She swallowed nervously. "What are you doing?"

"Your hair is all tangled." His voice was wavering and thin, and Ana heard something in it, something that made her vaguely uneasy.

She pulled her hair forward, over her shoulders, away from his disturbing fingers. "I should brush it," she said breathlessly.

He drew it back, all of it, drew it away from her hands, spreading it over her back. "Where's your comb?"

"No—no, really, I—"

"Where's your comb?"

"There's a pocket inside my dress. I—I think it's there. I was using Dolores's brush this morning, but I—I guess I should braid it."

He leaned over her, his arm pressing against her shoulder as he grabbed the brush from the table. She felt his first, tentative strokes through her hair, the way he held it carefully so it didn't pull, and the care he took melted her. He touched it as he had in Chagres, but not like that. Softer, more even strokes, tantalizingly hypnotizing. Strokes that made her realize how tired she still was, how weak. She felt as if her bones had dissolved, and the more he brushed, the more she realized she had no will left. She couldn't stop him. Didn't want to . . .

"You have beautiful hair, Ana," he said, his voice deep and quiet. "When I first saw you, I thought I'd never seen such hair on a woman."

"My mother's hair was this color," Ana murmured, eyes closed, bound by his magical stroking.

"Was it? What was she like?"

"Ummmm. Beautiful. Charming. She was English, and she had this lovely accent." Ana laughed softly at the memory. "She had a rule for every occasion. Things like: 'A lady always wears her hair properly, even when she's at home.' Manners were very important to her, but she also liked to have fun." Ana sobered. "Too much fun, maybe."

"You mean your father."

She felt wrapped in a deep, warm cocoon. "Yes."

"What was he like?"

"I never knew him," she said simply. "They met at a ball. She was a debutante, and he was a married nobleman. He was charming, handsome—or so my mother said. She fell in love with him."

"And then what?"

"Then what?" Ana sighed. His touch was like a drug, lulling her. "They lived happily ever after."

He stopped abruptly, his hands dropped away. Ana felt suddenly cold, strangely bereft. She opened her eyes to see him come around to stand beside her. He held the brush in his hand, and his face seemed pinched, there was a strange look in his eyes.

"What?" she asked. "What is it?"

He sat heavily on the stool, toying with the brush. "When I was six, my mother took her first lover," he said. "She flaunted them in front of my father, but he never stopped loving her. Stupidly, perhaps, but all the same, he never stopped. When she was dying, she lay there hurling curses at his head until she had no voice left. She always hated him. He always loved her. He was —very religious, and after she was gone, he became even more—severe. Punishing sin—punishing me—was the only important thing to him. I think, sometimes, that he blamed me for her death, or at least her hatred. He told me once that she'd started hating him the day I was conceived, but the truth was she hated us both. Me because I was a part of him, and my father because—because—I don't know." He paused as if remembering. "Sometimes I think of their spirits together now—" He laughed shortly. "His heaven, her hell. It was what they both deserved, I guess."

She stared at him unsteadily. "Why are you telling me this?"

"Because," he said softly, fastening his gaze on hers. "Because when I thought you were dying, I realized I didn't know anything about you. And I couldn't bear it, Ana. I couldn't bear it." He took a deep breath. "If it means I have to tell you all about my life, I will. If that's what it means. But I don't want stories from you. I don't want fairy tales. I want the truth."

Her voice felt forced from her throat. "Why is it so important to you?"

He looked at her. "Isn't it enough to know that it is?"

Yes, it was enough. The realization was startling, but for some strange, inexplicable reason, Ana wanted to smile. She knew she should be afraid of him, but when she looked at him, watching her with a question on his face and tenderness in his eyes, she felt . . . fragile, cherished.

It was a completely alien feeling. She didn't think she'd ever felt this way, or if she had, it was so long ago she couldn't remember. Ana had a sudden, piercing wish that she had met him when she was young. Before Dr. Reynolds, before her mother's insanity. Back when she was whole and life had been an open promise.

Before she learned how to protect herself from pain.

But it was too late for that, surely, and it didn't matter. She hadn't met him then, but she knew him now and they had somehow, miraculously, become friends.

She couldn't stand the thought of losing that, and she knew right now he was giving her the choice—and there was no real choice to make. She raised her chin. "What do you want to know?"

The guard left his eyes, he relaxed visibly. "I don't care. Anything. Tell me anything. What's your last name?"

"My last name?" Ana leaned forward, drawing her knees up and resting her elbows on them. "I don't have one."

"Ana—"

"No, it's true, I don't have one." Ana closed her eyes, remembering her mother's story. "She always thought he would come for us, you see. She believed it so much she wouldn't give me any other name. She thought he would give me his."

"What was his?"

"Simonov." Ana breathed the name, remembering the time, as a child, when she had called herself that to her friends, sure that any day, any hour, her father would come riding up and bestow the name upon her. In her daydreams, it had been like knighting a warrior. *My beloved daughter, in the sight of God and all those gathered here, I now knight you Anastasia Simonov* . . . "His name was Gregori Simonov."

"Ana Simonov." Cain tried.

Ana opened her eyes and shook her head. "Not Ana. My name—my real name—is Anastasia."

Cain raised a brow. "A good Russian name."

"Prettier than just Ana."

"No." He grinned. "I'm used to just Ana."

"You're easy to please."

"Always."

His eyes were dark, glinting with humor, and Ana suddenly found herself staring at him, captivated by his gaze. He was an attractive man, especially when he laughed. The realization sent a tiny thrill into her stomach, a heated shiver up her spine, and Ana blinked and sat back, startled into silence.

"Something wrong?" he asked. He was on his feet in a moment, leaning over, laying his hand against his cheek. "What is it, Ana? Did you feel dizzy?"

She stared up at him, licking her lips. Dizzy, yes, she felt dizzy, and disoriented, and—and strange. All because of his eyes . . . Ana sat up and pushed the hair off her face. "I'm fine. No, really, I'm fine." *Or she would be, as soon as he stopped touching her.*

"You feel warm," he said, backing away, his brow furrowed in concern. "You should sleep. You're probably just tired."

"Yes." Ana put her hand over her eyes, feigning exhaustion. "Yes, that's it. I'm tired."

But when he finally left the room, leaving her in dark silence, Ana lay there wide awake, staring at the shadows.

Chapter 25

"—Have you ever seen the sky so blue, *Señor* D'Alessandro?" *Doña* Melia sighed, leaning back against the *quincha* wall and staring up at the sky. "I have never seen it so blue."

"It's lovely," Cain replied absently, in Spanish. "How do you feel?"

"Wonderful." She flashed him a bright smile very much like Jiméne's. Then she laughed and pointed to the yard. "Look at little Enzo play—ah, such a wonderful boy he is!"

"Mama, you spoil him with talk like that." Serafina chuckled and looked up from her needlework. "He is a good boy, but he is still a boy, eh? Why, just last week . . ."

Cain closed his eyes and lifted his face to the sun, letting Serafina's words fade into a meaningless buzz. It felt good to be out here, just sitting, thinking about nothing, dreaming of nothing, hearing Enzo laugh as Amado piggybacked him around the yard and wondering where Jiméne was, and Ana—

His gut tightened, and Cain's eyes snapped open. Ana. Beautiful, enticing Ana. He didn't know what to do about her anymore, but he was damned sure he wasn't going to be able to control himself much longer.

He thought about her constantly, dreamed about her at night, woke up drenched in sweat and shaking because he heard her soft breathing across the room. He would lie there, huddled in his hammock, aching and wishing he could wake her up, wishing he could touch her with his fingers and his lips and his tongue.

It had been three days since Ana's fever had broken, three days since she'd smiled that soft, beguiling smile and told him about her life, and his need for her had grown until it was worse than it had ever been with whiskey. It was all-consuming, burning, inescapable even while he slept. The more he knew about her, the more they talked and laughed together, the more his desire grew, until just the mention of her name drove him almost insane with wanting.

She had lost her wariness. Now it was easy to get her to talk, to share her life with him—at least the part before she'd gone to Rosalie's Home for Women. He never asked about her life there, didn't really want to know. Thinking of her there, sharing her favors with paying customers, inflamed him. Cain never knew whether to be angry that she'd given herself to others but not to him or whether to be insanely, possessively jealous. Neither emotion was comfortable. Both made him too aware of just how vulnerable he'd become.

So he decided it was easier not to know about Rosalie's. At least for now. Later, perhaps, when Ana trusted him more—when he trusted himself more—but not now, when his feelings were still too raw, when he wanted her with an intensity that was painful. Now it was easier to think of her past in terms of her childhood, and of her present with him—though every day, he wondered a little more just what "with him" meant.

"Where is Dolores?" Jiméne walked up, blocking the sun and running a hand over his sweaty face. He frowned at the cane walls irritably. "She has said she would watch Enzo. I need Amado now."

"I'll watch him, Jiméne," Serafina replied absently, not looking up from her sewing. "Take Amado if you must."

"You are busy watching Mama." Jiméne pushed at his rolled shirtsleeves. "And it is Dolores who promis— Sweet Maria, look at this!" Jiméne broke into English, staring dumbfounded at the doorway.

"What is it?" Cain asked, twisting to see. The sun slanted into his eyes, and he tented his hand over his face.

He froze.

His heart stopped in his chest, Cain's throat constricted painfully. Ana stood in the doorway—but an Ana he had never seen before. She was dressed in a brightly patterned red chemise, the familiar native dress he'd seen on Panamanian women all through the isthmus.

But it had never looked like this. The dress was loose, hanging straight from a short-sleeved shoulder, but it clung to Ana's delicate curves provocatively. When she turned, he saw the fringe trimming the plunging back. Fringe that shivered when she moved. Fringe that swayed and shook and caught in the fat braid hanging between her shoulder blades.

Cain swallowed. His whole body felt hot. It took every ounce of strength he had to keep from jumping to his feet and dragging her off into the jungle. The strength of his passion for her amazed him. "Ana," he croaked. "Where did you get that?"

"Do you like it?" She smiled, turning toward him. "Dolores lent it to me. I couldn't stand the thought of putting the wool on again."

"You—you are beautiful, *cariña,*" Jiméne stammered.

"Isn't she beautiful?" Dolores gushed in Spanish. "She looks wonderful in this dress, yes?"

Ana looked questioningly at Dolores.

"She said you look wonderful," Cain translated softly. "And she's right, *querida*, you do."

Was it his imagination, or did she seem disconcerted by his words? She turned her head and looked down at the ground. Nervously, Cain thought, even demurely. He dismissed the idea abruptly. He'd seen Ana be many things, but never demure. After all, she was hardly a virginal debutante.

She took a deep breath. "I was tired of being in bed. I wanted to visit with everyone."

Beside her, Dolores smiled widely. "She wants to take a walk," she said in Spanish. She winked broadly at Cain. "But she is weak, yet, Doctor. She could use a companion."

He threw Dolores a glance of mock disgust, and then looked at Ana. "Dolores says you'd like to go for a walk."

"Yes—well, I—maybe not." She smiled weakly, motioning to the bench beside *Doña* Melia. "Perhaps I'll just sit here, with the rest of you."

"You should go, *cariña,*" Jiméne advised. "Amado and I must join Juan in the field, and Mama will go in shortly. A walk would do you good, I think."

"Then, Dolores—" Ana motioned with her fingers, pantomiming a walk. "Would you go with me?"

Dolores smiled and plopped down on the bench. "Doctor, would you tell her please that I must watch Enzo, as I promised?"

"It is about time," Jiméne grumbled.

Dolores crossed her arms over her chest and looked imperiously at Cain. "Please, *amigo.*"

"Dolores has to watch Enzo." Cain translated. He got to his feet and held out his hand to Ana. "Will I do?"

He could have sworn he saw nervousness cross her eyes again, and Cain wondered why. But before he could be sure, it was gone, and she smiled politely.

"Of course," she said, putting her hand in his.

"Do not go far," Jiméne teased in Spanish. "Just to the jungle and back!"

"We will be watching you, Doctor," Dolores joined in. "I will come running if I see any improper behavior."

Cain glanced over his shoulder and winked. "Why? Did you want to watch, Dolores?"

"Ah, such a rogue you are!" Dolores laughed.

He turned back to Ana, who was frowning thoughtfully.

"What was all that?" she asked.

"Dolores told us to be careful of snakes," Cain replied easily. "I told her we would. Are you ready?"

"Yes. Yes, of course." She withdrew her hand from his and started off, walking a few steps ahead of him. "Let's go."

There it was, that nervousness again. Cain watched her curiously for a moment, disturbed and not knowing why. She was different somehow, strangely quiet and thoughtful. He wondered if maybe it was the aftereffects of the illness, then discounted the thought. *Doña* Melia was fine. Tired but fine. No, he doubted illness could be the problem—

He looked up from his musings to see that Ana hadn't paused to wait for him. She was already at a copse of palms across the yard. Quickly he ran to catch up with her, stumbling when she stopped short suddenly and turned to him.

"I would like to do something for Jiméne's family," she said. "They've all been so kind."

"They don't expect anything," he said.

"Oh, I know they don't." Ana stopped. The sunlight filtering through the leaves dappled her skin, highlighted her hair. She looked up at him. "But I feel I owe them anyway. Haven't you ever wanted to do something just because it felt right?"

Cain's heart caught in his throat. *Yes. Oh, yes.* "What would you do?"

"I don't know." She shrugged. "I don't have any talents to speak of—" A shadow crossed her face, and she frowned slightly. Then she forced a smile. "But there must be something I could do to thank them for what they've done. And you. I'd like to thank you too."

He couldn't breathe suddenly. "No, I—"

She looked away, staring into the trees. "I wish I could cook, or make something." She laughed shortly. "The piano player at Rose's used to write songs for people he liked. I wish he were here now because, God knows, I can't write music."

"Ana—"

"What do you think?" She turned her gaze back to him, her brow was furrowed. "You understand them. What would you like if you were them?"

I'd like to touch you, kiss you . . . Cain closed his eyes briefly, pushing away the thought, and cleared his throat. He opened his mouth to tell her that he thought they needed nothing except her thank-you, but suddenly he couldn't say it. Couldn't say it because she was staring at him with rapt attention, the sun shining on her hair and shadowing her face, and he wanted nothing more than to kiss her. And because of that he forgot everything. "Christ," he murmured. "You're so beautiful."

He heard her quick intake of breath, saw her golden eyes, wide and startled as if he'd just said something shocking, and he was surprised to see the slight flush on her cheeks.

The sight of her that way—startled, embarrassed, aware—went straight to his heart, pulsed through him. He saw her nose, slightly reddened from the sun, and the strange, disconcerting shyness in her eyes, and the soft curve of her small breasts beneath the loose collar of the native chemise.

He saw it all, and his mouth went dry, the heat coiled in his loins. The way she was looking at him now—was that desire in her eyes?—Christ, it made him want to bury himself in her, to touch and smell and taste her. The pain of desire shot through him more intensely than ever, and Cain took a deep, ragged breath.

The sound was rough and startling, cutting through the charged silence like a shout. Ana stepped back convulsively, nearly tripping over a root, grabbing on to the trunk for balance. Her braid flopped over her shoulder, smacking against her breast, and she twisted around, startled. He saw the moment she realized it was only her braid—and not his hand—that touched her. Her shoulders relaxed, and she looked away.

When she glanced at him again, there was a slight, self-conscious smile on her face, and challenge in her eyes, and Cain knew he'd lost whatever moment there was. He had surprised her—something that didn't happen often, he knew—but now she was in control. Now it was as if those few charged minutes had never existed.

Disappointment unfurled inside him. He had been close. So close. Christ, what he wouldn't give to be able to get past that cool self-assurance of hers, to see desire in her eyes and know it was for him. What he would give to know if she had really felt something just then—or if it was just his imagination.

He pulled at the buttons on his shirt until he felt the slight breeze on his chest. "Maybe you could—maybe you could cook something," he said helplessly.

She looked at him doubtfully. "I could try."

"Maybe—" He floundered for a suggestion. "Maybe a cake."

"A cake?"

"Yeah. A cake."

"Cain," she said, smiling, "I've never baked a cake in my life."

He shrugged. "How hard could it be?"

She laughed then, relaxing against the tree. "I don't know. I've never tried. But I do know my mother couldn't do it. She would always ask Mrs. Williams to bake on my birthday."

"Who was Mrs. Williams?"

"Our neighbor. She cooked for us. It's all part of being a lady, you see, Mr. D'Alessandro. Ladies make tea. They do not cook." She said the last emphatically, with an exaggerated accent.

Her teasing was irresistible. Cain grinned. "I see. Ladies eat, though, I take it."

"Of course, though eating is vulgar, really. The thing to do is to take tiny bird bites at dinners, and then go home and gorge yourself on the servants' stew. That way, you at least look delicate."

"I suppose you were delicate even when you had your face buried in birthday cake."

"I did not have birthday cake," Ana said grandly. "I had bread pudding. It was my favorite." She closed her eyes at the memory. "Bread pudding with raisins and cherries. And brandy sauce that Mrs. Williams lit on fire. God, I loved that pudding." She opened her eyes again, sighing. "I haven't tasted it for years. Not since she died."

"Our cook used to make chocolate bread pudding with custard," Cain remembered. "I never cared for it much myself."

"No?" She raised an eyebrow at him. "What did you like then?"

He shook his head. "I don't remember."

"You do too," she accused. "There must have been something. Chocolate cake, maybe? Or custard? Perhaps lemon tarts?"

"*Not* lemon tarts."

"Then it was chocolate cake."

"No, it wasn't." Cain leaned against the tree beside her, close enough so their shoulders brushed. Heated desire shot through him at the touch, and he tried to ignore it, to keep his voice light. "It was marzipan."

"Marzipan," she repeated thoughtfully. "My mother liked it too. I have no idea how to make it."

"I think you grind up almonds with sugar," he suggested hopefully.

She laughed. "Sorry, D'Alessandro. *You* make marzipan if you want it. I don't even know where to get almonds here."

The sound of her laughter, the joyful teasing, made Cain feel so warm and good that he longed for it to go on forever. For the moment, he forgot his desire, and just wished for this camaraderie to continue. Perhaps they wouldn't ever have to go back to the *quincha*. Perhaps they could just lean here, against this tree, and talk about favorite foods and neighbor women until the end of time. Perhaps—

"I wish I knew how to make that bread pudding," she said thoughtfully. "I did watch Mrs. Wilson make it now and then."

"Do you remember it at all?"

"A little." She pushed away from the tree and shrugged. "Bread crumbs and sugar. I think—no, I know—there were eggs."

She looked so forlorn for a moment that Cain felt an overwhelming urge to touch her, but he knew if he did she would withdraw, and that was the last thing he wanted. So he restrained himself forcibly, crossed his arms over his chest. "Why don't you make it, then?"

She threw him a disgusted look. "Why don't *you* make it? It would probably be better."

"Probably."

Ana's eyes widened in disbelief. "Are you telling me you know how to cook?"

"Well." Cain shrugged with exaggerated humility. "A little."

"How much is a little?"

"More than you, if you can only make tea," he pointed out. "This is how I see it, *querida.* With your memory, and my skill, we should be able to turn out a pretty edible bread pudding."

"Your skill?" she asked doubtfully. "How much skill is that?"

"I can at least boil an egg," he informed her.

She laughed. "That's hardly a recommendation."

"It's more than boiling water. Do you want my help or not?"

Ana thought for a moment, and then she nodded. "Very well, you can help. But only if you promise not to take over. This is my thank you, after all."

"As you wish." He held out his hand to her. "Shall we get started?"

She knew she should not want so badly to be with him. After this afternoon, when she'd felt the power of his desire, and with it another startling stab of her own, Ana knew the best thing to do was to stay away from him. She had seen his kind of desire before, knew where it led, and was afraid of the hurt she would see in his eyes when she inevitably refused him.

If she refused him.

No, *when,* she told herself forcibly. Other men had made the mistake of thinking she cared about them, thinking she desired them as well. Those men she hadn't cared about, with those men she had welcomed the disillusionment of sex. Sex was just her job, after all, and the sooner they realized she felt that way, the better. But those men weren't Cain. She did care about him, and because of that, she wouldn't be able to face his disappointment once he realized her feelings were those of a friend only, not a lover.

Most certainly not a lover.

She felt stronger at the very thought. The words helped her discount her growing feelings for him over the last days and her strange reaction to him just now, outside. Helped her ignore the way her stomach clenched and her blood raced when he walked into the *quincha* carrying a bowl of eggs.

"Well, here they are," he said, setting them on the table. He looked up at her and smiled, a broad, flashy smile that warmed Ana to her very center. "I hope that's everything. I think Serafina and Dolores will rush in here in a panic if I ask for anything else."

Ana turned away, busily checking the items on the table, even though she'd checked them moments before he walked in. "Yes. That's everything. I think. No cherries, but I suppose the bananas will do." There was no yeast bread, either, just torn-up corn tortillas. But they were enough like bread, weren't they? They certainly tasted like bread . . .

"So." Cain rolled his shirtsleeves up and looked at her expectantly. "Tell me what to do."

"Well, I don't know." Ana eyed the table, trying to remember. What had Mrs. Wilson done? She had beaten eggs, Ana remembered. She looked up, smiling triumphantly. "I think we beat the eggs first."

"How many?"

Her smile died. "I—I don't know."

"Well, we've got seven here. That's probably enough, don't you think?"

Ana grasped on to his logic. After all, he knew and she didn't. "I'm sure it is."

"Good." He turned the bowl over. Eggs spilled out, rolling across the table, and together they grabbed for them. Cain winced as one hit the ground with a splatter. "Six eggs," he amended, chagrined.

Ana laughed. "I'm sure six is enough." She handed the eggs to him, one at a time, while he cracked them into the bowl, then stood back when he took up a fork and began whipping them wildly. Egg flew out of the bowl, spattered all over his white shirt.

Cain stopped and looked down, a disgusted look on his face. "Damn."

"There's probably one whole egg on your shirt," Ana pointed out with a smile. "If you're not more careful, there won't be any left."

He tossed back his hair and leveled the fork at her. "I don't need suggestions from you. If you want to serve this surprise for dinner, you'd best get started."

He was right, of course. Ana sat and picked up the knife, cutting the bananas into thin slices. The sun slanted over the table, glinting off the knife and warming her skin, and she paused and stared at the dust motes glittering in the light breeze.

This was so nice, she thought, watching the motes and listening to the low timbre of Cain's humming and the clattering of the fork against the bowl as he whipped the eggs. If nothing else was like those days in the kitchen with Mrs. Wilson, this was. This warm familiarity, the sense that she wasn't alone, that if she wanted to say something—anything at all—there would be someone to answer back. Or someone to just nod and smile and keep beating eggs. She hadn't even realized she'd missed it, and yet she had.

"Now what?" Cain put the bowl down and waited.

She looked up at him, smiling inanely until she realized he'd asked a question. "Oh. Well, then we add sugar. I think Mrs. Wilson used to soak the crumbs in milk. But there's no milk."

"What about water?"

She looked doubtfully at the shredded tortillas. "I suppose that would work as well. It's wet, anyway." She lifted the jug and poured a steady stream into the bowl, watching while the tortillas floated to the top. Gently she pushed them down again. She looked up at Cain just in time to see him breaking pieces off a cone of brown sugar.

"Do you think this is enough?" he asked, holding up the cone.

"I don't know. I thought you were the one who knew how to cook."

"This is a little more complicated than boiling an egg, Ana."

"An hour ago you were convinced that was all the skill you needed."

"Well, that was an hour ago." He laughed slightly, shaking back his hair. "Now I'm willing to concede this might be harder."

"Wonderful." Ana stepped around the table to stand beside him, and looked down into the bowl. The smooth, pale yellow eggs were dotted with hard lumps of brown sugar. It didn't look quite right, not how she remembered it, but it *had* been a long time ago. "That's fine. Now I think we just mix everything together and put it in the oven."

He stiffened. "The oven?"

"Yes, the oven." Ana reached for the bowl of tortillas. "It cooks for about an hour, I think—"

"Ana, what oven?"

"What oven?" She repeated, frowning. "Why, a regular ove—" She stopped short. "Oh, my God. There's no oven. Is there?"

"Just a clay pot." Cain started to laugh.

"This isn't funny," she protested. "There's no oven. What are we going to do?"

He sank onto the bench, still laughing. "Boil it?"

"That's not—"

"Or we could fry it."

Ana looked at him, and she felt her face begin to twitch, felt laughter move up her throat. She looked down at the bowl in her hands, at the tortillas floating in a pool of water, and she chuckled. "Good God, this is a mess."

"No, it's not." He took the bowl from her and poured it into the eggs and sugar, stirring it once. "Now that—that's a mess."

She looked at it, at the pieces of tortilla floating in watery egg and the rocks of sugar bobbing above it all. It looked nothing like she'd intended, nothing like she remembered. It looked suddenly—ridiculous.

She laughed then. "This is all your fault."

"My fault?"

"You said you could cook."

"I said I could boil an egg."

She pointed her finger at him. "You deliberately misled me, Cain D'Alessandro."

He grabbed her finger, curled it back into her palm and wrapped his hand around hers. "I didn't know how difficult this recipe would be."

Warmth seeped through her at his touch. Ana's mouth went suddenly dry, and the laughter died in her throat. "I—I told you I hardly remembered," she said.

"That's not what I heard." His voice was soft, his eyes deep and dark and infinitely beguiling.

"Then you only hear what you want to hear." Ana's heart thumped in her chest so loudly she thought he must hear it.

His hand tightened on hers, and he pulled her forward, closer until she was less than an inch from his chest. "I do not," he whispered.

"You do too."

"No."

"Yes."

His head dipped closer, dark hair falling forward. Ana caught her breath, her palms were sweating. He was going to kiss her, she knew it, and she felt suddenly faint, horribly out of control. Other men had tried this, and she had avoided it, but she couldn't remember what she'd done then, couldn't think of anything but the fullness of his lips, and his warm breath on her face. Good God, he was going to kiss her.

But he didn't. She knew the exact moment he decided not to, saw the desire in his eyes replaced by hesitation, heard the catch in his breath, the muttered sound that could have been a curse or a sigh. Then he dropped her hand and moved away, turning back to the pudding, and Ana knew he was going to pretend it hadn't happened.

That was what she wanted too. Yes, it was what she wanted. Ana waited for the relief to wash over her, but instead she felt disappointment so keen it was painful. A strange, gut-wrenching disappointment that made her throat tight and sent her heart racing so she felt dizzy.

She bit her lip and clenched her hands in her skirt, feeling absurdly lost. She watched him dump the bananas in the bowl, saw his muscles flex with the movement and the dark hair beneath the flaring of his collar.

And all she could think about was how much she wished he had kissed her.

Chapter 26

Ana tried the rest of the afternoon to forget. She helped Serafina and Dolores grind meal for tortillas, concentrating on the smooth stones and the scraping of grain, trying to tell herself she had merely been overcome by the moment, that she hadn't *really* wanted to kiss him.

She told herself that as she helped Serafina roast the beef for dinner, kept telling herself when Dolores took the bread pudding off the fire and put it aside. The smell of sweet custard, bananas, and corn overpowered the meat for a moment, and Ana's stomach flipped. *You felt nothing*, she reminded herself. *Nothing at all.*

But when they sat down to dinner, and Cain took his regular seat beside her, Ana's careful protestations fled. He sat close—too close. Their shoulders brushed, his thigh pressed against hers, and his breath was hot against her cheek when he leaned down to translate. She felt shivery again, but not from cold. *You felt nothing*, she told herself again. It was only that they'd spent a lot of time together lately, and she had come to care for him a great deal. The way she assumed he cared for her.

No. Not the same way. The niggling thought pierced her, and Ana sliced her knife into her meat as if the action would exorcise the thought from her mind. She didn't have to look at Cain to know his feelings for her had grown far past easy friendliness or concern. He wanted her. She'd seen the look on the faces of too many men to be deceived. She knew it intimately, knew the passion-dark eyes and the broken voice. He wanted her, and she knew that inevitably, he would push her far more than he had today.

But what she would do about that, she didn't know.

The buzz of conversation heightened, and Ana gratefully allowed it to break into her thoughts. *Doña* Melia said something, and they all laughed. Ana forced herself to smile politely.

"She says she is not a child. If Serafina wants to cut someone's meat, she should cut Enzo's." Cain leaned close, his whispered words like heat against her ear.

Jiméne chattered.

"He says Enzo can cut his own meat now." Cain's shoulder brushed hers, sending a tingle down her spine. "*Doña* Melia says Enzo is just a child." Pause. "And Jiméne tells her she is only an old woman."

There was laughter in the room. Ana dug her knife into her meat again, took a bite and chewed. The savory roast was like dirt on her tongue, her throat was too dry to swallow. She gulped her water, forced the bite down, and tried the fried plantain. It was impossible. She couldn't eat, she couldn't talk, she could barely breathe. Her throat felt closed, her stomach cramped.

Ana took a deep breath. She was being an idiot. He was just a man, he probably hadn't thought beyond getting her into bed. Once he slept with her, she knew he would soon get over his desire. They all did. In the brothel, she'd had only a few regular customers. For the rest, she had merely been a challenge. *"Ten dollars says you can't make the Duchess feel a thing." "Go on, Johnny, see if you can't bring a moan from her!"*

She'd heard the talk often enough. Rosalie had certainly taken advantage of it. *"The Duchess is my special girl, gents. She'll cost ye extra—she's a choosy lady. Very choosy."* Ana had been the elite girl, the one they all wanted.

What else they wanted from her, she wasn't sure. A moan? Or more than that? Had they wanted her to wriggle and gasp, to pretend she felt the same desire they did? She hadn't been able to do it. It was only a job, and a boring one at that, one client like every other. Each wanting the same thing. The second was like the twenty-second, and in the morning she'd been unchanged. Still the Duchess. Still the woman who walked down the hallway to the privy, smelling the morning-after odors of tobacco smoke, powder and perfume, the heavy, musky woman scent mixing with that of liquor.

"What makes you look so sad, *querida?*" Cain's voice was so sudden in her ear, Ana jumped.

She looked at him guiltily, for the first time since this afternoon. What she saw in his eyes made her pause. Dark, knowing secrets. As if he saw clear into her soul and understood. She caught her breath. "I—I'm tired, I guess."

"You guess?" A soft half smile curved his mouth.

"I *am* tired."

"I see." His smile widened. "I guess making bread pudding takes a lot out of a person."

She looked away, unable to face the promise in his gaze. "Yes, I suppose that's it." It would be easy, she thought suddenly. So easy to give to this man what she'd sold to so many others. She took a deep breath. "Dolores said we should have a real party to thank you now that *Doña* Melia can be part of it."

His glance was bemused. "Dolores 'said'?"

Ana laughed slightly. "Well, that's what I think she said."

He shrugged. "I don't need a party."

"Maybe not. But you deserve one after curing Jiméne and *Doña* Melia and me."

He smiled then. "Yeah, I guess maybe I did do that."

She saw the soft edge of confidence in his face, and it filled Ana with quiet pride. Yes, she would give herself to him if he wanted her. She would do it because there was nothing else she could give him, and he deserved something for the hell he had gone through. Even if it was only sex.

"Esta aqui!" Dolores came to the table bearing the frying pan that held the disastrous bread pudding. She smiled brightly at Ana and set it on the table with a flourish. Amado followed with a stack of clay bowls, his own smile wide and white as he waited for Dolores to cut the pudding.

There was respectful silence. Dolores dipped the spoon into the pudding and lifted it out.

Ana's heart sank. Egg ran in watery, curdled clumps over the sides of the spoon, plopping back into the pudding. Drenched tortilla pieces clung to it like limp paper. She saw Dolores falter, but then Jiméne's sister gained control, her smile never wavering as she spooned the pudding into bowls and passed them around.

"Oh, God," Ana said in a low voice. "Tell them they don't have to eat it, Cain. Tell them."

Dutifully he translated. There was a chorus of "nos" and jabbering, and then, like clockwork, each member of Jiméne's family dipped into a bowl and took a bite.

Ana's spoon hovered over her own bowl. She stole a glance at Cain, who was studying a spoonful with amusing consternation.

"Don't eat it," she suggested.

He shook his head. Then he took a bite. She saw his eyes widen, his throat constrict. He swallowed quickly.

"Well?" Ana asked.

"It was . . . good. Very good."

Ana looked around the table. They were all having the same reaction. Widening eyes, quick swallows. Their smiles looked pasted on, but dutifully, they each took another bite.

This time, so did she. It was on her tongue for less than a second before Ana gagged. She wasn't aware of flavors so much as textures. Limp tortillas, sweet, watery eggs, slimy bananas covered with clumps of curdle. She choked and put her spoon down, her eyes watering.

Then she looked at Cain, who was valiantly trying another bite. His jaw worked convulsively, she saw his quick shudder, the rigid swallowing—

She started laughing. "Please, stop," she said with a gasp, pushing her bowl aside. "It's—it's terrible!"

Cain nearly threw down his spoon. He took a huge gulp of water and translated quickly. The relief that broke out on the faces of Jiméne's family was comical.

"I do not think cooking is one of your talents, *cariña,*" Jiméne informed her somberly.

They all laughed, and Juan went to get his guitar.

It was later, much later, that Ana sat alone in the darkness. The evening had been over for some time, and while she had enjoyed Juan's sensitive playing and the songs they'd all sung, Ana was grateful to be alone. The day had been tiring, but though her body was tired, her mind was reeling. She had gone to bed only to stare at the shadowed ceiling, listening to Cain's soft snores on the other side of the room and feeling an uncomfortable, unfamiliar warmth in her belly.

Suddenly she had been unable to spend another moment in that room. She felt as if she were on the edge of something both frightening and compelling. For once in her life, she had no idea what to do about it.

"Ana? Ana, is that you? Are you all right?"

Cain's voice ran over her, deep and dark, shivering along her spine and up the back of her neck, and Ana wondered if he'd somehow heard her thoughts here in the darkness. It didn't seem silly, really. No, much more than that, it seemed entirely reasonable. He had always seen too much, felt too much, known too much. "I'm all right," she said softly.

He came closer. She felt his presence in the darkness, the familiar awareness of him that made the hair on her arms stand on end.

"What's wrong?"

"Nothing. I couldn't sleep, that's all. I didn't mean to wake you."

"You didn't wake me." He was suddenly so close she felt his heat. "That is, I didn't hear a noise." He laughed wonderingly. "I didn't hear your breathing. I think that was what woke me up. I didn't feel you there anymore."

The words swept over her, sank into her. She heard the care in them, and the warmth, and she felt shaky inside. "I was coming back," she said softly.

"Were you?" His hands were on her arms. Warm and strong, gripping her shoulders with a desperation she recognized from his delirium and her fever.

His palms opened, slid down to her elbows, over her bare arms. The touch sent shivers through her body, sent longing stabbing into her heart. But it wasn't as simple as that. Yes, he wanted her, but he wanted her with the innocence of a man who didn't know her past, a man who wanted to make love to a woman he cared for. He wanted a lover, not a whore.

She didn't know if she could be that.

Ana closed her eyes and took a deep breath. "Don't."

"Don't?" he asked. His hands moved up and down her arms, he spread his fingers over her skin, lingeringly, cherishing. "Ah, I wish it were that easy, *querida.*" His voice was a hoarse, raw whisper. "But I can't stop. I've tried and I can't. Today—today I thought I could control it. I was wrong. I can't. I want you so much. Christ, too much. Don't you think I would stop it if I could?"

"You only think you want me." She shook her head. "I—I'm not who you think I am."

"You aren't?" His voice was light, amused. "Who are you then?"

"No, really, I—" Ana twisted around, pushing away his hands. "You don't know me, you don't understand."

The moonlight lit his face, gilded his hair. He looked puzzled. "What don't I understand?"

"Those years at Rosalie's—they changed me. I can't explain, but—but they did. You want someone who can want you back. Someone who thinks this means something. You don't want me."

"You don't give yourself enough credit, Ana," he said gently. "You're right about one thing, I don't want the Duchess. But I do want you."

She looked down miserably. "We're the same person."

"Are you?"

"Yes." The admission was so quiet she could barely hear it herself, a whisper in the darkness.

"No." He didn't move, just stood there, watching her.

"You don't understand, do you?" she snapped bitterly. His steady watching angered her. Damn him, he was deliberately being obtuse. She was trying to *save* him, and he was standing there, pretending her words meant nothing. "They used to bet on me, did I tell you that? Probably not, I'd nearly forgotten it myself. I was Rosalie's prize. 'Melt the Duchess,' she used to say. 'She's cold as ice, boys—see if you can melt her.' "

"Did they?"

"No." She shook her head. "No one."

"Does that make you afraid? Are you afraid that if I touch you, make love to you, you won't melt? Or that you will?"

She looked away from him, toward the cane-slatted door. "You don't understand." Her voice dropped to a whisper. "You don't understand. I care about you, you're the only friend I've ever had. And I—" She swallowed painfully. "You expect too much. I don't want to disappoint you. Cain, don't you see? Don't you understand? I'm a whore. I can't give you what you want. It isn't—it isn't in me."

There was silence. Silence so big it seemed to fill the room and her heart. Silence so painful Ana wished she hadn't said anything at all, wished he hadn't awakened and found her in the vulnerable hours of night. Tomorrow, she knew, she would have been fine. Tomorrow, she would have been able to go ahead, to let him have her without feeling regret for the disappointment she would cause.

Tomorrow, none of this would have mattered.

She looked up at him, wishing she could see his expression in the darkness, her stomach sinking when she realized he was standing there, unmoving. She could only imagine what he must be thinking—

He took a deep breath suddenly. It cut the darkness like a shout. Then he turned and went to the door, throwing it open so the slats of moonlight became a flood. He stood there, silhouetted against the light. Then, very slowly, he beckoned to her.

"Ana, come here."

It was a compelling voice, one she wouldn't have been able to resist even if she wasn't feeling so lost and lonely. Ana got to her feet and went to him, pausing just before she reached the door. "What?" she asked.

He leaned against the door frame, his dark hair shadow on his shoulders, his face chisled by the light, and motioned for her to come closer. "Look out there."

She peered over his shoulder, staring out into the night. Moonlight pooled on the dirt ground, making shadows out of clay pots and stones, flickering through the long, fringed fronds of the banana trees with a whisper. She heard the jungle sounds, familiar now and not frightening. Soothing even. She smelled the breeze and the orchids and the sweet, lush scent of growth.

"I look out there, and I'm not myself anymore." His voice was quiet. "It's hard to believe I've ever been anyplace but here."

"I know," Ana said breathlessly. She felt suddenly as if they were one mind, one emotion, joined together. That no matter what she said, he knew she was going to say it, that no matter what she thought, he thought it with her. She leaned back against the open door, bracing her palms against the cane and staring out at the jungle. "I know."

"Do you think we can pretend, Ana?" he asked, the longing so strong in his voice it tugged painfully at her heart. "Do you think, just for a little while, we can pretend there's no past—nothing but us right now?"

She bit her lip. "I don't know if I can do that."

"No?" He turned to face her, his eyes glittering in the darkness.

Ana felt her heart fill her throat as he moved closer, closer. He was in front of her then, filling the darkness so she could see nothing but the hint of moonlight around him, could feel nothing but his presence.

"I want to make love to you, Ana," he said in a voice so deep it made her shake, and Ana felt the last of her reserve fading away, melting under the dark temptation of his voice, his heat. "Let me make love to you."

Chapter 27

She didn't say no, and Cain didn't know what he would have done if she had. God knew, he couldn't walk away, was physically incapable of walking away from her at this moment. Christ, she was so beautiful, all moonlit hair and eyes, with a soft wariness in her face he found infinitely precious. She was breathless and startled, and he wanted her more than he had ever wanted anyone—anything—in his life.

He touched her. He felt her jump as he traced her shadowed collarbone with his finger, the hollow of her throat. Touched her jawline and ran his thumb over the fullness of her mouth. Felt the warm rush of air from her gasp. But she didn't move. She didn't run, and it was enough for now. It was enough.

He wanted to tell her *I love you. I love you.* But he didn't, because he knew then she *would* run. Instead, he cradled her face between his hands and moved closer until he felt the heat of her body against his, until he smelled her elusive, citrusy scent. And when she looked up at him, he bent his head and kissed her.

Softly at first. He just brushed her lips with his, and the scalding, burning sensation that barreled through him was so powerful he nearly lost control. Oh, God, it had been so long. It had been so long and he'd never felt like this before, never had such all-consuming longing, never felt as if her touch alone could send him into climax. His hands tightened on her face, he felt the trembling beginning in his body, and Cain backed away, tried to catch his breath.

And heard her whimper.

It was his undoing. The sound broke through his control, and with a harsh groan, Cain took her mouth, urging it open, wanting, needing to taste the sweet, heady essence of her. Her tongue touched his, tentatively at first, and then with an urgency that surprised him. He felt her hands on his body, felt her breasts pressing into his chest. Finally it was going to happen. He felt faint at the promise.

But he knew if he didn't move now, he wouldn't be able to stop himself. He would take her right here, on the hard bamboo floor, and he didn't want that for her or himself. No, this first time, he wanted slow, languid pleasure.

Cain pushed himself away. His heart raced, and when he looked down into her face, heard the soft panting from her parted lips, it was all he could do to speak. He backed away farther, despite the inner voice that warned: *Don't give her time to think. If she backs away now it will kill you.* But he did it anyway. Stepped away and held out his hand and forced the sound from his lips.

"Come with me," he said.

She stared at his hand, and in that moment, Cain knew he'd made the wrong decision. She was going to back away. She was going to stop this insanity, and he couldn't bear it. *Ah, Christ, he couldn't bear it.*

"Don't be afraid," he said desperately.

She smiled, a soft, secret smile. She put her hand in his

and licked her lips unconsciously, erotically. "I'm not afraid."

But he heard the edge of doubt in her voice, and Cain wanted to reassure her, to show her with his body if not with words how much he loved her. He tightened his fingers around hers and pulled her with him, through the *quincha,* dodging shadows in the darkness until he got to their room. The room where he had sat, hour after hour during her sickness, afraid and lonely. The room where he needed her presence—her spirit—like a drug. Like wine. Without her, he was nothing. There was nothing.

He paused just inside the door, and she paused with him, pressing against his back, squeezing his hand, and Cain pulled her around so hard she fell against his chest, all warm and soft and willing. He pressed his hand against her cheek and buried his face in her hair, wanting to wrap it around him and feel it slide against his naked skin.

He ran his lips over her hair, over her cheek, breathing in the scent of her, finding her mouth in the darkness and urging it open, running his tongue over her teeth and twining it with hers. He untied the leather thong holding her braid in place, tossed it aside, and then grabbed the mass in his hands, felt it sliding through his fingers like heavy, heated satin. He fanned it over her shoulders, over her back, before he dug his hands in the heaviness of it and gripped her scalp, angling her head back so he could explore her mouth in deep, intimate strokes. He took the kiss deeper then, tasting her, breathing her, forcing her lips farther apart as if he could swallow her whole, take in her very essence. Humid, sweet, citrusy. He heard her soft whimper, felt the vibration in her throat, and it inflamed him. *Slower,* he thought. *Slower.* But he couldn't slow down, much as he wanted to. He would never be able to stop.

Don't stop. Don't stop. Don't stop. Ana was reeling,

pulsing, splintering. She had never imagined a man could taste like this, never knew this kind of desire could exist. She felt on fire, her skin was burning. She felt his fingers holding her prisoner with her hair, and then they were gone, moving along her back to her waist and then upward, molding the thin cotton shift against her body.

Nothing in her life had prepared her for this. Nothing. Not this sweet surrender or this heady yearning. She moved with him, wanting him to touch her, shifting so her breast filled his hand. At the touch, Ana lost the last vestiges of control. He had wanted her to forget the past; she forgot it. He wanted only Ana—here she was, wanting him with an urgency that was frightening. So she didn't think about it. She didn't think when his mouth moved from hers and traced the sensitive flesh of her throat. She didn't think when he dragged down the sleeves of her dress, revealing her breasts. She felt the warm, tropical air on her bare skin, tingling, curiously erotic. Then she felt his tongue, wet and hot, circling her nipples, urging them to taut, painful peaks, flicking against her skin until she nearly cried out with longing.

Good God, she'd never felt anything like this. His tongue made her insane; she felt everything with painful intensity. *Stop this,* she thought. *Stop it now, before it goes too far, before you lose control.* But she couldn't obey the summons, and in some dark part of her mind Ana realized she'd already lost control. She couldn't stop him if she tried, couldn't stop herself. God help her, she thought she would die if he stopped.

She plunged her fingers into his hair. The dark shadow of it pooled on her hands, soft and long and heavy. She gripped it with her fingers, pressing closer, holding him in place, trying to stifle her moans as he laved her breasts. *Don't think. Don't think.* Her hands moved over his hair, down to his shoulders, and suddenly she remembered the dark curls on his chest, and she wanted to feel them against her, feel his heat against the stiff peaks of her nipples.

Frantically Ana pulled at his shirt, urgency making her quick and clumsy. She heard the rip of cloth, and then his mouth was on her again and he was helping her, fumbling with his fastenings, pulling off the shirt without breaking the kiss. She ran her fingers over his chest, touching the wiry, springy curls, the flexing muscles, and she heard his moan, vibrating through her, shuddering through her. She clutched his shoulders, pressing her breasts against his chest.

"Please," she murmured into his mouth, not knowing what she asked for or even what she wanted. "Please—"

"Yes." He broke the kiss, sliding his mouth over her jaw, down her throat. His hands were on her back, sliding to her waist as he moved lower, taking her dress with him. His mouth fastened on first one breast, then the other, licking, nipping, teasing. Then he kissed the valley between them and dipped lower, to her waist, her belly, her navel. She felt his hands on her buttocks, holding her in place, a willing prisoner against his mouth, and she held on to his hair for support, arching, pressing, wanting.

God, she wanted him. She had never imagined such honeyed sweetness. Never imagined such insane longing . . .

"Ah, Ana," he whispered against her skin, making her shiver. "You are so beautiful. So beautiful."

The dress pooled to the floor at her feet, so she was naked before him. The air caressed her with its warm moistness, and she twisted in his hands, tossing back her hair. It was a heavy, soft curtain against the skin of her back, warm and soft and unbearably erotic. He'd said she was beautiful, and she felt it now. For the first time in her life, she felt beautiful, and sensuous. She felt—

She jerked in surprise as she felt his kiss on the soft fleece between her legs. Ana clenched his hair in her fingers, tried to back away. She'd never felt such a thing, never imagined it. "No," she protested softly. "No—"

"Yes." He whispered the word against the curls, forcing her legs apart gently with his hands, holding her in place with a strength she hadn't realized he had. Ana stiffened, her need fleeing in sudden embarrassment. But he would not let her go. She couldn't close her legs, couldn't back away, couldn't move.

And then she felt his kiss against the most intimate part of her. Wet, open-mouthed kisses. Hot, unbearable kisses. Gently, tenderly, and she forgot her embarrassment, forgot everything but the heat spreading from his tongue to her belly, into her heart. She was trembling. She clutched his hair, no longer wanting to pull away. Unable to pull away. Unable to resist him. It was so hard to resist him. His tongue circled her, pushed inside her, licked deeply. She thrust against him, wanting more, unable to control her movements or her broken moans, unable to stop her trembling. Oh, God, she was going mad. She couldn't stop it, couldn't stop—didn't want to stop. The tension grew inside her, growing and growing until she arched against him, held him tightly against her.

"Let it go," he whispered, moving his lips on her heated, tortured flesh. "Let it go."

She had no idea what he meant. All she knew was that she couldn't control it anymore. She wanted to give in to the pressure. It was moving over her, building, growing, exploding. *Ah, God, what was this?* She felt herself tighten, felt the resistance.

"Let it go, Ana." He spoke against the most sensitive part of her, and she surrendered. Release erupted through her, blacking out all thought, all sound. She shuddered against him, melted, fell into a dark whirling pleasure that left her throbbing even when he took his mouth away.

If he had released her then, she would have fallen. But

he didn't. His hands were steady, knowing, gentle and possessive at the same time. She felt him moving back, felt the light kiss against her curls, her navel, the tender touch on her breasts. She wanted to talk to him, wanted to ask *what was that?* but she couldn't make a sound. All she could do was stare wordlessly at him, as he looked at her.

"Did I make you melt, Ana?" he whispered, his eyes burning. "Sweet Christ, *querida,* I want to make you melt again . . ."

The words sank into her, into the dark need inside of her, and Ana felt the throbbing desire start again. *Yes,* she wanted to say. *Yes, make me melt. Yes* . . . But he was already pushing her back, gently pushing her until the bedstand pressed against the back of her legs and she was falling backward onto the mattress. He loomed above her, his dark hair spilling forward, hiding his face, brushing her throat.

Then, for just a moment, he backed away, and Ana heard her own soft whimper, reached for him with hungry hands. She heard his fumbling, and then he was beside her again, the naked, hard length of him pressed against her body. He kissed her, and she tasted herself on him, salty and musky, humid and strangely exciting.

"Ah, Ana, what you do to me," he murmured against her mouth. He kissed the sensitive flesh behind her ear, then followed it with his tongue, and Ana jerked, arching against him with a silent moan, lifting her throat to him as if she were a sacrifice and he were some pagan god. "God," he muttered. "Sweet Christ, I must be dreaming. I want you so much—I can't wait—"

He rose over her, quickly spreading her legs with his knee. She felt his hardness against her, felt the swift pressure. He thrust into her in one long, hard stroke, burying himself in her, impaling her.

It was familiar. Too familiar. Ana froze, clutching the blankets with her hands. She heard his groan, felt him bury his face in her throat, but she was suddenly rigid. Suddenly the Duchess.

She felt his invasion with every part of her being, and Ana squeezed her eyes shut. *Just a job.* Her own words rang in her ears, and she tried to fight them. She couldn't bear it, not now, not when she knew what there was to feel. "No," she whispered, begging to someone, something. "No." *God, no, don't take this away from me too. Not now.* But she couldn't stop it. She felt like ice, cold and sweating at the same time and horribly, desperately afraid.

And then she felt his soft kiss, moving up her throat, kissing the corners of her mouth, kissing away tears she hadn't realized she'd shed.

"Ana," he whispered. "Sweet Ana. Give yourself to me, sweetheart. Don't be afraid. Ah, Ana. Ana. Ana. Ana." Softly he said it. Soothingly. Over and over again, an endless cycle that repeated even as he drew back from her, easing out of her until he was barely inside then slowly, oh so slowly, rocking back. Touching her, kissing her, whispering her name until the memory began to disappear, until she began to forget the Duchess, began to believe that she was truly just Ana.

She felt him sink into her, gently increasing the rhythm until Ana felt the pressure building again. Slowly. Slowly. Building until her fingers loosened on the blankets and she ran her hands over the heated smoothness of his shoulders and back, until she locked her legs around his hips and rocked with him, until she felt branded with the feel and the scent and the taste of him.

Ana opened her eyes, looking up to find him gazing at her, his eyes dark and bottomless, his throat sinewy with the strain of holding back, and she clutched his arms and pulled him down to her, felt him slide against her sweat-slick skin, the coarse, erotic scratch of his chest hair on her sensitive breasts. She rocked against him, unconscious of her motions, knowing only that she needed him to fill the hollowness inside her, to be so deep there would be no telling where she ended and he began. She needed his compassion and his strength, needed him to save her. *God, yes. Save me.*

He grabbed her hips then, thrusting hard inside her, as if he understood her fear and desperation. Filling her. Taking her. Saving her.

The pressure was there again, filling her body and her soul, making her long to cry out in surrender. Swirling and rising and building . . .

Her release exploded over her, washing through her in waves so intense it was almost painful. Ana clutched at him, gasping words she didn't understand, trembling beneath him as he thrust deeper and deeper, faster and faster.

And then she felt him stiffen, heard his hoarse, strangled cry before he shuddered and collapsed, and she felt him throbbing deep inside her, hot and wet and unbearably sweet. *Yes. Oh, yes, this was what she wanted, what she needed* . . . His face was buried in the curve of her neck, his mouth moved against her skin. The heaviness of his weight felt good. So good. She wanted it to go on forever and ever.

But she knew it couldn't.

Ana squeezed her eyes shut, waiting for his inevitable withdrawal, the lonely chill she would feel when he was gone. She knew it well, knew she would feel cold and dirty and empty, knew she would pretend not to see his knowing, smirking smile. She would want him gone then, she knew that too. She would want him to grab his clothes and leave quickly—so she could start to forget about him.

If you can forget about him.

The thought came, unasked for and unwelcome, but she knew it was true. Tonight had been different. Her responses had been unstudied, the way she'd arched against him and whispered his name, the way she clutched him. She remembered gasping beneath his sensual onslaught, crying his name in her release—release she'd never imagined, never known. She could almost *see* herself writhing beneath him, begging for release, for salvation. Her hands in his dark hair, her limbs twined with his. The vision assaulted her in dizzying, confusing images, and she was aching suddenly, wanting something so far beyond her grasp she couldn't imagine it. Wanting him to stay there, wrapped around her, his arms and his legs and his hair catching in hers.

No. That wasn't real. He wouldn't stay, it didn't matter what she hoped for. It was only a dream, and one she didn't really want.

The thought brought sadness so deep she wanted to cry. Ana struggled to push it away. She clenched her fists in the blankets. *Leave,* she thought. *Please, just leave now so I can forget this.*

But he didn't. He rose up on his elbow and looked down into her face, wrapped a strand of her hair around his finger and smiled down at her.

"You all right?" he asked softly.

No. No, I'm not all right. Ana nodded slowly. "Yes."

He opened his mouth as if he wanted to say something, and then closed it again, glancing away for a moment as if she was too painful to look at. Ana's heart constricted. She waited for his next words, the ones that would thank her in a stilted, awkward tone before he pulled away from her and went to his hammock. She watched him, feeling frozen inside, waiting.

Then he smiled again and leaned over her, pressing his lips to hers in a gentle, open-mouthed kiss.

"You're perfect," he whispered. "Christ, you're so perfect."

Ana was suddenly wrapped in confusion so strong it took her breath away. Because she saw his eyes finally, saw the emotion shining from them, and everything dropped into place. She knew then why he didn't leave, and why he caressed her as if she was the most important thing in the world.

He loved her.

He loved her.

The knowledge made her numb with fear.

Cain felt her struggle in his arms. At first, he thought she was just moving to get comfortable, and he rolled onto his side and tried to cradle her in his embrace. It wasn't until she pushed at him with a little, choking sound of dismay that he realized she was trying to escape.

But before he could do anything about it, before he could even protest, she swung her legs over the side of the bed and rose. He felt the sudden ease of pressure on the mattress, heard its creak, and then she was skirting away from him, bare skin glowing in the darkness, shadowed by the heavy length of her hair.

He lay there, still not quite believing it, drugged into complacency by the strength of his release. He told himself she was only going to get a drink of water.

Then he heard the shuffle of clothing.

Cain sat up. "What are you doing?"

She didn't look at him. "Going for a walk."

"A walk?" He heard the sharp rise of incredulity in his voice and he struggled to control it. "A walk?"

"Yes, a walk," she replied with exaggerated care. "You don't need to worry about taking up the bed tonight. I'll sleep in the hammock when I get back."

He felt as if she'd punched him, and then cursed himself for being surprised. He had forgotten. For a time, he'd been so lost in sensation, in the warm, pulsing rightness of being inside her, that he'd forgotten she was not an ordinary woman. She was a prostitute. A woman who was used to selling her favors, to quick rolls that brought no warmth, little pleasure. The thought sent nausea clawing through him. Christ, he was just another man, another client.

But then he remembered. He had felt her pleasure, felt the quick, passionate responses of her body and heard her soft moans. No, he was not just another man. He had felt her throbbing against his tongue, had tasted her and kissed her. He had not mistaken her responses, he knew. Had not mistaken his. He had made love to her, and he wondered if any man before him ever had.

He looked at her and knew then that he was the only one. She was confused and uncertain, and for the first time since he'd known her, she wasn't even hiding it very well. She pulled on the chemise with shaking hands. He heard her bitten-off curse as the cotton tangled around her waist. No, she was not unaffected.

"Don't go," he said quietly.

She stopped. Her back was to him, but she half turned her head. "I'm just going to take a walk."

"Why?"

"Because I can't sleep. I'll just keep you up all night."

He grinned. "That's fine with me."

She turned away again. "No. Not again."

"Why not, Ana?" Cain whispered. "What's wrong? Didn't you like it?"

"You were—" She yanked at the chemise. "You were very good."

" 'You were very good,' " he mimicked. "That's not what I asked you, Ana. I asked if you liked it."

"Cain—"

"Did you like it?"

"Yes. No. I—" She wrenched on the fabric, ripping it in frustration, and spun around to face him. "What do you want me to say? 'I've never felt this way,' or 'You made me feel things I've never felt'—is that what you want to hear?"

"Only if it's true," he said harshly.

"You don't understand." She sounded near tears; the

chemise lay crumpled and abandoned at her waist. "This changes nothing—I told you it wouldn't. You don't understand."

"No?" Cain rose, trying to control his anger as he faced her. He had given her his heart, made love to her with his very soul. And she had done the same, he knew it even if she refused to admit it. "Pardon me for disagreeing, *querida,* but I think you've got things a little mixed up. It's not me who doesn't understand. It's you."

He advanced slowly. She swallowed and moved backward, grabbing at the edges of the torn chemise. When it didn't budge, she crossed her arms over her chest, hiding her small breasts from his view.

She swallowed. "Don't."

Her eyes looked huge and dark and frightened in the darkness, her hair a wild shadow over her shoulders. Like a trapped animal, he thought for the second time since he'd known her. Then he realized it was more than confusion she felt. It was fear. She was afraid.

The knowledge took his anger.

He reached out, running a finger down the softness of her cheek. She jumped, and then froze, and he dropped his hand. "What are you afraid of, Ana?"

She lifted her chin. "Leave me alone."

"Why?"

"Because I want you to."

"Why?" he whispered.

She stepped backward until she was against the wall. "I know what you think. I know you think you're different than the rest. But you're not. You're not. I didn't feel a thing."

Cain moved forward, so quickly she was startled, and grabbed her wrist, pulling her against his chest, and then he curled his fingers beneath her chin and forced her to look at him.

"Liar," he said softly. "I don't believe you."

"I'm telling you the truth," she whispered. "I felt nothing. Nothing."

"Really?" He ran the back of his hand down her cheek. "Not when I did this?" He touched her mouth with his finger. "Or this?"

She shook her head frantically. "No. No."

"Really? Then how about this?" He bent his head, brushing her lips with his, then slowly, achingly slowly, tracing her lips with his tongue.

"No." Her voice shook—or he thought it did.

Cain slid his hands around her waist. She stiffened as he touched her bare skin, he heard her rapid breathing. He backed her against the wall and then held her in place with one hand. With the other, he touched her nipple. It stiffened immediately. "Not this?" he whispered against her mouth.

She shook her head wildly, tearing her lips from his. "Don't do this to me. Don't do this."

"You keep saying that," he said, continuing his relentless teasing, knowing it was unfair and hating himself for it even as he couldn't stop. "Tell me, *querida,* what can I be doing to you? You said you feel nothing when I touch you."

She bit her lip. She was trembling. He felt her struggle in the stiffness of her muscles, the way she refused to look at him. "You don't understand."

"Then explain it to me," he said softly. "Explain it to me, Ana. Make me understand."

"I already tried."

He frowned. "You did?"

"Before—" She waved a hand, closed her eyes. "Before this."

It dawned on him suddenly what she was talking about. Their conversation before he'd made love to her had been lost in the exquisiteness of the act. He'd forgotten her fears. What had she said? *You expect too much. I can't give you what you want.*

He had discounted the words, refusing to believe them, knowing she still thought she was someone she hadn't been for a very long time. In his arrogance, he'd thought his lovemaking would make her see that. But that was his belief, not hers. He was the one who thought her whoring days were over.

Was it possible she had never intended that at all?

He swallowed, horrified at the thought, and stared at her. His hand stilled on her breast, and he felt her resistance, saw the fierce biting of her lip and her averted gaze.

"Ana," he said slowly. "I don't care about your past." With shock, he realized the words were true. The questions that had once seemed so important—why she became a whore, why she hated doctors—didn't matter anymore. "I don't care."

She lowered her eyes, took a deep breath. "I know."

"You're still—" he forced himself to say the words. "You're still planning to go on to San Francisco."

She threw him a quick look. "I told you nothing's changed."

"What if I asked you not to go? What if I asked you to stay here with me?"

She was silent, and Cain held his breath, for a moment wishing he could take back the words. He wanted to tell her he loved her, wanted to cradle her in his arms and make love to her again and again, until the idea of going on to San Francisco was anathema to her.

But he'd never said those words to anyone before. This was the only time in his life he'd felt worthy enough to say them. It was ironic, he thought, that the one woman who made him feel worthy was a woman practiced at artifice and lies, a woman who cared for no one herself—

No, that wasn't true. She cared for him, he knew it. Christ, he knew it. Cain pressed closer, and she pressed her hand against his chest, splaying her fingers through the curls on his skin, and looked up at him. He saw fear and confusion in her eyes, and because of that, he said the words he'd sworn not to say.

"I love you."

She shook her head, not even looking surprised. "No, you don't. You only think you do."

He laughed quietly. "How reassuring that you think so much of me. I don't know my own mind, is that it?"

"You don't know me."

"Yes, I do."

"No, you—"

"Shall I tell you how much I know, Ana?" he asked gently, pressing her against the wall, grabbing the hand she'd placed on his chest and curling his fingers around it. "Should I tell you who I see when I look at you?"

She struggled against him. "No, Cain, don't—"

"I see a beautiful woman who's afraid of being loved. Of loving herself, even. I see a woman who has convinced herself love isn't important."

She shook her head. Her hair fell over her shoulders, her breasts. "That's not true."

"Then tell me what is true."

She said nothing. She couldn't even look at him, and that alone sent pain knifing into his heart.

He sighed, tightening his hands on her skin, closing his eyes. "Ah, Ana, why won't you let me love you?"

"Because," she said, in a voice so soft he had to bend his head to hear it. "Because then I would have to love you back. And I don't know if I can do that."

He didn't know what to say to her. They were the saddest words he'd ever heard, and he didn't know how to answer them, how to do more than stare at her lowered head, at the hair falling forward to cover her face and throat, shadowing the small mounds of her breasts. She seemed so delicate then, and fragile, and it occured to him that he'd never seen her this way, had always seen her as indomitable, unbroken.

He had an intense urge to wrap her in his arms, to hold her safe and protected against the world. His Ana, who had never backed down from any fight, who had always confronted everything, stood half naked and trembling, helpless and alone.

Ah, Christ, the sight of her that way broke his heart.

Because she was lying to herself, he knew it. She thought she couldn't love him back; what she didn't realize was that she already did. He knew it, even if she didn't. Sometimes the words weren't important.

But she wouldn't listen to him if he told her that, and it suddenly didn't matter. She had given him confidence, she had given him back himself. For that, if nothing else, he loved her enough for both of them.

So he said nothing. Instead, he bent and kissed her, kissed her until her resistance melted and she curled her arms around his neck, kissed her until he heard her soft sob of surrender.

"I don't care what you say," he whispered then against her mouth. "I don't care what you do. I love you, Ana. That will never change."

And he showed her with his body just what he meant.

Chapter 28

She woke before he did. She was nestled against his body, cradled back to chest. His arms curled around her, one hand cupping her breast, the other lax against her stomach, and she felt his warm breath against the curve of her neck, stirring tiny tendrils of hair so they bobbed against her throat. She felt warm and protected there, held so tightly against him, as if he was loathe to let her go even in sleep.

Ana opened her eyes, staring into the pale dawn dimness. His fingers twitched against her stomach as if he felt her movement, and he pulled her closer, murmuring against her skin. His body hair was soft against her back and buttocks, coarse where her legs twined with his.

She had never lain with a man like this. Not through the night, not in the soft glow of morning. The men who used her body were always gone within the hour, leaving her alone to watch the sunrise. Sometimes she lay awake and stared at the light spreading across the cheap plaster walls of her room, feeling the warmth of morning move over her—her own private celebration.

Alone. It was how she wanted to be, how she always imagined her life. Not once had she dreamed about lying tangled with a man in the morning, or feeling his warm, possessive hands cradling her body. Not once.

She liked the feeling.

And that frightened her.

Ana closed her eyes again, blocking out the light, letting the darkness creep over her, and with it the panic that had assailed her last night. The panic that she'd let him kiss away. She was amazed at how easily he'd done it. One touch, and she melted. One kiss banished the fear. She had wanted his touch, needed it, because when he touched her there was no emptiness, no loneliness. No darkness.

She was no longer herself, but some stranger. Someone who craved his touch, who believed him when he said "I love you." Someone who believed that maybe, just maybe, he wouldn't hurt her the way she expected to be hurt.

She was someone like her mother.

The words jumped into her mind, unavoidable, undeniable, and Ana tried to blink back the tears behind her eyes. God, she was more afraid than she'd ever been in her life. Afraid because she was weakening, because she felt him touching her, holding her, and the touch was filled with caring even in sleep. Because she was losing control and she didn't know what to do about it. With Cain, there was no thought, no control. His touch had her aching for more, begging for more. The Duchess—the woman men had been trying to warm for years—had melted, puddled at his feet like an icicle in the sun. Even now, the heat of his fingers on her skin sent an excited tingle racing through her.

Oh, God, what had she done?

She wanted to clear her mind, to think about what to do, how to make this all go away, but she couldn't stop thinking about last night. Couldn't stop thinking about the way he made her feel. Heard over and over again the words *I love you. That will never change.*

He was so persuasive, and she was so weak where he was concerned. He loved her, and she knew he would stop at nothing to make her admit she loved him too. But she didn't know how to love someone back. She didn't want him to love her, didn't want him to expect so much from her. The sight of her mother flashed into Ana's mind; she saw again the excited smile that lit her mother's face whenever they received a letter from her father, and then the way the light in Mama's eyes dimmed the moment she read the words: "Not yet, my love. Soon, but not yet . . ."

How many times had Ana heard those words? How many times had her mother explained them away? Too many times, enough that soon Mama even believed the lies, had gone mad believing them. But Ana never had. She had never believed. All she had seen was pain, insanity—and destruction.

And that was all she believed in now. Cain had said the words. He had told her he loved her, and she believed him. He did love her now, and maybe he would forever. But that didn't mean he wouldn't hurt her. It didn't mean he wouldn't eventually destroy her the way her mother had been destroyed. He might not mean to, but he would.

She knew how much hurt was in "I love you," even if he didn't. Love stole from a person, a little at a time, insidiously whittling away, piece by piece until there was nothing left. Love wouldn't stop—Cain wouldn't stop—until he consumed her completely.

It was too much to give, even if she'd known how to give it. So she couldn't give him a chance to ask. She didn't trust herself anymore to refuse him. Last night had been proof enough of her lack of willpower. She had been swept away by passion and desire, had wanted him so badly she couldn't think or breathe. She was horribly afraid that if he touched her, it would happen again.

There was only one solution. She had to leave before he had a chance to touch her again.

The thought sank into her stomach like lead. Ana's throat tightened until she couldn't swallow. It would be best, she told herself. She already had a life mapped out, a future. San Francisco. Her own house. Independence. The things she had always wanted. The sooner she had them, the sooner she could put this journey and her feelings for Cain D'Alessandro behind her, the sooner she could get on with the life she had always expected for herself.

The life you want.

Yes, she wanted it. A safe, comfortable life without pain or confusion. Without Cain.

It would be best for both of them. He would forget her, and go on, and eventually realize that she wasn't the right woman for him. He would find someone who could love him the way he deserved to be loved.

Yes, it was better this way. Much better.

Ana blinked back her tears and began to plan.

Cain woke at her movement and lay there while she disentangled herself from his arms. He felt her rise from the bed, heard the light pad of her footsteps across the bamboo mat floor. He opened his eyes and watched her. It was morning already, and she was dimly lit by the sunlight breaking through the crack between the roof and the wall. Her back was to him, her movements graceful as she tossed back the long, thick curtain of her hair and reached for the dress he'd eased past her hips for the second time last night. She shook it out, holding it in front of her for a moment, studying the small tear in the bodice. Then, with a sigh, she stepped into it.

He said nothing as she dressed, liking how relaxed she was when she thought he was asleep, finding a certain voyeuristic pleasure in watching smooth hips disappear beneath cotton pantalets, round shoulders disguised by a lifted sleeve. Christ, she was beautiful. The most beautiful thing in his life. The only beautiful thing.

He wished she hadn't left the bed so quickly this morning. The slow awakening, feeling her buttocks wiggle into his groin, the slide of her feet past his leg, had brought him into a sleepy, lazy arousal. He wanted to make love to her again. Again and again. Like last night, before they'd fallen into exhausted sleep. He felt as if he could spend his whole life making love to her, hearing her soft moans of excitement, feeling the hot, slick depths of her pulsing around him . . . Hell, the memories made him instantly hard.

He rose to one elbow, raking a hand through his hair. "Ana," he said softly.

She tensed and turned to face him, wariness on her face. "Oh," she said, a small, breathless sound of surprise. "Good morning."

"Come here."

She smiled then, a shy, shaking-head sort of smile that made him smile in return. "It's morning."

"The best time of day," he said. "Come here and let me show you."

"No." She motioned to the door with a sigh and a limp-wristed wave. "They're all awake."

He heard them then, the noises of morning outside the room. Enzo's childish whining, the low, hurried voices of Juan and Amado and Jiméne preparing to go into the fields, the clank of pottery and the hiss of fire. He heard them, and he didn't care. "To hell with them," he said. "I'll just kiss you quiet."

She almost laughed, he saw the twitching of her mouth. But then she was somber again. She shook her head, the movement sent her hair flying, made the tear at the neckline of her dress gape a little wider. "It's late," she said. "And I promised Dolores I would help with the washing." She reached back and grabbed the mass of her hair, twisting it with smooth efficiency, searching the room for the leather thong that tied it.

Cain felt a swift stab of regret. She was disappearing already, the passionate woman he had held in his arms all night. The lustrous hair was pulled back, the dress hid her delicate curves, and her eyes were . . . Cain looked closer, disconcerted. There was something about her eyes, something strange. Suddenly he remembered her fear last night. She'd been frightened and unsure, and though he thought he'd kissed her fears away, he'd been wrong before. Perhaps he hadn't done enough. Perhaps she was still afraid.

He frowned. "Is something wrong, Ana?"

"Wrong?" She lifted her brow in question. "No, of course not. What could be wrong?"

"I don't know. Last night you seemed upset. I was just wondering—"

"I'm fine." She cut him off with swift finality. "You should probably get up too, before Enzo rousts you out."

Something *was* wrong, but Cain couldn't put his finger on what. There was no anger in her voice, she wasn't avoiding him exactly, but there was something about her manner and her words that was different. She was Ana, yet she wasn't.

He watched her thoughtfully. "We should talk."

She froze for an instant—so briefly he wasn't sure he'd even seen it—and then relaxed, spotting the leather tie laying on the table by the bed and reaching for it with studied casualness. "We can talk later if you like," she said. When he said nothing, she looked at him. "All right?"

He knew he should say no, should insist on talking to her right now, find out what lent the edge to her movements. But it was so elusive, and he knew it might be nothing at all, merely her own confusion. Even he was unsettled after last night. Perhaps she only needed time.

God knew, time was something he had plenty of.

He nodded reluctantly. "We'll talk later."

She was visibly relieved. "Good. I"—she motioned to the doorway—"I think I'll go, then." She turned, walking across the room, so quickly she was almost to the door before he found his voice.

"Ana."

She turned, one hand poised on the jamb. "Yes?"

"Don't I get a kiss good-bye?"

She looked confused for a moment. "A kiss," she repeated slowly, and Cain could have sworn he saw fear cross her face, though she recovered quickly. "A kiss. Of course."

She took a deep breath and crossed the room again, stopping just beside the bed. Cain had the feeling she was steeling herself. But just when he decided to pull her down and ask her why, she sat on the edge of the mattress and leaned forward, and he smelled her scent and felt her warmth, saw the gentle jiggling of her breasts against the fabric of her dress and the soft fullness of her lips. The hunger rose in him again, so sharply he could taste it, and he didn't care anymore about her strange reticence. All he wanted was the kiss.

So he took it. He put his hands on her waist, dragging her forward until she was almost on top of him, and brushed her lips with his. She started to pull away at the light touch, but he tightened his hold. He brought her as close as he could, pressing her lips apart, stroking the sweet warmth of her mouth with his tongue, tasting her, wanting her. Ah, Christ, how badly he wanted her, even now, when they'd made love all through the night. Wanted her just as badly as the first time—more, even, since he knew now what sweetness to expect—

She wrenched away from him, dodging his hands, and Cain opened his eyes in surprise, staring at her. She was shaking; she held her fingers to her mouth as if he'd hurt her, or as if she was startled that he had kissed her at all. He reached out to touch her, but she backed away, moving from the bed, forcing a smile that quivered at the corners of her lips.

"Ana," he whispered.

She blinked, shook her head slightly. "I have to go," she said, and spun around, hurrying from the room and him, disappearing into the shadows beyond the doorway.

Damn it, she was trembling. *Trembling.* Ana stopped just outside the door, leaning against the wall so he couldn't see her, and fought for control. She had not expected him to ask for a kiss, though she should have. He was never content to leave well enough alone; there was always something more he wanted, always something.

She closed her eyes and swallowed, clenching her fists. The problem was, the more he wanted, the more she wanted to give. A light peck she could have managed, but the kiss he'd given her—open-mouthed and erotic—left her shaken and confused, longing for more and hating herself for it. If only he'd simply brushed her lips, the way she thought he was going to.

But Ana suddenly knew with searing certainty that even that wouldn't have mattered. Even a light kiss would have the same effect. Her senses were tuned to his, her body was no longer her own.

It only made it more imperative that she leave soon. Today, if possible. She would wait until he left the room, take the steamer tickets and go. The only way to escape him was to run, fast and far away, so far away he couldn't touch her, couldn't even think about her—

"*Cariña,* are you ill?" Jiméne's voice cut into her thoughts. Ana looked up, realizing she stood in the main room. Dolores, Serafina, and Amado sat at the table, staring at her as if she'd lost her mind. Which wasn't far from the truth. It wasn't like her to so totally lose control, and certainly not in front of other people.

It was only another indication of how disconcerting her life had become since Cain came into it.

She unclenched her fists and pasted on a smile. "I'm fine, Jiméne. Only tired."

"You have not rested enough," he chided gently. "You are not well yet. Come now, you must eat. Serafina has made some fish."

"Really, I'm fine." Ana pushed away from the wall. "And I'm not very hungry."

Jiméne frowned. "But, *cariña—*"

"In fact, I think I'd like to take a walk."

"A walk?" He looked confused.

Ana nodded. "Just a short one. I—I think I need some air."

"Ah," he said thoughtfully. "Of course. The sun would do you good. I will go with you."

Panic surged through her. "No, really, Jiméne, that's not necessary."

"Of course it is not, but I should like to go just the same."

"But—"

"We can talk, eh, *amiga?*" He took her hand, nestling it safely in the crook of his arm. "We have not talked in a very long time."

Ana fought for calm. It was better this way, she told herself. She still had to steal the steamer tickets from Cain, and more than that, she couldn't very well leave without directions. Jiméne knew how to get to Panama City. There was no need to panic. Just as soon as she wormed the information out of him, she would be able to leave.

Her stomach clenched, she felt a sudden ache where her heart was, and Ana pushed it away. There was no time for it now. Her sanity was at stake. This was the best way, the only way.

She repeated the words silently as Jiméne led her outside. The sun had just risen, but already it was growing warm, she felt the prickles of sweat start in the valley between her breasts, the soft, moist humidity.

Jiméne patted her hand reassuringly. "You look much better, Ana. Perhaps it is too much to hope that my family does you good?"

Ana felt a momentary pang of sadness. "Your family has been wonderful to me, Jiméne. I will miss them very much."

"You do not have to go for days yet. Even then, if you do not wish to. We would all like it very much if you and D'Alessandro would stay."

"You have enough to take care of without us."

Jiméne was thoughtful for a moment. "Is it so important, *cariña,* that you go on to San Francisco?"

Ana drew away, feeling suddenly uncomfortable. "We must go at some point, Jiméne. We can't just stay here forever."

"No." He smiled. "Though I can wish it."

"The steamer leaves in a week."

"You will stay here until then?"

Ana nodded, though the lie felt heavy in her chest. "I think so. How far is it to Panama City from here?"

"Only a day." He motioned to the trees off to his right. "There is a path there—a road—that we take into the city when we go. It is very safe. Only peasants use it, and they have nothing to steal."

Ana tried to see through the trees, but the path was well hidden. "Is it wide enough for a mule?"

"Two mules," Jiméne boasted. "We made the beginning ourselves, Amado and Juan and I. It is wide enough for a wagon. A small one. Once you must go, Juan and I will travel a short distance with you. Perhaps, if you like, we will go with you into town."

"Perhaps." Ana felt like the worst kind of traitor. It was so easy, getting information from Jiméne, and though she should have been glad, she felt strangely . . . miserable. She pasted on a slight, thin smile. "We can decide then."

"Sí, we will decide."

They stood in silence for a moment, so long that Ana turned to go back to the *quincha,* opened her mouth to make some excuse for him to leave her here so she could hide. But before she could speak, Jiméne sighed heavily and turned to her. His amused countenance was gone, in its place a strange resignation.

It was so startling she stopped and stared at him. "Jiméne?"

"We are friends, are we not, *cariña?"*

She nodded slowly. "Yes."

"As I thought. Perhaps then, you will not mind if I ask a question?"

A trickle of discomfort seeped down Ana's spine. "Of course."

"Ah, then." His voice was a whisper, and he looked away. "Will you give me the truth?"

She stepped back warily. "If I can."

He nodded, stroking his mustache. "I will ask you this again, for a different reason this time. Must you go to San Francisco?"

Ana stiffened. His very demeanor made it impossible to dismiss the question as lightly as she had before. "Why do you ask?"

He pursed his lips, folding his arms across his chest and staring into the distance as if trying to figure out best how to say something. "I ask because of D'Alessandro."

"I . . . see."

"No, I do not think you do, Ana." He looked at her. "I do not think he belongs there."

"He doesn't have to go," she said breathlessly. "He's under no obligation to me. If he wants to stay, he can."

"Cariña—"

"We aren't husband and wife, Jiméne. You know that."

"Sí. Sí, I know." He looked at her with eyes that seemed to pierce her. "You would leave him behind so easily, then?"

Ana started. It was as if he knew. But then, he couldn't know she was planning to leave Cain. She'd barely determined that herself. Ana forced herself to remain composed. It was only her imagination, her guilt. She looked steadily back at Jiméne, but her words felt pulled from her throat. "I would have him do whatever he wants. It has nothing to do with me."

"It has everything to do with you," Jiméne argued softly. "You may not be husband and wife, *amiga,* not in words. But in your hearts . . ." He shrugged.

She looked away, denying the fear his words inspired, and the leaden lump in her throat. "You said you did not think he would do well in San Francisco. What did you mean?"

"I have heard there are many hard men there." He paused. "And hard women."

Ana felt his eyes on her face, and she refused to look at him. "There are people like that everywhere."

"Sí, there are," he agreed. "But it is not often that the woman a man loves is one of them."

She turned to him then. "I don't understand you."

"It is merely this, *cariña,"* Jiméne said simply. "D'Alessandro loves you. You will destroy him if you become again what you were."

"Why not just say it, Jiméne?" Ana stared at the horizon, tightening her arms over her chest. "A whore. I will destroy him if I become a whore again."

"As you say."

"I never stopped being a whore," she said, softly because the lump in her throat was so large.

"Only you believe that, Ana."

Ana squeezed herself, pressing her lips together in a thin line because it felt as if they would tremble if she didn't. She felt like a blight standing there in the bright sunshine, with nothing but darkness inside her. Darkness and fear so intense she couldn't speak, couldn't do anything but stare into the horizon and feel Jiméne standing there beside her.

Finally he touched her arm, startling her. Ana jerked around.

"I must go back," he said gently. "They wait for me to go to the fields. You will think about what I said, Ana? You promise me you will think on it?"

She nodded shortly. "I will."

"That is all I ask then." He took a deep breath. "I will see you later?"

"Yes."

"Then *hasta luego.*" He bowed slightly, and she watched as he strode back to the *quincha,* leaving her alone.

It occurred to her then that she should be grateful and relieved. He had left her by herself, left her without having to make an excuse to stay behind. She could wait until Cain left the *quincha,* steal the tickets, and borrow a mule without arousing any suspicion. It would be hours before anyone noticed, and by that time, she would be halfway to Panama City.

Yes, she should be relieved.

But all she felt was despair.

Chapter 29

Cain lay in bed, trying not to worry about Ana. It had been half an hour since she'd left, and he still felt the tingling on his lips from their kiss, but her obvious discomfort had killed his desire. Now all he wanted was to get her alone somewhere and force her to tell him what was wrong.

Because something was definitely wrong. Cain got out of bed and grabbed the clothes he'd left lying there the night before, shaking them out absently. The gentle *click click click* of insects hitting the bamboo floor caught his attention for a moment, but when he saw there were no scorpions, he let his thoughts unfocus again and shrugged into his shirt and pants. Damn, he could not get rid of this feeling. It was like a black cloud over him, an elusive warning.

He shook his head as if that could clear it away. She'd promised they would talk tonight, and for now that had to be good enough. Besides, he had no other choice but to wait. But the thought didn't make him feel any better, and Cain strode distractedly into the busy main room.

Serafina looked up from baby Melia and smiled, but the smile dropped from her face quickly. "My God, what has happened?"

Cain's frown deepened. He glared at her, trying to think. "What did you say?"

"Is something wrong, Doctor?" *Doña* Melia's face was lined with worry. "You look angry."

"Very fierce," Serafina added.

"Like a lion," Enzo offered helpfully.

"Like a lion," Cain repeated slowly. It dawned on him then that he was frowning. He sat on the bench next to Enzo, and rubbed his eyes. "I'm all right," he said. "Sorry."

"Are you sure?" Serafina leaned over him, peering into his face. "You do not look fine."

He leaned away. "I am fine. Just thinking, that's all."

"Is it usually such a painful process for you?" Serafina teased.

That forced a wry smile from him. *"Touché, señorita."*

Her forehead wrinkled. *"Touché?* I do not understand this *touché."*

"It means that you wounded me deeply with that comment."

"Ah." She nodded, her eyes twinkling. "Then perhaps some breakfast would make you feel better?"

"Perhaps it would." Cain waited, watching Enzo eat a banana with great gusto and sticky fingers, while Serafina went to the fire and dished out some rice and yams. He looked around the room. Amado, Juan, and Jiméne were no doubt already in the fields, minding the cattle.

When Serafina set a plate before him, he picked up his spoon slowly, trying not to ask the one question he wanted to ask. His willpower lasted about two seconds. He set down the spoon. "Where's Ana?"

"She should be doing the wash with Dolores," Serafina said.

His anxiety lessened. "Oh." He picked up his spoon again. "Where?"

Serafina laughed. "For a man with such a beautiful wife, you do not keep track of her well."

"Serafina," *Doña* Melia objected. "Behave yourself."

"I am only teasing him, Mama. Look, what a gloomy face he has. Cain, Cain, you are not in a good mood this morning, I can tell."

He regarded her dourly. "I've had better days."

"See, Mama? He could use some laughter today."

"Perhaps." *Doña* Melia looked at him measuringly. "You look as if you have the headache, Doctor. There is some water outside, perhaps it will do you good."

Cain sent her a grateful glance. It was what he needed, to be alone for just a moment more. He rose from the bench, trying to act nonchalant as he left his uneaten breakfast and went outside to the clay water barrel. But though the cool water didn't ease the ache in his head, it did help him compose himself. He spent a long time there, letting the water run over his skin, listening to the murmur of chatter from inside the *quincha* and waiting for his edginess to fade. By the time he went back inside, he felt at least able to hold a conversation.

Jiméne was seated at the table, polishing off the rest of Cain's breakfast. He smiled when Cain came through the door, pushing aside the plate. "We could use your help today, D'Alessandro, if you can."

Cain nodded absently. "Of course."

"Good." Jiméne rose quickly. "Then come now, we must go before Juan gets angry. The man has a terrible temper—have I told you that before, Serafina? Your husband is like a raging bull when he is mad." Jiméne motioned impatiently. "Come along, D'Alessandro. We do not have all day. The sooner we leave, the sooner you can return to your lovely wife, eh?"

He'd been wrong about the soothing effect of water, Cain thought wryly. Jiméne's words only brought back his unease. The last thing he wanted to do was work with Jiméne and the others in the fields all day, away from Ana. He'd be useless. Already he could barely concentrate on Jiméne's unending chatter as they went to the stable.

He couldn't stop thinking about her, couldn't stop imagining what it would be like tonight, when he saw her again. He wouldn't hold back, he decided. For once, he would tell her everything he wanted to. Tell her that without her, he was nothing, that he wanted her with him forever. Tell her he wanted to see her face every morning when he opened his eyes, that he wanted those long, dark evenings with nothing to do but sit in front of the fire and read and make love far into the night.

Tell her he wanted to see her grow heavy with his child.

Christ, the image was so strong it nearly made him shake. A child, a family. It was what he wanted, what he had always wanted. A real family, people who loved each other, who didn't use each other. A family to make him forget his past. She was his only hope for that, because he knew deep inside that if she refused him, he would never find someone to take her place. It was long past time to tell her that, whether she was ready to hear it or not.

When they reached the stable, he stood watching as Castañeras grabbed the halters from a pile on the floor and went to where the mule stood, chomping contentedly.

"*Perdición,* it is as I thought. Juan has taken the other mule." He turned to Cain apologetically. "One of us must walk to the fields, I am afraid, *amigo.*"

Cain nodded, barely listening.

It took a moment for Jiméne's words to register, but when they did, the breath caught in Cain's lungs.

One mule was missing.

"Christ." He heard his own oath, and it seemed to come from miles away, to echo strangely in his head. One mule was missing. One mule. The knowledge filled him with sudden, inexplicable terror. *It couldn't be. He was wrong. He had to be wrong.*

"Jiméne," he cut through the Panamanian's chatter abruptly, breathlessly. "Jiméne, where does Dolores do the wash?"

"Where?" Jiméne repeated stupidly. "At the stream—off the path just ahead. Why?"

Cain didn't bother to answer. He spun on his heel, ignoring Jiméne's gasp of surprise as he raced toward the trail. He hit the path at a fast pace, meaning to remain calm, but by the time he rounded the first bend, Cain had broken into a run. His heart pounded, he tried to contain his panic. But his desperation grew, the sense of wrongness washed over him in giant, suffocating waves. Christ, she had to be there. *Had* to be. She could be no place else.

He heard the stream before he saw it. Heard the bubbling water. Heard the slapping of clothes on the rocks. It took him only a moment to realize what was wrong. There was no laughing, no talking. Nothing but silence. As if Dolores was alone . . .

Cain burst around the corner, stumbling to a stop. Dolores gasped and dropped the shirt she was washing. It caught in the current, a flash of white drifting out of reach, and she looked up at him with round, wide eyes, her hand at her throat.

He couldn't help himself. "Where's Ana?" he demanded.

Dolores's fear was replaced with puzzlement. "I do not know. She never came to help with the wash. I thought she was with you."

"No," he whispered. He suddenly lost all ability to move or think or breathe. "Not with me."

"Well, I have not seen her."

Desperately Cain tried to think. Dolores had not seen her. She was not at the house. He broke out in cold sweat, denying what he knew was true. No, it was impossible that she could have left. Impossible. She didn't know the way; even Ana wouldn't set off through the jungle alone—

But she had. He knew it. Cain twisted around, leaving Dolores to stare after him as he ran back down the path. He sprinted across the yard, pushing through a puzzled Jiméne and Amado at the door, ignoring everyone as he flew through the *quincha* to the room he and Ana had so recently shared. He paused in the doorway, searching for his case and the burlap bag that held what was left of his clothes. It was there, on the other side of the bed, and he grabbed it and ripped it open, spilling his things onto the mattress. His frock coat, a ripped shirt, a pair of underwear.

He grabbed the coat, fumbling with it, turning it this way and that until he found the inside pocket. The pocket that held the steamer tickets.

It was empty.

He stared at it, unable to believe the tickets were gone. He hadn't been away from this room for more than half an hour. There hadn't been time . . . It had to be the wrong pocket. There were other pockets, maybe he was mistaken. He nearly ripped the coat apart, searching. But each pocket turned up the same thing: Nothing. The tickets were gone. Not just hers, but his as well. She had taken both of them.

So he couldn't follow her.

"I have to go," she'd said this morning.

He hadn't realized she meant forever.

Cain sank onto the bed. Ah, Christ, what had he been thinking? He'd known she was uneasy, but he hadn't thought— Hell, he hadn't thought she would leave him.

Just like that. Without a word or a note. Without anything.

But Ana had always run. He knew that. Hell, it was how he'd met her. And she ran not just physically, but emotionally. She withdrew inside herself, built that damned wall up around her. She'd told him she was incapable of loving, and he hadn't believed her. Had chosen instead to believe she just didn't know what she was capable of, that he could show her how to love—how to love him.

That was the biggest joke of all. He didn't know where the hell his confidence came from. He had failed at every other damn thing in his life, why was he so sure Ana was different?

Because you love her. Because you've no other choice but to believe she loves you too. Yes, that was true, but he was a fool to believe it made a difference, a fool to believe in happy-ever-after endings and loving families, children and good-morning kisses. Ah, Christ, what a fool he was.

The ache spread through him, nearly paralyzing him. Cain felt the hot sting behind his eyes, the frustration coiling in his gut. He had trusted her, had given her everything he could, and she had given him nothing of herself. Nothing.

"Oh, Ana," he breathed, looking up at the ceiling, then closing his eyes when the pain assailed his heart. "Sweet Christ, what you have done to me."

God, he needed a drink. The thirst came with his frustration, washing over him, wrapping him in blackness and desire, making him swallow in painful, tight weakness. Yes, a drink. It was familiar and beloved, it would ease the pain of losing her. Without her, there was no point in refusing it. And he wanted it so badly now. Red wine, *aguardiente,* bourbon . . .

Ana . . . He called up her name, and with it came the strength to send the craving away. The thirst dissipated as if it had been nothing but a mild temptation, and it was then he knew. He knew that he was wrong, that he was lying to himself. Ana had given him nothing? No, she had given him everything. She had given him a piece of herself. A piece she probably hadn't even realized she'd given away. Not yet. But she would. And until she did, there was nothing he could do, nothing he could say.

He wanted to chase after her, to take her in his arms and force her to admit her feelings for him, but Cain knew that would be a mistake. It was time for Ana to decide what she wanted; he could not decide for her. It was her life and she had to choose how to live it. If Ana loved him, she would be back. He had no other choice but to believe that.

Slowly he dropped the coat still clenched in his hands and moved away from the bed where he had taken her over and over again, where she had yielded to him her breath, her body, her soul. He heard the creaking of the bamboo mat beneath his feet with some far part of his mind, felt himself moving across the floor, through the door.

The family all stood there in the main room, still as death, watching him with curious, wary eyes—as if they expected him to break into lunacy at any moment. The sight of them that way, poised, waiting, anxious, made him ache, and Cain froze, not knowing what to say, what to do. Finally he just said it.

"She's gone."

Jiméne stepped forward and shook his head. "You are wrong, *amigo*. Where could she have gone? She was here only moments ago—when you were outside. She will be back."

"The mule is gone. She took the steamer tickets."

Jiméne paled. "The steamer tickets?"

Cain nodded.

"Gracias a Dios." Jiméne let out his breath slowly. "I

am *muy estupido! Amigo,* I fear you are right. Today—this morning—she asked me how far it was to Panama City. She asked me about the path."

Cain's stomach fell. "And you told her."

"I did not think anything of it," Jiméne insisted. "*Dios.* It is lucky the path is safe. There are only peasants on it. Ah, such a fool I am!" He headed for the door. "Quick, D'Alessandro, let us take the mule. We should be able to find her soon—she left only moments ago. She cannot have gone far."

"No."

Jiméne stopped. He turned slowly, confusion lighting his eyes. "No?"

"No."

"But—but you cannot mean it! You cannot mean not to go after her! You love her. She loves you!"

"Yes." Cain looked away. "But I'm not chasing her down, *amigo.* Not this time." *Not this time.* Slowly, feeling as if every muscle in his body was protesting, Cain went to the bench and sat down, put his elbows on the table and his head in his hands.

And waited.

Chapter 30

It was growing dark now. Ana huddled on the mule, wishing she had thought to bring a blanket. She had been too long at Jiméne's, had forgotten what it was like to be surrounded by the green twilight, to feel the constant, threatening pressure of the jungle. Alone, it was even worse. She felt vulnerable and afraid. Every little sound had her jumping in her seat, twisting to see imaginary brigands crashing from the underbrush. Any moment now, she expected to see Esteban's men bearing down on her again.

And this time, she had only herself to rely on. There was no Cain to wield a fatal scalpel. No Cain to hold her at night, to protect her against the aftershock. No Cain to keep attackers from using her as they wished.

No Cain.

The feeling of emptiness grew inside her, and she forced it back, as she had been forcing it back for the last hours, and concentrated on the rhythm of the mule's gait. *Trot, pause. Trot, pause.* The animal moved carefully down the twisting trail, setting each hoof down with deliberate, slow precision. From what Jiméne said, Ana had expected to reach Panama City before dark. But the mule was taking its own sweet time, and it was becoming obvious that she was going to have to spend the night in the middle of the jungle.

Ana eyed the darkening underbrush cautiously, wondering if there was a better place around the bend, or if she should make camp there. There was a large tree just beyond the path, leafy enough to protect her from the rain, though it wouldn't be warm. Not like the *quincha,* with its waterproof roof and bamboo floors.

Her fingers tightened on the reins. By now, surely, Cain would have noticed that she was missing. He'd only been at the side of the house when she went back to take the tickets, she'd heard him splashing at the well. Not far away at all. Perhaps he'd raised the alarm. Perhaps even now, they were riding hell-bent down the path, searching for her, determined to find her before darkness set in. Ana closed her eyes, imagining it. For a moment, the vision was so strong she actually thought she heard the sound of pounding hooves on the path above her, heard the faint echo of her name ringing through the jungle. *Ana! Ana! I love you. That will never change . . .*

A lump lodged in her throat. It wouldn't matter if he came after her, she would refuse to go back with him. It was better this way, better if he never came after her at all. Then she wouldn't have to argue with him, wouldn't have to look into those warm brown eyes and tell him that she would rather be in San Francisco, taking gold from men who wanted to use the body she'd given to him.

Your life, she reminded herself forcibly. *This is what you want.* Yes, what she wanted. To be in charge of her own life, to make her own decisions. She had dreamed of this day for years: Owning her own house, turning away the men she disliked and inviting the ones she wanted to her bed.

But there's only one man you want.

Ana winced. No, it wasn't true. She didn't want only one man, didn't want Cain in her bed again. In fact, the first thing she would do when she got to Panama City—the very first thing—would be to find some miner with money to spend. Perhaps that would exorcise this strange attraction she had for Cain D'Alessandro. Perhaps then she could forget him.

The thought sent a sudden chill over her, a wave of revulsion so strong she felt weak. Ana reined in the mule. Her hands shook, and she clenched them into fists, trying to control her emotions. She was tired, that was all. It was time to stop, to rest. By morning she would feel stronger.

Slowly she dismounted and led the mule off the path, through the trailing vines and dense undergrowth to the semiclearing beneath the large ceiba tree. The shadows were dense around her, the jungle eerily silent in those few moments before total darkness. She tried not to feel it as she unloaded the few things she'd brought with her, humming to herself as she took care of the mule. But the sound of her voice was disconcerting, high and thin, weirdly muffled in the lush curtain of foliage, and she soon stopped, finishing the chore quickly and settling herself at the base of the tree.

Ana closed her eyes and leaned her head back against the trunk. She was alone. At last. Soon all this would be behind her. Again she would be able to rely solely on herself. Again she would be the person she'd been in New York. Safe, alone.

Lonely.

Her heart felt clutched in a vise, the cold spot inside of her seemed to spread through her body, to her limbs. No, not lonely. Not lonely.

Liar.

The images came into her head then, images too strong to fight, rolling over her in great waves of miserable memory. She saw herself, standing in the chill lamplight of her room, wiping one man's seed from her body while she waited for the next, feeling nothing, thinking nothing. Saw herself moving through the salon at Rose's, detached and alone even in a crowd of people, rarely smiling, never laughing. Saw herself watching as they cleared the body of one woman away, dead from opium overdose, searching the room for items she might want to take for herself: a perfume bottle, perhaps, or a gown.

Remembered the darkness she'd felt all the time. The horrible, unending emptiness, the inevitable wondering if her own death would mean nothing to someone but the opportunity to acquire a pretty necklace.

She had not felt that way for a long time.

Not since she'd met Cain.

Ana swallowed. Sadness welled in her throat, a great, heavy weight made it hard to breathe. She had been used to those feelings before, had never expected anything different for herself, never wanted it. The memory of her mother had always been too strong, the memories of vulnerability, insanity all worse than that empty darkness.

It had been easy then. She had nothing to care about, no one who meant anything to her. The loneliness was easy to bear simply because she'd never felt anything else.

But that was before she'd known what it was like to feel. Before she knew anyone who cared what she thought. Before she'd been held late at night and made love to with slow, patient sweetness.

Ana closed her eyes, seeing Cain's easy, seductive smile, the teasing light in his eyes. She remembered him standing there in the sunlight with egg dripping in yellow ribbons down his shirt, remembered his tousled sleepiness when he woke in the morning and the way he grabbed her in his delirium—as if she were his life. More than all that, she remembered last night, and the warm, giving man who had made her forget her past.

Ana glanced at the burlap bag beside her. Inside were the steamer tickets she'd taken from Cain's coat. Both of them, so he wouldn't follow her, so he wouldn't show up in Panama City and sweep her away, take her back. They were her guarantee. As long as she had them, she was safe from him, safe from his all-seeing eyes and honesty. Safe from the words *I love you,* and what they meant. *I love you, Ana. Nothing will ever change that. I love you. I love you. I love you.*

She was riding away from all that now. Riding away because she didn't want to be vulnerable. Because she was afraid of madness. But she wasn't her mother; he was nothing like her faithless father.

And she was already vulnerable.

She didn't know when it had happened, or how, but Ana suddenly knew that her defenses had been down for weeks. Despite herself, she had already let Cain in, let him fill the hollow spot inside her. She had been fooling herself, pretending she was still the Ana she had been, the cold, collected Duchess who never let anyone close enough to hurt.

She had not been that person for a very long time. Jiméne had been right, Cain had been right. She was the only one who hadn't seen it. No, she was no longer the Duchess, no longer her mother's Anastasia. She was only Ana.

It was all because of Cain. All because of his belief in her, his never-ending belief that she was better than she thought she was, that there was something inside of her that was fine and good and honorable. Because he believed it, she had no choice but to believe it too. He had done more than simply understand her spirit—he had given it back to her.

And she was riding away. The only thing in her life that had ever been good, or right, and she was riding away from it because she was a coward, because she needed him, and she was afraid of that need and what it meant. It was safe where she was going. A world she understood. A world where nothing touched and nothing hurt.

A world where there was no laughter. No love. Only emptiness. A world where she could destroy herself. Because she *would* destroy herself, she knew suddenly. If she went back to being the old Ana, that darkness would swallow her up. There would be nothing. This time, she knew too much about love and belonging and hope to survive it.

She was afraid to become the Duchess again.

God, so afraid.

Ana drew her knees to her chest and wrapped her arms around them, trying desperately to stop her trembling. Her fingers were like ice. She felt the tears just behind her eyes and she fought them, forcing them back, blinking in an effort not to cry. She wished he were there with her, wanted him wrapped around her, his quiet breathing in her ear, the feel of his heat. Wanted to hear his soft words telling her not to be afraid, that everything would be all right.

Wanted to tell him she loved him.

Ana buried her face in her arms. For the first time since her mother died, she let the tears come.

"But it hurts, Doctor!" Enzo whined and shifted his small body away from Cain's probing hands.

"Be still, Enzo." With one hand, Cain anchored the boy firmly to the ground. Anxiously he pushed aside a lock of Enzo's dark hair, searching for the bump, looking for blood. There was none, which was a relief, considering how the boy had screamed bloody murder when he'd fallen off the cow moments before. "You're fine, little one," he said in Spanish, letting the hair fall back into place and rocking back on his heels. "It will stop hurting in a bit, just as soon as you—"

He broke off, seeing Enzo's eyes stare past him, into the field. Cain swiveled around, expecting to see Jiméne, or Juan.

He did not expect to see Ana, though he had been waiting for her.

She stood there, looking at him uncertainly, saying nothing. The red dress was torn and muddied, and her hair had loosened from her braid. It spread over her shoulders, tumbled down her back in a heavy wave of curls, glimmering richly in the sunlight. Her face was streaked with dirt, there was a bright pink scratch running along one cheek. She looked tired and worn, and so beautiful it made him weak.

He wanted to touch her, to make sure she wasn't an illusion, but he didn't. She was back, but he wasn't sure what that meant, and he couldn't bear it if she shrugged away from him. So he didn't touch her.

She looked at him, and then looked away, and he saw the shine of tears in her eyes. Saw the way she lifted her hand as if to stop him from saying something. Saw her swallow convulsively before she turned her eyes to his.

"I love you," she whispered. The tears welled, one slipped down her cheek, making a clean streak on her skin. "I love you."

Slowly he rose. It took every ounce of strength he had to turn to the boy at his feet. "Run on home, Enzo," he said gently. "Find your papa."

In moments, he heard the patter of the boy's feet across the field, and they were alone. Ana had not moved, had barely taken a breath. He saw the anxiety in her eyes, the way she watched him as if she were afraid he would tell her to go—God, as if he ever could.

"Ana—" he breathed.

She closed her eyes briefly, clenched her fists at her

sides. "I thought I could leave. I thought if I went far enough away, you wouldn't find me. But I—I didn't know . . . I didn't know you were already inside me." Her voice trailed off, a mere whisper in the breeze. She laughed slightly, as if embarrassed by the admission, and wiped the tears from her face with the back of her hand. Then she swallowed, painfully, and the tears welled all over again. "I was out there, all alone, and I thought—I thought: 'This is all there is.' This is what I have. Nothing. Nothing but so much—so much darkness."

She looked up at him miserably. "I thought I could go back to being the Duchess again. But I can't." She looked down at her feet, and her hair came forward to hide her face, her hands twisted in her skirt. "Even if you don't want me, I can't go back. I'm not—I'm not that person anymore. I don't know who I am. I don't know anything . . . Except that I love you, and I think—I know—I need you."

Cain stepped forward. He reached out, and took her hand, wrapping his fingers around it so it stilled on her skirt. Her fingers were cold.

She clenched his hand as if it were a lifeline. "I'm so afraid, Cain," she whispered. "I need you so much, and I'm so afraid."

"Ah, *querida.*" He ran his hand through her hair, twining its richness through his fingers, raising her chin. "Don't be afraid. Don't be afraid. I'm here. I'm not going anywhere, and I need you just as much. I love you just as much. God, how much I love you." He kissed the damp trail of tears on her cheeks, tasting the saltiness on his lips, his tongue, kissed her eyelids and the soft, downy hair at her temple. "Perhaps, *mi corazon,* we can save each other."

Her lips pressed together in a trembling, fragile smile. "I think it will be a hard job."

He kissed her again. "Not so hard," he said against her mouth.

"Yes," she said. "Not hard at all."

"Marry me," he told her. "Stay here and marry me so I can see you every morning when I get up, and hear your voice at night when I go to bed. So I can choke on your damned bread pudding and watch you brush out that lovely, glorious hair. But mostly—ah, *querida,* mostly, marry me so I can hear you singing lullabies to our daughter."

She grinned at him then, looked up at him with bright, shining eyes. "You know I can't sing."

He laughed out loud, holding her close against him, feeling as if the sun and moon and all the stars were shining down on him at the same time. "Then I'll teach you. Ah, my sweet, sweet Ana. I'll teach you."